THE WHITE GUY DIES FIRST

ALSO BY TERRY J. BENTON-WALKER FROM TOR TEEN

BLOOD DEBTS SERIES

Blood Debts

Blood Justice

THE WHITE GUY DIES FIRST

13 SCARY STORIES OF FEAR AND POWER

EDITED BY
TERRY J. BENTON-WALKER

CONTRIBUTORS:
Faridah Àbíké-Íyímídé
Kalynn Bayron
Kendare Blake
H. E. Edgmon
Lamar Giles
Chloe Gong
Alexis Henderson
Tiffany D. Jackson
Adiba Jaigirdar
Naseem Jamnia
Mark Oshiro
Karen Strong
Terry J. Benton-Walker

TOR PUBLISHING GROUP TOR TEEN NEW YORK

This is a work of fiction. All of the characters, organizations, and events portrayed in these stories are either products of the authors' imaginations or are used fictitiously.

THE WHITE GUY DIES FIRST

A Tor Teen Book
Published by Tom Doherty Associates / Tor Publishing Group
120 Broadway
New York, NY 10271

www.torpublishinggroup.com

The Library of Congress Cataloging-in-Publication Data is available upon request.

ISBN 978-1-250-86126-9 (hardcover)
ISBN 978-1-250-86128-3 (ebook)

Our books may be purchased in bulk for promotional, educational, or business use. Please contact your local bookseller or the Macmillan Corporate and Premium Sales Department at 1-800-221-7945, extension 5442, or by email at MacmillanSpecialMarkets@macmillan.com.

First Edition: 2024

Printed in the United States of America

0 9 8 7 6 5 4 3 2 1

COPYRIGHT ACKNOWLEDGMENTS

To my mom, Shirley.

Thanks for planting the horror seed early on.

A NOTE FROM THE EDITOR

The White Guy Dies First is a deeply personal project for me, so I took great care in curating this collection of short stories. Horror has been a beloved part of my life ever since I was a small kid climbing into bed with my mom to watch scary movies until *way* past both our bedtimes. And despite sometimes being frightened out of my mind, I could never quit horror.

Horror is so much more than just ghosts or gore or monsters. The genre has always been a medium to deliver terror that's most often intertwined with a deeper message, which can be far more horrifying than any superficial scare. Every story in this collection has a greater purpose beyond frightening you—and I had an incredible time discovering the beating heart of each one and helping them all stand out more and beat even stronger.

I am extremely proud to present to you *The White Guy Dies First: 13 Scary Stories of Fear and Power.*

Happy reading.

Terry J. Benton-Walker

CONTENTS

THE WHITE GUY DIES FIRST

GHOULFRIENDS ONLINE BLOG

"Missing Genius: Thirteen Years Later, Jakobi Warren Still Nowhere to Be Found."

Posted: Tuesday, July 16, 2024 at 2:22 A.M.

Welcome back, ghoulfriends! Once again, it is I, William, Blog Master and purveyor of the ghastly and terrifying!!! Today's post is special—because it marks the 13th anniversary of Jakobi Warren's mysterious disappearance.

In 2005, Jakobi graduated with a film degree from Morehouse in Atlanta and went on to found Level 13 Studios two years later, which was headquartered on the 13th floor of an old office building on 13th Street in the city of his alma mater. He'd claimed in a press release that the naming of his studio was a jab at all the people who'd said he was a fool for starting a business in such an "unlucky" location. But maybe they were right—because four years later, Jakobi Warren disappeared without releasing a single film.

When Jakobi's landlord went into the studio after Jakobi had been late with rent and utilities, he found the entire floor cleared, except for a single half wall set back from the elevator bank. On the wall hung 13 movie posters for 13 films that had never been seen by anyone but Jakobi. At the base of the wall sat a single cardboard box with 13 film reels and a note that read:

THE WHITE GUY DIES FIRST
—Jakobi

The back of the card read:

Inspired by real accounts of the supernatural.

Despite all the films being fully shot and edited, none of them were ever released. But here's where it gets weird: A story leaked from within the local police department—they were investigating the disappearances of 13 actors, all white males between the ages of 16 and 60. I know what you're probably thinking, *Thirteen dead white guys—meh*, but what's truly interesting about that article was that every one of those missing actors had a starring role in one of Jakobi's films. So what really happened to Jakobi and those white guys??? Some people have even gone so far as to suggest Jakobi murdered his own actors—onscreen and then in real life. Of course, all that attention led someone to track down and post Jakobi's *The White Guy Dies First* collection online. But that was back in 2014.

I didn't watch the collection until a few years ago, when I was 13—and that was one of the best decisions I've ever made. S/O to my dude Lex for sending me the link and convincing me to watch. Those films changed my life. They undeniably reset the horror canon for people of color, who, mind you, historically have had a really shitty time in that genre. But when I finished watching, my heart shattered into a bajillion pieces because I realized I'd never get to experience another Jakobi Warren film. And the world would never have another opportunity to explore another dark corner of his brilliant mind.

So where is he?

Well, the police officially closed the investigation into the 13 missing white guys back in 2015, because there was simply no evidence. It was like they all vanished into thin air. In a poof of privilege.

My love for Jakobi's *The White Guy Dies First* collection was what originally got me into all things horror and why I started *Ghoulfriends*—so I could share my undying love for creepy shit with the world. So, tonight, as you read your scary books or watch a slasher or play that survival horror video game, take a moment to think about one of the greatest to ever do it: Jakobi Warren, Unsung Hero of the Horror Realm.

Until next time, ghoulfriends.

—William

Comments

---

oZZZie Oz: This is the worst blog ever. I miss when Tumblr had porn.

> **Blog Master Will:** Blocked.

Will's Mom: I love you, honey bunches of oats!

> **Blog Master Will:** Blocked ❤.

(Anonymous User): He was racist and deserve to dissappeer. If white guy came up with a movie called black guy dies first, yall wud be mad!!!!!!

> **Blog Master Will:** White guys already did that. They just weren't bold enough to say it out loud.

Alpha of the Alphas: Bruh. You been at this for YEARS. Its a fool air and. You never gonna get famous off thiss weirdo shit. Give it a rest

> **Blog Master Will:** *You're
>
> **Blog Master Will:** But I WILL be famous one day, and when that day comes, you're still gonna be the same old troll who can't spell, squatting on his parents' wi-fi to bully strangers on the internet. Good luck with that. 🍀
>
> **Blog Master Will:** Oh, and BLOCKED. Obvi.

Jackie "Jumpscare" Jinkins: Ooo! FINALLY a *real* horror fan! This collection is so badass! What's your favorite? Mine's "The Golden Dragon."

> **Blog Master Will:** Hmm . . . It's hard to pick a favorite. I love them all?

Debbie Cutwright: Jakobi Warren was a freak and a murderer.

Thee Horror Aficionado: Why are you so obsessed with this dude? He's mediocre at BEST

Mikey Meiers: Yo! You ever hear about the collection of thirteen short stories that allegedly one of Jakobi's interns wrote after the studio closed??? I might have a lead on where you can read them. DM me . . .

Blog Master Will: HO-LY SHIT. Say less.

Jackie "Jumpscare" Jinkins: It wasn't just one intern, I don't think?? I heard these stories were collected from a few different places, but no less cool.

Jackie "Jumpscare" Jinkins: Hey . . . uhhh . . . can I get in on those stories too???

ALL EYES ON ME

FARIDAH ÀBÍKÉ-ÍYÍMÍDÉ

DAILY NEWS

The Circus from HELL

Following an explosive one-night circus in the town of Nowhere last week, a string of missing persons has been reported in the area.

Local authorities are currently treating these incidents as connected; however, there are no current leads on the case.

If you have any information that could help please contact the police department at 555–0125.

1987, Middle of Nowhere, America

A FEW DAYS BEFORE

Once upon a time, in the town of Nowhere, Helen Thomas was trapped in a box, slowly suffocating under the weight of the world, and scared she'd stay trapped forever, never to be seen or heard again . . .

"I've been thinking about this for a really long time now, and you're great . . . I just think we'd do a lot better if we had more time apart . . . ," Helen said to her reflection in the rearview mirror.

The car was empty and mostly quiet, save for the heavy pelting of rain against the metal roof of the beat-up Mustang, accompanied by the swishing of the windshield wipers, which made a disturbing screeching sound each time the blades cleared more rain away.

She sighed, cleared her throat, and tried again.

"Asher, I think we should take a break. It'll be good for the both of us. In a few weeks, summer will be over, and then it'll be senior year. You can finally focus on football and college applications. And I'll be working to save up for the move to Los Angeles. I want to focus on my future, and I don't think I can do that with a boyfriend . . . we can try again maybe in a year or so or . . ." She stopped herself mid-lie, slumping a little in defeat, but then a moment later, she sat back up again.

If she was going to do this, she had to do it properly. She had to be honest. But the truth was so much harder to acknowledge, let alone admit to herself in the dark.

She adjusted the rearview mirror, flicking the car's interior lights on above her.

Now illuminated, she could see herself more clearly, though it took her a moment to recognize that the girl in the reflection was indeed herself.

Or rather, an exhausted-looking version of herself. There was a subtle dullness to her dark skin, her relaxer-reliant hair a mess and frizzing up from the rain she'd gotten caught in minutes ago, and her red lipstick smudged from the day's wear.

Helen quickly pulled her bag onto her lap, dug around in it, taking out a small golden tube she'd swiped from her mom's dresser some weeks ago. After pulling the mirror down some more, she popped the lid off the lipstick and pressed it to her mouth, staining it bright scarlet. She pressed her lips together, smoothed her damaged hair down with her hands, and began her breakup monologue again.

This time with all intentions of telling the truth.

What was the truth? She wasn't sure anymore.

She'd been living the lie for so long.

Helen cleared her throat. Pulled on a serious face. And opened her mouth.

"Asher—" she began, but was immediately cut off by the sound of the car door being thrown open as the pale grinning face and bright blue eyes of the devil in question appeared before her.

Helen's heart stopped for a moment, her deep-brown eyes widening as the truth lodged in her throat.

"Shit, Asher. You scared me!" she said, placing her hand over chest and her now erratic heartbeat.

Asher scrunched his eyebrows together, his wet brown hair plastered to his forehead as he stared at her in confusion. "Were you just . . . talking to yourself?" he questioned, as he maneuvered his lanky body into the driver's seat of the car.

Helen felt cold rush through her, both from the open door and from the thought of nearly being caught. "No . . ." she replied—another lie.

He didn't look convinced, but it was obvious he found it all so amusing.

"I'm pretty sure I even heard you say my name . . . Were you having some *alone* time?" he asked, his voice dropping an octave as he placed his large pale hand on her dark brown knee. "Because if you were," he whispered, "I can help finish you off."

She watched as his hand slowly moved under her dress, and she quickly shoved it away. "Stop being such a dog, Ash. One, I'm not doing anything here with you. We're at a *gas station* because *you* wanted to stop and pee. Two, we're already late for the movie," Helen said sternly, pulling her dress back down over her knees.

"You're right. Let's get to the movie," Asher said, in an uncharacteristically resigned manner. The usual Asher would shoot back a retort of some kind, something that would definitely result in Helen rolling her eyes while ruminating more on why she was still with him in the first place.

But instead, Asher moved away, tipping his head back onto the headrest, his expression flat and subdued.

For a moment, she feared he'd heard her breakup speech. She wasn't sure why that made her feel sick, but it did. She didn't want to hurt him, though maybe him overhearing her would make things easier. It would mean she'd finally gotten this over and done with.

But then why did the idea of no longer being with Asher make her feel worse?

"Are you okay?" Helen asked hesitantly, waiting for him to turn to her with his big glassy puppy-dog eyes and tell her that she'd betrayed him or something, but instead he did something else entirely.

Asher shook his head but didn't look at her. "Bowie died over the weekend," he said.

It took Helen a few moments to process that sentence.

"Oh . . ." she said, blinking at him slowly. "The singer? I didn't know you were a fan—"

He shook his head and finally looked squarely at her, those eyes of his disarming her in an instant. "No, not the singer, my sister's poodle named Bowie. I guess she must've named it after the guy. I was pretty close to him even though he wasn't mine," Asher continued. "I didn't say anything before because I didn't want to ruin our date, but then you said the word *dog*, and I remembered—"

"Oh, Ash, I'm so sorry," Helen said, taking his hand and squeezing.

"No, no, it's fine, I don't want to bring the mood down. I'm good."

"You sure?" she asked.

He nodded and smiled at her. "Yes, I'm sure. Thanks for asking though. You being so caring is one of the many things I love about you."

Helen felt her stomach twist. She couldn't tell if it was because of the food truck burger she'd had earlier or if it was this whole situation with Asher. He looked at her with so much expectation, like there wasn't a doubt in his mind that she wasn't a liar.

She needed some fresh air.

"I think I'm gonna get a water from the 7-Eleven. You want anything?" she asked him, opening the car door as she did.

Instantly, the cold swept inside and the rain along with it, which grazed her arm and gave her goose bumps.

"Nah, I'm good. I've got everything I need right here," he said, stroking her arm now.

His touch felt like one thousand little critters dancing on her skin.

"Cool!" she said, pulling away from him and clambering out of the car into the rain. "I won't be long—don't get impatient," she said, then slammed the car door behind her and hurried into the 7-Eleven before Asher could *touch* her again.

She couldn't remember a time she'd actually enjoyed Asher's touch, and they'd been together for three years now. All through freshman, sophomore, and junior years. He was her first boyfriend, her only boyfriend. Her first everything really.

Was that weird? That she didn't like the feeling of making out with her boyfriend after all this time? Or holding his hand? Or telling him she loved him? Or doing anything intimate at all?

Asher wasn't perfect, but he wasn't a terrible person either. He liked watching films as much as she did, and he treated her nice. Got her expensive gifts. Complimented her all the time.

He'd always tell her how much he loved her hair, her skin, her body.

Her friends would see them together and remind her of how lucky she was to have a boyfriend who adored her.

But why did she feel the opposite of lucky?

The chiming of the store's bell as she entered the 7-Eleven disrupted her thoughts.

That was enough thinking about him now. She clearly couldn't end things tonight, especially not when his family dog had just died.

"Hello?" a voice called out from somewhere outside Helen's head.

Helen looked up to find a girl standing in front of her.

She had dark brown skin, a small coily Afro, and circular spectacles that framed her face perfectly.

"Do you need any assistance?" the girl asked, with an arched eyebrow and a smile. Her face was so striking, filled with all sorts of perfectly placed angles and contours. Helen almost forgot her words.

"Um, yes, water, I need water—a bottle of it preferably," Helen said, her voice a little high-pitched.

"I believe we do have that," she replied in an almost-teasing way. "It's over here. Follow me," the girl said, and Helen did.

As she walked behind the girl, she noticed her peculiar fashion sense. Not that Helen could judge much, seeing as her own go-to colors were boring earth tones.

But it was hard not to notice the brightness of the girl's orange waistcoat, light-green corduroy bell-bottoms, and her chunky bright red boots. They were colors that were meant to stand out. She clearly didn't mind being seen.

"Here we are," she said, sliding open one of the refrigerator doors and handing Helen a bottle, their fingers brushing together for less than a nanosecond as she did. Yet that fraction of time felt much longer.

"Th-thanks," Helen quickly said, and the girl smiled even wider, revealing an endearing snaggletooth.

"No problem at all. Need help with anything else?" Gas Station Girl (or GSG for short) asked.

Helen shook her head. "I should be, uh, good with finding the rest of the, um, stuff myself." Her words stumbled clumsily out of her mouth, like she no longer knew how to structure a sentence.

She didn't even know what else she was looking for or if she even needed anything else. She just knew she wanted to be normal again and was struggling to be right now.

"Okay, well, give us a shout if you need anything," GSG said, before turning away and going back over to the checkout station.

Helen couldn't help but watch her walk away. Taking in more details, like the lemongrass scent she left behind and her movements, confident and strong.

The more Helen looked at GSG's clothes, the more she found herself liking them.

It wasn't necessarily something Helen would wear herself, but they somehow suited this girl. Made her look good.

Helen's eyes traveled up to the girl's face, and she startled when she saw the girl staring right back at her. Catching her red-handed.

Helen shifted her eyes away, pretending to find interest in the jar of pickles in front of her, grateful to her own complexion for hiding the heat slowly creeping up her face.

A few moments later, Helen found herself in front of the girl once again, ready to pay and go back to the car, where she could no longer hide from her own man-made house of horrors.

She placed her items on the counter, and the girl smiled at her in this strange knowing way while tapping the objects' values into the cash register.

Helen pretended not to notice the girl's expression, looking instead at the bulletin board behind her, where several rows of the same bright poster hung on the board.

> **Circe Des Rêves**
>
> **—Here for One Night Only**
>
> **A circus like no other. Come and see our world-class acrobats, our trained circus pets, our fire-breathing men, and our terrifically terrifying Clowns!**
>
> **This special event will also be televised for the first time!**

Helen felt a jolt of excitement at the mention of cameras. Her sudden interest must have been obvious because the girl was now turning to look at the poster too.

"You like the circus?" the girl asked.

"I guess it sounds . . . cool," Helen said, which was a lie. She didn't care much for the circus itself but rather the fact there'd be cameras, which meant she could be seen by hundreds of people. Maybe even more than that.

"I wouldn't peg you for a circus girl."

Helen raised an eyebrow at her. "What kind of girl would you peg me for?"

"Hmm . . . I don't know yet. I guess that part is a mystery for now—oh fuck." The girl groaned as the bag she'd been placing Helen's purchases inside ripped. "I'll need to double this, hold on a moment," she said before turning around, sliding a footstool in front of her, and climbing up to get more bags from the storage behind the checkout.

Helen tried to watch as subtly as she could while the girl dug around.

"There we go. These should do just fine," the girl said, jumping down from the stool and turning back to Helen.

"Thanks," Helen mumbled, as she averted her gaze again.

Quiet crept in while the girl carefully double bagged her things.

"What's your name?" the girl asked suddenly, disrupting the silence.

"What?" Helen asked as a reflex. She hadn't expected a question.

"Your name. What do people call you?"

"Oh . . . Helen."

The girl nodded thoughtfully, but before Helen could ask for her name too, the girl was speaking again. "Helen, like Helen of Troy . . . the girl who launched a thousand ships. Very . . . *fitting*," she said, staring directly at Helen, or rather *through her*, like she was somehow reading all her thoughts, turning them over one by one.

Helen didn't know much about Greek myths, so she didn't know if that was a good or a bad thing.

"I'm actually named after my aunt Helena, but my mom didn't like my aunt much and so got rid of the *a*," Helen clarified, as GSG turned to grab some store coupons from the shelf. Helen tried not to look at her too closely once again.

"Well, then . . . Helen without an *a* . . ." the girl said, her back still to Helen. "In the future, you should ask a girl to dinner after you finish checking her out. It's only polite . . ."

Helen stilled, taken aback by the implication. "I wasn't—"

"I know. I'm just joking," GSG said, still smiling. "That'll be a dollar and fifty cents."

Helen's face grew even warmer.

She quickly slid across three fifty-cent coins and then took the bag off the counter. She wanted to leave before this whole exchange could get any more awkward. She mumbled a thank-you and goodbye and quickly turned to walk away, but she was stopped by the girl's hand on her wrist.

"Wait," the girl said, and Helen was forced to look up at her once again.

Helen's heart stuttered when she did.

GSG yanked one of the circus fliers from the board and handed it to Helen. "It's my uncle's circus. We're kind of a nomad family. We travel every few weeks to different towns and cities all around the world. You should come along."

"You work here *and* the circus?" Helen said. Those were all the words she could muster.

"Just the circus. I'm covering a few shifts to help an old friend of my uncle's out while we're here, but the circus is my main thing. I have this whole act where I dress up as a clown and scare all the kids with my evil clown laugh," she said with a wicked smile. "I promise it's a lot of fun and I'm not just saying that because I have a vested interest in all this."

Helen looked down at the flier and then back up at her. Helen nodded, feeling her heartbeat in her throat. "Oh, uh . . . yeah, I guess I'll see. My *boyfriend* loves this stuff, so it might be worth checking out," she said, cringing internally for using Asher to prove some benign point to this girl. The point being that Helen was the sort of girl who had a boyfriend. It all seemed so silly to even mention it in the first place.

It wasn't all a lie though—Asher did have a strange obsession with clowns. He'd even made her watch that *Poltergeist* movie that had come out last year for this reason alone. Yet she still felt like a fraud for bringing him up.

The girl did not flinch at the mention of Helen's boyfriend. She just smiled at her and said, "Good, I hope I do see you there. It was nice meeting you, Helen."

The way she said her name, combined with that snaggletoothed smile of hers, made it feel like they were playing a silent game of truth or dare and she had just issued a dare.

Helen nodded, smiling tightly back at her. Not quite accepting the dare, but also not turning her back on it either. "It was nice meeting you too . . ."

The girl answered Helen's unspoken question: "Beatrice."

"Beatrice," Helen repeated, liking the feel of her name on her tongue.

"But my friends call me *Tris*," Beatrice added.

Was that an invitation? Helen thought. *To be friends?*

"Oh right . . . Tris," Helen said.

Something in Beatrice's expression shifted, and Helen could tell then that she had won the dare.

Without another word, Helen rushed out of the 7-Eleven feeling breathless, as if she'd climbed ten thousand steps. The cold wet air coated her skin as she flung the car door open before climbing in quickly, as though Beatrice would catch her and expose more of her unuttered secrets.

The door slammed shut loudly behind her, the sound like a gunshot ringing in the air.

"What took you so long?" Asher asked when she got back.

She almost startled again, somehow having forgotten he was there. "I got distracted, sorry. Let's just go," she said.

He started the car once again and placed one arm back around her as he began to reverse out of the gas station. She couldn't tell if it was the vibrations from the car or her own internal shaking; either way she felt on the brink of collapse.

As Asher drove away, Helen did not look back to see if Gas Station Girl was visible in the window. Even though she so wanted to. Instead, she turned to look at her boyfriend.

She felt something inside her break at how underwhelming the feeling was. She truly felt nothing. No tingling when his fingers grazed her back. No nervousness when he looked at her as he drove along the wide stretch of the road, nor joy when he leaned over to kiss her forehead before returning his gaze ahead.

Just an underwhelming nothingness.

You should ask a girl to dinner first after checking her out, it's only polite.

Beatrice's teasing words echoed inside the dark corners of Helen's mind, and when she closed her eyes, she could see Beatrice again.

This wasn't the first time Helen had seen a stranger and felt weird, confusing things. Sometimes she felt this way when she was watching a film and some beautiful tall actress would waltz onto the screen; uncomfortable feelings would swirl inside, and she'd be overwhelmed by them all.

It was so much easier to switch off a movie when it got to be too much—much harder to switch off a person.

That didn't mean she couldn't try.

She squeezed her eyes shut, trying to erase the unease. She thought of things that made her truly happy. Like the future and what could come of it.

A future where she would no longer be an insignificant, unknown, unseen thing in an insignificant, unknown, unseen town. A day when everyone would know the name Helen Thomas, and she'd finally be seen on screens all over the world. In her dreams she would get to Hollywood, and she'd star in the most wonderful pictures. She'd be something. *Be someone.* Not just Asher's girl.

Something real.

Something of her own.

"Wake up sleepyhead, we're here," Asher said.

She felt his hot breath against her ear and everything inside her twisted and shriveled up. She opened her eyes, disappointed to see it wasn't the future yet. She was still in this car, still a nobody. "I wasn't asleep," she said, though she *had been* dreaming.

"Sure, you weren't. I'm gonna go grab some popcorn and collect our speakers for the film. Want anything?"

"I'm good," she said.

He nodded and went off to fetch the food, while she stared ahead at the giant screen and the many cars parked around them, waiting for the film to start.

They would be watching the 1966 *Batman*, a classic and also a favorite of theirs.

Looking into the other cars, she caught glimpses of couples making out. Some were chaste kisses, others accompanied by passionate heavy petting.

She thought about what it would be like to kiss someone and have it *not* be a lie.

She thought about what it would be like to kiss Beatrice. Helen guessed Beatrice was a good kisser.

Not that Helen would ever have the chance to confirm this suspicion.

There was a sudden bang on the roof of the Mustang, and Helen jumped, looking up as though she'd somehow be able to see what had caused the loud noise through the opaque material.

Just then, there was a knock on the window. She turned, but there was no one there.

Is it hailing outside or something? she thought, but the sky had cleared up since the rain from earlier; it was now just cold and damp.

Suddenly, she heard a third bang, but this time she saw something.

In the windshield, towering over the car, a face hidden behind a white clown mask appeared.

Helen froze as the clown's face stared down at her in the dark. She couldn't breathe. The clown moved slowly toward the driver's side of the car. The intruder stretched one hand up as if grabbing something from the roof. A *weapon*, she suspected. She felt air return to her lungs once more and started breathing fast. She heard the car door unlock and quickly scanned the interior for something that could be used as protection, but annoyingly, Asher's car was empty.

She wanted to cry, to run, to do *something*, but as usual she choked. Unable to flee even when everything in her screamed for her to do so. Instead, she sat frozen as the clown reached for the door handle.

She watched in horror as the car door opened, and the masked intruder casually slid inside, careful not to spill the popcorn in his hands.

Helen could hear a low chuckle as the clown lifted his mask, revealing the face of her annoying soon-to-be *ex*-boyfriend.

"Oh my God, you should have seen your face, Hel! Priceless.

Absolutely priceless—" He was cut off by Helen's hand swiping him across the head.

"That wasn't funny, Asher."

He smiled, rubbing his temple. "It was funny to me."

She folded her arms and sat back in the seat, annoyed that he'd do that to her. He knew she scared easily.

He leaned in close, placing his hand on hers. "I'm sorry, Hel. I just wanted to surprise you, raise the spirits and all."

"Yeah, well, I don't like my spirits raised in that way. Next time you pull something like that, I'm going to chop off your head along with that creepy mask and feed it to a pack of chickens."

Asher found this very funny; he threw his head back in laughter like it wasn't a serious threat. "Hel, you're hilarious," he said, plugging the speaker into the Mustang's radio compartment.

"Thanks, I want to be a clown when I'm older," she answered sarcastically.

"Well, you're halfway there with this mask and that hair of yours," he said with a jovial smile.

Helen self-consciously brought her hand up to her hair, smoothing it down gently. She caught a glimpse of it in the rearview mirror again. She was overdue on her next appointment but hadn't gotten a chance to go to the salon in a while. The relaxers burned her scalp, and she never looked forward to that feeling.

Helen thought about asking him what he meant by that, but she remembered his sister's dead poodle and decided to play nice.

It wasn't the first time Asher had made a strange remark about her hair, but for some reason, this time his words made something inside her burn. Like indigestion, but worse—deeper . . . darker.

She dropped her hands and her courage and decided to ignore his comment. "I think the movie's starting," she said instead, noticing the flicker of the big screen.

Asher sat up, eager as the movie began to play.

But Helen wasn't watching the screen anymore. She watched him.

If it weren't for Bowie, this might've been the perfect time to just come out with it. While he was still distracted and under the influence of cinema magic, but unfortunately, the dog was dead, and in many ways, so was she.

The film went on, and the crowd was mostly quiet; that is, until Lee Meriwether appeared as Catwoman. There were some jeers from the crowd, people whistling as the feline bombshell sauntered onto the big screen.

Helen had watched this movie more than once, and her reaction was the same whenever Lee came on the screen. She'd feel her heart pick up its pace, causing guilt to rise inside her.

Asher sat forward, grabbed a handful of popcorn, and stuffed it into his mouth, chewing loudly in a manner that felt unbearably obnoxious even though it probably wasn't.

"She's so hot, right?" Asher whispered, and Helen looked at him with an eyebrow raised.

"She's okay I guess," Helen said with a shrug. "I love Catwoman though. You know, I hope they do a Catwoman movie or show that I can audition for. I really want to play her someday."

Asher snorted. "*You* want to play Catwoman?" he asked in a tone she didn't like.

"Yeah . . . that's what I just said."

He shook his head.

"What?"

"You don't exactly *look* like Catwoman, I guess."

Helen narrowed her eyes. "What's that supposed to mean?"

"Well, for one—and I mean this with love, Hel—Catwoman is a bombshell. It would disturb the whole sanctity of the role, you know? I think she needs to be depicted correctly, not just by *anyone*. Also, you know I support any dream of yours, but I don't know, I just think it's better to be realistic. You don't get hurt that way."

His words pierced through Helen, digging out almost all the joy and hope inside her. Almost. She thought about arguing with him, mentioning Eartha Kitt and her iconic portrayal of Catwoman in *The Batman* television series. She thought about telling him how much seeing Eartha in that role had made her feel seen in ways she usually didn't. How seeing Eartha had made Helen realize she wanted to do it too, to go to Hollywood, to be an actress.

But she didn't say any of that; she wouldn't let Asher kill any more of her dreams.

"Didn't realize you were such a big fan of Catwoman," Helen simply said, her voice wavering only slightly.

He shrugged, stuffing more popcorn into his mouth. "She's okay, you know, for a *girl* supervillain. Lee Meriwether is so hot though, so I guess I am a fan."

Helen nodded and sat in silence. She took out the circus flier, focusing on it and ignoring the heaviness in her eyes and on her lashes.

She had to stop being such a coward about it. She had to end things before she was stuck in this lie, in this town, forever. Breaking up with him was her only way out.

When the film was almost over, she felt a little courage finally settle inside her.

"Hey, Ash . . . ," Helen said softly.

"Mm-hmm?" he replied, not looking at her. Too taken by the film.

"There's a circus in town tomorrow. We should go."

Asher's eyebrows shot up, and he finally looked at her, interested. "We totally should, make the most of our summer while it lasts. Maybe you can finally spend the night," he said with a smile.

Helen forced a smile. "Yeah, maybe . . . but you know how strict my parents are . . . so we'll see."

In truth, Helen's parents would probably be fine with her staying the night. They loved Asher more than she ever could. He represented everything they wanted for her. A white picket fence and an eternity spent in suburbia.

Helen had grown so accustomed to lying to herself that the lies she told others slipped out with ease.

She could end things at the circus, a place where he'd at least find some joy in the aftermath.

And secretly she hoped for other things at the circus, like maybe seeing Beatrice again.

He brought his hand up to her face, moving her hair back and staring directly into her eyes. His unsettling blue met her terrified brown.

He leaned in and kissed her.

She let him.

He tasted like sweet popcorn and entitlement.

She counted the seconds it took for it to stop, and when it did, she felt like she could breathe again.

Tomorrow Helen wouldn't have to pretend anymore.

Tomorrow she'd finally be free.

The circus tent had been set up at what felt like the edge of the world but was really just a field in a nonresidential corner of town.

It looked majestic. The cone-shaped tent, with its black, red, and white spiral stripes, jutted into low-hanging clouds, sticking out boldly against the evening's dark blue sky. The pattern on the stripes created an optical illusion, making it seem like they were swirling and moving around.

Helen had spent the entire journey practicing her speech in her head, as she had been for several weeks now, but it never seemed quite right.

Maybe it was because it seemed like she had no real reason to end things other than the feeling that something just wasn't right.

In an alternate universe, there was probably another her walking about whose dream it was to be with Asher forever. Sometimes she envied Alternate Universe Helen—*she* didn't have confusing thoughts and feelings. That imagined world was probably one of the many reasons Helen was scared to end things. But a life with him wasn't a dream for Helen in this universe, not even close.

"I didn't realize this was such a big deal. It's weird I didn't hear about it until you mentioned it—had they even been advertising it?" Asher asked, his hand clasped in hers.

She shrugged. "I didn't see the flyers until yesterday either. Apparently it's a family business or something," Helen replied, remembering what Beatrice had said.

They were in the long line outside the circus tent, waiting to enter, near the back because Asher had made them late again with his incessant need to pee every thirty minutes like a toddler.

Asher looked at her and laughed. "You look a little ridiculous with those sunglasses on. You haven't taken them off all day, and the sun has practically set now."

"They go with my outfit," Helen answered simply, even though that wasn't the reason she'd opted to wear sunglasses today. But she was sure he wouldn't like to hear that his comments yesterday had resulted in her crying herself to sleep. Her eyes were still red rimmed, and she'd prefer not to have questions asked about it.

She just wanted to get tonight over and done with.

"If you say so . . . ," he muttered, as they moved down the line.

Half an hour later, they were inside the tent (which looked much bigger on the inside than it did on the outside, if that was even possible). There were many townspeople, some people she recognized from around her neighborhood and others who were complete strangers.

It was so crowded, there was barely any space to think or breathe.

"Oh, look, Hel, they have video games," Asher said, gesturing to a row of gaming machines with small crowds of boys who couldn't be more than twelve gathered in clusters, watching the screens intently.

"You want to go and play? I don't mind doing my own thing for a while," Helen said, partly wanting to put off the inevitable as long as she could.

"You sure? I don't want to abandon you here," Asher asked, his eyes focused on the machines and not on her.

He *clearly* didn't want to leave her alone.

"I know you want to play, go ahead. I'll keep myself entertained. They seem to have a lot going on," Helen said, wincing at the bright lights and the loud noise of the crowd as people rushed about excitedly.

Asher quickly planted a kiss on Helen's mouth and whispered, "You're the best," before hurrying over to the crowded gaming machines with her red lipstick smudged on his lips, jumping at the chance to play games with like-minded people.

His smile was wide; he looked so happy.

Good, Helen thought. *At least tonight won't be all bad.*

She scanned the expanse of the large tent, looking for things to distract herself from the conversation she'd be having soon.

The one that would start with *I want to end things* and end with so many unanswered questions, like: Why did complete strangers excite her more than her boyfriend of three years? Why did the thought of kissing other boys instead of Asher make her feel just as uneasy as he did?

And why was the idea of kissing girls more appealing?

Helen squeezed her eyes shut, wanting to delete that last thought permanently from her mind.

When she opened them, her head was clear, but her vision was not. In her direct line of sight, watching her from the corner of the room was . . . a clown.

A very familiar-looking clown at that.

The clown's dark brown skin was painted white with a bold red smile, her hair a black Afro, her clothes bright and circus-like.

The clown smiled at Helen, raising her hand to wave at her.

And Helen, unsure of what to do with herself, awkwardly smiled and waved back.

It was like those cheesy movies Asher hated but Helen secretly loved.

That scene where the boy surveyed a busy crowd, looking for something of little to no significance, when he was struck by the thing that would forever change him. He spotted the girl of his dreams in the crowd, and he knew in that moment that today was the first day of the rest of his life.

Clown Girl, also known as Beatrice the gas station girl, smiled wickedly at Helen before pushing herself off the wall she was leaning against and making her way through the crowd over to Helen.

It felt like the girl was moving in slow motion; Helen couldn't quite believe that she was even here to begin with.

"Hello, Helen of Troy," Beatrice said, when she finally got to her. "Enjoying the circus so far?"

Helen felt like she could barely breathe, but she somehow managed a nod and a quick reply. "Yes. It's very . . . busy."

Beatrice's smile stretched even wider, her eyes searching like they'd done yesterday, sorting through Helen's thoughts, seeing right through her unstable exterior. There was something weirdly comforting about Beatrice's appearance.

"You look, um, really different," Helen said, wanting to contribute something to this conversation and not have Beatrice think she was uninteresting.

Beatrice looked down at her clown costume. "I do? I thought I always looked this colorful. That's disappointing."

Helen panicked. Had she accidentally insulted her or something? "I just meant you looked really good—cool, I mean, really, really cool. Better than usual even . . ."

Clown Girl's eyebrows furrowed. "You're saying I look better as a clown?"

Helen kept putting her foot in her mouth somehow. She wasn't sure why this strange girl made her feel so nervous; what was there to even be nervous about?

Clown Girl's expression broke into one of amusement. "I'm just pulling your leg, sorry. I'm a bit of a menace when I'm in costume. Helps with the character I'm building," she said.

"What character is that?" Helen asked, her arms folded, hoping her embarrassment at being so easily fooled wasn't noticeable.

The Clown Girl stepped close to Helen, closing almost all the space between them. "It's a secret."

Helen swallowed. "A secret?"

"Mm-hmm, and if I tell you, I'd unfortunately have to kill you," Clown Girl said in a low whisper, and then she stepped back, wearing that mischievous look on her face.

"Ah . . . Well, I quite like living, so I guess I won't ask."

"Good choice. It's hard to get blood out of polyester," Clown Girl said.

Helen nodded, gesturing to the girl's outfit. "Not to mention white. It's also hard to get blood out of white."

"Exactly," Clown Girl said, maintaining eye contact.

Helen smiled shyly, then caught herself and returned quickly to a neutral expression.

She anxiously searched for Asher, who was still by the gaming machines, but this time he was playing, and the crowd was watching and cheering him on.

"Have you managed to check out any of the attractions yet?" Clown Girl asked.

Helen pulled her eyes away from her boyfriend and back to her. "No, not yet. I was just looking around for something interesting to do while I wait for my boyfriend to finish playing video games. Got any recommendations?"

At the word *boyfriend*, Clown Girl turned back to the machines, her eyes searching the sea of people for the boy. Helen couldn't tell if she identified him, because Clown Girl turned back to her with a shrug. "Depends on what you fancy really. I can give you a rundown of how things work here?"

Helen nodded. "That'd be useful," she said. It was too overwhelming trying to figure it all out herself.

"All right then, follow me," the girl said with a smile and a wink.

And Helen did just that.

They circled the room, Clown Girl showing Helen the exhibitions, such as the fire-breathing acrobats, the clown balloon show that she'd be joining later, and the men on stilts. Then she showed her the random games they had to offer: pin the tail on the donkey, pinball machines, as well as other game machines, some much like the one Asher had been glued to, and others that all had some variation of smashing a ball into something and possibly winning a giant plushy toy.

"And lastly, we have this attraction. I recommend it for people who aren't so fond of the crowds but still want to be entertained." Clown Girl gestured up to a banner above this new section of the tent. The words read *Hall of Mirrors*.

"Sounds right up my street," Helen said, still reeling from all the information as well as the growing size of the crowd inside the tent.

Clown Girl smiled. "I take it you're more of a homebody, like to keep to yourself, unseen and whatnot."

Helen shrugged. "Sometimes, I don't know, I get overwhelmed. But I actually love being in front of people—in performance, not so much in the everyday. I guess being in a crowd when you're one of the faceless many is not the same as being in front of a crowd when everyone has come to see *you*." Helen wasn't sure if she was making any sense, but Beatrice didn't seem confused.

"Performance? You're into singing?" she asked, and not in a way that felt mocking, but instead with a genuine curiosity.

"Acting," Helen corrected.

"Wow, I see that. You've got the looks for it. I'd pay to see you," she said.

Helen felt her face warm. "Thank you. My boyfriend tells me girls who look like me aren't big-picture material, so that means a lot."

Her face screwed up, and darkness fell over her features as she looked directly into Helen's eyes. "He has no idea what he's talking about, Helen. None at all. Don't listen to him. No offense to your boyfriend or anything but men aren't that bright."

Helen smiled a little at that. "No offense taken."

"So, the hall of mirrors it is?" Beatrice asked.

Helen nodded, looking ahead at the dark room through the attraction's entrance. "It's not scary, is it?"

"Not at all, kids love it. Some say it's like facing up to all these versions yourself and coming out better in the end with a new clarity. A kind of spiritual experience, I guess. But if you do get scared, you can just knock on any one of the mirrors, and someone'll be right out to help you."

Helen felt better hearing that. "Thanks, that helps."

"I'll let you go in then. Have fun, and tell me how it goes," Beatrice said with a smile, before stepping away.

Helen nodded, looking back as she walked away, then shifting her gaze over to the games, where Asher seemed to be wrapping up and talking to the guys around him now.

She quickly slipped inside the hall of mirrors before he could spot her too.

Like a coward, she hid, wanting to buy as much time before the truth had to come out.

As expected from a place with the name *hall of mirrors*, there were mirrors everywhere. On the walls, where she could see herself pass by. On the ceiling, where she could only see her head and shoulders and not much else. And on the floor, where it felt like she was walking all over her own shadow.

Beatrice had been right about this attraction. It was much quieter.

Eerily so.

The only sound Helen could hear were her kitten heels against the plastic of the mirrored floor.

It really did feel like she was alone, the only person left in the whole entire world.

As she walked along, her reflection followed her, staring back at her with the same bewilderment she felt about herself, her present, and her future.

She watched as her reflection suddenly turned and stepped away, abandoning her in the dark and leaving the mirror empty. Helen stopped walking, blinking fast, wondering if this was real.

How this was real.

She quickly walked over to the next mirror panel and saw herself again, but this time it wasn't a version of herself she recognized.

She looked a few years older, exhausted and withering away. *Alternate Universe Helen*, she immediately thought.

Helen moved to the next panel, and there she was again.

This time, mirror Helen was dressed in a white gown and wore a long glittering veil.

When she got to the next panel, she almost gasped at the sight of Asher, who stood behind this version of herself. She looked back in the room, searching for the real Asher, but he wasn't there. She was alone.

This Asher was a mirror fake, holding on to the rounded stomach of mirror Helen.

Another alternate universe, one where she stayed with Asher, choosing a life with misery—the third wheel in their unhappy marriage. This Helen had the white picket fence her parents coveted for her. When Asher went out into the world and worked, this Helen remained at home, hidden in the shadows of suburbia, her body a factory for pumping out kids to populate their own house of horrors.

Helen frantically moved past the other frames, watching this potential life unfold in front of her.

A life with Asher, trapped together in this town of Nowhere, where she stayed imprisoned in her skin, never becoming anything, never being seen by anyone.

In the next panels, mirror Helen shrank in on herself, until she became nothing but dust. But Asher was still there, smiling at her menacingly. In some frames, he was laughing, others he was judging her, and the rest he was just grinning.

"*I can't breathe,*" Helen whispered in the dark hallway to herself and all the versions of herself trapped behind the glass.

She needed to get out of there.

Helen looked around frantically, her vision shaky, her limbs vibrating as she paced around before finally taking off into a run when the terror got to be too much for her to stand still.

She stumbled as she ran through the haunted halls, then banged into a mirror at a dead end. She turned back, running the other way, but found herself running into another wall with no exit.

She was trapped; there was no way out.

Her breaths became uneven as she turned to find another mirror reflection of herself. This Helen was crying. She couldn't tell if this one was real. If this one was really her.

"Helen," she heard a voice say from somewhere in the dark, and she saw Asher again in the mirror, stepping out from behind her.

"Leave me alone, please," she whispered.

Silence followed, then footsteps.

"What happened?" he asked, his eyebrows bunching together.

"I need to get out," she said, her voice rising. She felt itchy and tired.

"The exit is just over—"

"I don't want this. I don't want to be trapped forever hating myself and hating you," Helen said, shaking her head, blinking hard to erase him forever.

"Helen—" false Asher said, stepping forward into a different panel, his arm almost lifelike as it reached toward her.

She panicked and screamed. "Get away from me!" Despite knowing none of this was real, she felt something overtake her completely as she shoved him away from her, hard. She waited for the feeling of the impact, waited for the stinging in her palms, expecting it to feel like her hands were hitting the plastic mirror, but instead she felt the familiar softness of his chest.

Helen watched in horror as Asher, who suddenly seemed to be real, stumbled backward, losing his footing completely and hitting his head on the sharp corner of the wall.

Helen heard a crack as he slumped to the ground.

He's real. Asher was real.

And he was lying there like a doll, unmoving.

"A-Asher . . . ," she said quietly, hoping his eyes would open. But he didn't move an inch.

"Asher, stop playing," she said, stepping closer to him. Her voice was wobbly as she watched the life slither out of the boy. His eyes were open wide, his jaw slack.

"Asher, please," she said, getting on her knees, her hands shaky, searching his neck, his wrist, his chest for a pulse, but she realized quite quickly that she had no idea how to check if he had one.

Everything about him was so quiet. So unlike Asher.

She felt sick.

What had she done?

"Helen . . . ," she heard again, feeling her heart stutter as Asher mumbled her name once more.

He blinked and opened his blue eyes, which were luminous under the bright spotlighted ceiling.

Thank God, she thought.

She slowly helped him to his feet.

"I'm so sorry, Ash—oh my God, you're bleeding!" she said as she looked down at the ground and saw splatters of red.

Asher placed his hand at the back of his head before presenting his bloody fingers to her. "Why . . . ?" he started, blinking quickly. "What were you doing in here?"

She didn't know what to say in response to that, so she said nothing.

"You said . . . you hated me . . . that you were trapped," Asher continued.

"I don't—I didn't," she began.

He shook his head, his brows furrowed. "You did say that though. I *heard* you."

He was right; she had said it, and she'd meant it. And from the way he was looking at her now, she could tell he knew that too. The truth was written all over her face, smudged by the tears on her cheeks.

"I think we should break up," Helen finally said.

There was a beat of silence, and she watched Asher's face for a change of expression, but he just stared at her in disbelief.

"Why?" he said, placing his hand on the back of his head again, presumably to stop the bleeding.

"W-we just have different futures . . . and goals . . . I—I want to g-go to Hollywood, star in pictures—"

He scoffed in her face. "Hell, that's not a real reason."

She felt her nerves thrumming through her bloodstream, or perhaps it wasn't nerves at all but something else. "It is—" she replied, cut off by his laughter.

"Fuck, Helen . . . you can't just go to Hollywood. That's not real. Not for people like us. Who's the last person from Nowhere that you heard starred in a picture? That's right, no one. You've been going on about this for years, and I hoped you'd start to take life more seriously, but you just keep picking at this dream of yours—"

"What's wrong with dreaming?" she said, cutting him off this time. Her voice was cold and hollow.

He looked at her, almost pityingly. "Well, Hel. You gotta wake up at some point, right? Even if a girl from Nowhere could make it to the pictures, that girl probably isn't you . . . for one, all those fancy actresses are blond and, you know . . ." He hesitated, not saying the quiet part out loud. "You gotta wake up, realize how good I am for you, how good we are—fuck, my head kills."

She didn't let herself take in his opinions. They didn't matter anymore.

"I am wide awake, Asher, believe me," she said.

She heard him laugh again, but before he could say more demeaning things to her, he was interrupted by fate.

Fate being the familiar figure of a clown behind him.

Helen watched in what felt like slow motion as the clown raised her hand high, revealing a large butcher's knife, which she plunged into Asher's shoulder.

The sound he made could only be described as inhuman. Bloodcurdling, shrill, and filled with unfathomable agony.

It was the sound Helen heard inside too, every time she told herself a lie.

No more.

Helen stepped back, her limbs shaky as she saw the clown appear in every reflection. The clown tilted her head at Helen, as if asking, *What now? It's your call.*

The knife was still deep inside Asher, the clown's gloved hand gripping the handle.

Asher pleaded, crying out for help. But his voice just echoed, bouncing off the reflective surfaces, only to be swallowed whole by the dark. He frantically reached out for Helen, but she was only focused on the clown, who nodded at her and grinned wide as she yanked the knife out of Asher's shoulder—which only made him scream more.

She watched Asher fall to the ground like a puppet whose strings had been cut.

As her ex-boyfriend squirmed on the ground, Helen held her hand out for the knife, finally answering the clown's silent question.

What now? It's your call.

Asher lay on his back, looking up at her, his eyes wide and afraid. He started kicking and clawing at the ground, groaning as he tried to escape.

The clown handed her the knife, and Helen took a deep breath.

Now she would finally end things.

Raising the knife above her head, Helen took three confident strides over to Asher. Then she let every lie, every muted emotion, every version of herself she had played spill out as she sank the knife into his heart.

Another scream ripped from him. Helen knelt and took him in her arms as his voice began to fade. The last thing he would see was her. Her statement was the last thing he would hear before he was fully devoured by the endless sleep that was death:

"Let go, Ash, go to sleep. There is nothing wrong with dreaming," she whispered, and then he fell still.

For a few moments, the world followed suit, still and silent, and then Helen remembered she was not alone.

She turned to find the clown, Beatrice, still standing in the corner.

"I'm glad you got your clarity," Tris said.

"What now?" Helen asked, in a state of shock. She couldn't believe what she'd just done. Couldn't believe she had *killed* someone. That someone being Asher.

Asher was dead because of her.

She caught sight of herself in the mirror once more. The reflection staring back at her was different. A new iteration of Helen, this one dressed like a clown, blood dripping all over her, from head to toe. Her clown smile, much like her regular smile, was a performance, painted on for the world to see.

Beatrice walked over to her, and Helen pulled her eyes away from the reflection, her gaze now on the crime scene.

"Now . . . we take him to my uncle's trailer, and I'll handle the rest."

As the circus raged on, the sound of laughter and high spirits in the air, the two girls dragged Asher's body out into the night, careful not to drop him.

The area was deserted enough that they were able to walk along the path in the field to where the trailer was parked.

Helen did not look Asher in the face. It would be like staring directly into the truth, something she had never been good at doing.

Nearby, the sound of people talking rang out, and Helen felt like throwing up.

"We need to hurry," Beatrice said, watching over Helen's shoulder as the group's shadow loomed around the corner. "We're almost there."

Thankfully, they made it to the door of the vehicle. Tris quickly opened it, and on the count of two, they hauled Asher's body inside.

He fell to the ground with a thud, and Tris sighed. "Wow, your boyfriend was *heavy*," she said.

He's not my boyfriend, Helen wanted to say, but she couldn't bring herself to.

It didn't matter anymore.

"I need to run back and get some supplies real quick. Wait here, okay?" Beatrice said.

"You want me to wait in here alone? What if your uncle comes back, or what if someone finds me—?" Helen started.

"He won't, they won't, you're safe here, and I won't be long, I promise," Beatrice said.

Helen wanted to fight back, but she wasn't sure what other options she had at this point, so she nodded, and the girl smiled at her and then left Helen alone in the trailer with nothing for company but Asher's corpse.

Five minutes passed, then ten minutes, then twenty, and the girl still hadn't returned.

It started to dawn on Helen that she didn't know this girl at all. It was very possible that Beatrice had set Helen up. Maybe that was what she was doing right now: calling the cops.

Any moment now, they'd be here, and Helen would be put in handcuffs and escorted straight to the local county jail.

Helen let out a shaky breath. This had to be one of her twisted nightmares. None of it felt real. Not the versions of herself she'd seen in the mirrors, nor the fact that she was standing right next to Asher's dead body.

She felt dizzy and unwell, like she could die right then and there.

She needed to get out.

Helen nearly stumbled over Asher's body on her way out of the trailer, her breaths getting more uneven as she burst out of the supposed safety inside and out into the scary unknown.

Helen walked a short distance from the trailer and felt tears anchor her eyes closed as she took a deep breath of the crisp night air, almost choking out a cry but was stopped by the sound of something terrifying.

"Helen?" a voice said in the dark.

Her eyes flew open.

She'd been found. It was too late for her. Someone had finally seen her, and she was screwed.

She turned toward the voice, and relief almost knocked the wind out of her.

It was just Beatrice, standing with a worried expression and what looked like another dead body at first but revealed itself to be a medium-sized rug all rolled up.

"Are you okay? Did something happen?" she asked.

For a few moments, Helen didn't say anything, she was still reeling from all the events of the night. Or rather, all the events of the past hour. "I—I'm f-fine, I—I j-just couldn't b-breath in that trailer a-alone."

Tris nodded. "That's okay. I'm here now," she said, reaching out to squeeze her hand. Helen felt herself immediately relax. "Let's head back in."

Helen nodded reluctantly. They returned to the trailer, and she let Tris go back inside first before following suit.

But when they returned, something had changed.

"What the—" Beatrice began as they stepped back into the cramped trailer. Helen came in behind her, her eyes following Tris's gaze over to the empty space on the ground where Asher had been only minutes before.

Helen's heart stopped altogether as the rug slipped out of Tris's arms and onto the ground with a thump.

"Wh-where did he—? How—?" Tris began, turning back to Helen with a look of horror.

Helen shook her head quickly. "I—I don't know."

Beatrice rushed forward, looking under the bed in the corner of the trailer, then in the built-in cabinets, even in the small sink cabinet, as though Asher had somehow come back to life and hidden himself away.

Then again, this was the most likely of the scenarios playing out in Helen's mind.

The first scenario being that Asher had vanished into thin air, leaving no trace of him, living or dead, behind.

The next was that Asher was now a ghost and had slipped out of the trailer through the walls because there was no other way. There was only one door, one exit, and the two girls had been standing right next to it, meaning they would have seen him if he'd somehow managed to get up and get away.

"Okay, so . . . new plan: We need to get out of here as quickly as possible," Tris said, turning to Helen, who was on the brink of a meltdown.

"But A-Asher, h-he—"

"Do you trust me?" Tris asked her earnestly, placing her hands on Helen's shoulders to ground her again.

Helen looked at Tris, whose clown makeup was partially wiped away, leaving behind her soft striking features and intense gaze.

Could she trust a stranger? She wasn't sure, but her gut told her she should trust this one.

She nodded slowly. "I think so."

The girl nodded. "Okay, this is going to seem weird, but you're going to need to change clothes."

A few minutes later, Helen was dressed in a clown costume identical to the one Tris wore.

The girl knelt by the dresser, pulling out an assortment of face paints as well as an instruction guide.

"I've left a note for my uncle explaining that I left early and told him I will be meeting him at our next pit stop in Los Angeles. We're traveling in the trailer registered to the circus, so you need to blend in when we get there. Once we're there, you're free to become whoever you want or need to be. Here you go. Follow this guide to do your face paint. I'm going to make sure the engine is good to go; meet me out front when you're done," the girl said, smiling softly at Helen before stepping out of the trailer and into the night once again.

The girl's words echoed in Helen's mind. *You're free to become whoever you want or need to be.* Something about those words made her feel light.

Helen looked down at the paints and the painting manual and then at her reflection in the mirror on the side.

She almost gasped at the sight of herself. So different to the mirror images she'd seen before.

Those visions trapped Helens in various picturesque scenarios, they'd resembled the parts of herself she recognized and hated most.

This Helen, however, the one in the reflection right now, she was unrecognizable, and something about that . . . excited her.

She picked up a brush and dipped its edge in the paint pots, following the instructions until she was yet another version of Helen she didn't recognize.

When she was done, she stepped out again, this time as a new person, one who didn't want to be scared anymore but couldn't help still feeling petrified.

She knocked on the window at the front, and Tris opened the door, letting her inside.

Helen took a seat on the passenger's side, feeling exhausted. She'd gone through so many emotions in such a short time frame, it felt like her brain could combust at any moment.

"Engine's running fine," Tris said quietly to Helen.

But Helen wasn't listening; she still couldn't shake the guilt that eclipsed her.

"My parents . . ." she said. "I won't get to say goodbye to them."

"I'm sorry," Beatrice said. "Maybe we can make a quick pit stop—"

"It's okay," Helen said, shaking her head. "It would just raise more questions, and they might try to stop me . . . might even turn me in." She remembered just how much they loved Asher.

Asher whom she killed. Asher whose dead body had disappeared and could be anywhere.

"I'm so fucked . . ." she whispered, mostly to herself.

Tris's eyes burned fiercely with what resembled pain as she stared at Helen in the dark. "You're not fucked, Helen. Not in the slightest."

"You don't know that," Helen said, looking down at her fingers, which were still trembling and stained with Asher's blood.

Not his real blood, of course, just the blood her guilty conscience kept conjuring and making her see.

Tris slipped her fingers into Helen's, stilling them. "I do know that. Because I know what fucked actually looks like. Being fucked looks like having an abusive alcoholic dad who'd come home each night and beat the shit out of your mom. Being fucked looks like your dad driving your mom out of the house and turning on you next. Being fucked looks like being driven over the edge by such a fucked-up environment and then while retaliating, literally giving your dad some of his own medicine, you get your *clarity*. And then you go to your favorite uncle, the weird one who owns a traveling circus, and he lets you escape your mistakes. *That's* fucked, Helen, and you're nowhere close."

Helen didn't know what to say to all that. It was so much, and it made her understand why Tris was so willing to help her.

"I'm sorry that happened to you," Helen finally said after moments of quiet.

"Didn't say it did," Tris replied, and then leaned in close. "You aren't the first person who found *clarity* in the hall of mirrors either. We have a lot of people get their clarity there."

"What do you mean by that?" Helen asked. But she was pretty sure she knew what Tris meant. That the circus wasn't only a circus. It was a place where people got to shed their demons, real and imagined.

"I mean . . . that you aren't alone. You get a fresh start. You get to escape and write your own future."

"I get to escape," Helen repeated in a whisper.

"Yes, you do," Tris said softly.

"Okay," Helen said, "I'll do that."

"Good," Tris replied, moving in even closer.

"Before I do, though, I have a question," Helen said, once their foreheads were touching.

"Go on," Beatrice whispered. She placed her hand on Helen's face before sliding her fingers behind her neck.

Helen felt the truth weighing on her like it always did, but this time she didn't turn away from it.

"Can I kiss you, Tris?" Helen asked, and it was the most courageous thing she had ever done.

Tris smiled. "I thought you'd never ask," she said, closing the gap between them.

Far, far away from the town of Nowhere, Helen Thomas finally lived.

HEDGE

KALYNN BAYRON

"Tyler, it's just like it was before—no bones, no blood, just . . . skin," Brandon's mom said.

Brandon tugged at his earlobe, tried not to disturb the scab that had formed there from the constant irritation of his pulling and tugging at it. He pushed himself deeper into the shadowy space under his bed. He heard his mother sigh. From his hiding spot, Brandon could see her feet stuffed into her ugly work shoes, the deep-brown skin of her ankles showing below her scrubs.

"Hang on a minute, Tyler," Brandon's mom said. She'd taken refuge in Brandon's room, not knowing he was hiding under the bed, listening, holding his breath even as she called for him. She pulled the bedroom door open and yelled, "Wesley! Wesley, find your brother. I don't have time for this! I have to be at the hospital in twenty minutes, and it takes me thirty to get there."

Sometimes his mother's voice was like the brakes on a train: screeching and hissing, unable to stop.

"He's in the house somewhere, Ma," Wesley yelled from downstairs. "Just go. I'll find him."

She shut the door to his room again and lowered her voice. "Everything straightened out? Everything good with the permits?"

There was a pause, and Brandon could hear a muffled voice on the other side of the phone. The words were impossible to make out.

"That's good," Brandon's mother said. "I'd burn it to the ground if I thought I could get away with it. Yesterday a woman called the hospital asking if we had any John Does. Her son is missing. White male, thirty years old, tattoos on his right forearm. You want to guess the last place he was seen?"

Brandon heard a muffled yell from whoever was on the phone with his mother.

"Exactly," his mother said. "And, Tyler, he was *a developer*, just like James."

Brandon flinched at the sound of his father's name. He hadn't heard it said aloud in a long time. Behind closed doors and praying hands, sure. But just spoken aloud? Like his father might have come walking in at any moment? No. Brandon's fingers found his earlobe again, feeling the rough surface of the scab under his thumbnail, a small comfort.

"Apparently this guy was out there measuring, taking pictures, planning on making a bid to buy it and turn it into a high-rise. I didn't have the heart to tell her that the county coroner paid us a visit, asking if anybody had come through the ER who fit the description of a John Doe they had on ice—Caucasian male, age indeterminate but probably under fifty. It was hard to get a description when the only thing left were a few scraps of skin. Some of the tattoos were intact, but not much else. Might be the same guy, but I'm not sure."

Brandon's stomach turned over. What did that even mean?

There was another long pause. "No," his mom said. "You heard me right. They *had* him on ice—as in past tense." Brandon's mom sighed. "Tyler, the remains are gone."

Indiscriminate shouting erupted from the phone again. Brandon heard a few curse words and not much else.

"I'll call you later, and we can talk," Brandon's mom said, and after a brief pause, she walked out of Brandon's room.

"There's money for pizza on the kitchen counter," she said, as she rushed down the stairs. "Love you, baby."

"Love you too," Wesley said.

The front door creaked open, then slammed shut, rattling the entire house. Brandon wriggled out from under his bed and poked his head into the hallway. Wesley was standing there, glaring at him, his arms crossed tightly over his chest.

"Why don't you answer her when she's calling you?" Wesley

asked, as he sauntered down the hall in his stockinged feet, the boards creaking under him.

Brandon looked down at the floor. "I dunno."

"Do me a favor and speak up next time." Wesley clapped a hand down on Brandon's shoulder. "She's already stressed. She doesn't need to be worrying about you too."

Brandon rolled his eyes and pulled away from his older brother. He knew Wesley was right. She was stressed, but so was Brandon. Losing a parent wasn't something you just got over, especially not under the circumstances in which Wesley and Brandon had lost their father.

Their father had gone missing a year ago. Two weeks after he disappeared, some local kids found his body—or what was left of it—at McCannon's Topiary Garden. Brandon was still numb. He couldn't wrap his mind around the fact his dad wouldn't be coming home ever again. There had been no goodbye. Brandon just assumed he would see his dad when he got home that evening, so he hadn't bothered to say *bye* or *I love you*. The evening came and went, and Dad never came back.

They couldn't even have the casket open for his funeral because of what had happened to him, which was—well, Brandon didn't know. Nobody had any answers about what, exactly, had happened to him. But their mother knew. At least Brandon thought she did. She had to, right? He remembered when she'd gone to the hospital to confirm what they all hoped wasn't true, and when she returned, she didn't speak for three days. She just sat in her room and stared at the wall. Brandon was too afraid to press her about it. His father's name was added to the long list of people who'd died under tragic, sometimes mysterious, circumstances at the now condemned topiary garden. They had all tried their best to move on, but Brandon felt like the sadness would cling to him forever. He could feel it. Like a heavy cold hand on his shoulder, weighing him down, always batting away happy memories and heaping grief on him until he felt like he was going to collapse in on himself.

Brandon went downstairs and sat on the couch. He flipped on

the TV and scrolled through the channels, searching for something, anything, to distract him from the terrible ache in his chest.

"Anything good on?" Wesley asked, free-falling onto the couch, sending Brandon half a foot into the air.

"Nope. Same old shit."

Wesley winced. "Watch your mouth."

"Why? *You* don't." Brandon tried to scoot as far away from Wesley as he could, but Wesley reached out and pulled him close, then dug his knuckles into the crown of Brandon's head.

"Ouch!" Brandon yelped. "Get off!"

Wesley sat back, a little smile on his lips. "You, sir, need a lineup. *Damn.*"

Brandon pulled at the back of his neck. "It doesn't matter. Nobody cares anyway."

Wesley sighed. "Listen," he said softly. "I know you're having a hard time. We all are. But the only way we get through this is together. Don't start showin' out. If you're sad, you can cry. If you're mad, you can say that. But don't do that thing where you shut everybody out."

"She never should've let him go out there," Brandon said, as he pulled his ear until it hurt. He blamed his mother, even though he knew good and well it wasn't really her fault. But he needed somebody to blame, otherwise his father had died for nothing, for no reason, and that just didn't seem fair.

Wesley narrowed his eyes and sighed. "*Let* him go out there? Brandon, Dad wasn't a kid. He made his own choices. You know how hardheaded he is—was." Wesley swallowed hard, then cleared his throat. "Mom didn't know what would happen. She beats herself up about it enough as it is."

Tears stung Brandon's eyes, and he clenched his jaw until his temples ached.

Wesley softened his grip on Brandon. "We have each other, and that's what matters."

Brandon looked at Wesley, who flashed him that funny little smile, just the slightest gap between his two front teeth. He looked just like their dad—big brown eyes, dark brown skin, high cheekbones. Brandon looked more like their mother—toothy smile, square jaw, stout. He was glad. It hurt to look at Wesley, and Brandon couldn't imagine having to look at himself in the mirror every day and feel that same hurt.

"And you should really watch your mouth." Wesley flicked the back of Brandon's ear. "You're fourteen. You're still a baby."

Brandon gave him a half smile. He'd been practicing in the bathroom mirror; every time he found out about a new curse word, he'd put it in a sentence and say it until it rolled off his tongue, but never loud enough for his mother to hear. She would have lost her whole mind.

"Come on," Wesley said, hoisting himself up out of the deep folds of the overstuffed couch. "Mom's working a double shift again, so it's just you and me till tomorrow."

Brandon liked to give Wesley a hard time, but deep inside, Brandon knew he wouldn't have made it all this time without his brother. Wesley could never replace their dad, but he tried to ease the pain of his loss by filling in where he could.

Brandon followed his brother into the kitchen of the old craftsman-style house his mom had inherited from his grandma after she died. It was a little run-down, needed a new coat of paint and new glass in the upstairs windows, but their dad had sworn he was going to fix it up one day. Brandon didn't know who would fix it now.

"What sounds good? Fruity Pebbles? Pancakes?" Wesley asked, as he rifled through the cabinets.

"Oreos and milk?" Brandon asked.

"No way. Mom would kill me if I let you eat that for breakfast."

"You're no fun." Brandon knitted his brows, and pressed his mouth into a tight line. "Aren't older brothers supposed to help you get away with stuff?"

"Yeah, but Mom's insurance doesn't cover silver teeth, so no cookies for breakfast."

They settled on orange juice and chocolate chip pancakes, which

Wesley whipped up with the authority of a chef. Brandon gobbled up his stack and returned to his place on the couch.

Summers were the worst. The air was hot and sticky, and the house didn't have air-conditioning. There were ceiling fans in every room, but all they did was push the heavy, moist air around the house in rolling waves. By midafternoon, Brandon's shirt was clinging to his back, and he was ready to get out of the house.

"Wesley," he called from the bottom of the stairs. "Let's go to the park or somethin'. It's hot as hell in here."

"Watch your mouth, Brandon!" Wesley yelled back.

Brandon turned and sat on the last step.

Ding-dong!

Brandon jumped up as Wesley came bounding down the stairs and opened the front door. Three boys all but fell into the front entryway, talking among themselves. Brandon rolled his eyes so hard, he thought he was probably looking at the inside of his own skull.

"What's good?" one of them asked, slapping hands with Wesley.

"Chillin'," Wesley said.

Brandon sat back down on the step. The Harrison brothers, Kel and Teddy, had been friends with Wesley since elementary school. And Chris was one of Wesley's friends from his job at the movie theater.

Of the three boys, Brandon hated Teddy the most. Teddy was the oldest of the Harrison brothers, same age as Wesley, seventeen, but Teddy was infinitely more annoying. He was tall, brown-skinned, and eternally ashy. Brandon couldn't stand it when he palled around with Wesley.

"You babysittin'?" Teddy asked, staring at Brandon.

"Yeah," Wesley said. Brandon caught the little bit of resentment in his tone.

"I don't need a babysitter. I'm fourteen," Brandon chimed in.

"Ohhhh shit!" Teddy said. "He's a grown-ass man." He reached for Brandon, like he was going to mush his forehead with his pointer finger, but Brandon slapped his hand away.

An angry scowl stretched across Teddy's face.

"Listen," Kel said, nudging Wesley's shoulder. "Chris and I were thinking we should go out to McCannon's."

Brandon stiffened. Even hearing the name of the place where his father had died was still too much.

Chris yawned and stretched his arms high over his head, making his already-too-tight T-shirt come up over the brown skin of his stomach. He was a big, solid dude who played football for the local high school. He was a linebacker and looked like a whole-ass man, complete with a close-cropped beard.

"Are you on steroids?" Brandon asked. He was pissed at Chris for bringing up the topiary garden, so he figured now was as good a time as any to mess with him.

"No," Chris said, like he was deeply offended. "This is all natural." He flexed his biceps. "Why? Did somebody say I was taking something?"

Brandon scowled at him. "Maybe," he lied.

Wesley playfully shoved Brandon back. "Chris, he's joking. Relax."

Chris eyed Brandon suspiciously, then turned his attention back to Wesley. "So? We going out to McCannon's or what?"

Wesley looked like he wanted to throw up. "Why would you ever think I would want to go out there?"

Chris raised an eyebrow. "It's finally getting torn down, and I got about fifty pounds of fireworks in my garage. I say we light the place up. Give it the send-off it deserves since it's getting demolished anyway."

"Wait. What?" Brandon asked, standing up. "What do you mean it's getting demolished?"

"The city's tearing it down," said Kel. "After all the fucked-up stuff that happened out there, I think they just want to bulldoze it to the ground and start over. Sounds like a good idea to me. You don't think so?"

Brandon and Wesley were silent. Brandon knew the park was permanently closed, but he didn't remember hearing anything about it being torn down. It should be demolished, right? Brandon wished every day that the place would disappear off the face of the earth, but that wouldn't bring his dad back, so did it even matter? He wasn't sure how to feel about it.

"We're not allowed to go out there," Brandon said. The conversation he'd overheard his mother having stuck in his head. *No bones, no blood, just . . . skin.* Brandon shuddered. "Mom says we're not supposed to go anywhere near that place."

"Hey, who asked you?" Teddy snapped.

"Shut up, Teddy," Kel said, rolling his eyes at his brother.

Kel wasn't as bad as his older brother, but his beady brown eyes and the way his cornrows were never braided all the way down at the back of his head made Brandon uncomfortable.

Teddy shoved his hands in his pockets. "Well, Wesley? You coming or not?"

Wesley hesitated, then turned to Brandon. "I know we're not supposed to go, but if they're tearing it down, we might not ever get the chance."

"You *want* to go to the place where Dad died?" Brandon asked, confused. "Why?"

Wesley shrugged. "I just—I feel like I need to." He sighed and put his hand on Brandon's shoulder. "We won't be out there long. You said you wanted to get out of the house."

"Who invited *him*?" Teddy asked, holding his hand up to block Brandon from going out the door. "No kids."

Brandon tilted his head and looked at Teddy like he was small. "You're only three years older than me. You're still a kid too."

Teddy rounded on Brandon, but Wesley stepped between them. "You walking all the way out to McCannon's?" Wesley asked. "Last time I checked, I'm the one with the ride." He reached into his pocket and pulled out his keys, giving them a little jingle in front of Teddy's face. "Be nice, or you can take the bus."

Teddy grumbled something under his breath and walked out onto the porch.

"What's his problem anyway?" Wesley asked.

"Tracie broke up with him," Chris said in a whisper.

"*I* broke up with *her.*" Teddy's voice faltered, and he cleared his throat.

Brandon was sure Teddy was about to cry. He craned his neck to watch. Teddy caught sight of him and shoved his hands in the pockets of his sweat suit, a sweat suit with holes in the legs and a torn neckline. Brandon couldn't tell if it was supposed to be like that or if he'd just been in a fight.

"Your girl left you, Teddy?" Brandon asked. "Is it because you spent all your money on that Yeezy tracksuit tryna impress her, but instead you look like Freddy Krueger whooped your ass?"

Kel and Chris laughed so hard, they had to jog away from Brandon to collect themselves.

Teddy spun around, his fists balled at his sides.

Wesley put his hands up in front of him. "Brandon comes with me, or I'm not going. He's just a kid, Teddy. Ease up a little."

"Tell him to keep his mouth shut about Tracie," Teddy said through gritted teeth. "And about my outfit. Shit was expensive."

Wesley shot Brandon a cautionary glance, and Brandon ran off to grab the pizza money and his shoes.

Brandon, Wesley, and the rest of the boys piled into the car—a black Plymouth Road Runner that was about to break down at any moment. Wesley had saved up for two years to buy that beater. The paint was chipped, and the interior smelled like a mixture of Black Ice Little Trees and the funk from Wesley's gym bag, but Brandon knew Wesley loved his car almost more than he loved anything else. Brandon called shotgun but was overruled by Teddy, so he joined Chris and Kel in the back seat as Wesley slid in behind the wheel. The engine turned over, and they backed out of the driveway and sped off toward McCannon's.

McCannon's Topiary Garden and Recreational Area looked like a place people go to die. Tucked away in the rolling hills, it had once been a nature preserve, but the rich folks who lived close by in the

'70s wanted tennis courts and concrete fountains and softball fields. They pooled their considerable wealth and bribed a few members of the city council to open the area up to development. They got their members-only swimming pools and their racquetball courts. They even got a hedge maze, something one of Brandon's teachers said was a giant waste of money because nobody was going to use it for anything good. That was how McCannon's came into being, and from the jump, things had gone wrong.

Brandon had heard the rumors. Death haunted the place. People went in and came out in body bags, and there was always something weird about the deaths themselves. Overdoses shouldn't have left people's mortal remains unidentifiable. Accidents incurred by trespassers shouldn't have had the coroner's office struggling to confirm if the remains were even human. What kind of slip and fall makes your skin peel off? The only thing more broken than the bodies that came out of McCannon's were the families left behind. Brandon knew that pain all too well.

The park was closed. Permanently. Had been for years. It was closed when Brandon's father came out here—and it had still found a way to take him away. Brandon felt like the park was always taunting him, keeping the truth of what had happened to his father a secret.

Wesley swung the car around and skidded across the uneven pavement in the parking lot. There were cautionary signs posted on the chain-link fence warning trespassers to *KEEP OUT.* Bits of yellow police tape still clung to the fencing, and Brandon wondered who else's broken and bloodied remains the local authorities had found inside.

Kel got out, then climbed up and over the fence, while Wesley and Brandon squeezed through the padlocked front gate. Teddy rummaged around in the trunk and took out the fireworks they'd picked up on the way over and two cases of beer. He passed them through the fence to Wesley.

"You can't drink," Brandon said.

"*You can't drink,*" Teddy said, mimicking Brandon's tone. He squeezed through the fence and took one of the cases from Wesley. "Shut up, Brandon."

"Yo," Wesley said. "You gotta chill. I already told you—he's just a kid."

Teddy huffed as he hoisted a case of beer onto his hip and walked away. Chris stood on the other side of the fence as the boys looked back at him.

"Come on, Chris," said Wesley. "You want me to push the fence open for you?"

"No, it's not that." Chris stared past Brandon, into the shadowy park. "I just—you sure you wanna be here?" Chris suddenly sounded like he was having a change of heart and that made Brandon nervous.

Wesley glanced over his shoulder, staring into the park. "I mean, no. But I wanna fuck this place up. Come on."

"I'll go around," Chris said.

"It's two blocks' worth of fence," said Kel.

"I'll jog," Chris said.

"Whatever," Brandon said, as he followed Wesley into the park. Brandon used to think the weird stories and rumors were just to keep kids from trespassing on the condemned grounds, but now he wasn't so sure—not after what had happened to his father.

Brandon let his gaze sweep over the park. The once green fields were brown and overgrown. Many of the trees sported branches so long, their fingerlike offshoots scraped across the ground as a gentle breeze kicked up. The tennis courts were fractured, and all kinds of weeds had pushed their way into the cracks. Brandon hadn't been in the park since his father's death, but it seemed the only people who enjoyed the park now were vagrants and kids who snuck in beer and cigarettes, used too many curse words, and pretended to be grown.

They walked for a while before Teddy set down his case of beer on the ledge of a huge fountain that stood midway through the park. The fountain featured a giant Liberty-esque statue in the middle. The water had long since evaporated. Dirt and leaves and empty beer bottles littered the concrete basin at the foot of the statue. Teddy tore open the case of beer and popped the top on a can. He tossed a closed one to Wesley, and Wesley tossed it back.

"Oh, come on," Teddy said, rolling his eyes. "Your brother's got you wrapped around his little finger."

"I have to drive us home, remember?" Wesley said.

Teddy grumbled something under his breath as Brandon took a seat on the edge of the fountain.

"Check this out," Kel said, scaling the statue in the center to dangle from its extended arm.

Just then, a loud crack made Brandon jump, and Kel almost fell but caught himself at the last second. Chris emerged from behind the fountain on the opposite side, firecracker in hand, smoke still billowing from its spent core, his face ruddy and tight from laughter.

"You scared me!" Kel said, scampering down the marble statue and doubling over, clutching at his chest and panting like a dog. "I'm about to have a heart attack!"

"You should check your drawls," Wesley said. He sat on the rim of the empty fountain, howling with laughter.

Kel swiped his hand at him as if to say, *Shut up*, and Teddy tossed Chris a beer.

Cloudy purple ribbons fanned out across the sky as the sun sank low. Teddy had a beer, then two more. Kel and Chris joined in, and they were through the case by the time the sun set. Wesley wasn't drunk, but he was falling all over himself, laughing as his friends made fools of themselves. Brandon sat watching his older brother, who had held their family together after his father's death, laugh from the gut for the first time in a long time. It was nice, but the fact he was doing it so close to where their dad's remains had been found didn't sit right with Brandon. He didn't think that was disrespectful? He didn't think it was weird?

"We should check in with Mom," Brandon said.

Wesley glanced over at him. "I already texted her. Told her we're at Chris's house."

Brandon huffed. He'd been hoping bringing up their mom

would make Wesley cut their little field trip short, but it looked like he already had all the bases covered.

"I'm starving," Brandon said, trying another excuse. "Mom's gonna be pissed you didn't feed me."

"Calm down, little man," Chris said, breathing hard into Brandon's face. His breath smelled like tuna and beer, and Brandon tried not to breathe as Chris slung an arm around his shoulder. Chris shoved a pack of saltine crackers into Brandon's hand and slapped him on the back.

"Why do you have a pocket full of crackers?" Brandon asked.

"You said you wanted a snack," Chris said.

"Thanks," Brandon said.

He opened the pulverized crackers and dumped the crumpled contents into his mouth. He leaned back and stared into the overgrowth of maple trees. Their branches intertwined with each other as their roots snaked out of the ground and broke the pavement apart. The wind rustled the leaves, and the trees seemed to shift. Brandon sat up straight and squinted into the dark. He thought he saw something move between the trunks.

No. It was just the trees themselves, and still . . .

Chris chucked a half-empty can of beer at Brandon, striking him in the shin.

"Hey! You're wastin' it!" Kel seemed like it caused him physical pain to see the beer spilling out into the empty fountain's basin and mingling with the bits of trash and broken leaves.

"Tracie is everything," Teddy said, as his words began to run together. "*Everything*—I'm telling you."

"Nah. Kayla Malone," Wesley said. "*She's* everything."

Wesley and Teddy slapped hands and laughed as Brandon rolled his eyes. He was sure Wesley didn't even know Kayla Malone in a way that mattered. All he ever did was talk about her, but he was too shy to talk *to* her. Brandon hopped off the fountain's wall and wandered away from the boys, who had decided to start a small bonfire in the low-lying brush. He added it to his mental checklist titled *Things to Tell Mom.*

Brandon walked down a gravel path and made a quick right, before descending a steep flight of stairs and stopping at a short wrought iron gate. A small sign hung on a crooked post.

McCannon Topiary Garden est. 1948.
A place to be at one with nature.

The inner gate was padlocked, so Brandon put his foot between the bars and hoisted himself up. He leaned his chest against the top bar and started to pull himself over when some movement in the garden caught his eye. He stopped.

In the dark, Brandon saw three hulking shapes. Breathing. No. Were they breathing? He shook his head and eased his feet back onto the ground. The shadowy shapes slowly came into focus as Brandon's eyes adjusted to the gloom. They were hedge sculptures that looked as if they had once been trimmed to resemble human figures, their original forms long since lost to an overgrowth of foliage. Vines sprouted from misshapen arms and legs, trailing off like tentacles in the encroaching dark. And there was a rustling. Brandon craned his neck to see where it was coming from but couldn't make it out. He took a step back as unease swallowed him whole. He pulled at his ear.

Just beyond the strange figures, Brandon spotted the entrance to the sprawling hedge maze. The opening was at least nine feet tall and looked like a giant doorway, with two paths snaking off—one to the left and one to the right. Brandon squinted, trying to see how deep the maze went. He couldn't tell, but what he knew for sure was that somewhere in there was where his father had spent his last moments. He looked at the pavement under his sneakers. His dad must have walked over this exact spot.

A knot worked its way up Brandon's throat. He turned away from the hedge maze and ran right into Teddy. He screamed, and Teddy clapped a sweaty hand over his mouth.

"Shhhh!" Teddy said, spewing a tunnel of fetid air into Brandon's face.

Brandon pulled back. "You scared the shit out of me," he said angrily.

Teddy threw his head back and laughed himself half to death.

Brandon started to walk away.

"Wait a minute. Were you . . . were you gonna go in there?" Teddy asked, peering down toward the maze.

"No."

"Yeah, you were," Teddy said. "You *want* to go in there? That's where they found your pops—or what was left of him, right?"

Brandon clenched his jaw.

"What's wrong?" Teddy taunted. "You scared?"

"No." Brandon wanted to tell Teddy fuck off, but he could hear Wesley's voice in his head telling him to watch his mouth.

Teddy mounted the fence and fell over the top. He fell hard on the pathway, and Brandon couldn't help but smile. Teddy stood up and walked in a halting, jerky sort of way toward the entrance of the maze.

"What are you doing?" Brandon asked. A sudden chill ran up his back, and he felt his skin prickle. He looked at the once human-shaped hedge nearest to him. He seemed to remember it being in a slightly different position before. He blinked, trying to clear his head. Had it moved?

"Havin' . . . some . . . some fun." Teddy's words ran together like his tongue was too big for his mouth, the alcohol clearly getting the better of him. "Don't be . . . such a crybaby."

Teddy disappeared into the maze.

Brandon waited for him to pop back up at any moment. *He's going to try and scare me. I* know *it.*

Minutes passed in the dark. Brandon's mind raced between wanting to go get Wesley and not wanting to be labeled a baby. He was the tagalong. Wesley didn't seem to mind, but everyone else did. They liked scaring him, blowing ringlets of smoke in his face, and teasing him about whether he had even kissed a girl yet. He hadn't. But that wasn't the point.

I'm gonna go get Wesley.

Brandon turned to retreat up the path when there came a rustling from the garden. Everything inside him told him to run, but he didn't. He turned and glanced over his shoulder. The hedges seemed closer than they had been before.

He stepped back.

He turned toward the path, and then, from behind him, there came another sound. This one more subtle, caught in the breeze. He almost missed it. Brandon cocked his head and turned his ear back to the maze. A whimper, like a dog begging to be let out to take a piss. The noise climbed in pitch and fervor until it became a wail, a moan of absolute anguish. Brandon heard a rush of footsteps, staggered and heavy. He craned his neck and peered down toward the maze entrance. He didn't see Teddy, but he wondered why he was walking around in there like that—like his feet were made of lead, making all that noise. Brandon knew Teddy was drunk, but was he faded enough to be dragging his feet around?

Brandon's heart began to gallop. The sound of blood rushing through his veins muffled the nighttime noises all around him. He turned and ran away from the garden, pumping his legs and arms as hard as he could. Something was following him. He heard a rustle in the grass that had, in some parts of the park, grown to waist height, and his heart lurched in his chest.

Brandon barreled into the opening where the fountain stood illuminated by the bonfire the other boys had stoked to a roaring blaze. He skidded to a stop in front of Wesley, Kel, and Chris.

"I don't get what she sees in him, man." Chris slurred his words, and Brandon saw a line of spit hanging from his chin.

"Tracie's not the only girl out there, Chris," Kel said. "You've gotta expand your horizons beyond your friend's girl. It's . . . weird."

"It's not! She's *beautiful*!" Chris shouted.

"Okay, Chris. Okay," Kel said.

"Wesley! You gotta come with me!" Brandon blurted out, trying to catch his breath.

"What's wrong?" Wesley asked, concern coloring his voice.

"Teddy is messing around in the maze. He's trying to scare me!"

Wesley chuckled, and Kel sat up.

"There's a maze?" Kel asked.

Brandon was annoyed at his brother's lack of urgency. He was just sitting there like an idiot. "Get up! Go tell him to stop!"

"Okay. *Okay,*" said Wesley, raising his hands in front of him and climbing to his feet.

"What's-a-matter, Brandon? You scared, sweet little boy?" Kel said in the same condescending tone as his asshole brother.

"Shut up and come on," Brandon snapped. "Teddy went into the maze, and then I heard . . ."

Kel seemed to come out of his drunken haze as he stared at Brandon. "You heard what?"

Wesley came close to Brandon, looking concerned. "What is it?"

Brandon looked up at Wesley, and, like big brothers so often do, Wesley gave Brandon a reassuring little smile.

"It was—like a whining noise," Brandon said quietly, afraid to speak it aloud. "And then it sounded like Teddy was dragging his feet on the ground, like something was wrong with him."

Concern spread across Wesley's face. "Come on," he said. "Let's go check it out. Teddy's probably just messing with you."

Chris wiped his chin, and Kel huffed loudly and stood up. They all followed Brandon down the gravel path and down the concrete stairs to the little fence by the maze.

Wesley reached into his pocket, and his mouth turned down at the corners. "The flashlight on my phone is broken. I'm not gonna be able to see shit." He glanced back up in the direction of the fountain, shrugged, and hopped the fence in one smooth motion.

"What are you doing?" Brandon asked. Something sank into his chest—a terrifying sort of primal fear that left him unable to move. "You—you can't go in there. You can't see! It's dark!"

"You told me to make him stop. That's what I'm doing," said Wesley. "I should burn this damned place to the ground while I'm at it."

Kel hopped the fence, and then Chris went over like a slug goes over a stick. They walked toward the hedge maze's entrance that by now looked like a great black hole in the mountain of tightly packed foliage. Brandon watched the not-human hedges. They seemed to be in their original positions, and Brandon shook his head. Of course, they were. They weren't moving on their own.

"Just stay put," Wesley called.

Kel turned and went into the maze, taking the path on the right. Chris went left, and Wesley paused.

"Stay put. Five minutes, ten tops," Wesley said.

"Ten. Tops," Brandon called back as he pulled at his ear. The scab suddenly came loose, and Brandon could feel the sting of the open wound. Blood wet his fingertips, and he quickly wiped his hand on his shirt.

Wesley disappeared to the left, and Brandon pressed his waist into the metal gate. He didn't want to go into the maze, but he didn't want to be alone on the outside either.

There must have been owls nesting somewhere nearby, because their calls pinged back and forth. Brandon saw their shadowy shapes crisscrossing in the sky above him. They hooted and hollered . . . Why were they screaming? He'd never heard an owl cry out like that before, and he wondered if that was normal.

He watched them soar overhead. Screeching. They swooped low, disappeared into the hedge maze, then zoomed back toward the sky. The scream came again. Brandon whipped his head around and saw someone standing in the entrance of the maze. The scream was coming from that direction, from whoever was standing there.

Brandon tensed his body, his muscles preparing to explode into a run. The figure came forward, groaning and sputtering. It lurched forward just enough for Brandon to see its face.

Chris.

"Stop it!" Brandon yelled. "You're scaring me!" He was done pretending to be brave.

Chris's head snapped back, and he made a gurgling noise as if he were trying to speak through a mouth full of liquid. His body twisted in an unnatural way as a tangle of vines ensnared him, circling his midsection. It yanked him backward, and his back bent right in the middle with a loud snap.

"Chris!" Brandon shouted.

Chris was pulled back into the maze, to the right and out of sight.

Brandon put his trembling hands on the fence. "Wesley!" he screamed, his voice cracking. "Wesley, where are you? Get out of there!"

Another scream came from somewhere in the maze, and Brandon heard quick footsteps, a snarl like a wild animal, and the snap of branches—or maybe bones—breaking.

"Wesley! Kel! Chris! Please! I'm scared!"

At the entrance, another figure stumbled out. Brandon recognized him right away and heaved a sigh of relief. Wesley.

Wesley would take him away from this place. Wesley would protect him.

"Wesley! We gotta get out of here!" Brandon scaled the fence and stumbled toward his brother. Wesley turned toward him, and Brandon stopped.

A stream of warm piss rushed down his leg.

"Bran—don," Wesley wheezed. His left arm was gone. The bloody stump was ragged and spurting. Wesley lumbered forward and Brandon reared back, falling hard onto the ground, unable to move or scream or blink.

Wesley staggered toward him. Small tendrils of vines squirmed in the hollow sockets of his eyes. The eyes that had once been so much like their father's were gone. His skin had a wrinkled, loose appearance, and something beneath its surface undulated. The right side of Wesley's face hung off the bones at an odd angle, like the flesh was draped over the skull because all the muscle beneath was gone. A gash in Wesley's abdomen should have had his guts spilling out, but what hung from his body was a writhing mass of vines and bloodied leaves.

Brandon scrambled back. His heart cartwheeled in his chest, his mouth went dry, and his screams turned to pitiful whimpers. Wesley jerked upward, straightening his back. He tilted his head up and looked at the sky. In the glinting moonlight, Brandon watched in terror as a squirming mass of vines pushed their way out of Wesley's gaping mouth. Smaller tendrils burst from his bare forearm and from the tips of the mangled fingers on his remaining hand. Wesley leveled his head, now held to his neck with a stitching of thorny stems, and lumbered toward Brandon.

Brandon could do nothing except look up at his brother as he loomed over him. "Wes—Wesley?" he stammered.

"Wesley." The voice that came from his brother's body was *not* Wesley's. It sounded like the crunching of dead leaves and the slither of snakes all at once.

A white-hot pain ripped through Brandon's leg, and when he looked down, he saw a barbed length of vine ripping the flesh from his bare legs, embedding itself beneath his skin, writhing through his veins. He tried to scream but managed only a high-pitched whistling sound as his throat was torn away. In the dark, something fell from Wesley's torn pocket.

His phone. Their mother's face lit up the screen as it vibrated on the ground. Brandon wanted to reach for it, but his body was not his own anymore.

Brandon, his big brother, Wesley, the Harrison brothers, and their sidekick Chris, were gone—and five new almost-human hedge sculptures stood just beyond the entrance of the hedge maze in McCannon's Topiary Garden.

A *place to be at one with nature.*

THE GOLDEN DRAGON

KENDARE BLAKE

The Golden Dragon! Delicious Chinese Food!

That was what the red-and-yellow sign above her family's Chinese restaurant shouted at Sophie Kim as she swept the front walk.

She didn't know why it seemed like the sign was shouting—it's not like there were actual exclamation points on it—or why it was shouted in a bad fake-Asian accent—*the Go-din Dwa-gon! Dee-wricious Chinese Food!*—but that was how it was. Every time. The only part that didn't ring off the insides of her head was the generic red-and-blue neon OPEN sign just beside the glass door.

Maybe it was because the dragon on the sign seemed so excited about everything. He—or she, or they; because Sophie didn't know anything about dragon gender—was stretched across the white background, tail curled and claws outstretched, mouth open in a happy and decidedly hungry grin, showing sharp teeth and a bright red tongue. Claws reaching for their famous egg rolls, their dad liked to say. Jaws open to eat lazy daughters who slacked off sweeping the front walk, said their mom.

Sophie picked up her broom to dust off the dragon's feet. She wondered if the dragon was as bored as she was. Or if it was more like her dad, eyes on the horizon and nostrils flared for the sight or scent of new customers. Sophie had liked that dragon when she was a kid. With its eyes, red as rubies, and its long serpentine body covered in yellow scales, it had seemed like their family mascot. A protector. The guardian of the almond chicken. But she wasn't a kid anymore. And now the dragon just looked kind of . . . crazy. Happy crazy, like their uncle Jo-Jo when he showed up to family dinners already drunk and laughing at jokes nobody understood, but crazy.

She banged imagined dust off her broom bristles. "Welcome to the Go-din Dwa-gon," she whispered. "May we seat you near da Go-din kitchen?" She snorted. Her Asian accent was even worse than the customers'. But that seemed about right coming from a Korean-American girl whose Korean-American family ran a Chinese restaurant.

The glass door beside her swung open. Her older sister leaned out.

"Hey. Can you hurry up?" Summer asked. "You still have to top up the spicy oil, and then there's about a metric ton of vegetables to wash."

Summer pushed her glasses up—they were forever sliding down the bridge of her small nose—to study Sophie's broom strokes, back and forth, back and forth, no strength behind them, bristles barely touching the cement. "You are so lazy."

"Yeah," Sophie replied. "I'm trying to get the dragon to eat me so I won't have to wash vegetables."

Her sister glanced up at the sign overhead. Summer was older by two years, a senior, already promised a nice, fat scholarship to a private college in Michigan. *Who wants to go to Michigan?* Sophie'd asked when the acceptance package came. *It's fine,* their mom had said. *A long way from Colorado, but a good school.* A school that would pay, was what she'd meant. Nearly full ride. All the Kims would have to cover was a few thousand per semester plus book fees.

"Dad's ordering a new sign next month," Summer said.

"That's what he always says."

"No, really. I heard him talking to the vendor on the phone, arguing over the price to redesign the dragon. And add 'try our famous egg rolls' to the bottom."

"Don't let him do that," Sophie groaned. "How exactly are the egg rolls famous? How exactly is our food 'delicious'?"

"It's better than saying '*authentic.*'" Summer snorted. "Mom'll tone it down. Maybe it can say 'home of the best egg rolls in town.' That would at least be true."

The only other Asian restaurant in their western Colorado suburb was Dragon Wok, a Chinese/Vietnamese place in a strip mall and their egg rolls were horrible. When it had opened, their dad paced back and forth for a month, asking why they were so stupid that they couldn't come up with another name, why they'd cursed their town with *two* dragons, and how their Golden Dragon was going to cut the head off that wok dragon and put it on a stick.

Sophie sighed, and Summer started ragging on her again about her sweeping when a black BMW sedan rolling down their block caught Sophie's eye.

"Oh, here take this." She shoved the broom into her sister's hands.

"No. No way." Summer pushed the broom back, but it was no use. Sophie was already gone, trotting down the sidewalk.

"I'll make it up to you on the weekend rush," Sophie called over her shoulder as the BMW slowed and the back window rolled down to reveal Stevie's lovely face, pink-cheeked and smiling, as Emily snaked her carefully tanned body through the passenger window to wave.

"There is no weekend rush, you little brat," Summer yelled, but her shout was muted, as if she didn't want her little sister's rich friends to hear. Jacob, Emily, Stevie, and Sean were seniors with cars and big houses and no need for scholarships. No need even for applications; they would end up going wherever their parents had gone or wherever their parents sent the money to build a new science lab.

"Kumiko!" Emily and Stevie exclaimed together. It was their little nickname for her, something they'd gotten from an old karate movie. Both girls were older and cooler—and the kind of pretty that wasn't the least bit threatened by Sophie's black hair and round cheeks.

Summer shook her head. "That's not your name. It's not even Korean!"

"Yeah, well, Summer's not really your name either, *Sung Mei*," Sophie said, and her sister scowled. She had no comeback for that. Sophie really was Sophie's name; her parents had let go of the last of the traditional stuff for their second kid.

From the slowing car, Stevie and Emily waved at Summer in a sort-of-friendly way, then pretended she wasn't there. Summer wasn't worth bothering with. She was no fun, always working or studying, and she never gave them the time of day either, even though they were in the same year at school.

"There she is." Jacob smiled from behind the wheel. Sophie made sure to smile the shy, closed-lip smile he expected, the one he liked. "You up for a house party?"

"On a Wednesday?"

"My parents left for Barbados again," Emily said, her arms flayed out in exasperation. "Again! Like, they never get bored of that place. So, you coming?" Her green eyes sparkled. Her makeup was always so good, and her skin had never known a blemish, something she credited Sophie for after begging her for Korean skin-care secrets, which Sophie had given, after watching the same ten-step tutorials that everybody watched on the internet.

Jacob stopped the car and got out, like an actual gentleman, and Sophie said, "Just let me clear it with my sister."

"They're not really your friends," Summer whispered, when Sophie returned to her beside the blinking OPEN sign.

"How would you know?" Sophie asked accusingly. "You don't even know them, do you?"

Summer lowered her gaze. Her mouth had drawn closed in a tight, angry line. "I know *you*," she said, and looked Sophie dead in the eyes. Her sister did know her. She knew that Sophie didn't really like these vapid rich assholes. Except that sometimes she kind of did. They were funny once in a while and, on occasion, surprisingly kind. Besides, even if she didn't like them, it was hard not to like how it felt to be around them. Their world was not the same world she and Summer had grown up in. Their world sparkled, and everything in it was so easy.

"Look," Sophie snapped, "just cover for me, okay? And the next time Emily gives me one of her cast-off handbags, I'll split the take with you off Poshmark." The last little gift had been a brand-new Dior minibag that Stevie had accidentally bought two of. Sophie had resold it online for two thousand bucks.

"Kumiko!"

Sophie turned and saw Stevie leaning out of the back seat window.

She slapped her manicured hand against the BMW's sleek black paint. "Come *on*!"

"I gotta go," Sophie said to Summer, and turned to jog to Jacob. He raised his arm so she could tuck up underneath, and he smiled and gave her a kiss—a surprise right there in front of the restaurant, and Sophie didn't need to look at Summer to know she'd be scowling.

"Thanks, Summer," Jacob called. Then he winked. "Don't wait up."

Sophie hurried to the back seat without another glance at her sister or the restaurant—not because she was ashamed, she told herself, or embarrassed by the kiss. She just didn't need any more grief. She got in next to Stevie and Sean. Jacob got back in the driver's seat and adjusted the rearview mirror so he could see her eyes. Summer said he was only after her to bang an Asian, to mark one off on his international-bang bingo card. Summer thought she knew everything.

"Bye, Summer!" Emily said. She waved before ducking in the car to whisper, "See you at school tomorrow, smelling like General Tso's." She turned in her seat—no need for seat belts when you were as invincible as Emily, so she just buckled it underneath herself to stop the car from beeping. "How is it that you're so sweet and fun, and your sister has such a stick up the ass?"

"Sticks up the ass are good for scholarships," Sophie replied, and in the mirror, Jacob grinned as the BMW squealed away from the curb. She ignored the crack about General Tso's, even though she spent hours above the grease traps, too. Emily wouldn't have said it if Summer weren't so shitty to them.

Sophie leaned back and looked around the car. Even though they'd been hanging out for a couple of months, Sophie still wondered what she was doing there. Maybe it was just that Jacob and Emily, Stevie and Sean were bored to death of one another. But whatever the reason, it was better than staying at the restaurant all night and getting her fingers slick with oil or freezing them off washing vegetables.

Jacob veered the car onto the on-ramp for the highway, putting the pedal to the floor, pushing the engine harder than he needed to because who cared? The BMW was an old toy already—a gift from one of his father's clients for Jacob's sixteenth birthday. One of his father's clients. Not even his father himself. That always drove Sophie a little crazy—how grotesquely rich did one have to be to buy a brand-new BMW for their accountant's *son*?

And how spoiled did one have to be to drive that gift like they were trying to use it up as fast as possible?

"Yo, Kumiko," said Sean from the other side of Stevie, "next time how about you bring me some fries from that restaurant?"

"It's a Chinese place, you ass," Stevie said, and elbowed him in the ribs. "They don't have fries."

"We do, actually," said Sophie. "They aren't on the menu, but enough people ask for them that my dad always keeps some to throw in the fryer."

"That's so sad." Emily gripped the headrest as Jacob veered across two lanes. "That you have to Americanize your menu like that."

"Duh," said Sean. "It's all Americanized. You think orange chicken is authentic? Have you ever even been to Japan?"

"It's a Chinese restaurant, stupid," Stevie said, and thumped him again.

"Yeah," Sean said, squinting as he gave her a shove, "but who goes to China?"

"I've been to China." Jacob glanced at Sophie in the rearview mirror. "My dad took me to Hong Kong when I was like eight."

"What was it like?" Emily asked.

Jacob seemed to think for a moment, like he was trying to remember or put it into words. Then he shrugged and said, "Just like Japan," and they laughed.

Sophie cleared her throat. "Hey, you guys? Where are we going? This definitely isn't the way to Emily's." She watched as a look passed through the car from one person to the next until it settled in Emily's green eyes.

"You caught us, Kumiko . . . Surprise! We're breaking into the Japanese Gardens!"

Sophie's eyes widened as Stevie and Emily cackled joyfully. Sophie shifted in her seat. She knew they had done things like this before. They bragged about it so often that Sophie gave them fun alliterative categories in her head: Dabbling in Delinquency with Drugs. Sampling Suburban Slum-life through Shoplifting. But this was different. If they got busted breaking into the gardens, it would be no big deal for them—Stevie's mom was some high-powered lawyer—but Sophie doubted the immunity would carry over to the kid from the Chinese restaurant.

When they reached the Japanese Gardens, Jacob at least had the sense to park outside it and climb over the gate. The way he abused the BMW, she'd been worried he would use the car to ram right through it. Sophie got out hesitantly, so hesitantly that Stevie pushed her a little from behind.

"Come on," Jacob said, and held out his hand. "It'll be fine."

She didn't take it, but she followed them into the park, definitely the least graceful over the gate. Jacob had to catch her on the other side when her foot got caught and she fell. Emily and Stevie hopped it like ballerinas, then held hands and skipped, squealing happily down the groomed paths, the hedges and shrubs dark on either side, blossoms pulled in for the night. The boys raced ahead, Sean making as much noise as a stampede of cows. Sean, the beautiful moron whose handsome looks and boundless cash could solve any problem. As they passed around a bottle of something, their ease and lack of care spread through the warm spring air, and Sophie relaxed. Everything would be fine. Just another night of drinking and smoking pot. They'd probably get bored of the gardens and leave after twenty minutes.

"Down there," Stevie said, and pointed to a spot by a brook. "Isn't it pretty?" They walked down carefully in the dark and sat on the grassy slope above the banks of smooth round pebbles. The moonlight showed a bridge nearby, plus silhouettes of carved stones and a temple in the distance.

"What is that, Sophie?" Emily asked. "Is it, like, a church or something?"

"I don't know," Sophie replied. "I've never been here before."

"I'm going to go climb it," said Sean, and Emily smacked him.

"Show some respect," she said.

He jerked away and made like he was going to hit her, and she laughed. But before they could actually argue, Jacob gave Sean a shove.

"Just chill," he said. "Enjoy the moment. Try not to get us all arrested."

"Whatever." Sean flopped onto his back and lit a joint, the bottle tucked into the crook of his arm.

"Getting arrested might actually be good for him," Sophie said, and everyone laughed. Even Sean, laughing around the wet end of the joint, his chuckles gray puffs of smoke in the moonlight.

Sean would never get arrested. There was no karma for people like these. Not even the universe wanted to upset them. And Sophie didn't want to upset them either. As much as she resented them, she adored them, too. Watching Emily lean against Stevie and share a joint, exhaling smoke like the dragon on their restaurant sign, was like watching a scene from a black-and-white movie. Something about starlets, and glamour, and friendships that last lifetimes. Their lips shimmered and their jewelry sparkled; they were as pristine as the white curves of a sculpted vase. They almost weren't even real.

So, when Jacob held out his hand for Sophie to follow him across the bridge, she went. And when he had her on her own, pressed against the side of the temple, hidden among the sleeping flowers, and she said, "Hey, I'd rather not," she wasn't surprised that it seemed like he didn't hear her.

She gave his shoulder a small shove. "Hey, I mean it. I'd rather not do this here."

"Come on," he said. "It's the perfect place. It's why we came."

"Well, no one told me that."

He whispered in her ear, pretty, flattering compliments that sounded insincere. But mostly, and this was the thing that set off alarms, they sounded half-hearted, like it didn't matter if she believed them or not. It didn't matter if she gave in or not. He would still have his way.

Jacob always got his way.

"I said knock it off." She forced her hands up between their chests, balled into fists.

"And I said, *relax*." He grabbed them and wrenched them back down.

Sophie's heart started to pound, pumping good, strong blood to her muscles and brain as the night of celluloid perfection evaporated. This was real life and her real body, and Jacob was pressing it against a temple in an empty Japanese garden.

She tested the grip of his hands on her wrists and tried to squirm away, to slide right out from between the temple and his chest. It didn't work. She barely moved. Jacob wasn't a big guy, not built like a football player. But he was still strong. Much stronger than she was.

Sophie's body went rigid as her mind raced, and she felt his grip on her loosen as she stopped struggling. Maybe he thought she'd given up or given in. She didn't know how he'd think that, when she was breathing hard, so scared she was actually trembling.

"That's good," he said, kissing the side of her face as she turned away. "It's going to be good."

Sophie grimaced. She raised her hands, alternating from fists to claws, maybe to shove, maybe to grab. She listened to his whispers and thought about just letting it happen. Maybe it would be ok, and Summer was wrong and Jacob really did like her, and she would become his girlfriend, and be able to hang with them a little longer. She tried to relax for a minute, but she couldn't. It felt gross. It felt wrong.

"Can we seriously not do this here?" She gave him a shove. He just had to get the message. See that she was serious. Then he wouldn't do what it seemed like he was going to. "Emily and Stevie are right over there—I don't want them to think—"

"It's cool," he said. "They know."

They know. Of course. Because Sophie wasn't really part of their crew. She was a novelty. A pet. *Let's take little Kumiko out of the Chinese restaurant for a night. Ask her how to get rid of our zits. Dress her up in our clothes. Take her to the Japanese Gardens so Jacob can do her in her natural environment.*

All things she had let them think, and it had worked out pretty well, until now.

"Sweet, soft Sophie," Jacob whispered, and tugged at her jeans.

He wasn't even looking at her. He didn't know her at all, didn't know that at home her dad called *her* the golden dragon, for how much fire she breathed and how sharp her claws were.

She grabbed a fistful of Jacob's hair and yanked it hard.

"Ow!" His head jerked to the side. He blinked at her. "Are you crazy?"

"I said I'd rather not." She hit him across the face. They struggled, and he dragged her to the ground, and for a few shining moments, her anger kept her afloat. But it didn't last. He hit her back, and she saw stars. He called her names that sounded more at home on his tongue than the compliments had.

It would have all gone a different way were it not for the sound. The creaking low groan that came from inside the temple.

"Shit." He froze and looked from the temple to Sophie, and his hands relaxed on her arms like they were friends again. "Did you hear that?"

She took advantage of his distraction to worm her leg up between them and kick hard, hoping to hit his crotch. He yelped and rolled away, and Sophie clawed up from the grass and ran through the gardens.

Not back to the car. Even with terror and anger controlling her body, she knew she would find no allies there. She hid in the woods. She listened to Emily and Stevie call for her, and eventually, Jacob, and even Sean, who called her name like he was bored, like he thought she was a pain for holding them up.

After a few minutes, they got in their car, and when they drove past, Sophie pulled out her phone for a rideshare.

It wasn't that late when Sophie got home—her parents were still in the kitchen doing prep for the next day's buffet—so she snuck through the closed restaurant and up the back stairs to their apartment, past Summer's closed door, and into the bathroom. She switched on the light and locked the door, then looked at herself in the mirror.

She looked like she'd been attacked. But not by a person. Most of the scrapes were from the branches of trees and the Japanese holly she'd fallen into as she fled. Her lip wasn't split. Her eyes weren't blackened. Her cheek was going to swell where Jacob had hit her, but not that bad, and she had round cheeks anyway. If she kept her hair forward and her head down, who would notice?

She tensed at the sound of footsteps and said a quick prayer that her mom wouldn't rattle the doorknob and demand access. But it wasn't her mom. It was Summer.

"Hey, you home already from playing China doll?" she asked angrily. "Whatever little presents they gave you are mine—you owe me for doing your chores!"

Sophie thought of all the things Stevie and Emily gave her sometimes: Last season's outfits. Designer makeup they didn't want anymore. She'd taken it all and never figured on needing it to cover up bruises.

Summer pounded on the door. "Are you alive in there? Or are you still pretending to not speak so good Eng-wish?"

"Very funny," Sophie said, her voice tough. "Go away."

"I am not covering for you anymore, do you hear me? You can hang out with those assholes *after* you finish your work. They don't even really like you, you know. You're like a pet to them. And they probably think you know karate."

"I do know karate," Sophie half shouted through the door. "And so do you, Summer. You just have to reach deep, deep down inside yourself and *focus* . . ." Sophie dropped her hands to the sides of the sink and started to cry.

Strong arms wrapped around her. She didn't know how Summer had gotten past the lock, and she didn't care. She just let her big sister clean her up and tuck her into bed.

His goddamned phone was missing. Jacob searched all his pockets, and in between the seats of the beamer. He retraced his steps through his house, and the garage, and down the driveway, even though he hadn't been out there. Maybe Sean or Stevie had it—he reached for his phone to text them, but of course, there was nothing to reach for. And besides, he knew where it was.

In the grass in the Japanese Gardens. He must've dropped it after Sophie went nuts.

He had to go back. She could have picked it up, be planning on using it to . . . what? It wouldn't prove anything. And he hadn't done anything, except he supposed he shouldn't have hit her. But man, could she fight! Not like that sister of hers who'd barely said no and who was dumb enough to think he was going to keep on dating her afterward. But Summer hadn't said anything either. That was the nice thing about Asian girls. They were quiet. The worst thing about them was they sometimes kicked him in the balls and made him lose his phone.

Groaning, Jacob dragged himself out to his car and drove all the way back to the gardens.

When he got there, he jumped the gate again and winced. He was tired, and his legs were sore, and his crotch ached. He picked his way through the park to the temple and bent down, searching the grass and wishing he had the flashlight that was infuriatingly on his missing phone. And then there was that sound again. The same sound he thought he'd heard with Sophie. Like a groan or the low creak of a door opening—if that sound could come from a throat.

"Sophie?" Maybe she was still here, waiting for him. Maybe they could straighten all this out; maybe she'd come to her senses and changed her mind.

Her shape drew up from the blackness inside the temple, and his shoulders squared with happy pride, impressed with himself and his lingering horniness despite the kick. But the shape in the temple wasn't Sophie. It was too tall, and the hair was too long, hanging down the shoulders and across the eyes. And Sophie hadn't been wearing a white robe, had she?

"Sophie?" he whispered again. The woman's head jerked in his direction, and he gasped. *Run,* he thought, but his legs wouldn't move. *RUN!*

The woman's black hair seethed like it was full of insects; her elbows jerked like a marionette's. She hobbled toward him, bent over and moving so oddly, he wouldn't have been surprised to see her feet on backward.

"Are you okay? Do you need me to call someone?" he asked ridiculously, because she clearly wasn't, and he didn't have a phone. He expected his words would make her stop. Make her disappear. Because this wasn't real. This was a dream.

Her white fingers hooked onto his arms, and she dragged herself up, her terrible face so close, and he smelled water and stone and spices. She breathed that creaking sound into his ears, and Jacob began to weep.

After the night in the Japanese Gardens, school was just like Sophie knew it would be: Stevie and Emily ignored her. They didn't shout for her to get in their car and go off campus for lunch. Sean brushed past her like she was a ghost, and as for Jacob, she didn't see him at all.

At the restaurant, she put in extra shifts and covered Summer's chores, a thank-you for being there that night, an *apology* for leaving her holding the broom. And it was a good thing, too, because Summer suddenly seemed to have a lot of shifts that needed covering.

A few days later, she caught her sister slipping out the front door just before closing and said, "Hey, where are you going all of a sudden? Is there some secret math camp happening that I don't know about?"

But Summer only grinned. She looked a little tired, a little pale. Her eyes were bloodshot, and there was something different about her hair. "It's astronomy club, dumbass. You know I hate math."

"Stop defying so many of our stereotypes," Sophie teased, half shouting because Summer was already gone. She sighed and grabbed the broom to sweep the sidewalk. The last thing she expected was to look up and see Emily's Tesla creeping to the curb like one of those curious white whales at the zoo.

And she definitely didn't expect the face that greeted her from behind the wheel.

Emily looked like shit. Bags under her eyes and no makeup, and her hair—usually a shiny brown—limp and a little greasy.

Sophie leaned down. Stevie was in the passenger seat, and she didn't look much better.

"Hi, Sophie." Emily smiled, but it wasn't her usual smile. It was shaky, and her lips were dry. "Can we come up and talk?"

"What, like, in my room?"

"Please? We really need to ask you about something."

Sophie wanted to say no. But it was so oddly fascinating to see them haggard—she kind of needed to watch it play out. "Park up there." She pointed up the street, then waited while they parked. As they approached, they walked weirdly, their shoulders hunched and their eyes all shifty. Stevie didn't seem to want to go near the dumpster for some reason.

"We can talk upstairs." Sophie led them through the restaurant. "Mom, this is Emily and Stevie," she said as they passed her in the kitchen, Mom wearing her white apron and her hair net, a vegetable cleaver in one hand. "We need to talk about school stuff; I'll be right back." Behind her, Emily and Stevie smiled and nodded. Emily did this weird half bow thing, and her mom, confused, did the same.

"So you, like, live up here," Emily said once they were upstairs. They'd never seen her family's apartment and were no doubt scandalized by how small it was and that it smelled like fried rice.

Sophie ushered them into her bedroom and closed the door. "So what's going on?" she asked.

"Have you seen . . . ?" Emily started. "I mean, have you heard of . . . ?"

"If you're wondering if I've heard from Jacob, no, I haven't."

"No, no." Emily pressed her palms against her eyes, hard. "That's not what I'm asking."

"Just spit it out, Em," Stevie snapped.

Emily whirled on her. "Shut up, Stevie! How am I supposed to spit it out? What am I supposed to say that doesn't sound fucking crazy?"

"She'll know, or why else are we here?"

"Fine! Just shut up and let me think! Shit." Emily turned and stepped closer, and Sophie realized that she could smell her, like she hadn't showered in a while. "Sophie, Sean's dead!"

"What?"

"He's dead, *okay*? We saw it. It came up from under that bridge in the gardens and snapped his fucking neck!"

"What are you talking about? You saw *what*?" Sophie must have misheard. They must be messing with her. "Look, if you're worried I'm going to tell someone about what happened that night with Jacob—"

"I *knew* it!" Stevie pointed a shaking finger. "I told you, Emily. I *told* you it was his fault. He raped you, didn't he, that night—?"

"No," Sophie said, her eyes narrowed. "Though it wasn't for lack of trying."

That shut them up.

"But if he didn't . . . ," Emily murmured, and looked at Stevie.

Stevie stared at Sophie hard. Then she said, "But he tried, didn't he? I think that's still enough."

"Enough for what?" Sophie asked. "What are you talking about?"

She watched, mystified, as Stevie pulled out paper after folded paper, things she'd actually printed out, and spread them across Sophie's bed in an unhinged trail of internet research. On them were pictures of a pretty Asian girl and photos of the Japanese Gardens. Early sketches, too, plans from before the garden was complete.

"We thought Sean was just joking around. Or that we were seeing things," Emily muttered, pacing. "But we saw it, Sophie. We saw it kill him right in front of us, and we weren't on anything!" She pointed her finger when she said that, like she was daring Sophie to call her a liar.

"Someone killed Sean," Sophie said carefully. It couldn't be true, but something had definitely happened; she'd never seen them so disheveled. "Did you go to the cops?"

Emily pressed her fists to her eyes like Sophie was being frustratingly stupid. "It wasn't like that."

"Like what?"

"We ran," Stevie said. Her voice was low; she still sounded more angry than scared. "It was the only thing we could do. We just hoped that it wouldn't follow us. That it couldn't follow us out of the gardens."

"What couldn't follow you out of the gardens?"

"*Her.*" Stevie leaned down, and her finger struck the girl's photo. "Haruko. In 1911, she was raped and killed." She reached for another paper. "Her dad was this big land developer. He went crazy afterward. Killed himself. But before he did, he built the gardens as a memorial to her. And that temple." She pressed her finger into the paper so deep, it was like stabbing, and Sophie leaned in.

"That's the same temple we were at," she muttered.

"No shit!" Stevie grabbed pages in her fists. "And it woke her up, do you get it? It's like Jacob was singing her song! And now she's in our mirrors and under our cars and fucking everywhere!" In a rage, she tore the photograph of Haruko and let the pieces flutter to the carpet. "He just had to go back to the same place," Stevie growled. "The same temple in the same garden where he did Summer last year. He just had to be sick *and* sentimental, and now we're all going to die!"

"What?" Sophie asked. Jacob and Summer? That couldn't be. "But . . . my sister didn't even know him," she said quietly.

"Well." Stevie snorted. "She used to."

"She never told me," Sophie whispered. It made sense suddenly, how certain Summer had been that Jacob was a creep. How much she seemed to hate them all. Summer had tried to warn her. Sophie just hadn't listened. "Wait. If Jacob did that to my sister at the same temple last year, then why didn't this girl or whatever wake up then?"

Emily blinked. "Because they were, like, practically dating. It wasn't like what he tried to do to you." She grabbed Sophie by the arms. "Listen, we're sorry, okay?"

Sophie glanced between them. They didn't seem sorry, mostly scared, and Stevie was mostly pissed.

"We didn't think he would—we didn't know—it just never occurred to us that you wouldn't want to." Emily's green eyes wobbled. "But now there's this thing, Sophie, and it's after us. And we need your help."

"My help? Why?"

"Because it's a *Japanese* revenge ghost!" Emily flapped her hands in Sophie's general direction. "*You* must know how to stop it!"

Sophie looked from Emily to Stevie. "A Japanese revenge ghost?"

"Look, we know how it sounds," said Stevie.

"Yeah, like you can't get enough of messing with your little Kumiko." Sophie pointed to the door. "Just get out. I'm not going to say anything. Nobody would believe me if I tried."

"Sophie." Stevie pressed her fingertips to her temples. "It's not about that, I *swear*."

"It probably doesn't matter anyway," said Emily. There were real tears on her cheeks, but Sophie had seen that before. Emily could cry on command, to get a new iPhone or to get out of doing something she didn't want to do. "We haven't seen or heard from Jacob since that night. We tracked his phone to the temple, and that's . . ."

"That's where she got Sean," Stevie finished in a flat voice.

Sophie took a deep breath. She was about to shove them physically through the door when Emily screamed, "The mirror!"

She pointed to the vanity behind Sophie.

"What?" Sophie asked, but Stevie shoved Sophie face-first onto her bed before she could turn to look. Stevie grabbed Sophie's aluminum softball bat from the corner and swung it with a cry. The mirror shattered, and glass shards went flying. Downstairs, Sophie heard her mom shout to ask what had happened.

"You broke my mirror!" Sophie cried.

"Is she gone?" Emily shrieked. "Is she gone?"

"No, she's not gone," Stevie shouted at her. "She'll never be gone!" She held the bat aloft, ready to swing at anything. They had actually lost it. Sophie had to get them out of her room. Out of her family's home. She looked down and caught a sliver of her reflection in a piece of broken mirror. The swelling in her cheek was gone, the scratches from the shrubs healed. It was like nothing had even happened. But she was still the dragon, even if she didn't have the battle scars. She didn't know why they were playing this prank or what their endgame was, but she didn't care.

Let them mess with their little Kumiko. Let them see how Kumiko can mess right back.

"Okay," Sophie said, and Stevie turned, surprised. "If what you're saying is true, and *if* she's real, she can be banished with a Buddhist-consecrated sword."

"Where . . . where do we find that?"

"My dad has one hanging in the restaurant. Let's go."

A Buddhist-consecrated sword. Stevie nor Emily said anything when Sophie took the sword off the restaurant wall and brought it with her into the back seat of the Tesla, so if their grand plan was to get her alone in the gardens for Jacob to humiliate her again, then she at least wouldn't be unarmed. The sword was dull, just for display, and never once touched by a Buddhist, but it was pretty heavy, and she was pretty sure she could beat the hell out of him with it if she had to.

By the time they got to the gardens, it was dark. They got out of the car, and Emily hugged herself and shivered even though it wasn't cold. She took a deep breath and started to climb over the gate again, with much less fervor than the last time.

"Wait, why do we even have to go?" Stevie asked, lingering by the Tesla. "Sophie's got the sword. *She* can take care of it."

"We're not going to ask her to go alone to save our asses," Emily hissed. "And besides, it's after *us*. Do you want to stay alone by the car, or do you want to follow the sword?"

Sophie clambered over the gate, ignoring their argument. It was just a park at night. There was nothing out there, nothing after them. Though she had to admit they both really could be actresses, the way they were carrying on.

"It came out of my mouth when I was brushing my teeth," Emily whispered. "All this long black hair, like I couldn't breathe, like it was going to choke me—"

"Like you were a big cat," Sophie muttered, shouldering the sword. "Tell me more. About Haruko."

"What more do you need to know?" Stevie asked. "Is the sword not going to work?"

"Well, is she buried here?" Sophie asked casually. "Like, are her remains here? Or is this the very spot that she was murdered? All these are important details."

"We don't know any of that," Emily said. She glanced over her shoulder and flinched, moving so close to Sophie that she thought Emily was about to ask for a piggyback ride.

"All right." Sophie turned. "Enough of this. You got me out here. So where's Jacob? Where's Sean? What's your big plan to humiliate me?"

"We're not trying to humiliate you!" Stevie shrieked. "What is wrong with you? Why don't you believe us?"

The temple loomed behind them as Sophie waited, but neither Stevie nor Emily said anything more. They just clung to each other, bewildered eyes big as dinner plates.

Sophie sighed. She turned back around and kept walking as Emily and Stevie gripped the back of her shirt in their fists. They were so unnerved, or so good at pretending to be, that even she held her breath when they walked inside and adjusted her grip on the sword handle.

There's nothing in this temple, she reminded herself. Probably not even Jacob and Sean. The idiots would have gotten bored with this game and wandered off after ten minutes.

"Come on out," she called, and took a step. Her shoe slipped in something wet. She looked down.

Something wet and dark. And thick . . . Her eyes adjusted and followed the path of it through the temple as Stevie turned on her phone's flashlight, and Emily screamed.

It was blood on the floor. And on the walls. More blood than Sophie had thought could fit in a body. And it hadn't been splashed or dripped, but slathered, like a bleeding corpse had been dragged back and forth, up and down, all over the place.

"Where's the body?" Stevie asked. "What happened to their bodies?"

"Jacob's phone!" Emily gasped. She spotted his phone lying on the floor and raced to it, then tried to unlock it even though it was covered in blood. What did she expect to find? Explanatory texts? Snapchats from beyond?

It could still be a joke. That was what Sophie told herself as she held the sword in her shaking hands. It could be red paint—except how to explain the smell? Maybe it was cow's blood, easily collected from a butcher shop. They could have done it all themselves, and Sean could be in a bush somewhere, filming her reaction.

"Okay, this is no longer funny," Sophie said. "Where are they?"

"Are you blind?" Emily shouted. She gestured to the walls.

"Emily! Behind you!" Stevie gripped Sophie's shoulder hard enough to hurt as Emily spun to see the shape in the corner.

Sophie couldn't believe what she was seeing. And she couldn't see it very well because Stevie seemed unable to make herself shine the flashlight straight at it. But even in the shitty light, the white robe and the long black hair were clear. So were the eyes, shot through with red veins. Whatever it was took a jerking step toward Emily.

"Kill it," Stevie screamed, and pushed Sophie forward. "Use the sword!"

"This isn't real; my dad got it in a gift shop!"

"But you said—you lied! Why would you lie?"

"Because ghosts aren't real," Sophie shouted.

"You bitch!" Stevie spat as she backed away. "We came to you for help!"

"And why would you do that? This is a *Japanese* revenge ghost, and I'm *Korean*, you shits! And I was born in Boulder!"

Emily's mouth dropped open. Both girls screamed. Maybe Sophie screamed, too; she couldn't tell. What she did know was that they pushed her down as they ran for the car. Face-first into Jacob and Sean's cold congealing blood. They took the flashlight, too, but she could still hear: the creaking moan, the dragging footsteps.

Sophie shoved herself up and ran, sword in hand like a baton in a relay. Emily and Stevie were way ahead on their long legs, screaming their heads off, so they probably didn't hear her when she called, "Wait! Don't leave me!"

The Tesla's lights came on, and Emily threw it into gear. She backed up without looking and nearly hit Sophie when she peeled out of the parking lot, the car bouncing as it jumped the curb.

"Damn it!" Sophie spun around, breathing hard, ready to convert to Buddhism and do what she could with the sword. But there was nothing there. No shambling ghost with too much black hair. No blood. No croaking, wheezing groan.

Curiously, she looked back at the white Tesla as it sped along the curving hill road. What was it Stevie had said? She was everywhere now. In their mirrors. Under their cars.

"Jesus Christ, Emily, shut up! Just stop screaming!"

Stevie jerked the wheel of the Tesla and slammed down the accelerator, taking her anger and fear out on the car, the stupid, so-called self-driving thing that she could barely keep on the road. It was Emily's car, and Stevie was scrunched behind the wheel—she had longer legs, and there hadn't been any time to adjust the seats. She shouldn't be driving at all, except Emily was clearly in no condition.

"What are we going to do?" Emily moaned. "Stevie, what are we—?"

"Shut up! You're going to shut up, and I'm going to drive us the fuck away from here. That's what we're going to do." Stevie swung the car out onto the main road without braking, making the tires screech and the Tesla slightly fishtail. "Then we're going to find ourselves some real help and stop this bitch from—"

Her words cut off abruptly as the driver's side window shattered and a thin pale arm snaked inside. The ghost pulled itself up from the underside of the car, clinging to it like a spider, and Stevie finally screamed, too. She fought the ghost for the wheel, trying to steer through the cold, iron-strong grip of the dead girl's fingers as they clamped onto her face.

"Em, help me!" she cried, but Emily only screamed and screamed, pressed against the passenger door. The ghost lurched in farther through the window, and the front seat filled with that sound, that goddamned creaking sound, and all that seething black hair, and the scent of water, and stone, and cooking spices. As Stevie looked into those wide bloodred eyes, she hit the brakes too hard, and when the ghost jerked the wheel, she heard the tires squeal before she felt the car flip.

I'm not wearing my seat belt, she thought detachedly, just before her head crashed through the windshield.

Sophie flinched at the rubbery screeching of tires and the loud crash when the Tesla went off its wheels and started to flip. After the noise ended, she ran forward a few steps. The car had landed on its back, one headlight broken, the wheels spinning in the dark.

Sophie stood in shock, half expecting to see Emily open the door and curse out the inconvenience of the wreck. But it wasn't Emily who crawled out. Or Stevie either. Emily and Stevie were dead, as dead as Sean, as dead as Jacob. Much more dead than the white-clad thing that slowly made its way back up the road toward Sophie in the parking lot.

I should leave, Sophie thought. *I should run.* But run where? Back to the restaurant, to bring the ghost home? To the police station, where they'd call her crazy?

She watched the ghost amble closer with its jerking steps, the white robe so bright in the dark, it was like a patch of fog. But the closer it came, the less its legs jerked, and the less white it was, until it was just a shape, a person, and just walking.

Until it was just Summer.

"What?" Sophie breathed. Her sister's hair was still wrong, and her eyes were still wild. Her face was still too pale.

"Don't be scared," Summer said, and Sophie almost laughed. "It's just me."

"It's not *just* you," she said, and Summer did laugh.

"No. It hasn't been 'just me' since last summer, right down there." She turned to look into the garden, at the silent shadow of the temple.

"How? What—?"

"I don't know. I think she took pity on me. Or maybe she knew that she had to stick around so it wouldn't happen to you." Summer's bloodshot eyes narrowed, red as rubies. Her nostrils flared, and her hair gave an irritated twitch. "I knew what he was up to when he picked you up. It was right there on his face, like a dare. Daring me to do something about it. So I did."

"Summer," Sophie said weakly as Summer moved beside her to look down at the wreck of Emily's car.

"And they say *we're* bad drivers." She clucked her tongue and reached out to wipe Jacob's blood from Sophie's cheek. Sophie tried not to jerk away. The night was quiet, too pleasant for all the death nearby and too normal for the thing standing at her side, the thing that had exacted a revenge she hadn't asked for, the thing that both was and was not her sister.

"Everything's okay now," Summer said, and sighed, almost fully Summer again, the same annoying, bossy Summer she always was. Their dad had never called Summer the dragon. Only Sophie. She watched warily as her sister reached into her pocket for her glasses and put them back on, balanced on the small bridge of her nose. "But be careful, Sophie.

"Once I leave for Michigan, you're going to have to take care of your own shit."

BEST SERVED COLD

H. E. EDGMON

Hunger is a strange animal with many names, and I've been hungry a lot in my life. Hungry for things I could touch and things I couldn't, for things I could name and words my tongue had been robbed of.

And I really, really used to hate my brown eyes.

Boring, basic, shit-colored eyes, with nothing exciting or romantic about them—nothing at all like green eyes. I *hungered* for green eyes, even going as far as buying cheap, probably toxic colored contacts from a stand at the mall, only to have a sobbing fit on the bathroom floor when I realized my natural eye color was too dark to be hidden under the film.

It was my brother, Kai, who helped me feel better. He lifted me off the ground and turned me to the mirror, pointing to my reflection staring back at us, and said, "Those eyes are our ancestor's eyes. They're always watching you. Are you going to make them proud, EJ?"

And then, years later, Kai brings a boy with the most beautiful green eyes to the Pow Wow. His name is Isaac.

My parents let me skip school on Friday to make the six-hour drive from our home outside Detroit to the Upper Peninsula for the four-day-long celebration. A year ago, they never would've agreed to that. But a year ago, I was sixteen and confused, angry for reasons I couldn't put into words, and when they looked at me, they didn't know who they were looking at—a problem I'd had myself for a long time.

Kai helped. He'd moved out three years earlier, fresh out of high school, and started his journey toward reconnection, making friends with seed traders and building relationships with folks out on the rez, and—in his own words—discovering the parts of himself that'd been stolen by colonization. He saw my suffering and our parents' confusion, and he handed me the words to finally talk about the things I was feeling. Words like *two-spirit* and *ancestral trauma*.

It turned out I was *angry* because I was playing a game whose rules had never been designed for me to win.

Our parents still don't really get it. Our mom calls herself white because *white people* think she is, because she passes in their spaces—even though her grandfather spent his childhood at a boarding school in Oklahoma and his adulthood beating the religion they gave him into her own mother. Our dad's parents grew up together on a rez in Florida but moved to Chicago before he was born, and he spent his formative years hearing how they'd gotten themselves out of there to give him a better life.

They don't understand Kai's and my drive to reconnect. They don't see how they, too, have been stolen by a kind of violence. But still, they'd do anything to make sure I don't go back to who I used to be. That's as much as I can ask for.

Drums and bells mingle with the sounds of elders chanting and babies laughing and the sobs of those in between, and I find myself thinking, not for the first time this weekend, that I never want to leave.

I spent Friday night catching up with Kai and the friends I've made on my trips up here over the past year. Eating fry bread, and salmon and deer jerky, fresh berries, and roasted hominy. Curling up in front of a bonfire and listening to men play music, watching women bead at a nearby table and little kids stomp barefoot in the lake, and dozing in and out with my head on Kai's shoulder.

And on Saturday morning, his new friend Isaac joined us.

Apparently, they met a few months ago, in a hunting club they both belong to. Hunting, like fishing and farming, tends to attract people on polar ends of the spectrum. One look at Isaac, with his eyes like new money, his blond ex-military haircut, and the Patagonia jacket fitted over his broad shoulders, and I worried he was at the *wrong* end. I think other people at the Pow Wow worried the same. I noticed the looks he got, the narrowed-eyed suspicion of elders that followed wherever he went. If either Isaac or Kai noticed, they didn't let on.

Maybe they were just letting me come to my own conclusion. And later that night, I did. I had been too critical. As far as I can tell, Isaac is a good guy. We spent the day getting to know each other—talking, and eating, and dancing. He grew up here, and he cares about this land and the people who come from it. That's what got him into hunting in the first place. And he seems to love Kai. If none of the rest was important, the latter would be all it took to convince me.

Now the celebratory mood of yesterday and this afternoon has largely faded. A few leaders in the community have come out to speak about MMIWC (Missing and Murdered Indigenous Women and Children) in our area. All night, we've heard awful stories about human trafficking and abuse and state violence, stories of women and children and queer people being lured away from their communities and never seen again. This isn't *ancestral* trauma but ongoing danger.

The feeling I've been clinging so tightly to, that thread of community and comfort I've never felt so strongly anywhere else, has shifted. It's just as strong, maybe even stronger, but there's pain threaded throughout it that demands to be acknowledged. To ignore the pain would be to dishonor the community.

Isaac is still attracting stares. When speakers talk about white men targeting Indigenous communities, people glance in his direction. It's not like he's the *only* white guy at the Pow Wow, but he's the only one who looks like he'd be just as at home at the Republican National Convention as he seems to be here.

But Isaac doesn't shrink under the scrutiny. He doesn't seem to feel guilty or uncomfortable, and that says a lot, doesn't it? He has one hand on my brother's shoulder, leaning to whisper in his ear. I wonder—and not for the first time—if they're friends *and*. Kai is nebulously queer, I know, and even if he introduced Isaac as a friend, the vibe between them is clearly intimate. It's not like I'm hunting for clues, but I can't help noticing the small touches, the lingering glances, the closeness that *should* be okay in a totally heterosexual male friendship—but isn't, really, at least not most of the time.

Maybe Isaac feels me staring, because he tilts his head, catching my eye. He nods, an acknowledgment of something more than just the shared glance, and I offer him a half-sad small smile in return. Mourning music thrums in the air all around us.

"EJ," Kai groans on Sunday evening, slamming the trunk of my car closed after helping pack it up. He turns to me, big brown eyes sad and soft. "Do you really have to go tonight? It's just one more day."

"Mom and Dad already let me skip Friday," I remind him.

"Yeah, so what's so different about missing Monday?" He raises his thick eyebrows, his expression indignant when I chuckle at him.

I have to laugh it off. If I don't, I might actually start listening. It would be enormously shitty of me to take advantage of my parents' fragile new trust to spend another night at the Pow Wow.

Even if I *really* want to.

"Let them be," Isaac chides, stepping up from behind him and putting a hand on Kai's shoulder. The glow of my taillights makes his eyes look more yellow than green. "There'll be other trips."

Kai groans, waggling a finger at me. "You better come up this summer—spend a whole week with us. No, a month!"

"I'd love that." I can't think of anything else I'd rather do.

"Me, too." Isaac grins.

Us, I think. Definitely gotta ask my brother about that later. I guess it shouldn't matter what he and Isaac are to each other—but I'm nosy.

Kai sweeps me off my feet, and I bury my face in his neck, my own arms curling around his waist to lace my fingers at his back. I want to remember everything, everything about this weekend and this moment and the feeling of being present and whole and connected to something so much bigger than myself. I never want to go back. I try to remind myself that going home right now is *not* the same as backsliding; I can take this weekend with me.

When he sets me on my feet again, Kai swipes his hand over his eyes and sniffs. "I'm just—I'm really proud of you, you know? Watching you find yourself here—the way you've let your guard down so you can be part of this—just—We're all just really lucky to know you, kid."

It makes me want to cry just as badly, but I can't. I think if I do, I might not stop. I need to get on the road. It's already going to be well after midnight by the time I get back to our suburb. "I'm driving home, Kai, not going to war."

"You know what I'm talking about," he mumbles. Finally, taking a deep breath, he takes a step away from my car and waves his hand at it. "All right. Okay, okay. Get going. Text me when you get there safe."

"I will." I swallow past the lump in my throat and wave one last goodbye to Isaac and climb in the driver's seat.

With that bittersweet ache stronger than ever, I put the Pow Wow behind me, feeling farther and farther from home the closer I get.

I don't make it all the way there, though.

It's dark in the middle of nowhere when my car's low-fuel light blinks to life. No big deal. Light on means at least thirty miles to empty, and *empty* means another twenty if I'm lucky. It is weird, though. This is the second time since leaving the Pow Wow that the light's come on, and last time I stopped, I filled up the tank. She's not a Prius, but my car can handle more than *this*. But fine. It's fine.

Only it isn't. Because I don't make it fifty miles or even thirty miles. Less than five miles later, the car sputters, chokes, and dies, the steering wheel locking up in my hands as I wrestle her over to the side of the road.

"You've got to be kidding me," I announce to the car. She does not respond.

I tug my cell out of my pocket. 10:11 P.M. And absolutely no service in Fuckall Nowhere, Michigan. I could truck it down the road on foot, but I don't remember the last time I saw an exit sign. There could be a gas station half a mile up ahead. There could also be nothing for hours in either direction.

I tap my phone against the palm of my hand, staring out my car windows. I can only see as far as my headlights. A stretch of dirt road, with cornfields on either side. The lights cast shadows on the nearest row of stalks, creating shapes where they don't exist.

It's just my mind playing tricks on me, but I swear one of the shadows in the field looks like someone watching me.

"Grow up, EJ," I chastise myself, ignoring the way my heart tries to climb out my mouth.

I never should've left the Pow Wow. But I did. So, what to do now?

Walking for miles isn't an option. Even if I wanted to, it's not safe. The stories from the MMIWC ceremony flash in my mind.

No service, so I can't call for help.

There's no way I'm making it to school tomorrow. But my parents can't actually be mad at me for this, right? I mean, I get points for trying, right?

I tug off my sweatshirt before balling it up and shoving it under my head, leaning against my window.

Okay. I'll hang out here until dawn. Maybe some nice farmer will drive by on their way to work. If not, I'll feel a lot better about trying to walk for help in the daylight.

There's nothing watching me from the cornfield. I'm safe.

Totally safe.

I triple-check the car door locks, though. Just in case.

I wake to the sound of pounding on glass and inhuman yellow eyes watching me from outside my window. The scream bubbles up and out of me before my mind even knows to be afraid, my body reacting with an animal's instinct—trying to crawl to the other side of the car.

"EJ! Hey, hey, it's okay. It's me. It's Isaac."

Isaac?

Halfway over the middle console, I freeze. My heart is still trying to gallop its way out of me and into the field, but I narrow my eyes and twist my head to get another look at the thing outside my window.

It *is* Isaac. He's holding a flashlight, and when the glow catches directly into his eyes, they turn that yellow shade I saw right before leaving the Pow Wow. He lowers the light to offer me an awkward wave, and suddenly they're green again.

I shove myself back into my seat before pushing open the door and stumbling out into the road with him. It's still black out. The late-night mist has settled over the cornfields, making everything darker than it was when I fell asleep. The only sounds are our breathing, the hum of Isaac's truck parked behind my car, and about a million different bugs. Goose bumps prick along my bare arms, and I rub my palms over them.

"What are you even doing out here?"

"What am *I* doing out here?" He huffs, holding out his arms at his sides, as if to demonstrate the complete lack of anything at all. "What happened to you? Are you okay?"

"I'm fine." *I'm safe.* Just cold and hungry and irritated that I left the Pow Wow for this. "I ran out of gas. I was just gonna wait for morning."

"To do what? EJ, the nearest gas station's like . . . twenty miles from here." He gives me a pitying look.

"Yeah, well, I didn't think it was gonna be *fun*." I frown at him. "Seriously, though. Why are you here?"

"Got an emergency work call and had to take off last minute." He sighs, reaching over me to push my car door closed. "And you're lucky I did. There's some real weirdos out here. But c'mon. I'll get you where you need to be."

When he puts a hand on my shoulder and starts steering me toward his truck, my stomach knots, my fingers tightening at my sides as if to reach for something, but I'm not sure what. I remind myself I'm being paranoid and judgmental, just like all the grandmas and aunties giving him the side-eye over the weekend. Kai wouldn't be friends with someone who couldn't be trusted. He definitely wouldn't be *more* than friends with them, or whatever he and Isaac are to each other. I really should be grateful he showed up.

And still, my stomach doesn't unclench.

Isaac drives a lifted pickup. By the time I actually make it into the passenger seat, I'm out of breath. He—badly—hides a snicker, cranking up the heat when he sees me shiver again. Shouldn't have left my sweatshirt in my car. Oh, and—

"Shit. I left my phone." I grab for the truck handle, but Isaac waves a hand at me, shifting into Drive.

"Don't worry about it. You're not gonna be able to use it anyway."

My heart plummets. I stare at him, my fingers trembling around the plastic lever, an icy chill creeping down my arms that has nothing to do with the temperature.

He raises an eyebrow. "Because there's no service out here?"

Oh.

Right. Of course, that's what he meant. Slowly, I let my hand fall away and sink back into the seat. I scold myself for being such a wimp, while Isaac turns the truck around, and we start driving off in the direction we came from.

"How long were you out there by yourself?"

I glance at the digital clock on his display—1:32 A.M. "A few hours."

"Damn. You hungry?"

Summoned, my stomach unknots from its anxiety enough to give a pitiful snarl. My cheeks heat. "Uh. Yeah."

He snickers again and motions to the back seat. "Snagged some food for the road before I left. Help yourself. There's water, too."

He *brought* food? From the Pow Wow? Oh, score. Absolutely enormous W.

I twist at the waist to reach into the back, rifling around until I come back with a canteen of water and a bag of popcorn. Only after I've taken two swigs of the former and no less than three giant handfuls of the latter do I ask him, "So, what's the work emergency?"

"Some rare game spotted up this way not too long ago." Isaac shrugs. "Fresh meat's easier to catch at night. And less people on the road means faster trips."

Right. After he left the military, he got into the *meat* business. He'd mentioned that, I remember now. He sources "avant-garde protein" for rich eccentrics in the Great Lakes. Whatever that means. Nothing about the job sounded interesting, so my brain put the information on a shelf.

"Kai was real sad to see you go," he continues, changing the subject. "You two really have a beautiful relationship."

I cup my hand over my mouth to yawn. I've always been a night owl. This is far from truly *late*, where my chaotic sleep schedule is concerned, so I don't know why I'm exhausted like this. Maybe it's all the adrenaline of the night finally leaving my system now that I'm safe, leaving my bones heavy. I can barely keep my eyes open. "Yeah. I miss him a lot. But you two—you seem . . . close."

Again, I wonder at the real nature of their friendship, but I don't ask. If I'm wrong and Isaac is a straight white man, I really don't want to run the risk of him not appreciating the question. Especially not while I'm stuck in a truck with him. More goose bumps flutter to the surface of my skin at the thought.

He seems to know exactly what I'm saying without saying it because the next thing he says is "yeah. I was worried about it, at first. You know, befriending a guy who clearly has a thing for me. But it's worked out well."

Blink.

Blink.

Maybe it's just because I'm so much more tired than I was when I got in this truck, but something about the way he says that makes the hair on the back of my neck spike up. Yeah. Yeah, no. I'm just tired. "What do you mean?"

"Well, I find him pretty repulsive. But if it weren't for him, I never would have met *you*."

I must be hearing him wrong. That's possible. My head is swimming. I don't remember ever being this tired in my life. What the hell is wrong with me? I scrub my knuckles into my eyes, fighting to keep my head up. "Um—I'm sorry, what? You find him what?"

When I pull my hands away to look at Isaac's face again, his head has turned ninety degrees to stare directly at me. He's speeding down the dirt road, but he's not looking at anything but me. "We can talk more about it later. We'll have all the time in the world now."

"I don't—what does that—?" In a haze of green and white, we pass the exit sign. In the distance, I can make out a gas station just over the hill, then in our rearview. "Where are you taking me?"

Isaac doesn't answer. The last thing I see is the blur of his green eyes becoming more and more yellow as my own vision fades entirely, the taste of buttered popcorn and something chemical on my tongue.

I'm freezing. That's my first thought when I come to.

My second is something along the lines of *fuckshitfuckfuckfucknonononono.*

I jerk upright, my hands flying to assess my naked skin for injuries.

Naked. Why am I naked?

My body *seems* fine, other than the lack of clothes. No cuts or bruises or any pain from broken bones. Even my head feels better, my thoughts clearer and sharper. There's no soreness to indicate that something else might've been done to me while I was unconscious and stripped.

The painful spark of relief is short-lived. I'm still *here,* discarded like a carcass in the middle of this room.

It's smaller than my childhood bedroom but bigger than a closet. Everything is gray and silver. Gray walls and a gray floor and a silver generator humming at the back and big silver hooks hanging from the ceiling. Gray and silver all morph together into one colorless abyss, lit by only a single white bulb hanging from the center of the room.

I blink at the hooks, the black shadows the light bulb casts on them hitting the gray wall, shadows that look like claws stretching down toward the ground, toward my bare legs. The ceiling is too high for me to reach them on my own, and all I can do is watch as they loom over me.

Hanging hooks. My brain turns it over and pokes at the thought but can't seem to grip it tightly. What are hooks like these used for?

On the other side of the room from the generator is a door with a massive metal handle shaped like a steering wheel. When the wheel starts to spin, I scramble to my feet, curling one arm protectively over my chest, my other hand dipping down to shield between my thighs.

The door clicks open, and Isaac steps through, pushing a little metal rolling cart—and whistling. Before he can close the door behind himself, I catch a glimpse of what's beyond, outside this room. It looks like . . . a house. A normal living room, with log walls and a fireplace. A cabin? Warmth leaks in from the fire, but it's doused as soon as he slams the door closed again.

"Glad to see you finally woke up, EJ." He smiles at me. Grins, like we're in on some kind of joke together. "You scarfed down a lot of that food. More than I thought you would."

Popcorn. *Drugged* popcorn? Evil.

"Please don't do this. Please—Kai loves you. He trusts you." I know I sound pathetic. The argument isn't convincing, even to my own ears. "What kind of person would rape their best friend's little—"

"*Rape?*" Isaac has the gall to look offended, glancing over at me from where he's sorting through tools on his metal cart. "I'm not going to *rape* you. That's disgusting."

Maybe it should be comforting. If anything, it only makes me more afraid. If that's not why he brought me here, what's his plan? Why the hell am I naked and standing in the middle of what looks like some kind of walk-in freezer?

The hooks hanging from the ceiling.

Fresh meat's easier to catch at night.

No.

No, there has to be another explanation.

Isaac turns to me, lifting a cleaver from the cart. The sharpened edge glints in the shadowy glow from the single light bulb.

When my back slams against the generator, a rush of cold air frosting my skin, I realize I've been backing away from him. I hold my hands up, palms out, no longer granted the luxury of caring to cover myself.

"No, no, please, this can't—"

"You know, I told you I felt kinda weird about making friends with Kai at first. I didn't want him getting the wrong idea." Isaac holds a hand—the one not carrying a giant knife—to his chest. "I'm not homophobic. I'm just not interested in him like that."

Why is he giving me a speech about not being homophobic while he stalks me across his walk-in freezer, where I'm pretty sure he's about to butcher me for meat?

"But one day he said something to me that really stuck. Someone asked him how he could claim he was pro-environmentalism when he hunts. Like, those two things are at odds, right? And Kai said his people have been hunting the animals here since the beginning of time. Always taking only what they needed—and never letting a single part go to waste." Isaac smiles, like he's reliving the conversation. "And then I knew. He was exactly who I'd been looking for."

"You—" I shake my head. "No. No, this isn't—I'm not an animal!"

Isaac shrugs. He closes the space between us, and his free hand curls around my bicep. I stomp at his boots, claw at his fingers, trying to wrench away from him, but he doesn't budge. He presses me down onto the metal cart, forcing my palm flat against it. It's so cold in the freezer that it feels warm under my skin.

The cleaver's blade presses into the back of my wrist.

My stomach climbs its way into the empty cavern of my chest where my heart used to be before it leaped from my throat. The fingers on my free hand dig into the skin of his face, neck, anything I can touch, but I know I can't stop him.

"Why are you doing this?" I whisper, as hot salty tears track over my cheeks.

Isaac's green eyes meet mine. Behind his head, the single light bulb flickers. "Because I can."

At the first sight of my own pink flesh and white bone, his blade splitting me open like a holiday ham, I start to scream. I don't stop until I pass out again.

I wish I'd started reconnecting sooner.

The bloody bandage wrapped around my missing fingers looks almost orange in the weird glow of the overhead light bulb.

Isaac's eyes look yellow again when he sits down across from me. He sets a platter between us. Smoked meat, like a plate of sausages.

My stomach growls for it. I wish he would kill me.

I *know* different nations have stories about cannibals. I can feel them on the edge of my mind, frayed ends of a blanket I want to wrap myself in but can't quite grasp. There are monsters who walk among us. They used to be human until they slaughtered their own and feasted on their bodies. Now they only *look* human. But they're cursed to walk among us forever, insatiable for human flesh.

At least, I think that's the story. Or one of the stories.

"You should eat something." Isaac picks up a piece of meat from the tray. "There's no use going hungry. It'll only make you feel worse."

If I'd reconnected sooner, I could be sure of the stories. I might even know how to get away from one of the monsters.

I wish I had a real blanket. It's so cold in here.

"Suit yourself." He shrugs, and I watch Isaac suck the crispy skin from one my severed finger bones.

When he comes for the rest of my hand, I try to crawl across the floor, as if I might actually escape him. I can't run. I'm missing my right leg from the knee down.

He lifts me up by my hair. "Do you want to go on the hooks?"

I don't want to go on the hooks.

There's a part of me that whispers he won't do it, though. I think he likes me like this—he likes prowling across the cold room, hunting me like we're two animals in the wild. It wouldn't be nearly so satisfying if he could just take what he wanted from a shelf. At that point, I'm no different than a frozen dinner.

Isaac grips my wrist, flattening my palm against the top of his cart. The cleaver *whooshes* through the frozen air before connecting with the metal under my hand with a sound that makes my teeth tremble, the blade undeterred by bone or flesh. I watch my thumb roll away, too numb to really feel the pain, and try to bite back the humiliating flare of gratitude that at least he didn't take the *whole* hand.

But I do wonder, as he starts sewing on a new row of stitches to curb the bleeding—*when* did he take my leg?

It sits under the light bulb and licks barbecue sauce from my tibia. The yawning emptiness in my gut is louder than the sound of its smacking.

This thing isn't Isaac at all. I know this, though I don't know how. It wears his face, but with a *wrongness*, his skin stitched over its decaying insides, its movements inhuman, its bones twisting his limbs in ways that don't make sense. It is almost Isaac, almost human, almost close enough to convince me, but something older than me screams a warning in my marrow. This monster sits beneath the yellow light and watches me, blood and drool slicking the sides of its face.

I realize I'm chewing something only when I start to choke. I shove the fingers on my remaining hand down my throat, try to make myself gag, throw up, but I can't. I force myself to swallow, rolling over onto my hand and knee, sucking in a breath, then releasing one that crystallizes right in front of me.

I'm alone in the freezer. Isaac isn't here, and neither is any monster. It's just the meat.

"You know, you were really nice to me the weekend we met. Not everyone was. Some of them treated me like I didn't belong there. You never did. I really appreciated that."

Isaac says this as he closes a new line of stitches at my hip. I say nothing. I watch the hooks overhead, the shadows stretching from their sharpened tips, and imagine a benevolent monster reaching out its clawed hand to me. I imagine curling my fist around one of those hooks and using it to crack open Isaac's chest.

I imagine an alternate reality where Isaac is a fish at the end of my hook and I'm one of those straight boys on a dating app, holding up his bloated corpse for the camera. I can't tell how delirious this thought actually is.

He doesn't seem to mind my silence. Maybe he doesn't notice the blood in my eyes. "Guess it worked out fine. That way no one missed me when I went and fucked with your gas tank."

There is a part of me, the one warm and fleshy bit that's survived this freezer, that knows I should feel something about his words. I can't dig deep enough to reach it.

When loneliness comes, I could swear I hear Kai's voice in the cabin beyond the freezer.

I lie still, a puddle of mottled flesh and jutting bones, my hair thinning and falling out, my vision gone perpetually blurry from the grayness of this room and a diet of nothing my mind will let me remember. Isaac has taken the fingers from one hand, one leg from the knee down, a sirloin of my thigh, thin strips from my back, and one ear.

One ear? I reach up to touch my fingers against the place where my ear used to be, connecting with a bandage flat against my skull. I remember it on some level, but I have no idea when that happened either.

I wrap my arms around myself again. I listen to Kai's wails. I wish I were home with him. I'm just glad he isn't really here with me.

Something is wrong with Isaac.

Obviously.

Something *new* is wrong with Isaac. He pushes his cart into the freezer, and it jostles beneath the shaking of his hands. He's always seemed so disturbingly happy, like he's enjoying my company. He smiles, tells me about his day, compliments me. But today there are new shadows on his face, dark circles brought out from lack of sleep.

I know it isn't me he's losing sleep over. From my corner, curled up to frost, I watch him.

"Unfortunately, EJ, I have some bad news." He sighs, picking up his knives to examine them, his trembling hands uncertain of which one he wants. "Our time together must finally come to an end."

A pitiful spark of joy. Then a realization sets off the first spark of panic I've felt in . . . I don't actually know how long I've been here.

When Isaac abandons his cart to unlatch two hooks from the ceiling, my throat tightens.

My voice is more of a breath than anything else, as if my words have forgotten how to make themselves heard, when I ask, "Why now?"

Only when he shoots me a startled look do I realize I don't remember the last time I spoke either.

The surprise passes. Isaac turns the hooks over in his hands. I watch his knuckles whiten as they clench and unclench around the metal. "Your brother won't leave me alone." Spittle flies on the last word. "He's pitiful. And he wants to be here *constantly.* He's going to see something he shouldn't."

Kai's voice. It wasn't my mind playing tricks on me. He was here.

How close was he to the freezer? How many feet were between us, while he laid open his grief about his missing sibling?

He could have seen me. Could have heard me if I'd just screamed.

Stupid. Stupid, foolish, naive, idiot child. I could have saved myself.

No. No, I can still save myself. I can survive this. I can get out.

Just not if Isaac puts me on the hooks. No matter what happens here tonight, I cannot let him get me on those hooks.

He sighs, moving toward me. The warm metal wall presses against my back, a caress against my frozen shoulder blade.

"I wanted us to have more time," he tells me. I think he means it. I think he's sad about this. "When you're gone, I'm actually going to miss you. Isn't that odd? I've never felt like—"

Without a yell or a curse or a warning of any kind, I grab for the hook in his hand. Adrenaline floods my body, wet and slobbery and warm, not cold, not compared to the freezer. Isaac has the audacity to look *confused,* not even angry—and when I force the jagged end of the hook up and into the underside of his jaw, into the soft tissue of his mouth, into the cavity of his skull . . . to look betrayed.

He makes an awful choking, gagging, coughing noise, stumbling toward me as I scramble back away. The hook tears through flesh when he does, ripping open his tongue, the vulnerable meat of his brain. He isn't *him* anymore—the last pieces of primal instinct left are puppeteering his dying body, and they claw at his lips, wasting the dregs of his energy trying to wrench the metal free. I grip the edge of his cart to keep my one good leg standing, and I don't let myself look away.

When he hits his knees, he tilts his head back to look up at me. Blood soaks the silver in his mouth. He tries to speak, though no words are formed.

I don't know why it sounds like a warning.

I can't open the door, not with only one hand, not with the wheel locked in place. But it doesn't matter. I'm alive. I killed the monster, and I'm still alive, and I just have to keep myself alive until Kai comes for me. Anytime now, Kai will come for me.

Kai doesn't come for me.

Sometimes I forget Isaac's body is in the freezer with me. Other times, I wake up and find I've crawled toward him in my sleep, burrowing into his side like a dog that stays at its master's grave.

Other times still, the monster shakes itself alive and crawls along the edges of the freezer. It stays away from the light. It watches me in shadow. I know it needs a new body.

It knows I'm weak.

I am so hungry.

Kai will come. Even if he doesn't, *someone* will find me. I only have to stay alive long enough for them to get here.

Human beings become monsters when they taste their own people's flesh. It's a fitting punishment. They've abandoned their kind, so they no longer get to *be* their kind.

But I haven't abandoned anyone. I didn't choose this. I wouldn't be punished for surviving, would I?

Would I?

I wake up curled into Isaac's side. My face is pressed into his neck. His neck, chewy and tough and bloody, is in my teeth.

This time, I don't choke, only swallow. The dim light bulb overhead pops and explodes, and the freezer plunges into darkness.

The monster breathes down my neck, its claws trailing my stitched-together spine with something like tenderness. I am too tired and too hungry to try and push it away.

When I hear Kai's voice the next time, a muffled, too-far-away call for Isaac through the cabin, I don't hesitate to call for him. I can't seem to remember how words are formed, can't make myself say his name, can only scream. It bubbles up and out of me, guttural and loud and wet.

Kai's voice again, louder, closer.

The sound of metal screeching.

Light plunges into the freezer. My brother's dark eyes find mine. "EJ? No, I—oh my God, EJ."

When he gathers me in his arms, his skin is so hot, it hurts. I whine at the pain.

"What happened?" he asks around tears. "How—are you—? Did Isaac do this to you? Where is he? I'll kill him."

Too late. I turn my head toward Isaac's body.

Where did it . . . go?

The corpse I grew attached to has disappeared, leaving nothing but a smear of dried blood on the gray floor.

I can't have eaten *all* of him.

When I don't answer, Kai lifts me and carries me from the freezer. Like his skin, the warmth of the cabin beyond is too hot. The nails on my remaining hand claw at my tattered skin, aching to be back in the cold.

He sets me down on a too-plush couch. Drags a blanket over me and wraps it around my naked butchered body. The sensation of *touch* makes me want to scream. The soft fabric feels like a web of nettles. "You're safe. Everything's going to be okay now. You're safe. Oh, EJ, I'm so sorry."

He pulls out his phone, but his scorching hand never leaves my shoulder.

I'm safe.

I tilt my head away from his face to find my own reflection in the cabin window. Something slithers, unrelenting, inside my belly.

I'm safe.

Unfamiliar eyes stare back at me in the window glass. My vision is still so blurred, I can't decide if they look brown or yellow.

I'm safe. But I don't think anyone's going to be proud of the thing I've become. Or what I have to do next.

My stomach growls. I reach for my brother's hand.

THE PROTÉGÉ

LAMAR GILES

On Saturday morning, before everything went wrong, the grand gong of the doorbell groaned differently. It was a bloated sob that ricocheted off the walls of Troy's home until it petered into a distant scream before vanishing altogether. Troy would later think of that twisted sound as an omen—a sign that whoever stood uninvited at the threshold of his family's normal, happy life should not be acknowledged, even if it meant never opening their front door again.

Darius, Troy's big brother, answered anyway.

Their parents wouldn't be back for a whole week—the longest they'd ever left the boys alone—because their anniversary cruise was hitting *four different Caribbean islands*. Mom had said she was going to buy a dress at each stop. Dad had said he was bringing back as much rum as he could. They'd both said the boys better *answer their phones* whenever they called to check in.

"Don't make us regret this," Dad had told them while they loaded luggage in the Range Rover.

This was low stakes for Darius, who was off to Georgetown University in August, but Troy had three long years left under their parents' roof. Any missteps would mean doom for Troy and Troy alone. This weighed on him, just not so much that he expected trouble at eight in the morning.

The odd moment of queasiness Troy felt at the sound of the doorbell passed quickly, and his curiosity about the early-morning visitor was the excuse he needed for a break from practicing the Ambitious Card. It was a trick where you placed a specific card—the ten of diamonds, for example—into the middle of the deck, then had someone pull that very card off the top. The idea being the card was so *ambitious*, it moved up in the world!

It was one of those "simple" tricks that was supposed to be "easy." But Troy kept spilling cards across his comforter. He abandoned the deck of splayed cards then and barely reached the banister overlooking the foyer when his brother called.

"Troy," Darius shouted. "Mr. Meridian!"

Shit. Jack Meridian was their next-door neighbor who'd taught Troy the card trick. Mom called him "an eccentric" and Dad said that was her way of saying "weirdo" nicely. Mr. Meridian loved it, though. His response: "Is there such a thing as a stage magician who isn't?"

As good-natured as Mr. Meridian was, his popping up felt like he'd stopped by to give Troy a grade—hopefully not on his Ambitious Card trick.

"Coming!" Troy yelled back.

He darted down the stairs, stumbling on the last two steps.

Darius snagged his elbow before he fell. "Slow down, man. Don't need you breaking your neck on my watch."

Darius looked and sounded like Dad. Everyone thought so. They were the same kind of tall—not quite six feet, but close enough to claim it—and the same kind of handsome. Darius was more muscular because he wrestled, and Dad liked to ride his Peloton, so if you saw just them, you'd assume they were a fitness family. If you then saw Troy, those assumptions would fly into the ether like his mishandled cards.

Five foot seven in boots, a little less wide than he was tall, Troy was the fun house mirror version of the other men in his family. His home was a loving place, though. Mom and Dad never shamed him about his body by suggesting he eat differently or less. Even Darius's clumsy gym invites felt more like bonding attempts than veiled judgment, though Troy had only ever joined him once. All that grunting, clanking metal plates, and *musk* wasn't his vibe. Troy felt comfortable in his own skin at home. Elsewhere . . . was another story.

Family couldn't protect you from the outside. Not always.

Maybe that's why Troy had taken such a liking to the man in their foyer. Jack Meridian was retired from his days of performing magic and illusions ("There is a difference, Troy!") in Vegas. Having purchased the home next door five years ago, and to this day, graciously sharing the basics of his craft with a kid he clearly took pity on, Jack had earned a great deal of admiration from Troy. Shorter than Troy and rail thin, Jack still seemed like a giant in all the ways Troy wanted to be.

For all the love and kindness Troy's family showed him, they never hid their confusion over Troy's affection for the old . . . *eccentric*.

Jack tugged his cherry-red sunglasses away from bloodshot eyes. He looked paler than usual, and that was saying something since he'd never been the kind of white guy who hit the beach, a tanning salon, or even stood outside for long periods of time. His sequined tiger-patterned jacket twinkled with a thousand bursts of reflected summer sunlight. It was a garment only Mr. Meridian could pull off. Though Troy couldn't help but wonder how he might look in something like it, under stage lights.

"Mr. Meridian," Troy said, getting out of his own thoughts. "What're you doing up so early?"

"Sorry to disturb. I was hoping to catch your parents, but I'd forgotten they were away. I need . . . a favor."

"Yeah, sure."

Jack shook his head. "Let me ask first. Never give away too much up front. Remember."

It was one of his many *Philosophies for Show Biz and Life Biz* (the working title of his in-progress memoir).

Troy said, "Okay. What is it?"

"I'm expecting a package soon, but I need to run downtown to Gossamer's."

"The magic shop?" Troy had only recently learned such a store existed and was still awaiting a promised trip.

"Yes. The package is quite valuable, and as such, I don't want it left alone on my porch, so I was wondering if you'd be willing to accept the delivery just until I return? You can say no. I won't be mad."

"Is it big or something?"

Jack mimed the approximate size and shape of a toaster.

Troy shrugged. "Okay, I'll hold on to it for you."

Jack chewed his bottom lip and glanced over his shoulder. "Just until this afternoon. This evening at the latest."

Then Jack did something so *eccentric*, even for him, that Troy felt the first tickle of crawling skin. The old magician hugged Troy with the heft of someone going off to war.

Why war? Troy thought, recalling the lessons on analogies from language arts class. But then Jack pulled away, taking that strange thought with him.

Jack said, "Thank you, Troy. You really are a fine young man."

Low heat warmed the boy's cheeks. "I been working on the Ambitious Card."

Jack grinned. "How's it going?"

Troy thought about saving face but felt a strong urge to be honest in the moment. Like he'd regret Jack leaving with a lie between them. "I'm having trouble with the card passes. My fingers feel clumsy."

"Mine did too when I learned all my tricks. Every spectacular magician I know can tell you stories of the many decks they sent flying in the early days. You're in good company. Keep at it!"

Mr. Meridian backed toward the door and snapped his fingers. A blue-purple flame leaped into the air and vanished.

"Whoa!" Troy beamed.

"Always exit like a showman, Troy."

Then he left.

Troy closed the door and made a note to ask about that snap-flame trick. The doorbell rang again. Mr. Meridian must've forgotten something. But when Troy tugged the door open, no one was there. A plain cardboard box rested on the welcome mat, though.

Troy stepped out, looking for the delivery driver.

He saw no one. Just the box.

With Jack Meridian's name and address scrawled in bold marker. No shipping label with the barcode thingy. No return address.

Troy picked up the package, gave it a shake—a slight rattle. He brought it inside his home, as promised.

Where it was safe.

Darius's friends arrived in the late afternoon. Some of his old wrestling teammates and a few upperclassmen girls Troy recognized from the school hallway, followed by a DoorDash delivery of Chinese food *and* pizza. The group was loud, and one of those wrestlers should've showered before arriving, but no one seemed to mind. Much.

Troy scavenged the deep dish and moo shu pork leftovers, then entered the family room as a Nerf football spiraled end to end and a wrestler-turned–wide receiver made a flying leap to catch it. The big boy came down hard on the wraparound couch with the ball in hand, the frame making a distressing *KA-RACK!*

"D," Troy said, "a word."

Troy led his brother to the kitchen for a summit. "Darius, if Mom and Dad found out we had people over—"

Darius held up a halting hand. "I'mma stop you right there. One, nobody leaves their kid at home and believes people aren't coming over. Facts. Two, it's not '*we*' it's '*me*.' Something goes wrong, I'll eat it. Three, where are *your* friends, Troy? You should be inviting people over, too. Not dragging me in here to review the rule book."

"I—I mean . . ."

There was a thunderous *BA-BOOM!* that could only mean property or bodily damage followed by a wailing "the fuck, bro?"

The brothers ran into the family room. Darius's wide receiver friend sprawled on his back, prodding his busted lip.

Darius said, "What happened?"

"Tripped over that." The boy pointed at the box resting in the middle of the floor.

Mr. Meridian's package.

Troy snatched it up, furiously scanning the room. "Not cool, guys. Who moved this?"

Low grumbles all around. No one copped to it.

Troy had *one job*. Look after this box! And these dicks—who weren't even supposed to be here—were about to mess that up for him. If the contents were damaged, Mr. Meridian wouldn't trust Troy with anything again.

"It's not yours!" Troy yelled. "You shouldn't have touched it!"

Darius, not unsympathetic, placed a hand on Troy's shoulder. "Chill. I'll handle it." Then, to the room, he said, "For real though, I told y'all about touching my people's shit!"

A girl fiddling with the remote said, "Well, can you come touch this remote and get your TV to YouTube? I'm trying to watch the new Marvel trailer, but I can't get it off the news."

Darius sighed heavily. Maybe regretting his host-with-the-most role this evening. He took the remote and attempted to fulfill the request. The TV remained on the local breaking news.

"Maybe it's the batteries," Darius mumbled.

No one paid attention to the report. Except for Troy. Because he recognized the storefront bathed in strobing red and blue emergency lights. Gurneys rolled black body bags to waiting transports.

Troy snatched the remote and turned the volume all the way up. The batteries seemed fine.

The reporter was in the middle of an explanation: "*. . . don't have confirmed details, but the situation here at the Hidden Hares strip mall is intense. There are a lot of police. Initially, there were reports of an active shooter, though those accounts seem false. There are, apparently, fatalities. Our source says, and I quote, 'It's worse than guns in there.'*"

Darius pried the remote from Troy's hand, unconcerned with the tragedy described on-screen. Troy wanted to rage, but he knew he'd done it plenty of times, too. Some war in another country. Some horrible highway accident three states away. Terrible stories that had Mom and Dad shaking their heads and proclaiming how horrible the world had gotten. Catastrophe mattered most when it was yours.

And this mattered to Troy. Because Hidden Hares strip mall was where Gossamer's Magic Shop was. It was where Mr. Meridian *hadn't* returned from to claim his package.

Darius had asked where Troy's friends were, and Troy feared this news report was answering the question in the worst possible way.

And what of that package?

I'll take better care of it, that's what! Troy thought. *Because Mr. Meridian's okay, and I'll be handing him a pristine box to show him how trustworthy I am so he'll teach me bigger and better magic.*

"Fuck it," Darius said, abandoning the remote and turning on the Xbox in the television cabinet. The TV automatically switched inputs, bringing up the console's profile screen. "Who trying to get washed in NBA 2K?"

A wrestler snatched the player-two controller. Everyone else groaned, then scrolled on their phones. Troy cradled Mr. Meridian's package and went for the TV in his room. He sat the box on his bed, gently, then turned his TV to the ongoing news broadcast and sent several texts to Mr. Meridian.

The news camera focused on another body bag being rolled to its final destination; the bag leaking pus-yellow gore. Someone with a badge on their belt thrust their hand in front of the camera to obscure the disturbing view.

Troy: **Mr. Meridian your package came and I'm taking real good care of it. You'll see.**

Troy: **If you want to pick it up tonight you can. Doesn't matter how late. I'll stay up. Just let me know.**

Troy: **Please.**

Mr. Meridian: **Who is this?**

Troy's heart plummeted.

The magician didn't put people's names in his contacts. Everyone had an alias. One day, after Troy had grasped a complicated sleight of hand gesture, the magician showed Troy his assigned designation with pride.

"You're earning your nickname today." Mr. Meridian held his phone for Troy to see.

Troy's cheeks and forehead burned. He had to look away because he was so moved. It said *The Protégé.*

"Why?" Troy asked, his voice so low that if Mr. Meridian hadn't heard him, he wasn't sure he'd be willing to repeat it.

But Mr. Meridian did hear. He squeezed Troy's shoulder and said, "Because someone who showed me there was more to life than the limitations I placed on myself once called me her protégé and told me we outsiders never need to introduce ourselves to one another. I won't insult you by saying we're the same because you're going to be better than me! I can smell it!"

Troy smirked. "*Smell* it?"

"Feel it. Smell it. You know us old eccentrics get *tied-tongue* sometimes."

"Tongue-tied."

"My point exactly."

Troy knew Mr. Meridian sometimes mixed things up, but people didn't get *tied-tongue* in a text. If Mr. Meridian were answering his own texts—if he *could* answer—he'd know who Troy was.

Troy nearly responded to the message with his whole name, but some aggressive intuition shoved him to a different course.

Troy: **Can you have Mr. Meridian give me a call?**

Mr. Meridian: **You might need a Ouija board for that, Protégé. That poser ain't calling anyone ever again.**

Mr. Meridian: **So do what's smart and tell me where you and MY package are?**

Mr. Meridian: **It'll be worse if you make me work for it.**

Troy's thoughts knocked around like rocks in a can. Before he could respond, his phone chimed with an incoming photo.

It's worse than guns in there.

Troy gasped. His phone clattered to the floor.

"Darius!" Troy shrieked. "Darius!"

Thunder cascaded up the stairs, and then Darius turned the corner into his room. "Dude, what's wrong?"

Nearly hyperventilating, Troy pointed at the facedown phone.

Darius retrieved the device. "Is it Mom and Dad?" When he flipped the phone and saw the photo there, he tilted his head, disgusted. "The fuck?"

He swiped the photo away to get a view at the messages. "Dude from next door sent this to you?"

Troy blubbered, "Someone's . . . got Mr. Meridian's . . . phone."

"Someone got your man's phone and sent you picture of a gutted animal? Why?"

Darius hadn't noticed the little details the way Mr. Meridian had taught Troy to do. Seeing everything at once helped him be a better showman. Along with the wet, glistening viscera and the jutting pink ends of snapped ribs, Troy saw the red-framed sunglasses in a jacket pocket and the sequined fabric reflecting the camera's flash through all the blood. Not a gutted animal. A gutted magician.

But Troy was too busy sobbing to explain.

Shay, the girl Darius had been hoping to get some alone time with, said, "Your brother good?"

"He will be. I think."

It was a little after ten, and they were on the porch, where the late-night june bugs bounced off the yellow light bulb overhead. Her car keys jangled. She was the last to leave.

She stood on tiptoe to give him a too-brief good night kiss. "Maybe we can chill some next week."

Next week. Fuuuuuck. Through a forced smile, he said, "I'd like that."

Darius watched her little Prius putter out of the cul-de-sac, pushed what could've been from his mind, and focused on his brother crying upstairs.

After stopping by his room to change into some sweats and grab a sleeping bag, Darius then returned to Troy's and dropped his gear in the floor. Troy was still whimpering. What would Dad say here?

Darius settled on "you don't *know*, for sure, something happened to Mr. Meridian."

Troy's tear-drenched face did not look convinced. "Why hasn't he come back for that?"

The box was still on Troy's bed. Maybe there was a good answer to Troy's question, but Darius didn't have it. If the nasty pic was really Jack Meridian's body, then yeah, his brother's weirdo old magician friend had gotten axe murdered or whatever, and how did you get a fifteen-year-old kid right from that?

Yet another answer Darius didn't have. So he unrolled his sleeping bag, then bundled up on the floor. "I'll be down here all night. Okay? We'll see what's up in the morning."

Darius squeezed his brother's hand, and gratitude radiated from the distraught boy.

Troy cried himself to sleep. Darius killed the lights and dozed right after. Neither of them heard Mr. Meridian's box move in the night, but they felt it in their dreams.

This didn't feel like any dream Troy had ever had before. First, he wasn't himself, but a woman. The star of this show.

It felt like playing a first-person shooter. A Call of Duty *cutscene where you were a character you didn't choose and couldn't control. SHE got dragged kicking into a dank room where overhead pipes dripped, and disturbing rust-colored splotches stained the concrete.*

Troy saw her curvy legs like they were his own. Those legs bucked against the golden chains looped around her ankles and knees, chains with symbols engraved in the links, symbols that glowed like magma. She swiped her manicured hand across the snarling white face of a man lifting her roughly by the torso; her nails raked permanent deep gashes in his flesh. Luminescent tattoos ran down her brown arm; they had the same angry glow as the symbols on her restraints.

"Get her down," the man with the torn face yelled. "Now!"

A new chain snapped from the dark, whipped around her wrist, and held fast. Thin wisps of smoke rose where the chain seared flesh. Troy felt it and screamed! Or tried to. He didn't exactly have a mouth here, but the woman whose body he inhabited did. She screamed plenty for them both.

The scarred man said, "Stop squirming. You know these restraint wards better than any of us. You're not going anywhere."

The woman was dropped onto a table, where the chains, moving on their own, affixed their dangling ends to the furniture, allowing the man with the bloodied face to step back and catch his breath.

Why did he look familiar? Troy wondered.

The woman's head whipped toward the shadows, where other faces emerged. White. Mostly male. Various heights and sizes. All wearing rubber smocks like they were expecting a mess.

The scarred man prodded his wounds. "I told you this would be worse if you made me work for it." Then, to the room, he said, "Where's the chainsaw?"

The woman bucked again. Futile.

A redhead, the only other woman in the room, handed the scarred man an electric chainsaw that seemed bigger than her. Apprehension crept into her voice when she said, "I was expecting a more surgical approach. Won't this damage the segments?"

"Belinda, you can take your foot however you want. Okay?"

Belinda, satisfied, returned to the shadows.

The scarred man revved the chainsaw. The woman Troy was connected to spit in the man's face.

A shiny glob of saliva dripped off his chin. "Nona, you could've just taught us what you know. We would've paid well. But I don't mind saving a few bucks."

He revved the chainsaw again before addressing his accomplices. "Why y'all looking so squeamish? We're magicians. Sawing someone in half's like the oldest trick in the book."

He lowered the churning blade. When it touched bare flesh, the soul-shredding pain sent the woman (and Troy) into convulsions and—

screams. Troy's and Darius's.

Troy awoke shrieking and gripping his stomach, where the chainsaw had . . . had . . .

He fell from his bed into the gap closest to his window, while Darius ejected from his sleeping bag and backpedaled into Troy's dresser, knocking various action figures to the floor and clutching his own stomach.

Troy, still pushing through the fog of sleep and nightmare, said, "Were you there? Did you feel her, too?"

Darius nodded in quick jerks, admitting what would seem ridiculous in the light of day. "Who the fuck was she? Who the fuck were *they*?"

"Magicians," Troy mumbled, those blazing symbols on that woman's restraints seared into his memory as was the face of the white man she scarred. Where did Troy know him from?

The alarm clock said 6:02 A.M. Still dark out. He snatched the TV remote off the nightstand and turned to the local news.

"What are you doing?" Darius asked.

"I want to see if they're still talking about what happened at the strip mall."

And they were. Sort of.

The blond anchorwoman stared directly into the camera. ". . . gruesome and bizarre turn in the massacre that took place at the Hidden Hares shopping center last night. The body of one of the victims, Larry McDonald, better known as retired stage magician Jack Meridian, appears to be missing . . ."

It cut to a frazzled man in blue scrubs standing in a brightly lit corridor by a directional sign that read MORGUE: "We don't know if there's been some sort of processing mix-up, or something else altogether, but we can't find him. It's like he vanished into thin air."

Troy hit MUTE. He couldn't focus on processing mix-ups or whatever. They said "the body" was missing. Jack was gone. "He's really dead. He's—"

Darius shushed Troy with a wave. "You hear that?"

Thump. Th-th-thump.

The boys frowned. It came from the hall.

Th-th-thump. Thump.

Troy rounded his bed. Darius grabbed an old tennis racket from the closet. They entered the hall, peering down the corridor.

The golden-hour rays of the rising sun seeped through drawn blinds to light their path, but not much. Not enough. Whatever was making that sound remained obscured by early-morning gloom, forcing them to draw closer, to investigate, to do the things a hundred horror movies had told them not to. It was different when it was real, though.

Halving the distance between them and . . . whatever, they were better able to identify it. Yet it didn't make sense.

It was Mr. Meridian's box.

The object, which should've been inanimate, bumped the far wall. Repeatedly. It slammed itself forward—*THUMP*—then went for weaker ramming action—*th-th-thump*. Small cracks webbed along the drywall from the point of impact.

Darius lowered the tennis racket. "You had an animal in that box this whole time?"

"Not an animal," Troy said, thinking like a showman. "Magicians never give you exactly what you expect."

"What then?"

"I'm not sure."

"So let's open it."

"I can't. I—" But why not? Mr. Meridian hadn't said he couldn't. Even if he had, did it matter now?

Troy crept toward the animated box, then grabbed it like he would a finnicky cat. In his hands, it was still. He tore away the brown wrapping paper, then worked at the taped seal. Darius raised the tennis racket again.

"On three," Troy said, preparing to fling the box open. "One . . . two . . . !"

He popped the lid and shook the box so the contents landed on the hall runner.

Darius backpedaled when the thing landed within inches of his toes. "Shit."

Not an animal.

It was a polished human jawbone with two glistening gold-capped molars.

The boys shrieked when the doorbell rang.

"Mr. Meridian!" Troy said, hoping against hope because the jawbone had to be some sort of prop, right? So maybe the trouble at Hidden Hares was part of some elaborate trick. A hoax! That was why Mr. Meridian's body was missing. Magicians didn't give you what you expected; they gave you want you needed. Troy needed Mr. Meridian to be alive to explain this insanity.

He descended the stairs with so many maybes, he barely heard Darius saying, "Wait! Don't open the—"

Troy tugged the door halfway open and recoiled.

The man on the welcome mat extended a badge across the threshold and said, "I'm Detective Monroe with the police department. Is there an adult home? I have some questions about an incident involving your next-door neighbor. Went by the name Jack Meridian."

Darius bolted down the stairs like something was on fire, then stood protectively before his brother, his nostrils flaring.

The man lowered his badge. "You boys okay? Do you need help?"

They'd been taught from a young age that the only thing they should ever say to a cop was they wanted to call Mom and Dad and/or a lawyer.

This was different, though, because this man was not a cop. Everything out his mouth was lies. They knew because of the puckered old scars stretched across his face. They remembered his chainsaw. They'd seen the truth of him last night.

There was more than the dream carnage splashing red recognition across Troy's mind. This close, in this light, Troy knew this man's name. Had seen him many times in his controversial TV specials and grotesquely compelling YouTube videos. This was the Macabre Marauder, Danford Dread.

Not so much a magician as a shock artist, Mr. Meridian had once explained when he caught Troy watching Dread's videos on his phone. Dread's thing was painful acts of endurance. He once hung himself on a meat hook in a slaughterhouse freezer for twenty-four hours. His signature Vegas act involved pinning his assistants to boards like science-class frogs and dissecting them in front of the audience.

"He perverts the art," Mr. Meridian had said. "Plays to the worst in people. He's dangerous."

Recognizing this man and recalling his reputation did not ease Troy's mind.

Dread said, "Can I come in?"

"No," said Darius. "Come back when our parents are here."

He tried to close the door, but it wouldn't budge.

There was nothing obstructing it that they could see. Darius strained, and Troy added his own weight, changing nothing.

Dread sighed. "We got to this part sooner than I anticipated."

Dread's left hand hung at his side, the fingers working in a fluid rhythm that Troy knew in his gut was somehow keeping the door ajar. There were illusions, and there was magic. Mr. Meridian had been adamant about that. This was the latter.

Dread flashed his hand toward the boys. An invisible force sent Troy and Darius sprawling across the marble floor.

"Come on!" Dread called over his shoulder. Two individuals who'd been standing just out of view entered the home with him. Another flash of Dread's hand, and the door slammed shut, sealing all five of them in.

Troy rolled to his knees, groaned. His breath caught when he recognized the petite redheaded woman—Belinda—from his dream. The third intruder, a tall man, wasn't a face he knew, but that didn't matter now.

Darius, wincing, got his feet under him. Then he darted forward, low, attempting to scoop Dread by the legs like one of his wrestling opponents. He'd always been brave like that.

The magician made another hand gesture, freezing Darius in place. The air around Darius's limbs shimmered against his straining muscles. Troy, more terrified than he'd ever been in his life, choked back a frightened whimper and squeezed the muscles at the base of his belly so he wouldn't pee his pants like a baby.

Dread turned his nose up, inhaling slow and deep. "I smell magic here. Which one of you is the protégé?"

Troy locked eyes with his brother and felt some relief from the fear he saw. If Darius, the bravest person he knew, was also afraid, then that meant Troy wasn't being a baby. Or soft. Or something so drastically different from the courageous men in his family. In this moment of shared terror, Troy wanted to comfort Darius as his brother had done for him so many times. He wanted to tell Darius everything would be okay.

Darius told Dread, "Let me go, you bitch, and we'll find out."

"Brave." Dread leaned into Darius, sniffing him like a dog. "But not you."

The magician squeezed his hand into a fist. There was a wet crack as Darius's sternum caved in, creating a sickening indentation in his chest. Darius's eyes rolled to the whites. His own bones crushed his heart like a steak in a vise.

Troy shrieked.

His brother was well beyond all comforts now.

"Rick," Dread demanded.

The tall man, Rick, tugged the destroyed boy to his feet.

Dread sniffed Troy. "Jack's magic's all on you, protégé. Like lilacs. Pussy magic."

Troy could barely form a thought. "My brother."

Dread gripped his chin. "Told you not to make me work for it. Where's my package?"

Belinda sidled next to Dread, pointing toward the staircase. "Hey, Dan!"

The jawbone sat at the top landing. Then it tipped, toppling to the ground floor as if it'd been tossed. It hit the marble with a *CLACK!*

Dread approached the prize he'd come to claim. When he reached for it, the jawbone flung itself into the air with force and crashed through a window facing Mr. Meridian's house. It was almost silly. Troy would've cackled with Darius about it if Darius weren't dead and Troy weren't completely hollow right then. Glass shards rained to the floor, and a second crash could be heard as it continued its trajectory through Mr. Meridian's window and into his home.

Dread, Belinda, and Rick exchanged concerned looks.

Belinda said, "It ever do anything like that when you had it?"

Dread shook his head. "We need to get in Jack's house."

"I tried last night," said Rick. "It's warded."

Dread said, "Not against his protégé, I bet."

Belinda voiced her concerns. "What kind of wards?"

Dread looked appalled. "You're scared of Jack Meridian's shit magic? For that, I should make you go first. Come on."

Troy got dragged away from his brother's body, wishing he'd said no when Mr. Meridian asked him to claim the package. Wished he'd said no the first day Mr. Meridian offered to teach him one damned trick. But in all their talk of magic and illusions, wishes had never come up once.

"Jack ever tell you about us, protégé?"

Dread chattered like he did in his videos. Nonstop. Incessant. Troy had wondered if that was his way of distracting marks from his sleight of hand. Now it felt like goading. Another form of torturing those around him.

"We're the Order of the Veil. Ancient magic. Brutal shit. Jack tried to worm his way in with us once but couldn't hack it." Dread nudged Troy on Mr. Meridian's porch. "Now get us past Jack's wards, or I'm going to break some ribs."

Mr. Meridian had a keypad lock. Troy knew the code to that but knew nothing of "wards"—he'd been fumbling the Ambitious Card just yesterday. Yesterday, when Darius was still . . . still . . .

Troy sobbed.

Dread didn't bother with magic, just delivered a hammer fist to Troy's side, buckling his knees, though Rick held him upright.

With a shaky finger, Troy punched four digits into the pad; the dead bolt retracted. Dread waved Belinda closer, and she laid a hand gently on Troy's shoulder. He still flinched.

All three of the magicians maintained physical contact with Troy as he opened the door.

"Cross the threshold slowly," Dread instructed.

Troy extended his right foot into Mr. Meridian's home. He'd crossed this threshold many times, but he'd never felt what he did in this moment. It was like dipping a toe into a pool. That instant of breaking the water's surface. A scrim of something barely tangible stretched across the entrance. And now, in the doorframe, Troy saw what had never been visible before. Symbols drawn on the wood. Squiggly lines and sharp angles glowing with amber light.

It's because I'm with them, Troy reasoned. Their magic and Mr. Meridian's were *reacting* somehow.

Troy also reasoned if he was the key and Mr. Meridian's magic was the lock, then he might have a chance here . . .

He continued across the threshold, his head and the shoulder Rick gripped breaking through the magical scrim.

Then he ran, ripping free of the magicians.

Only Rick's hand had crossed the warded threshold. As soon as he lost contact with Troy, there was an electric crackle, like a mosquito in a bug zapper, followed by what seemed to be an optical illusion. For an instant, time slowed. Rick's arm remained extended, the part beyond his wrist—beyond the threshold—slid down. It left a slug trail of blood on what presented like a pane of clear glass. On the other side of the barrier, where the hand had disconnected from Rick's arm, a clean cross-section of skin, fat, muscle, and bone was visible, as neat as a biology diagram.

Then Rick snatched himself away. Time sped up. His severed hand plopped on the floor.

The man screamed, clutching his spurting stump. Neither Belinda nor Dread offered aid. They only stared at Troy.

Dread calmly said, "I'm going to skin you for that."

Dread began chanting in an unrecognizable language and making gestures with his hands that looked like martial arts stances, with every strike aimed at a glowing symbol in the doorframe. One symbol vanished in a whiff of smoke. Dread focused on the next, and the same thing happened. It would take some time for him to erase all twenty plus that prevented his entrance, but not much. Not enough.

Troy went for the phone in Mr. Meridian's kitchen, dialed 911, but instead of an operator, he heard Belinda's voice whisper-chanting in a language he didn't know, though the sound made him queasy. He dropped the phone.

He considered taking the back door, hopping the fence, and running. But where? Where was safe from the fuckers who'd killed his brother with a flick of the wrist?

Before he could take his chances, he spotted Rick limping along the side of the house to cut off any backyard escape.

Thump. Th-Thump.

The sound came from the walk-in pantry. Troy flipped on the light.

The jawbone. It threw itself at the back wall over and over between toppled cans of soup and a ruptured bag of macaroni. Settle, hurl. Settle, hurl. Like a practical effect in a goofy old horror movie where you could see the strings. Noodles crunched under Troy's feet as he approached, cautious.

There was a door, moderately hidden, a light Mr. Meridian must've left on shining through the paper-thin seams. Troy swept everything to the floor, searching for a latch. The jawbone continued its battering ram act. There was a subtle ring embedded in the wood. Troy tugged it, needing a bit of extra strength to slide aside all the food he'd knocked to the floor. When the gap was wide enough, he wedged himself through.

The jawbone followed.

It flung itself down a short flight of stairs like a grisly boomerang, then hit a hard aerial U-turn. Troy chased it but skidded to a halt when he saw what the jawbone collided with.

A coffin.

It was composed of wooden planks. Cheap. With gaps between the slats wide enough to slide a pinky through. It was propped upright against the basement wall, and rusty hinges on its side were slick with fresh oil. The jawbone bashed against the upper portion of the coffin repeatedly, with speed and force that would soon break the wood or the bone. One gold tooth knocked free and skipped across the floor like a tossed die.

A wave of nausea hit Troy at the thudding footsteps overhead. Dread had broken the wards.

"Hey, protégé! You're gonna think your brother got off easy when I'm done with you."

Since Darius's brutally quick death, Troy had been drowning in fear and sorrow. But hearing Dread speak of Darius so . . . so . . . smugly made something in him surface. From the moment the light had left Darius's eyes, Troy understood he'd probably die today, too. Dread might even keep his promise and kill him horribly. But horrible wouldn't mean easy. Troy assessed his surroundings. Mr. Meridian's worktable was within reach, atop it a few of the everyday carry items a magician might have—a Sharpie marker, a deck of cards, a simple wristwatch. Then there were actual tools that *might* double as weapons: a ball-peen hammer, a wrench, a box cutter.

Thump. Thump. Thump.

What was in that coffin?

As the footsteps drew closer, Troy had nothing left to lose. No discovery more terrifying than the torment Dread had in store for him. His only slim chance for a fighter's death, if not salvation, was bravery in this very moment. He grabbed the jawbone as if it were the hilt of a sword, felt energy vibrating in it, then flipped the coffin's lid.

Oh God, Oh God, Oh God . . .

It was a person. Maybe a woman. She was naked except for gauze shrouding her biggest joints—the shoulders and hips—while neat stitching zippered her exposed flesh at smaller joints—ankles, knees, wrists. Her flesh was as dry as the jerky Darius had snacked on incessantly during wrestling season. Her eyes were milky glass. She looked to be screaming, but that was because anybody with a missing jaw would look like they were screaming.

The jawbone in Troy's hand no longer jerked with ramming speed. An invisible force tugged at it, steady but not quite strong enough to break Troy's grip.

Release me.

It was as faint as a whisper in a dreamer's ear. So low, Troy misheard. The voice repeated, clear with purpose.

Unleash me.

Dread thundered down the basement stairs, an orb of swirling fire hovering an inch above his hand to light the way. Belinda and Rick trailed. A gleeful trio of monsters advancing on cornered prey.

Rick said, "Let me take his fingers. One by one."

He collided with Dread when the leader froze in his tracks, clearly unsettled by the corpse standing upright in the coffin like a wax statue from Hell. "Nona?"

UNLEASH ME!

The jawbone jerked in Troy's grasp.

Belinda, her voice shaky, said, "Hey, kid. Bring that bone over here, okay?"

Troy's gaze flicked from the jawbone to his brother's murderers.

"Don't let it go," Belinda said. Begged.

Troy said, "A showman never gives the audience exactly what they want, but he does give them what they need. I think you need this."

"No!" Dread rushed forward.

Troy released the jawbone.

It flipped end over end before affixing itself in the right spot on the desiccated corpse as if magnetized. Troy would reflect on what happened next for decades to come.

The entire basement blazed in amber light so bright, Troy thought he might be permanently blinded. But it did recede. Into the coffin. Into Nona.

Her once dried flesh was brown, supple. The stitches holding her joints together fell away, unnecessary now. The tattoos Troy and Darius had dreamed of during her gruesome dismemberment glowed with the same power that had robbed them all of sight a moment before. Her glassed-over eyes weren't that anymore . . . they were rage and damnation, but not for Troy.

Belinda said, "Nona, wait! Please—"

Nona ejected from the coffin, her arms limp, her toes inches off the ground, and levitated to Belinda in a breath. Nona's head cocked sideways as the flesh of Belinda's cheeks split in bloody tears, exposing her full set of teeth. Then the skin peeled backward while Belinda screamed. Kept peeling from Belinda in wide strips that exposed the musculature of her entire shrieking skull. Kept peeling until it sloughed away beneath her clothes and spilled unsettling amounts of blood. Kept peeling until she was writhing meat on the floor. Then she was still.

Clutching his ruined hand, Rick sprinted for the stairs, but only halfway up, Nona cut her eyes at him and shouted something in a language that reverberated like she'd spoken three times from three different mouths. The steps under Rick's feet opened into a black portal that he fell through. A second portal opened in the far corner of the basement, six feet above the floor. Rick hollered, his head and good arm dangling from the aperture in space-time like he was peeking through a skylight. He tried clawing his way free, but ragged gray hands kept clutching at his clothes, hair, and skin, dragging him back.

"Nona, I'm sorry! I'm sorry!"

Nona uttered another reverberating foreign phrase. The sound was like a spike through Troy's skull, and fresh blood trickled from his nostrils. The portal winked away, severing Rick's remaining hand. Though that was likely the least of the man's concerns.

Dread did not run. Did not beg. He was all defiance and, maybe, a bit of pride. "I guess Jack Meridian's tricks weren't all shit. I thought he only had a few pieces. No clue he'd pulled all of you back together, Nona. I got a few new tricks, too. Care to—"

Nona winked away. There and gone like a popped soap bubble.

Troy's heart sank. "No, no, no, no, no!"

Sorcery Lady, don't exit like a showman now!

Dread didn't seem shocked. "Bitch knew what was good for her. Bad news for you, though, protégé, because I keep my promises. And since I'm not getting her jawbone back, I'll take my time claiming yours."

Troy grabbed the hammer off Mr. Meridian's workbench. Dread flicked his hand, and the hammer flung itself away.

"Did Jack tell you about any of this, protégé?"

Troy looked for something to fight with. Anything.

Dread drew closer. "My order, we're extreme knowledge seekers. We hunt objects infused with great power. Some years ago, we stumbled across a woman who radiated more power than we'd ever seen. It was in her blood *and* bones. So we acquired her. Divided her among ourselves. Jack Meridian had known her, been her friend. When he started stealing her pieces from my brothers and sisters, I thought he was simply trying to take us down a peg. I never even considered he might be reassembling Nona." He turned contemplative. "Wonder what would happen if I caught her and chopped her up again?"

He shook off the grisly thought and refocused on Troy. "I owe you some pain. But I'm going to give you a chance to decrease your burden. What sort of things did Jack teach you?"

Troy didn't understand.

"Tricks, boy!" Dread roared, and produced that tiny sun in his palm again.

Troy peered over Dread's shoulder. "Th-the Ambitious Card."

Dread motioned to the deck on Jack's worktable. "Show me. If you do it good, I'll kill you quick."

Troy shook the cards out, did a hasty side shuffle, then showed Dread a ten of diamonds. He reinserted the card in the deck, and it was at this point he should do the slide-control move Mr. Meridian had shown him to transfer the ten of diamonds to the bottom of the deck, where he could do more with it. But Troy had already messed the trick up because he couldn't stop looking over Dread's shoulder. At Nona.

Dread savored Troy's fumble. "Ah, well, I guess it's agony for you. Too bad, protégé."

Nona was close enough for her newly restored breath to rustle a lock of Dread's hair. He understood a second too late as Nona's fingers sank into the soft skin of his neck as if his flesh were clay.

Dread shrieked. Then the sound multiplied by a hundred, a whole stadium of agony. Troy clapped his hands over his ears. He wished he'd closed his eyes, though. Because as copies of Dread's face—eyes, nose, screaming mouth—puckered all over the magician's body like blisters, Troy found he was unable to look away. Every visible inch of skin was occupied by faces, one butting against another with only a razor-thin divider of unmarred skin between.

Nona yanked her bloody fingers free, and all of Dread's faces hollered.

Nona grinned, then slashed a hand across the air.

Dread collapsed into a pile of evenly divided faces. Not dismembered but diced.

All the faces kept screaming.

Troy felt his sanity slipping. If it was close before, his entire mental sanctity was now tipping at the edge of a void.

Nona—terrible, terrible Nona—levitated to him, avoiding the gushy screaming pile of Dread. Troy couldn't bring himself to run, and when Nona reached for him, he braced for pain. But her hand was gentle.

"I'm sorry you've seen so much," she said. "Away from this cursed place."

Troy slipped into a dark sleep.

He awoke in his own bed but didn't even start down the road of *it was all a dream* because Nona sat in the chair beside him dressed in jeans and a Hampton University sweatshirt she must've taken from Mom's closet. She looked like someone about to make a Target run, not a—a—

"What are you?" Troy asked.

"Someone who's grateful to your former teacher. I could hear him, you know. The more of me he reassembled. He was chatty while he worked. He spoke of you fondly."

Troy sat up, stared into the hall, thought of Darius lying beyond. "You were dead, but you came back. Can you bring my brother back too?"

She shook her head. "They didn't kill me. Just divided me. I repaid the favor."

"What's the difference?"

"Peace. Believe me when I say your brother's the lucky one."

"But . . . but . . ."

Nona placed a hand on his knee. The blood on her fingertips was dried and crusty. "You can choose to stay. I assume you have people who will return. But you've been exposed to a hidden world, and my scent is on you now. More like Dread will come. They will do to your loved ones what they did to your brother."

"They'd kill my mom and dad."

"Or worse. And their friends. And their friends' friends. The truly demented in our circles know no boundaries, particularly when pursuing power. I got sloppy, and I paid a steep price. It won't happen again. That won't stop them from trying."

"What am I supposed to do?"

"Supposed to? I can't say. Your choices are your own. But *if* you choose to come with me, I will honor Jack Meridian. I'll teach you, protégé."

"You mean leave? Forever?"

Nona shook her head. "Forever? No. However long it does take, when you're ready, you can return and protect your loved ones. You can get your own vengeance."

Troy's phone rang. The caller ID said *Mom*. He was supposed to pick up, no matter what.

But the boy Mom was calling was not the same boy she'd left behind mere days ago. There were new rules in the world, and to give his family a chance, he had to play by those now.

He placed his phone on his comforter. Took Nona's hand. They vanished from his bedroom as the call went to voicemail. It wasn't a showman's exit because no one was around to see it, but Troy would return. He'd come for the remaining members of the order that had taken Mr. Meridian and Darius—that he swore.

When he did, he'd show them all.

DOCILE GIRLS

CHLOE GONG

It was the night before the end-of-year dance, and Adelaide Hu sat less than an inch away from a gory cluster of intestines.

Beef intestines, of course. In a plastic bag. And though the bag rested by her feet, it was rather see-through, which made a gruesome picture under the blue-white glow of the school parking lot lights. Adelaide kept nudging it farther and farther under the car seat, but its putrid stench remained. Her older sister, Tara, had a fussy dog who was fed better nutritional value than Tara's actual children. The whole car smelled like blood.

"Five more minutes," Adelaide said anyway.

They had been parked for a while, idling in the lot. Each time there was movement, Adelaide peered through Tara's tinted windows, watching the rest of the dance committee pull in. She had delayed enough now to make herself late for their intended start. Not that anyone cared, even if she was the head of the committee and tonight's decoration efforts were entirely a result of her work.

"I don't understand why you won't just quit the committee." Tara reached over to turn on the interior light. Adelaide immediately turned it off to avoid anyone seeing her inside the car, lurking like a loser.

"It's almost over," Adelaide replied. "I just have to get through tomorrow."

"Is that a healthy approach?"

Adelaide shrugged. "These pissfaces attack the same way each time. It's fine."

The thing was, they hadn't been pissfaces just last week. Last week, they had been Adelaide's best friends.

Then Jake Stewart had dumped her out of nowhere during one

of their after-school coffee shop hangouts, saying that they were "graduating next year" so it was time for him to "get serious" about what he "really wants out of life." The conversation was over before Adelaide even finished her coffee. Despite the rush of tears in her eyes, she stayed calm, asking what she'd done wrong. *I can fix this*, she thought. This wasn't the end.

But Jake replied, "Come on, Ad. Don't be like that." He was already standing, putting on his jacket. "This was fun, wasn't it? But you knew we were never going to last after high school. I'm looking for something different."

The rest of her friends had stopped speaking to her in a matter of hours because it turned out they were actually *Jake's* friends, and when Jake was done with someone, they were done too. Fuck. *Pissfaces.*

Adelaide picked at a nail. Blood welled up at her cuticle for a quick second before she wiped it away. The smell of bagged intestines was getting unbearable now.

"Stop tensing," Tara commanded, squeezing her shoulder. "You're ruining your posture."

Adelaide tried to relax her shoulders. It wasn't working. This was going to be miserable. The six of them would make sure of that in a cohesive effort, and she was obviously outnumbered.

God. She couldn't believe how the group had found it within themselves to switch up that fast, as if she were only an extension of Jake to be removed and discarded at will. Adelaide had made such an effort to make sure each of them liked her. She and Madison had just gone dress shopping together, giggling each time the sales assistant brought an armful of fabric. She and Kayla had been texting for hours the day before the breakup, deep in discussion about the latest romance novel they were reading. And the boys . . . Robby, Liam, and Chris had helped her campaign for head of the dance committee, had sacrificed multiple afternoons to put up posters in the hallways. Yet, after Jake broke up with Adelaide, Robby moved seats in English with his nose pinched to feign smelling something bad while Chris had thought it particularly funny to text that night:

lol do u send.

Adelaide finally sighed, opening the car door. "You'll pick me up at ten?"

"Sure." Tara tapped the wheel. "It's not too late to bail."

Of course it was. Adelaide had been friends with these people for a long time, had observed exactly how they worked. In their eyes, every person at school either stood with them or against them. The moment Jake had shoved her out, they'd decided it wasn't good enough to let her fade into obscurity; they needed to keep reminding her that she had been rejected and it was repulsive to continue existing.

"You wouldn't get it."

Tara was nine years older. She'd gone to a different high school before they moved here in the suburbs, had had an entirely Asian-American friend group. Meanwhile, there were three Asians in the entirety of Adelaide's otherwise very white, very small high school—*including* her. She couldn't just do whatever, especially when she still had a whole year left to go. They would continue to attack, and she would continue to take it. If she antagonized them in return, she would be accused of being the unreasonable one, which meant the whole school really would turn on her.

"Mèimei—"

"Shhh!" Adelaide looked around the parking lot. Guilt gnawed on her stomach, but it didn't stop her from closing the door without a goodbye and hurrying off.

The dance was being held in the gymnasium, located behind the main school building. It had been built as a separate unit so that the rest of the school wouldn't be tarnished by its sweat and unsavory smells, which was also convenient for their decorating committee. Adelaide had been worried she would need to coordinate with the school to gain access after hours—especially since they had recently installed a security system controlled from the front office to ramp up safety procedures—but Mrs. Smith had waved her off, saying the cleaners could leave the gymnasium entrance open even after locking up the rest of the school. It wasn't a safety concern, as long as the double doors that connected the back of the gym to the main school building stayed locked. They only needed to make sure to lock the gym's front door once they were finished.

Adelaide trudged a path beside the main building, stomping her shoes into the grass as she headed toward the gym. The whole complex—with its hulking, tall shape and dark-painted exterior—was out of range from the parking lot lights. The twilight evening shadowed the building, some cryptid lurking in wait for its next prey, armed with a fancy alarm system that turned its innards into a giant crypt.

"It can't be that bad," she whispered under her breath. "It can't possibly be that bad."

The moment she pushed through the entrance, the others inside turned so fast that their heads practically moved in unison.

"Hey, A-Lay."

Robby's greeting came from the corner. He sat with one hand pulling a length of string off the wall and the other running through his blond hair. Though she stared at him evenly, his words pricked like nettles, the epithet warming her cheeks. She wanted to take back her past two years. Forget leaning over to talk to Jake in their bio lab that first week of freshman year, forget going on that movie date, forget saying yes to being his girlfriend and feeling like she was someone to be respected when she merged into the table that everyone at school wanted to sit at. People like her were never granted that kind of power.

Not like Robby. Not like Jake.

As if summoned by her thoughts, Jake emerged from one of the back rooms, carrying a box. Madison and Kayla both trailed after him, neither holding anything in their arms, yet they somehow looked even busier. With Robby and Liam cleaning the motivational posters from the walls, and Chris off in the corner typing furiously on his phone, that made the entire dance committee . . . and Jake's friend group. They all had the time to kill. Empty evenings structured around a lack of responsibilities, activities taken on if they enjoyed them and tossed aside when they got bored. It didn't matter how badly they screwed up. Life would continue, the years would go on, and when they each inherited their houses or whatever the fuck else so-called all-American families passed on, the portraits on the wall would still be smiling with white teeth and white faces.

"So where should we start?"

Adelaide shook herself out of her thoughts, turning around at the quiet voice. She barely held back her eye roll. Elaine stood behind her, pulling her cardigan sleeves over her palms. Elaine Zou wasn't on the committee, but she was a shoo-in for valedictorian and did every extracurricular under the sun to add to her college applications, so she had volunteered her time tonight. Adelaide didn't particularly like her, but that was mostly because people always confused the two of them for each other. It made no sense. Elaine barely uttered a peep in class unless it was to answer a question, and Adelaide used to be at the social center; Elaine wore the same dowdy shirt and jeans every day, while Adelaide changed her wardrobe every season; Elaine never even showed up to the cafeteria during lunch because her math textbook was her best friend. She was a perfectly nice girl, yet Adelaide couldn't help bristling because Elaine was exactly the person everyone at this school expected *her* to be, and it felt impossible to get away from the stereotype when Elaine was doing it all.

Adelaide tried to stifle her annoyance. She surveyed the gym, looking for a starting point to answer Elaine's question. "We could move the tables out of the way—"

The main door slammed back suddenly, bringing Devon Aldrich in like a jump scare. This time Adelaide actually rolled her eyes. As committee head, she had known Devon would be showing up: he had been assigned as help to save the teachers from having to watch detention on a Friday night. Devon was a notorious troublemaker, which—if you asked Adelaide—was embarrassingly cliché, alongside the multiple tattoos, the leather jacket, and the smoking habit that had stopped being cool about twenty years ago.

Devon nodded in Adelaide's direction. Adelaide nodded back. He was a nuisance, but they had been in the same tiny art class since sophomore year, so at least Adelaide was used to it when he let the doors close behind him with a thunderous noise.

Jake, meanwhile, threw his box down in annoyance. "Are you trying to break the gym?"

"Hell yeah," Devon answered immediately. "Don't be sad. You can flex your shrimp muscles in the hallways too."

Jake frowned. "Weirdo."

Adelaide cleared her throat. "I *said*, let's maybe start with—"

"There are balloons that still need inflating in the back. Everyone make yourselves useful," Jake cut in.

Before Adelaide even had the time to be offended that Jake was taking over, Robby kicked an inflated balloon in her direction, adding, "You're good at blowing, aren't you, Adelaide?"

Adelaide took a deep breath in. A deep breath out.

Since the breakup, she had tried the route of complete apathy, and she had tried the route of displaying great despair. Nothing got Jake's friends off her back for long. It wasn't about how she responded so much as it was about them egging one another on for a job well done. Robby was the type of person to make anonymous burner accounts so he could comment mean things to niche internet microcelebrities. Adelaide knew this because he'd shown her his accounts once with pride.

"Real mature." Devon gave the balloon a hearty responding kick, sending it flying back to Robby. "Any more stupid sh—"

Music blasted to life from the speaker that Kayla connected to her phone, drowning out the rest of Devon's taunt. She looked up innocently, twirling a finger around a lock of hair. Unperturbed, Devon made a scoff and headed for the back rooms.

Adelaide wavered. A few seconds later, she sidestepped Elaine—who had started to pick through the balloons already on the floor—and pushed through the left-side door into the back rooms too, catching Devon before he turned the corner.

"Devon, hold on."

The back rooms were off a single corridor that wrapped around one end of the main building, with entry doors on the right and left sides of the gymnasium. This back hallway housed a bunch of storage rooms on one side, while the other contained only the locked double doors that led to the south wing of the school. Most of the storage rooms back here had their doors propped open, their insides overspilling with basketballs and hoops and nets and other gym things.

Devon paused to wait for her. He peered through the entryway of the nearest room absently, moving aside a scrimmage vest and picking up an electric air pump.

"This will be helpful for the balloons," he said, more to himself. Even here, she could barely hear him over Kayla's bass-heavy pop music.

Adelaide hurried up to him. "Did Mrs. Smith give you the keys?"

Devon frowned. "What keys?"

"The keys to lock up." Adelaide walked a few more steps to turn the corner, where there were two other open storage rooms on her right, then the double doors into the school at the end.

"Um." Now Devon strode ahead of her, swinging the air pump in his hands. "Why would she give me the keys?"

"Because she said she would?" Adelaide returned. "I didn't have time to stop by her office, and she was out today. But she said she was seeing you in yesterday's detention so you could pass them on."

"Wait, but . . . why?"

This was such a waste of time. There was so much decorating to do, and instead she was talking in circles with someone who wasn't even on the committee. The gym didn't require much fiddly work because it was only a rectangular block, but it was *large*, which meant it was going to take *forever* to get everything set up.

"Because we need to lock up, Devon. Come on."

Devon took a moment to think. Adelaide couldn't comprehend how someone could forget whether they had been given a set of keys or not. Eventually, Devon shrugged. "I dunno what to say, dude. Maybe Mrs. Smith gave them to Jake instead. I saw him talking to her outside detention for a while yesterday."

Adelaide barely bit back a snarl. Of course. She wouldn't be surprised if Mrs. Smith had suddenly decided that Jake should be the committee head instead, that he was more suited for it.

"All right," Adelaide muttered. She turned on her heel, leaving Devon to his rummaging.

In the gymnasium, Kayla's music still blasted loudly enough to tremble the walls, drowning out what appeared to be an argument between her and Chris. The light outside was rapidly fading with the sunset, and the small windows high on the walls of the gym were glowing with faded orange. Jake was nowhere to be found. She hadn't seen him in the back, so maybe he'd stepped out . . .

Adelaide tugged the main door to check. It didn't move.

The music cut off abruptly.

"—I fucking *told* you, they're already in my downloaded library."

A prickle of unease crept down Adelaide's neck. Kayla was always prone to dramatics, fancying herself a Manic-Pixie-Dream-Girlboss blend, but this didn't seem like her usual type of prank. Adelaide gave the door another tug. It didn't budge. Maybe a cleaner had hit the panic button from the main office by accident. The security system would automatically trigger a lockdown in emergencies.

"What's going on?" Jake emerged from the back rooms with a large box of tinsel in his arms. The right-side door banged shut after him. "I heard yelling."

"We have no cell service," Kayla snapped.

"What do you mean?"

Kayla hurled her phone at him.

With a surprising quickness, Jake barely caught it with one hand, shooting her a nasty look. "Jesus, Kayla." He peered at her screen. "Just go outside and—"

"Door won't open."

Adelaide's voice echoed in the gym. Crawled into the little corners, shuddered when Madison looked up from detangling cords and offered her full attention.

"Did you lock it?" she asked.

"No. I didn't lock it." *Obviously*, Adelaide held back. "Maybe something is jammed up against it, but it feels more like the magnetic security system got activated somehow."

Jake heaved a sigh. He set his box down, then started rolling his sleeves up as he came toward her. "Here, let me—"

"OH MY GOD, OH MY GOD, OH—"

At once, everyone in the main gymnasium looked toward the back rooms, startled by the screaming. Adelaide recognized Liam's voice in an instant, but there was something unnerving about his shouts looping over and over, high-pitched and nonsensical.

Someone in the corridor would surely get to him first, but Adelaide lunged toward the left-side door, rushing past Jake before he could grab her. She pushed through. The corridor had turned pitch-dark. The overhead lights had all gone out, and something smelled . . . *metallic.* Just like Tara's car.

"Liam? Where are you—?"

Adelaide collided with someone. Her eyes were still struggling to adjust, but she felt cold leather press against her hands.

"Sorry, sorry," Devon said, trying to steady her. "I think the light switch is right here . . ."

The overhead bulb flared on again. It lit the space just as Elaine and Madison appeared from the opposite end of the corridor, having run in through the gymnasium's right-side door. Liam's screaming was coming from one of the rooms—the same one Devon had been rummaging in before to retrieve the air pump, though now its door was half-closed.

"Jesus, Liam." Adelaide pushed the door open. "What is—?"

For several moments, she couldn't comprehend what she was seeing.

A chainsaw was still winding down in the corner, its sharp teeth dripping red and painting the floor around it. Liam had tripped over his own feet near the door, tangled on the floor with a volleyball net around his legs. He glanced up with terror when Adelaide came through the entryway.

Robby, however, was on the other side of the room, surrounded by miscellaneous gym equipment.

Well . . .

Two *parts* of Robby, sliced completely in half lengthwise—his skull split down the middle, the generous incision line extending straight to his groin. His separated legs were closer together than his separated torso. There were lumps of organs spilling out from the casing of his chest, pink and formless against the flashes of white rib bone displayed in the fluorescent light.

But the smell was worse than the sight. The room was drenched with an animalistic stink; distantly, Adelaide thought of that school trip they'd taken to a farm during sophomore year, when the cow gave birth wrong and out came a screeching mangled animal covered in gore.

Adelaide didn't register the rest of the committee standing behind her in the corridor until she felt the splash of vomit against her leg. She jolted, a fresh rush of horror sinking into her stomach, prickling her arms, roiling against her throat.

"Everyone, take a step back," she said. "*Now.*"

They were too shocked to argue. Too horrified to be annoyed that Adelaide was the one giving the instructions, and when Adelaide reached down to haul Liam to his feet, he actually seemed grateful that someone was getting him out of there, even her.

"He—he—he—"

"Liam, what *happened*?"

"I don't know! I found him like this!"

Adelaide slammed the door to the storage room shut. Blocking out the smell and the incomprehensible sight.

"Go! Go!" she commanded. "Back that way!"

No one protested. It wasn't until they had all rushed back into the main gymnasium that her former friends started to screech at the same time. Elaine, meanwhile, fumbled for her phone, sniffling. Devon was also trying to call someone, but they had both missed the conversation about cell service being down, and there was clearly nothing going out.

"What was that—?"

"It's gotta be a prank, oh God, maybe it wasn't—"

"You *saw* the blood."

Silence. They had seen more than just blood.

"So did someone attack him?" Elaine asked quietly.

A hush fell over the group. Chris retrieved his phone from his pocket, his face as white as a sheet of paper. He slicked his hair out of his eyes, sweat plastered to his forehead, and said, "Nothing is sending. Signal is always bad here, but we should still be getting Wi-Fi."

Adelaide reached for her own phone. When she navigated to the Wi-Fi screen, it wasn't only that the school network wouldn't connect—there were no networks showing up at all, which never happened unless there was an area-wide power outage. Adelaide put her phone away quietly, digesting the situation they had found themselves in.

The main doors were locked. Their phones weren't working. And one of their classmates had been severed in *half*.

"Jesus, okay," Adelaide whispered to herself. Sooner or later, someone was going to look for them. Tara was picking her up at ten. Jake's parents were anal about his eleven o'clock curfew because he would always stay out late to prove that he could. If he was out too long, they would call the police in an instant, and then someone would find them. Precious, prized Jake—whom the world would fall over to save even when he was getting into trouble on purpose. They couldn't stay locked in this gym forever.

"I think we just need to stay out here," Devon said levelly. His eyes were latched in the direction of the back rooms. "Whoever did this might still be hiding nearby."

"You're kidding, right?" Elaine's voice was hoarse when she spoke up. She hugged her arms around her middle. Kayla and Madison were arguing with each other now about whether they could use Bluetooth to send a message out, making a racket that echoed off the walls and almost drowned Elaine out. "Those rooms are tiny. Where would someone be hiding?"

Kayla and Madison fell quiet. Madison's hands were shaking as she pressed them to her mouth, as if to keep another wave of nausea back.

"What about the double doors into the school?" Madison asked.

"It's locked," Adelaide offered.

"But don't we have"—Madison heaved a breath—"the keys? We were supposed to lock the main doors when we left. It's all on the same key loop."

A pause.

"They're gone." Elaine's voice had turned so quiet that Adelaide almost couldn't hear her again. "Mrs. Smith gave them to me. I didn't say anything because I was going to check my car first, but I know I brought them into the gym. Someone stole them."

And in the time they had been inside the gym, those double doors had stayed locked.

Adelaide glanced around. Chris gulped, the visible gleam of sweat on his forehead growing. He had offered Liam his arm for support before, but now he had taken a step away. Kayla and Madison both shifted on their feet. Created a layer of space.

"I don't understand how someone got in then," Devon muttered. He was the only one still intently thinking, trying to figure out how they had a murderous intruder. Everyone else had started looking at the other people in the room.

"The more likely explanation," Elaine said unsteadily, "is that one of *you* killed Robby when you were in the back."

A sudden chill settled over them. Elaine was Miss Valedictorian, after all, and the committee latched on to her logic fast, taking it as truth.

"Devon was in the back when it happened," Madison exclaimed.

"Yeah, making confetti sheet by sheet on that stupid tiny machine," Devon fired back. "If we really want to talk about who was in the back, I saw Jake *and* Madison walk by right before Liam started screaming."

"For five seconds to get that stupid strobe light," Jake snapped, pointing to the fixture he had plugged into the corner. "Definitely not enough time to get a chainsaw and kill my best friend!"

Silence. Madison gagged again.

"How could we have not heard a *chainsaw*?" Kayla said, almost to herself.

"Your shitty music was too loud," Devon answered.

Madison stomped her foot. In the next second, her lip was wobbling, and then she was heaving loud sobs with no tears in sight. "You"—she pointed a finger at Devon—"are not helping. And"—she exaggerated a hiccup that trembled her shoulders—"as the only one in the vicinity, I think *you* did it!"

"Oh, fantastic." Devon threw up his arms. "We're going around baselessly accusing each other of murder now."

"What's the alternative?" Madison cried. She waved at herself. "That *I* could do something like this? *Me?* Meanwhile, you've threatened to kill Robby before. We've all heard you."

Adelaide knew that their situation had been tense to begin with, but Madison's fake crying was so grating that it was giving her a headache. The tears were fun when they were at the mall trying to skip the line for the dressing room; now they felt out of place.

"Madison," she said. "Come on, enough."

"Enough?" Madison screeched. "We're going to let a possible killer go loose?"

"If we're talking possible killers," Devon returned, "Liam was the one who went back with Robby. How did *he* not hear a chainsaw running?"

They all turned to look at Liam. He blanched, his mouth opening and closing. "Because I split off to find the extension cords! For fuck's sake, how are you going to say *I'm* the killer with Incel James Dean Dupe standing right there?"

"Look, *look*," Adelaide interrupted before the argument could devolve further. "Let's just stay put. Whoever did this to Robby can't target us all at the same time."

It was already fully dark outside. The windows showed an ink-black night.

"We should try the windows," Elaine said, pointing up when she traced Adelaide's line of sight. Everyone ignored her this time. It was an idiotic suggestion, especially because the gym walls soared high enough that there was no way to get up to the windows, but Elaine continued: "I think we could break the glass."

"I think we can bring the main door down," Jake said, pivoting without any acknowledgment he had heard Elaine, who was tapping on her phone now, likely trying to send a text despite everyone else's attempts.

"You can't," Adelaide said immediately. "The security system's activated. The locks are magnetized. Honestly, the double doors into the school would be a better—"

"No one asked you, Adelaide."

Jake was shaken, his lips pale. Perhaps he treated her with such derision only because the situation was tense, only because he wasn't thinking straight. Or maybe he had always been like this.

"Jesus Christ, I'm trying to help before you break your knuckles trying to defy basic physics."

"It's not helping, as usual, so—"

The gym slammed into complete darkness.

A short scream echoed through the space. Elaine, maybe. Or Kayla. Adelaide's first instinct was to flinch back, bewildered at the sudden loss of one of her senses. While everyone else panicked and shouted and shoved, Adelaide stayed unmoving, letting her eyes adjust. Their silhouettes took shape. Jake and Chris were shoving each other. It was clear where they stood because their voices were so loud, tossing accusations back and forth. Adelaide blinked. Once. Twice.

There were nine of them tonight, weren't there? With Robby gone, they were down to eight, and she should have counted seven figures in front of her.

A strange thump echoed by her feet.

"What the hell was that?" someone demanded. Liam. His voice was closest, still rough from his screaming. "What did I just kick? Something *wet* landed on me."

Adelaide felt something on her leg too.

"Chill," Jake demanded. "Get your phone flashlights out."

One by one, their flashlights turned on, cutting beams into the gymnasium. When Adelaide turned hers on, she didn't point it at her classmates' shocked faces as they were doing to one another.

She fumbled to point the light down to where she felt something splashing on her leg . . .

Adelaide dropped her phone, right into a puddle of blood.

She screamed. The sound was hoarse, that feeling in nightmares when senseless terror loomed at full force without the dreamer comprehending what the matter was. A feeling devoid of all logic except dread. Though she hadn't yet digested what she was seeing, it was *wrong*, so horrifically *wrong*—

Her classmates scrambled to attention. Their arguments cut off; their phone lights pointed down until the sight at their feet was as clear as day.

Madison could have fallen, tripped over her kitten heel, and taken a tumble. Those were her legs. That was definitely the fabric of her sundress. And her arms held close to her body. She even had her phone still clutched in her hands.

Then, just a bit higher, there was the stump of Madison's neck. That protrusion of slick white bone: the end of a spine severed perfectly at one of the vertebrae, surrounded by throbbing pink flesh exposed to the air, blood still spurting onto Adelaide's leg with a nasty squelch at each weakening pump.

"I'm going to be sick," Kayla wheezed.

Adelaide lunged forward, closing her hand around Kayla's wrist to shine her light to the left. After Liam's kick, Madison's head had rolled away, facedown with her blond hair tangling at the back like a cheap wig on a mannequin.

Adelaide's stomach threatened to upheave too, but she swallowed hard. The blood had started to spread, though something was sitting at the edge of the puddle, disrupting the smooth unfurling.

Slowly, Adelaide crept closer, careful not to step in more blood.

"Ad," Jake said sharply. "The hell are you doing?"

"Wire," she reported, pointing at a silver coil of it on the floor. "Razor wire."

"It's Devon," Liam declared at once. "Devon is doing it. Madison accused him and he killed her."

All the flashlights swiveled to Devon.

"Excuse me?" he demanded, throwing up an arm to shield his eyes from the bright lights. "I don't even know what razor wire *is*."

"Then why do you have blood on your sleeve?"

Devon looked at the sleeves of his jacket. He recoiled, startled to find a splatter of red along the worn leather, then pointed at Liam and retorted, "The fuck? You do too!"

The lights swiveled again. Sure enough, Liam had a splatter along his front, soaking into the cotton of his white T-shirt. The moment they looked around, though, they realized they were all blood-splattered in some manner. A murder had happened before their very noses.

"I want to see everyone's hands," Adelaide said. Whoever did this would surely have gotten blood on their palms while handling the wire.

No one listened to her.

"I've had enough." Jake marched off toward the back rooms. "You can all stay away from me until we get out of here."

"What the hell?" Devon demanded. "You know you look really suspicious right now going off on your own!"

Jake ignored him. The beam of his flashlight waved erratically with his swinging arms, disappearing with him through the left-side door that led into the dark back corridor.

"Jake! Stop!" Kayla shouted, rushing after him and sniffling. "Separating from the group is dangerous!"

"Hey, hey!" Liam hurried to follow. It prompted Chris to move too, and then their little group of assholes was barging through the door, arguing among themselves about who was getting too close and who needed to keep distance.

Adelaide's chest felt tight. Only Elaine and Devon remained with her.

Four in there. Three out here. Something felt off. Menacing.

"I'm going to go too," Adelaide announced.

"What if they're dangerous?" Elaine hissed immediately. All the same, Elaine followed close on her heels as soon as Adelaide started to move, and Adelaide barely prevented herself from rolling her eyes despite the terrible feeling squeezing her stomach. She didn't want to have to babysit Elaine while their lives were under threat.

As if on cue, the moment Adelaide pushed into the corridor for the back rooms, there was a scream.

"Oh my God! There's *another* severed head!"

Her heart flew to her throat.

"Kayla! That's a fucking hockey mask!"

A dense plastic sound thudded against the wall. Someone's phone light flashed in an arc, illuminating enough for Adelaide to guess that the mask had been picked up and thrown.

God, it's so damned dark in here, why are we walking around here entering the individual rooms instead of being out there where we could safely camp out in a corner—?

Adelaide felt the hairs at the back of her neck prick up.

Then:

A blur of motion in the corridor. Adelaide couldn't see very well, but she felt the rush of air against her side. Fear hurtled down her spine, froze her in place. Her awareness of the world turned so staticky that she couldn't tell whether it had been someone rushing from behind or from ahead. Until Kayla screamed in feral, raw pain.

"Kayla?" Adelaide bellowed.

No one's phone light was shining straight anymore. They turned entirely unpredictable, spinning left and right in an attempt to spot who was running around.

"Someone *stabbed* me!"

Complete havoc broke out. Footsteps thundering. The others were hurtling into the rooms and slamming the doors shut, intent on locking themselves away. Adelaide didn't know what she could do. She merely stood there, petrified for what felt like an eternity, listening to the arguing voices and the clatters and—

"Adelaide!"

She blinked. What was that? Had it come from one of the rooms?

"Adelaide! Help me!"

It sounded like Elaine.

Adelaide finally rushed forward, following the call into a closed room. The moment she slammed through the door, she almost smacked her head against a volleyball net. Adelaide recovered fast, struggling to place the sound of nearby whirring before realizing Devon must have left the confetti machine on. Beside it, there was a phone facedown, its flashlight shining up. Crying echoed through the room, then grunting, and when Adelaide closed her hand around the phone and pointed, she found Elaine struggling to hold Liam off her, wet tear tracks reflecting off her cheeks.

Holy shit. Holy shit, holy shit, holy shit—

Elaine had a basketball jersey clamped over Liam's face, barely keeping him an inch away while he loomed over her, his hands pressed to her shoulders in attack.

"Adelaide, *pleasepleaseplease,*" Elaine screeched. "Please, help, help! He's the killer! He tried to stab me!"

Liam made a muffled noise into the jersey. Elaine's head tipped to the side. Sure enough, a knife lay with the batons, dripping with red.

Adelaide didn't waste time. She grabbed the nearest heavy object—the confetti machine, still plugged in—and brought the dense square of metal over Liam's head to knock him out.

Only she hadn't realized the source of the confetti machine's whirring was the blades on its underside. The very moment she made contact, it sliced efficiently, whip-quick metal gouging into skin and sending a viscous splatter of blood and tender bits of flesh in every direction.

Liam bled out in seconds.

Bits of his scalp flew wide, stringy viscera wads decorating the room like freshly cooked macaroni. They landed alongside the shiny confetti that had been left from Devon's task, some macabre addition to the existing color scheme. By the time Adelaide realized what the machine was doing and tossed it to the floor with a screech, the blades had already done enough damage.

He swayed. When he slumped off Elaine, the jersey stayed

around his face, covering whatever expression had frozen in place with death. Even after he stopped moving, his head continued bleeding, the initial frantic spray slowing to rivulets.

Adelaide felt a sticky sensation in her eyes. A delicate wipe along her cheeks didn't seem to help; she blinked once, and her whole vision blurred red.

"I killed him," she muttered. She couldn't tell if she needed to cry or hurl. If the sweat at her neck was hot or cold.

"I-it was s-self-defense." Elaine panted shakily. She rose to her feet, coughing as she caught her breath. Her phone had landed on the floor again. It lit a section of the room in electric silver, the angles wrong and the shadows distorted. "He would have attacked you too."

"Why was he trying to kill you?" Adelaide screeched. "Why did he kill Robby? And Madison?"

Elaine's bottom lip wobbled. "I don't know." She picked up her phone and tapped the screen to check if it was okay. Out of nowhere, the corridor lights came back on, pouring into the room through the half-open door. "He just . . . he attacked me out of nowhere with that knife."

Why?

The door creaked wider on its hinges. Devon peered in, his face pale.

"Sirens," he croaked.

Robby's body had disappeared.

Jake was pacing the gymnasium, his posture tense. From the corner, Adelaide kept her eyes pinned to his every movement, because if she didn't, then she was inclined to stare at Madison's detached head instead, and that didn't sit well with her stomach. Kayla, meanwhile, was in the other corner, bleeding profusely from her side. She hadn't seen who had stabbed her in that corridor, but she hadn't questioned it when Adelaide announced they'd caught Liam red-handed. Then again, Kayla didn't have the energy to do much else except sit and clutch her side to staunch the bleeding, wincing every few moments and drawing terrified looks from Chris, who held himself close to the left-side door.

The sirens were still faint outside, but they were getting louder. It sounded like the police were going to the school first, which meant it wouldn't be long until they saw the security system had been triggered in the gym, and it wouldn't be long until they were found.

"There was no time for Liam to have taken Robby's body," Jake said tightly. "I could hear him talking beside me until he disappeared into that room. He must have an accomplice."

"You're being ridiculous." Adelaide tried to wipe her hand on her jeans. "There are only the six of us here. Who are you trying to accuse?"

Pointedly, Jake looked at Devon.

"I felt a rush of air when someone brushed past me in the corridor. The only other people behind me"—Jake stabbed a finger at Adelaide and Elaine—"were you two."

"A rush of air," Devon said drily. "Nice. Let's go to court with that."

"You fucker—"

Jake took a step toward Devon. At once, the gym plunged into darkness again, triggering screams from Kayla and Chris. This time, though, Adelaide was prepared. She was already standing near the strobe light. She lunged for it, then flipped the switch.

Flash.

Jake scrunching himself down in fear, his hands held before his face.

Flash.

Devon rushing for the front entrance, pounding his fists on the doors as the sirens drew nearer.

Flash.

At the other side of the gym, Kayla was screaming loudest. It wasn't until the strobe flashed again that Adelaide spotted the knife handle sticking straight up from the center of her skull.

It took three more flashes before Kayla stopped screaming.

On the fourth flash, she was on the floor.

Adelaide breathed in shallowly.

On the fifth, someone yanked the knife out of Kayla's head.

On the sixth, Elaine turned around, the knife in her hand.

"What the hell?" Adelaide whispered under her breath. "What the *hell*—?"

Jake had his eyes squeezed shut. Devon was facing the main door, entirely focused on trying to get out. The only other person who had spotted Elaine was Chris, and he was paralyzed by the sight of her heading toward him with the knife. Adelaide should have done something. She should have shouted, used some of that adrenaline that had rushed through her when she was trying to fight back against Liam.

Liam wasn't the killer. It was never him . . .

Instead, for a reason she couldn't fully comprehend, Adelaide turned the strobe light off. She squeezed her eyes shut too, like that would erase what she had seen, like that would protect her when the knife came for her next.

When the overhead lights flared back on, Adelaide's eyes flew open too. No less than twenty seconds had passed, but she felt as though she might have been rooted in place for two decades, made into another support beam for the building, another brick for the walls outside.

Chris was dead—or at least close enough to it. His intestines trailed out of his opened torso, the engorged pink rope making a clustered pile on the gym floor. He was still twitching a little, in the same way that insects scrambled inside an electric trap when their legs had already been burned off. Each weeping cut was jagged and long, striving to pull his soft insides entirely outward.

And in the middle of the gym, Jake was holding the knife now.

"Christ." Jake dropped the knife like it had burned him. It clattered to the floor. "Someone shoved that into my hand, I *swear*!"

Adelaide finally understood.

Elaine was standing near Devon, a weeping gash cut across her forehead. It soaked blood down her face and onto her T-shirt, obscuring the other stains across her front—the ones that had actually come from Kayla's brain matter and Chris's intestines.

When she'd killed them.

"Stay away," Elaine sobbed at Jake.

Devon held his arm out too, trying to protect Elaine in case Jake lunged.

"It's *him*," Jake insisted, gesturing at Devon. "He's framing me!"

"Are you deranged? You were the one holding the knife!"

"It's not me—"

"What if it was me?"

Jake swiveled suddenly to look at Adelaide, his brow furrowing at her interruption. "What?"

"It could have been me," Adelaide said. Her voice carried an eerie calm that she didn't feel. "Why would you accuse Devon when he has no reason to get you in trouble? I have plenty. After how you've treated me."

A beat passed. Silence grew thick within the walls. The sirens got closer and closer outside.

And then Jake—even now—*rolled his eyes*. "Adelaide. Come on. Be serious."

She had spent three years with Jake, and yet it hadn't changed his mind about girls like her. In the very beginning, he had said that he loved her for how much she agreed with him. That should have been her first warning sign.

"I *am* being serious," Adelaide said. "You felt someone run past. Now all your friends who have tormented me relentlessly are dead, and you're being framed for it. Why wouldn't it be me?"

"Cut it out, Ad." There was no room for argument. "You couldn't."

He didn't say, *That's not you*, or *You're too kind for it*. He said *couldn't*. As if there were something physically limited about Adelaide, some shortened spectrum on her emotions that meant she would never push into the most visceral part of human vengeance. She wasn't really a person in his mind—not someone with wants and desires, the good and the ugly existing in tandem. She was an exotic smiling accessory to slot at his side until the time came to find a *real* girl. Someone who could be taken home and would blend right into the family photos. When he needed her, she was always around. When he discarded her, she would scamper off to nurse her wounds. Why would Adelaide Hu be anything other than accommodating?

Anger bubbled in her stomach. It was red-hot, like she had swallowed a bowl of liquid metal. She could think of nothing else. She wasn't afraid of Elaine despite the threat she posed; Adelaide wasn't worried about anything outside the next few seconds—and how this scene was going to unravel in front of her.

"Adelaide," Devon warned when she took a step toward Jake. "Be careful. Stay back."

"No, it's okay." She clenched her fists hard. "I have this handled."

Jake looked at her, perturbed by her tone. Perhaps, in that moment, he finally saw her for what she was capable of. She wanted to believe that she might have earned Jake's respect for once in his life.

They lunged for the knife at the same time.

And when Adelaide's hand wrapped around the handle first, she brought it up in an arc, cutting right across Jake's throat.

The sirens were directly outside the gym now.

Jake fell to the floor, gagging as he tried to take in air. Just as Adelaide turned around to Devon's startled shout, Elaine pulled another sharp blade from her sleeve and put it straight through his neck.

The motion was so quick that he wouldn't have had any moment to fight back. Devon gasped sharply. His hands flew up to scrabble at the blade.

Then Elaine tugged the knife out. Wiped off the handle. Chucked it to the floor. Devon, before he could do anything more, teetered onto his side, rivers of red gushing and gushing onto the floor.

"Jesus, Adelaide," Elaine huffed. "I was going to let Devon live. You had to do it right in front of him. Messed up my entire plan."

Adelaide had the bizarre instinct to apologize. She heard Elaine as if there were water in her ears. A droning sensation hummed through her head too, her thoughts scrambling to play catch-up with her actions. Devon was dead. She should have been afraid when she was the last one remaining, but she wasn't. If Elaine had wanted to kill her too, she would have done it by now.

"Your plan," Adelaide echoed slowly. She pictured the scene Elaine had set: Jake, holding the knife. "It wouldn't have worked."

"He would have been caught red-handed. Devon was an eye-witness."

"Please." Adelaide had seen every responsibility Jake had shirked over the years, every bit of trouble his family had gotten him out of. Jake Stewart wasn't an easy person to set up to take the fall for anything—hell, he hardly took the fall for matters he was *actually* guilty of. "That wouldn't be anywhere near enough. His expensive lawyers could spin a sob story out of this in hours. Think of his potential. A boy with so much to lose, so much life to live."

Elaine sighed. "Well, you've still made this a little difficult, given we don't have a culprit anymore."

The humming in Adelaide's head had mostly faded, yet Elaine continued to sound . . . different. Her words carried a hollow echo, like her throat had fathomless empty space inside it, extending and extending. Perhaps Adelaide was just as bad as Jake. Perhaps Elaine had always been like this, only it took Adelaide until now to realize it.

"What's wrong with you?" she snapped.

Elaine examined her nails, scratching some dried blood out. "Me?"

"Yes, *you*." Adelaide gestured around them, her arms erratic. "How can you be so flippant? You're *killing* people."

"No"—Elaine cricked her neck—"I'm killing *white* people. Don't tell me you've never wanted to do this. I gave you a chance, and you racked up a body count yourself."

"To *help* you. Which I only did because you were lying about Liam attacking you."

"Was it a lie?" Elaine returned just as quickly.

The gymnasium entrance suddenly shuddered. Police, calling that they were trying to come in. While Adelaide's attention whipped over, Elaine didn't look bothered.

"They're not getting in until I release the lock, don't worry. I knew they'd get an alert as soon as I triggered the lockdown, but I figured it would take some time to check out a low-priority security glitch after school hours." She took out her phone, glancing at the screen briefly. "Enough time to see all this through, at least." Elaine put the phone back into her pocket. "My mom was his nanny, did you know that?"

Adelaide almost didn't follow the topic switch. Then she caught sight of Jake in her periphery, nothing more than a pale, graying corpse now.

"He made sure to remind her at every moment that she was supposed to be waiting on him hand and foot," Elaine continued. "Imagine being ordered around by a nine-year-old—imagine your charge pulling his eyes back and calling you slurs if he didn't like being told it was bedtime."

"That's terrible," Adelaide said quietly. She hadn't known. Jake hadn't mentioned it.

Elaine shrugged. "This little group formed back in middle school, so they all took their turns tormenting her at the house when they went over to hang out. Jake, Robby, Liam, Chris, Madison, Kayla . . ." She said their names like a final roll call—a checklist of the dead. "She finally quit after he started high school. Before your time, so I guess you've never seen them in action. She still flinches when she sees them in the pickup line though. Hard to forget that kind of behavior."

"I . . ." Adelaide's mouth opened and closed. "I didn't know."

"Of course not." Elaine's gaze snapped over, locking with hers. "They haven't done it in years. Then, for some reason, they started again last week. Yelling and hooting at her across the parking lot. Nothing terrible, of course. Nothing I could report. But it terrified her all the same."

Last week, when the breakup had happened. Last week, when

Adelaide had been booted out of their group. Maybe it was a coincidence. Or maybe Jake was just insidious enough for it to be connected.

"So this is your revenge?"

The thudding on the door had turned louder. The police were using a battering ram.

"Of course."

"*Murder* was the best option?" Adelaide demanded.

"They're all murderers, one way or another," Elaine said easily. "Should we wait until they inherit their future companies and raze people's homes? Should we let Jake use his inheritance and shake hands with every judge in the district first? I'm only evening out the scales early, getting them before they can get *us* later."

There was no other way out from the gymnasium. Adelaide was at Elaine's mercy entirely . . . and yet it still didn't seem like Elaine intended to harm her.

"What are you going to do about me?" Adelaide asked. "Are you going to shut me up?"

Elaine pressed her hand to the cut on her forehead, stemming some of the blood. She shook her head. "I always admired you, you know. You fit in so well. It was as if they didn't even see you differently. As if they were willing to look past it for you."

"They didn't." Adelaide gritted her teeth. "They let me in for as long as they set the rules."

The door tremored hard.

"Yeah. I realized that pretty early on." Elaine pulled her sleeves up. Nothing more hid within the fabric. "That's why I decided I didn't want to try fit in. I wanted them to stop setting the standard. I wanted them in pieces."

Dimly, Adelaide told herself that this was the part where she ran, where she outwitted the killer and served justice. Instead, she asked, "You had the keys the whole time, didn't you?"

Elaine narrowed her eyes. "Yes."

"Give them to me."

Adelaide could have used them to escape. Elaine hesitated, but she must have read something in Adelaide's expression. She passed over the keys, and Adelaide hurried into the corridor, sidestepping every foul puddle and unsavory splatter. She unlocked the double doors into the school. Threw them wide open.

When Adelaide came back into the main gymnasium, Elaine had her phone in her hand, her thumb hovering over the screen. Elaine looked over, and with blood still splattered across her face, she grinned at the sight of Adelaide's return, as if there were something triumphant about the matter.

Adelaide nodded once.

Elaine crumpled her face and started crying. Adelaide ran to her side as if she were barely functional, grabbing Elaine's arm and crumpling to the floor with her in loud sobs that weren't really producing any tears. The police would find what they expected to see: docile girls, who didn't have enough humanity to do terrible things, who only lived to please, caught in the middle of such a terrible incident.

The doors flung open.

When the police charged in, Elaine sobbed harder and pointed to the back. "He went that way! We saw him! The killer went that way!"

The officers gaped at the scene. They likely hadn't expected to find complete carnage, but they were quick to react, shouting into their radios at once and running for the back rooms, for the open doors that could have taken an intruder away from the scene.

One officer crouched in front of them, his eyes scanning the damage. "Are you girls hurt?"

Adelaide took a shaky breath.

"No," she whispered. "My friend and I hid together."

GRAY GROVE

ALEXIS HENDERSON

A fog lay thick over Gray Grove, and the demon was still asleep in the muck of the marsh the night the girls arrived.

They rode side by side in silence, Rumi in the passenger seat, slumped against the window, fitting a fresh battery into her video camera, and Kaitlin with her hands locked in a white-knuckle vise grip around the steering wheel. The headlights of the truck snared on the eyes of animals in the brush. A cat. A possum. Perhaps a deer, or something wearing its skin.

The two girls found their way to Gray Grove as part of their shared podcast, *Girls and Ghosts*, which launched investigations into the many haunted locations throughout the South. Tonight's episode centered around Kyle Adams, who was said to have disappeared at Gray Grove more than forty years prior.

It was a big night, their first time recording an episode on-site, but Rumi wasn't in the mood for filming that evening. The day before, while Kaitlin had been partying at a friend's house, Rumi had pulled an all-nighter to finish her research on Kyle's case.

Kyle had been a blond-haired, blue-eyed varsity quarterback who had found his way to Gray Grove while chasing William Jones, a Black boy he'd been bullying for the better part of the school year. William was the last person to see Kyle alive, and in the wake of his disappearance, many suspected William of a murder they couldn't prove. Ultimately, he wasn't imprisoned for Kyle's death, but that wasn't to say he walked away unscathed. He'd gone down on drug possession charges and remained behind bars for the rest of his life.

Rumi recalled the day she'd interviewed him at the beginning of that very summer. She'd driven up to the Northborough Georgia Penitentiary for the occasion, during visiting hours. William was waiting for her when she arrived, sitting on the other side of a plexiglass window, dressed in a lurid orange jumpsuit. He was older, pushing sixty, and looked almost nothing like the frightened boy Rumi had seen in the black-and-white newspaper photos, beneath headlines like MURDER AT GRAY GROVE? And QUARTERBACK KILLER. But his eyes were still wide and soft.

"How did things escalate between you and Kyle that night?"

"His girl was sweet on me," William said into the receiver in a broken whisper. "Kyle didn't take that well. He followed me home one night, after my shift at the docks. But you have to know it wasn't me who killed him. Kyle was out for my blood, but I didn't want his spilled."

"Then what happened?"

For the first time, William had locked eyes with Rumi. "That night, when Kyle pulled his switchblade from his pocket, something from the marsh protected me. I don't know what."

Kaitlin pulled Rumi from her memories and back into the present. "You know we're doing a good thing here," said Kaitlin. "For Kyle. For his parents."

And for the listeners and the brand sponsorships they afforded, Rumi wanted to add because she knew that was nearer to the truth of it. But she bit that back. "Kyle's parents have been dead for twenty years."

"Well, his siblings then."

"He didn't have any. And both sets of his grandparents died—"

"Rumi, *enough*. You know what I mean. We're here doing a good thing. Kyle was a victim, and he deserves justice, and tonight we're going to give him that by allowing him to tell his own story. We'll let the dead speak for themselves."

Rumi wanted to argue that if every cold case could be solved by talking to the ghosts of those involved, there wouldn't *be* any cold cases. But she knew that would turn into a fight, and they couldn't afford that tonight.

"Are you mad at me? Again?" Kaitlin asked at last, squinting through the windshield at the fog-hazed road. A devout supernatural enthusiast, it was usually Kaitlin who let her fears get the best of her, Kaitlin who suspected paranormal activity where Rumi only saw shadows and tricks of the light, Kaitlin who was most afraid. But tonight things were different. She seemed impervious to the dark legends of Gray Grove, and it was Rumi who felt afraid.

"I'm just tired. I was up all night researching Kyle . . . It left a bad taste in my mouth. William was right, he was a racist dick."

Kaitlin's hands shifted around the steering wheel. She didn't look at Rumi. "Well . . . yeah. But everyone was racist back then. It was the eighties."

This was one of Kaitlin's most common refrains. As long as the racist in question was older than them, their racism could be excused, if not forgiven entirely.

"Besides," Kaitlin said, "he's dead. So we'll never know for sure. Not unless we ask him anyway. And we've got the spirit box for that. I think it's going to change *everything*."

Rumi fought the urge to roll her eyes. Every time Kaitlin mentioned the spirit box, all she could think about was how that money could've gone toward new sound equipment instead of what was essentially a digital Ouija board. According to Kaitlin, and the description she'd read on eBay, the spirit box was a radio device purported to transmit the frequencies of the spirit world into decipherable sounds, even full sentences. The plan was to use it during that night's séance, in the ruins of the Gray Grove plantation house, to commune with Kyle and discover what had happened on the night of his disappearance.

Kaitlin kept driving.

The darkness that enshrouded Gray Grove plantation was unlike the darkness Rumi had experienced anywhere else. Here there were no streetlamps. The sky—what little could be seen of it through the dense canopy of the moss-draped oaks—was untouched by the distant taint of city light pollution.

Rumi could smell the marsh long before they approached it, a familiar sulfurous stink that made Kaitlin wrinkle her nose and crank up the air-conditioning. Kaitlin was new to the South. She'd moved only three years before, halfway through their freshman year, when her father, a Marine officer, was transferred from Alaska to Paris Island, a military base off the coast of South Carolina.

After years in the South, Kaitlin was still greatly bothered by things most Northerners noted—the pollen and the persistent humidity, the marsh stink and the sand gnats that descended in hungry swarms as the sun set. Prone to sunburn and heatstroke, with an allergy to mosquito bites and a terrible fear of snakes, Kaitlin was wholly unprepared for life in the South. It was Rumi who'd befriended her when she'd first moved into their neighborhood. Rumi who had taught her to scrape away the tentacles of a jellyfish with a credit card after she'd been stung by one and rub wet sand on the sting to ease the pain. Rumi who'd taught her to stay out of high grass for fear of ticks and rattlesnakes. Rumi who'd translated the intricate linguistics of the South, carefully explaining the meaning of *cattywampus* and the importance of a well-placed *yes, ma'am* when talking to your elders.

But despite their initial kinship, lately Rumi had felt a distance yawn open between the two of them. The rift was widened by little things, like who Kaitlin chose to sit with at lunch or what she made of her closeness with Rumi when questioned by the friends they didn't share (all of them white girls with no friends who looked like Rumi). Sometimes she felt that Kaitlin was more invested in what Rumi could do for her—bolster her online presence, edit her vlogs, build the platform she yearned for—than the pure friendship they'd once shared. But Rumi couldn't bring herself to say that to Kaitlin. Lately, there were a great many things she couldn't bring herself to say.

Kaitlin rounded a tight corner, and Gray Grove, or what remained of it, appeared, cast in the beam of the headlights. The entire east wing had crumbled to rubble. Allegedly, it had collapsed amid an earthquake that struck the night those enslaved at Gray Grove revolted. From the road, Rumi could see that the west wing was mostly intact, whole rooms still standing, some of them half-furnished with the leavings of the last owners of the house, eerily pristine despite the passing centuries. Unlike other abandoned plantation houses, which were often graffitied or occupied by the homeless, Gray Grove was remarkably untouched.

In fact, the left side of the building was so pristine that Rumi half expected to see people behind the windows living their ordinary lives, tucking children into bed, washing their faces and settling in for the night. In comparison, the right half of the house was a startling contrast to the left. Nothing more than the rubble of bricks, half toppled into the marsh. When the tide came in, Rumi imagined the brackish waters would swell high enough to drown the ruins. The whole house looked like it was one strong hurricane away from being entirely swept out to sea.

Kaitlin pulled the truck to a stop in front of the ruins. She cut the ignition, pulled out the keys, and for a while, the two girls sat there in stony silence, staring through the fogged windshield, watching the ruins. Perhaps they had known then, without really knowing, the way their night would unfold. But if they did, if they had some small suspicion, neither of them voiced it then, content to let the silence lapse between them, until Rumi opened her door and stepped out into the road. Kaitlin followed suit.

Once one of the most prolific rice plantations in the South, Gray Grove had spanned more than nine hundred acres. Over four hundred men, women, and children were enslaved there, and the plantation had passed through several generations before it was razed in the fracas of the Civil War, destroyed by the very enslaved people it had exploited. Over the years, it was said that the souls of those people still roamed the ruins and the grounds that surrounded it. For many years, these paranormal sightings made Gray Grove a favored haunt of drunken high school students, sent there on dares, and paranormal investigators who traveled from hundreds of miles away to try to record the supernatural activity rumored to occur there.

Rumi, a true skeptic, didn't believe in the folktales and urban legends. Her investigations into Gray Grove had centered on the tangible horrors, accounts of the enslaved people who had lived and died there, the crimes of their masters, and . . . of course Kyle.

"Did you ever get that filming permit?" Rumi asked, folding her arms over her chest. It wasn't cold, but she'd been plagued with chills ever since they turned off the highway.

"We don't need one. My sister's best friend didn't when she got married in the west wing." The house's west wing was a favorite wedding venue of Southern brides (and a few Northern ones too) who favored Gray Grove for its haunting beauty. "That was a whole-ass wedding, and they took loads of pictures. All we're doing is recording a quick episode, and then we'll be out of here."

Rumi said nothing as she clipped a microphone to the camera and tested the sound. *Girls and Ghosts* was a podcast, but lately, Kaitlin insisted that they film everything they could so they'd have further evidence of their paranormal findings. Privately, Rumi suspected Kaitlin's budding fascination with filming instead of just audio recording had less to do with assembling evidence and more with her hopes of launching a solo career as a vlogger.

Kaitlin rummaged through the contents of the duffel bag slung over her shoulder and then touched up her makeup. She'd done a dramatic winged eyeliner look with a deep damson lip, wanting to channel what she called a "chic nouveau-grunge ghost-hunter aesthetic." She'd attempted to dress the part too, wearing all black with Doc Martens platforms that she'd borrowed from Rumi and never bothered to return.

"I have a good feeling about this one," said Kaitlin, starting toward the house.

Over the years, many ghost hunters, paranormal reality TV shows, low-budget horror movies, and urban explorers had covered the horrors of Gray Grove. But Kaitlin was confident they'd capture what no one else had. That night, at the heart of the Gray Grove ruins, they would record a séance, one that Kaitlin firmly believed would solve the mystery of Kyle's disappearance. Kaitlin had called this idea brilliant, a way to set their podcast apart from the dozens of others that had covered Gray Grove in the past. To Rumi, it was a gimmick, but she didn't say that to Kaitlin.

Together, with their flashlights in hand, Rumi and Kaitlin tramped through the ruins of what might've once been a front porch but had now been reduced to a heap of rotting planks. As they approached, their spirit box, which normally emitted nothing more than the roaring static of a TV set to channel zero, picked up a snatch of what sounded like voices.

"Holy *shit*!" Kaitlin shrieked and clapped her hands. "Did you hear that?"

A chill carved down Rumi's spine. "Yep. Sure did."

They ducked under a collapsing threshold and stepped into a wide grand foyer with what had once been a double staircase but was now just one set of steps curving up to the second floor, the other side having crumbled away with the rest of the eastern wing. To the left, the west wing of the house, strangely undisturbed and sparsely furnished. To the right, an empty wall open to the marsh.

"Wow," said Kaitlin, looking around. "It's beautiful."

"It's surreal," said Rumi, and she made sure to capture it, raising the camera to take sweeping shots of the room, panning left and right to capture it from all angles. The light clipped to the top of her camera lit the room beautifully. She zoomed in on the furniture: The scraps of a Persian rug, blooming with algae and reeking of mildew. The dust-frosted table that ran along the wall by the entrance to a corridor, the lamp standing atop it. The crystal chandelier dangling precariously overhead.

"I can't believe no one bothered to rob this place," Rumi said from behind the camera, still filming. "All this stuff must be worth a fortune."

"They say it's cursed," Kaitlin said. "A museum once emptied the house of all its furniture. Days later, it burned to the ground, and the only items left intact were those stolen from Gray Grove. The curators returned the furniture to its proper place in the ruins of the house to end what they called a 'horrible haunting.'" Kaitlin delivered this line—wide-eyed and grave—as though she were the one who'd written it, and Rumi gave her a thumbs-up from behind the camera.

Just then, the spirit box roared, picking up what sounded like the fragments of an ongoing conversation. Rumi was quite certain she caught the distorted jingle of a car-insurance ad, a riff from a rock song, a radio host laughing. But there were other sounds too, beneath those, daisy-chained together into an eerie chant. "It's . . . coming. It's . . . coming . . ."

Kaitlin shrieked and dropped the spirit box, but Rumi caught it a split second before it struck the floor.

"See!" said Kaitlin, pointing at it. "They're talking to us. They know we're here."

Rumi held the camera trained on Kaitlin, stabilized thanks to the expensive gimbal they'd splurged on a few months ago. In her other hand, the spirit box roared and shrieked, a harsh cacophony of static and what sounded like a chorus of voices, the gospel hymns Rumi had heard sung in her grandma's church as a kid. "I don't like this," she said.

"You're . . . scared?" said Kaitlin, her eyes wide with relish and delight.

Of the two of them, Rumi was the one to keep a cool head amid their investigations. But Gray Grove was getting to her in a way other places didn't.

Kaitlin snatched the camera and turned it on herself. She was so busy gloating, it seemed she'd entirely forgotten to be afraid. Rumi cringed back and held up her hand to cover her face as Kaitlin came closer, laughing. She zoomed in close enough for viewers to count Rumi's pores. Camerawork had never been Kaitlin's gift, and she certainly hadn't made a point to practice or improve her skill in any way.

"Stop," said Rumi, but she laughed a little too. "You know I hate being on camera."

"Well, the people want to see you," said Kaitlin. "They keep spamming the comments under all our posts asking for more footage of you."

"I'm not the talent," said Rumi, and she snatched the camera back. She cut the spirit box off, tired of the roaring static. "Now let's film the intro and quick. You've got a séance to perform."

Kaitlin delivered the lengthy intro in a near-perfect single take. She was good in front of the camera, Rumi had to give her that. With practiced ease, Kaitlin recounted the history Rumi had written about

Gray Grove and its inhabitants. About Kyle and William. "Kyle's body was never found. After a years-long investigation, William was cleared, and Kyle's case was closed. In the wake of the investigation, William was imprisoned on charges of marijuana possession." Kaitlin paused slightly, and Rumi thought she saw her wrinkle her nose. "William died two weeks ago in the solitary confinement cell where he spent the final years of his life."

"That was great," said Rumi, lowering the camera. Her voice came out small and strained, and she swallowed the lump in her throat. Talking about William always made her sad. He'd died just a few weeks after she'd last spoken to him.

Kaitlin frowned. "I think we should cut that last bit. About William."

"Why?"

"Because we're not here for him. We're here for Kyle."

"But he took the blame for what happened to Kyle. He didn't do it—"

"Exactly. He didn't do it. He's not why we're here. He was just some drug dealer who—"

"*Drug dealer?*" Rumi demanded, stunned. "Did you even read the case summary I sent you? I spent hours compiling all that research."

"I read . . . some of it."

"And let me guess, you skimmed the rest?"

"Whatever," Kaitlin snapped. "I read enough to know that William was found with drugs in his room the night he was arrested. That's why he was in jail."

"Weed," Rumi corrected her. "He was found with weed in his room. That hardly makes him a drug dealer. Any more than it makes you one for smoking at that party last night." Rumi had seen her Snapchats. "And by the way, while you were having the time of your life, I stayed up to finish my research on this case and write the script for this episode."

"Here we go again," Kaitlin said, and she started for the staircase, which, like the rest of the west wing of the house, was miraculously untouched. "Let's just get to the ballroom and film this séance so we can leave. The humidity is getting to me. I feel like I can't breathe."

They turned the spirit box on again as they climbed the steps. For a while its hissing static was the only sound. Every minute or so, Kaitlin asked it a question, but the only answer she received was more static. At the top of the stairs, a long hallway delved into the dark of the west wing. Kaitlin brandished her flashlight in silence and started toward the ballroom, or what remained of it anyway. It was a large space, cleaved down the middle, as though split in half with a giant axe.

Kaitlin made quick work of setting up the séance. From the duffel bag slung over her shoulder, she produced a hefty box of table salt, which she poured in a wide ring at the center of the room. Also from the duffel bag, she removed several thick pillar candles, which she arranged at the center of the salt ring and lit. As Kaitlin worked, Rumi set up the mics and cameras around different angles of the room, fidgeting with the tripods, checking the night vision. Kaitlin insisted that she take a temperature check, and the room registered a full fifteen degrees lower than the reading they'd taken downstairs—a sign of paranormal activity.

Encouraged by this evidence, Kaitlin turned up the volume on the spirit box, which began to emit a series of earsplitting shrieks that sounded a lot like the wailing of a baby. Or perhaps the screams of a mother who'd had her baby ripped from her arms.

"Holy shit," said Kaitlin, her eyes wide with what Rumi could only describe as . . . *delight*. She was enjoying the screams. "It's Kyle."

Rumi stepped into the salt ring. "What makes you so sure?"

"I mean, isn't it obvious? These are cries of pain."

"Kyle's disappearance wasn't the only bad thing that happened here. This was a *slave* plantation. Other people suffered too. Why are you so sure it isn't their voices carrying over that spirit box?"

Kaitlin rolled her eyes. "Here we go again. You just care about them because . . . because—"

"Spit it out," Rumi demanded. "I know you want to say it. Because they're Black, right? You think that's the only reason why I care."

"It's just that ever since we first arrived, you've been fixated on making Kyle out to be the villain of his own murder. It's victim blaming."

Rumi felt a flare of anger tear up her spine like fire. "Kyle was a raging racist."

"So, you're saying he deserved to die?"

"I'm saying that if we're here to tell his story, then we should at least tell the truth while we're at it. Kyle chased William here, a boy he tormented for *months* leading up to his death. Moreover, this isn't just an artsy wedding venue. This is a slave plantation. Kyle wasn't the first person to die here. He wasn't the first person to suffer. If his story deserves to be told, then so do theirs."

"No one's stopping you," Kaitlin shot back, tossing an arm to the camera. "I just think we should focus more on the *actual* victim of this story? Instead of, you know, giving listeners a high school history lesson about the people who destroyed half this house—"

"This house was built by those people. It was theirs to destroy."

"I'm not saying it wasn't. It's just that . . . violence is never the answer."

"Isn't it violence that brought you here tonight?" Rumi demanded, almost screaming at her now. She wanted to cry, she wanted to rage—she wanted to tear down what remained of the wretched Gray Grove plantation house brick by brick. "You came here because you think this is where Kyle died. I suppose violence isn't the answer unless, of course, it breeds the kind of content fodder you need to get your views. Because that's what all this is about, right? You don't give a shit about the rest of it."

In the flickering light of the candles, Kaitlin's big blue eyes turned strange and ugly. "The podcast belongs to both of us. If what you're saying is true, you're no more innocent than I am. At least I admit what I want. You can't even do that."

Rumi's cheeks felt hot with shame. As much as she wanted to make Kaitlin take back that ugly accusation, deep down Rumi knew she was right. She *did* want the views and attention as much as Kaitlin did. Maybe more, even. After all, it was Rumi, not Kaitlin, who had sunk countless hours into the preparation for this podcast. It was Rumi who'd spent weeks building their small audience from the ground up. The podcast had been her idea to begin with, and every comment, every listen, every new episode they uploaded felt like the hard-won spoils of her efforts. And still, she wanted more.

The truth was, Rumi hadn't come here for William or the nameless souls who'd revolted in Gray Grove years before. She had come to gawk and spectate, to process their pain and grief, their fear and their anguish, and turn it into digestible content for public consumption.

It was wrong, Rumi realized then; all of it was so wrong.

"You're right," said Rumi, lowering the camera. "I can't keep doing this. I quit."

Kaitlin's face contorted into a nasty sneer. She seemed to want to say something, but the words got stuck behind her teeth, and—in a moment of frustration—she lurched forward and ripped the camera from Rumi's hand with so much force that Rumi tripped over an upturned floorboard, and fell, clipping her head on a loose brick as she struck the ground.

She felt a sharp pain, saw a scattering of stars. The darkness and the marsh smeared sickeningly before her eyes as her vision failed her. Stunned, she touched her temple, and her fingers came away sticky with blood.

Rumi looked up at Kaitlin, and when their eyes met, something died between them. But it would be a long time before Rumi allowed herself to mourn it. Kaitlin seemed to sense it too because she clamped her mouth firmly shut, finally falling silent.

It was the first death of the night. But it wouldn't be the last.

Kaitlin took a half step forward. "Rumi, I—"

The wind began to howl so loudly, it drowned the rest of what Kaitlin said. The spirit box screamed along with it, and beneath the roar, Rumi heard a horrid chorus of voices singing hymns. All the candles went out. The salt ring scattered. The light on the camera flickered and dimmed.

Then the wind died.

A moment's quiet, and then downstairs, from the direction of the marsh came the sound of water bubbling. Through the break in the wall, Rumi watched in horror as the waters of the marsh appeared to boil, steam rolling off its surface in thick clouds. What still remained of the Gray Grove plantation house began to shake violently. Kaitlin lost her footing, dropping to her hands and knees beside Rumi. The house kept shaking. Plaster fell in sheets around them, shattering upon impact with the floor. A voice rattled over the speakers of the spirit box: "He's . . . here."

Rumi locked eyes with Kaitlin. "We need to run."

The two girls pushed to their feet and raced downstairs, dashing down the hall and clearing the staircase in a matter of moments. The first floor of the house appeared empty. Rumi saw a dark shape materializing from the murk of the mud and marsh water. Something big. Bigger than any gator she'd seen before.

Kaitlin saw it too. Hastily, she raised the camera and turned it on the water.

"What are you doing?" Rumi demanded. "Let's go!"

Kaitlin ignored her. She held the camera fast, filming the creature as it scrabbled up from the marsh. It wasn't human, not even remotely. Steam rolled off its hunched shoulders, thickening in the darkness around it, making it hard to distinguish its true form, but Rumi could tell it was tall (well over eight feet, even while doubled over) and wiry. Its flesh was the raw color of a freshly scraped knee, as if it had been skinned alive. The creature's thin fangs looked like baleen, and they were slick with spit and chattering. It was hungry. Very hungry. As if it hadn't had a proper meal in many, many years. Perhaps not since Kyle had ventured there, decades before.

It was William's protector.

The Demon of Gray Grove.

Kaitlin's eyes went wide above the camera. There was fear in them, but something else too, something worse . . . *greed*. She didn't run. She didn't move. She raised the camera higher, then turned the lens to zoom out, capturing the full scope of the creature. "We're going to be famous."

Rumi caught Kaitlin by the arm, trying desperately to drag her back. "No, *don't*!"

Kaitlin didn't listen. "Just let me get this shot—"

The demon sprang, and Kaitlin screamed when its jaws closed around her ankle. It tore her feet out from under her, dragged her toward the marsh as she thrashed and struggled helplessly. Somehow, she still held the camera fast.

"Rumi!"

Rumi—dizzy, still bleeding from the gash in her forehead—tried and failed to find her feet, watching in horror as the creature dragged Kaitlin through the ruins of the Gray Grove house and into the muck of the marsh. Kaitlin cried for Rumi; Kaitlin screamed and raged and tantrumed. But in the end, it was no use.

The demon felt no mercy. Only hunger. It disappeared into the murk of the water, and Kaitlin cut a final gurgling scream as it dragged her down with it. The last Rumi saw of her was her hand, still clamped around that camera.

The voices crackling over the spirit box fell silent. Gray Grove was quiet. Deep beneath the surface of the marsh, tunneling through the mud with Kaitlin's leg between its teeth, the demon disappeared.

SIX YEARS LATER

Rumi had always known that there was a special kind of frenzy reserved for disappeared and dead girls who looked like Kaitlin. But the media circus that followed the events at Gray Grove was worse than anything Rumi could have imagined. Millions of listeners flocked to the *Girls and Ghosts* podcast, picking apart every episode, analyzing each sound bite for evidence or an admission of guilt. All at once, Rumi found herself alone in the eye of a media storm so vicious, it threatened to tear her apart.

In her grief, Rumi did nothing to stop it. She released no statements, did no interviews, except the ones with the police and later with the lawyers Kaitlin's family had hired to cross-examine her testimony. Rumi told the same story every time, a story that wasn't her own, but one passed down to her from William and the others who'd escaped the Demon of Gray Grove unscathed more than a century before.

After an extensive search of the plantation, after the marsh had been pumped and the surrounding forest thoroughly searched, all the police had to show for their efforts was Rumi's camera—badly mangled, the footage destroyed—and one of Kaitlin's torn and bloody sneakers, both items recovered from the reeds at the far side of the marsh, half a mile from Gray Grove. An alligator's den was found nearby, and after much speculation, the police concluded their search and declared that Kaitlin had been attacked and devoured. Rumi hadn't challenged this declaration publicly . . . until now.

Rumi, now a senior in a college, set up a makeshift recording studio in the closet of her dorm room. She had spent weeks preparing for this night—squeezing in time to write the script between her classes and assignments—knowing she only had one chance to tell this story and tell it right. To clear her name and let the world know, once and for all, what had really happened. To tell Kaitlin's story.

Rumi stared at the screen of her laptop. She adjusted the microphone and clicked the RECORD button. "Hi, everyone. It's been a while, and I'm sure at this point you know the reason why. On today's episode of *Girls and Ghosts*, which is the last one I'll ever record, I want to tell you the real story of what happened to Kaitlin—"

Her voice broke on the name. It was the first time she'd said it aloud in years.

Rumi cleared her throat. Squeezed her fingers to still their shaking. She stared down at the script that lay on the desk in front of her, the words she'd typed blurring a bit before her eyes. She took a deep breath, willed herself to read them. "A fog lay thick over Gray Grove, and the demon was still asleep in the muck of the marsh the night Kaitlin and I arrived."

EVERYTHING'S COMING UP ROSES

TIFFANY D. JACKSON

Case # 22-0539

Evidence Item: 18-B

The following are excerpts from the journal of Leesa Nelson at age eighteen.

Hey You,

I know. It's been MONTHS! But better late than never, right? It's really not my fault this time. See, Grandma forgot to pack you in my hospital bag and then always forgot to bring you during her visits. Then, I came home and found that Grandma had let the garden go to shit. You wouldn't believe the amount of weeds that could pop up in six months. It was a mess. Between that and home school, it's just been busy. But we can play catch up! Like real friends. Not that I have many of those. How about I start first with some good news because you're never going to believe this. I got a job! A REAL job. I'm going to be working part time at Home Depot in the gardening department.

Okay I know what you're thinking. Dr. Lewis specifically said that I needed to find a different hobby other than gardening. He thinks I'm a little, what's the word, obsessed? I don't think so. I just think I'm really passionate about stuff. But I promise, I'll take up chess or something just to keep the scales balanced. And technically, this isn't a hobby—it's a job! I'll get to work with plants while making money. Plus, I'll get a pretty sweet discount and can buy anything I need for the garden. The best of both worlds.

Grandma swears we don't need the money, but I've seen a few of those overdue bills in the mailbox. And those notices are starting to come again, claiming they're going to tear our house down which is really scary. I mean, we've lived in this old place all my life.

Well, gotta go. Grandma is calling me down for dinner. Tuna and rice, yet again.

Love,
Leesa

Hey You,

Today was my first official shift at Home Depot. I was given a tour and . . . dang it's all just so perfect. I'm going to be surrounded by hundreds of plants, trees, seeds, and bags of dirt. I was so excited I could barely sit still during this morning's training. Well, I didn't really need a lot of training. I've been gardening all my life. No one knows their way around planter pots better than me. We actually have tons of them in our garden in the backyard. We mostly have flowers. Red, white and pink roses in giant pots. You know, growing roses isn't easy. It's a lot of work trying to keep them safe.

Speaking of which, I bought another planter pot. I'm thinking about adding a few more bushes to the garden. Maybe near the back, who knows.

There is just one thing . . . my new boss, Joey Tanner. He's this short white college guy with one of those weird mustaches. He seems a bit controlling. Towards the end of my shift, he kept making comments about how I wasn't organizing the orchids correctly. It's not my fault he doesn't know the difference between a moth orchid and a laelia. Also, he keeps staring, as if he's trying to figure me out or something. It gives me the creeps. I know Dr. Lewis says, whenever I feel unsafe, I should start by closing my eyes and counting backwards by ten. I tried but I can still feel him staring. Even when he's not in the room. I can't tell Dr. Lewis that. He'll think I'm imagining things again. Which I'm totally not. I've been really good.

I told Grandma about Joey and she just asked me to be careful. To not let him upset me. "You know what happens when you get upset." Blah blah blah. She's probably worried about me losing my job but really she has nothing to worry about. This is the best job I've ever had. No way I'm going to screw this up. I swear.

Later,
Leesa

Hey You,

I got my first paycheck today! I cashed it, bought two giant bags of topsoil (it'll be great for the new roses I planning to get) and gave the rest of the money to Grandma. She seemed so surprised. I know I told her I was working. Maybe she just forgot.

I think Joey has a little crush on me. He followed me yesterday to the parking lot, claiming that he wanted to give me some "life advice." Same way Lamar once did. Guys can be so sweet sometimes. But I don't need Joey's advice. I listened to him go on and on but told him I didn't need his help. He didn't like that very much.

Later,
Leesa

Hey You,

I didn't have work this afternoon because I had an appointment with Dr. Lewis. Dr. Lewis is by far my favorite doctor. He gets me, you know? And it's so hard to find real friends. He says were not really friends, that we have a doctor/patient relationship. I think he's just saying that so his other patients don't get jealous. He has a really really nice house. I've never been inside, but he has huge hydrangea bushes. I told him he shouldn't overwater. He told me not to come to his house ever again. That I was crossing lines. I mean, I was just trying to help! Give him some advice, the way he always helps me. His wife probably planted those years ago because if they were roses, they would've needed a lot more work.

I didn't have work today but that didn't stop Joey from calling to ask where I put the new inventory of tulips. I told him I used a wheelbarrow to bring them outside. That they would've wilted if I didn't. He was really mad. Told me that the floor plan was set up for a reason. I apologized even though I really wasn't sorry. Dr. Lewis always says that sometimes we have to do things we're not comfortable doing. I hope I don't have to do that too many times.

Later,
Leesa

Hey You,

Today, I helped someone pick out the perfect perennials to plant in their brand new front yard. I wish we had a front yard. Grandma says we need to keep our gardening in the back, where no one could see us. She's worried we might get in trouble which is just silly. It's only some plants and dirt. What's so wrong with that? But Grandma's always been a worrier. It's one of the reasons I never lie to her and try to tell her everything. Even the not-so-good stuff.

I've lived at Grandma's house my entire life. I was sort of a surprise for my mom. I don't think she really wanted kids. She said she didn't even know who my dad was. She used to scream stuff like that when she had too much of the dark stuff and throw things around the house. That's why Grandma and I spent so much time in the garden. Grandma's the real reason why I got into plants and stuff. We'd spend hours in the backyard together, just me and her. Me and Grandma, we're best friends. And best friends keep each other's secrets. Mom didn't want to be our friend. She didn't want to be in on our secrets. And she was really mean to Grandma.

Anyway, I have to run. Still have schoolwork to do. Also, I have a surprise to tell Grandma.

Later,
Leesa

Hey You,

Okay, so I wasn't totally honest about the job. I mean, yes I'm excited to work at Home Depot, excited to finally have money, and yes, I love the discount. But that's not the only reason I got that job, specifically.

See, Home Depot is in the Beach Shopping Center. And Lamar Howard works right across the way at Best Buy. It was easy to figure out where he works based off his TikToks. I mean, he took pics in his blue uniform. That's as good as an announcement if I ever did see one.

I know what you're gonna say but . . . it's different this time. Really. We're no longer in school together (he made sure of that with our little misunderstanding). And I'm still staying fifty feet away like I'm supposed to. But during my lunch breaks, I park just close enough that I can watch the Best Buy entrance, so that maybe I can catch a glimpse. Don't worry, I'm being careful.

I did see that while I was away that Lamar took Brittney Shaw to prom. She looked pretty in her dress and her hair is growing back nicely. Like I told the principal Mr. Cunnings, it really was accident. Everyone knows chemistry is a really hard class and I wasn't expecting the fire to shoot up so quickly. And, of course, I always carry pruning scissors on me, just in case I see any beautiful flowers on the way home from school. So really, I saved her. She would've been bald if I didn't cut her ponytail before the fire burned it all off.

After all that, Grandma and Dr. Lewis thought it would be best to do school from home for a while. Which I guess is fine. Means I can spend more time in the garden with the people I love.

Later,
Leesa

Hey You,

Work is SO awesome. Today I helped this old lady choose the right grass seedlings and convinced her to plant tulips rather than daisies. She was so grateful when I helped her load everything into her car that she gave me a tip. That happens a lot, people tipping me, telling me how great I am. Wish Lamar could see me the way others do. Maybe he wouldn't be so mad at me anymore. Like I told him, Dr. Lewis and all the other doctors . . . it really was just a misunderstanding.

Only thing that sucks about work is my boss, Joey. Everyone is really nice to me. Except him. He thinks I shouldn't be working there. I think he's mad because I know more about gardening than he does. Hopefully I can just keep away from him.

Well, have to run. More tuna and pasta for me.

Oh. And I bought a new shovel. Grandma made me burn the last one.

Later,
Leesa

Hey You,

My boss is really really mean.

He threatened to tell my social worker that I've been taking extra-long lunches. It was just one time, and it was a total accident. See, I was up late working in the garden, and I fell asleep in my car. But then when I woke up, I saw Lamar in the parking lot, helping a customer load one of those huge flat TVs in the back of their car. It was too big for him to manage alone so I jumped out to help him. He freaked out. I tried to explain that I just happened to be nearby but he wouldn't listen. I realized I was late for work so I ran away. Joey was waiting for me at the front door and said he was going to dock an hour of pay. It's so not fair. I mean, it's the first time it happened. But what could I do? I couldn't tell him the real reason why I was late. He wouldn't understand.

Tonight, the police called the house and asked what I was doing bothering Lamar again. Grandma is really worried now. She reminded me that he still has that restraining order but I measured it myself . . . Home Depot is way over the 50 feet *distance required. Plus, I don't want to go back to the hospital. It really sucks in there.*

Later,
Leesa

Hey You,

Today I tried to tell Dr. Lewis more about my garden but he kinda got upset at me first.

See, I just wanted to know if he ever found the dog he was looking for. They posted missing dog flyers all over his neighborhood. It was just an innocent question. He didn't have to be so mean about it.

Then I told him how far my garden has come, and he got really quiet. He asked me more questions, about the roses, Lamar, and Grandma. He started to sound like some of the doctors from the hospital. I didn't like that. It felt like he was . . . judging me when he's supposed to be my friend.

We're going to have to have a talk. But not now. Today, I picked up an extra shift at Home Depot. It can be really hard, trying to keep up with Lamar's schedule.

Later,
Leesa

Hey You,

Today at work, Joey was so annoying. Telling me I was taking too long with customers when I was simply just trying to help.

Then when I got home, Grandma found my empty pills bottle in the recycling. She asked me what I did with all the pills. I didn't want to lie to her. I really didn't. But those pills make me so tired. It's hard to get off work and still have energy to work in the garden. And she of all people knows how hard gardening can be. Grandma tried to call Dr. Lewis but he hasn't been returning any of her phone calls. Hope his wife and kids are okay.

Later,
Leesa

Hey You,

Today . . . wasn't a great day. When I got home from work, the police were waiting for me. They asked me a bunch of questions about Dr. Lewis. They say that I was the last patient he had seen before he disappeared.

I told them there must be some mistake. I still talk to Dr. Lewis, I have been for weeks. We still have our sessions virtually. Except, we don't have a computer.

They started asking me more questions like who's car I was driving and why I wasn't in school. Then, they asked me where my mom was, and I told them she was in the garden. Grandma looked upset when I said that.

When they left, Grandma said that she wants to move. Go someplace far away, but I told her we couldn't! I mean, who would take care of the garden if we're gone?

Later,
Leesa

Hey You,

I am so mad. It's Joey again. He's accused me of stealing a pair of hedge shears. Me? I mean, why would I steal something I already own. Besides, I promised Dr. Lewis that I wasn't going to steal things anymore and I meant it. If it's really mine, it would be mine.

Good thing I kept all the receipts of everything I bought in this journal. I knew it would help me out someday.

My mom used to steal a lot. Like I said, she really didn't want to be a mom or even a daughter. She used to come and go as she pleased, stealing anything she could get her hands on for money, including Grandma's social security checks. This went on for a while . . . until I stopped her.

Later,
Leesa

Hey You,

There's a rumor going around work that I was in the crazy hospital. The only way they would know that is if a manager somehow read my file somehow. I think it was Joey, because he got in trouble for accusing me of stealing.

Dr. Lewis hates that term, crazy hospital. I don't really mind it. I guess because I really don't feel much of anything nowadays.

Later,
Leesa

Hey You,

There are so many ways you could kill someone with stuff at Home Depot. There are axes, hand saws, bolt cutters, machetes, sledgehammers, even cultivators if you're desperate. Then when you're all done, there's rope, plastic tarps, shovels, gravel, mulch, concrete, and industry strength bleach.

I know I shouldn't think this way. That it's not right to think this way. But I can't help it. I'm really just observant. At least I don't say these things out loud anymore.

Yesterday, I decided that we should have a fire pit in the backyard. It's probably going to be a lot of work but I can probably buy most of the stuff needed with my next paycheck. Grandma doesn't want to help me. She just sit in the kitchen and cry. I wish she didn't get so upset all the time.

Later,
Leesa

Hey You,

Tonight, I told Grandma I wanted to plant more roses and she started crying, begging me not to. She keeps saying the garden is pretty enough, that we don't need anymore. But I really want it to be beautiful. Because there just isn't enough beautiful things in this world. I don't know what she's so upset about. I mean, I got my love of gardening from her. We both love roses so much.

Think I'm going to turn in early.

Later,
Leesa

Hey You,

Most of my shift are in the afternoons and on weekends. But Simon called out sick so they asked if I could cover his shift. I was so excited because that meant more money and a chance to see if Lamar would be at work today. But then that also meant I had to close the store with Joey.

He cornered me in the Bird feeder section. Saying that he knows the truth about me. About what I did to Lamar. I didn't do anything to Lamar. Yes, I crawled into his window and was waiting for him to get home, but it was only because he said we would talk "Later." I didn't know what time later meant so I just decided to wait for him at home. I brought him some roses from my garden I cut earlier that day. I was so tired that I fell asleep in his bed. When he woke me up, I was so started that I swiped my pruning shears at him. It was an accident! I swear. But the police arrested me anyway. They didn't believe me. That's when I started seeing Dr. Lewis.

But Joey doesn't understand all that. No one ever understands me. And you know what. I'm getting really tired of people not understanding me.

Hey You,

Joey was no call no show at work today. They sent someone to his house but he's nowhere to be found. It was fun watching Joey's every move these last few weeks. I knew from the very first day that he yelled at me that he would make perfect shitty compost for my garden.

I cut up Joey with the pair of hedge shears I found in his car.

You know, the ones he accused me of stealing. It did a pretty good job, but I had to use my axe to chop up the rest of him.

Grandma hasn't been feeling good. She says all the stress is hurting her heart. I told her to take one of my pills, that it would help calm her down but she said she's already tried that. She also said that doesn't want me to garden anymore. Grandma asked if I'm going to bury her in the garden. I told her she's already back there. But I don't want to think about her dying again. Not when she's all I have.

Grandma kept talking louder and made me promise not to tell anyone about all the plants or I'd end up in jail again. She's even making me stop journaling, just in case someone happens to find this book, so this is the last time I'm going to write to you. It's fine. Without Joey, Dr. Lewis, or Lamar . . . life is kind of boring so I won't have much to write about. Maybe we should move after all. Start fresh with a new garden. Maybe Grandma will finally let me have a front yard.

Later,
Leesa

Notes:

After the Nelson home was demolished to make room for a new city highway, developers made a startling discovery in the backyard of the once abandoned property. Human remains, ten bodies in total. To help identify the bodies, they dug up the remains of the previous homeowner, Gloria Nelson and found what appeared to be her granddaughters journal, buried beneath the rose bushes. Detectives were able to track Leesa Nelson, now age thirty-one, down to a nearby Home Depot in Florida, where she worked as an assistant manager. Her defense attorney submitted a plea of not guilty and claims the journal was fabricated.

HEAVEN

ADIBA JAIGIRDAR

Even in my dreams, I see the dead. Their bodies limp and lifeless, their eyes open, staring up into the heavens. Like in my waking world, I move toward them on heavy limbs, too aware of my own aliveness. But when I light the fire, the dead scream.

When I wake up, drenched in sweat, I can still hear echoes of their cries, like they've pierced the veil of dreams.

"Eshaal!" The call from outside the door—not a scream, though close enough—is real. Not a continuation of my nightmare. At least, that's what I tell myself as I roll out of bed and fling the door open. Derrick is waiting in the hallway, his blond hair disheveled and his clothes rumpled as if he's just woken up too. It's a relief to see his familiar face after my nightmare.

"I've been knocking for ages," he says. "Orla sent me. She . . . ," he pauses, looking down at his feet instead of at me, ". . . wants us to clear out Juliette's apartment."

I must have heard him wrong. "But we have another day," I say.

"Actually, it's more like twelve hours," he clarifies.

"But we don't even know exactly *when* she left. How can they say her time is up?"

"If this is too difficult for you, I can take care of it," Derrick says. "But orders are orders."

I turn away and close my eyes, but instead of finding peace, I'm bombarded by the images from my nightmare. Except this time the dead wear Juliette's face. Even my subconscious has given up any hope of finding her.

"Okay," I say, even though it's the last thing I want to do.

* * *

When Derrick and I go to Juliette's small apartment, I almost expect to find her there.

Stepping through the front door, I take in the stack of books piled high on the small dinner table, the loose papers scattered all around, the unwashed dishes in the sink. Once everything has been cleared out and sent to headquarters for sorting and redistributing, the place will be ready for new tenants. It'll be like Juliette was never here at all. Like our first date wasn't sharing secrets over her terrible cooking at that dinner table, or our first kiss wasn't an awkward fumble of hands by her front door.

"I'll pack up here," Derrick says, pointing at the mounds of books. "Why don't you take care of the bedroom?" He's looking at me like he knows my mind is not exactly occupied with getting rid of Juliette's things and like he's okay with it. If there's one other person I can trust in this world, it's Derrick. Ever since the two of us got paired up together for work, he's had my back. And I've had his.

Juliette's bedroom is as messy as anything else. Her bed is unmade, and there are stacks of notebooks, papers, and folders dedicated to her scientific research on her bedside table and desk. We already searched through it all when we realized she had left Heaven, but nothing useful turned up. But I have to believe there's something we missed.

Instead of packing it all away into boxes, I start going through everything. Because I have to know the reason Juliette left out of the blue. Why she went so far that for the six days we've been searching, there's been no sign of her.

Not even a dead body.

Juliette was happy in Heaven. She had found her calling doing biological research. She was convinced that with enough time, we would be able to finally destroy the Sunken and go back to some semblance of the life our ancestors knew. She scoffed at the dissenters when they marched on the streets demanding that they be allowed to go out in search of humanity, of land, of things that don't exist anymore. So I'm having a hard time understanding why she'd go—and why she didn't tell me.

The answers are here; I just have to find them.

But all I find are buried memories. Folders of research trips outside Heaven that Juliette would tell me stories about. Old photos of her parents and grandparents from before the world outside sank underwater and everything changed.

I pocket the only photo of Juliette among her things: one where she's standing in front of Heaven's gates with a nervous smile, ready to embark on her first research trip with her parents.

"Eshaal." I'm not sure when Derrick appeared again in the room or how long he's been saying my name. Everything is a blur. Between my pounding head and the emptiness eating me up inside, nothing seems to make much sense. "Our shift is about to start, but I can tell Orla that you're sick. We'll find someone to fill in for your shift today and—"

"No. I'm fine. Just . . . give me a minute."

Derrick sighs but nods. His footsteps sound too loud as he exits the bedroom. I stand up, taking in the room one last time. The last of this will be packed away by the time we're back in Heaven.

I take out the photo of Juliette, running my fingers over it like that'll help me commit her face to memory. I flip it over to find Juliette's familiar scrawl, though it's less legible than usual. There's a hastily drawn map, and beside it are quickly scribbled words in Juliette's handwriting:

go north until you find land

Tracing the words with shaky fingers, I feel something akin to hope flutter in my chest.

I pocket the photo and take one last longing look at the place. There are so many memories of Juliette here, but they can't be my last ones. Because Juliette is still out there—she *has* to be.

Derrick and I walk through the dark alleyways of Heaven, past pitch-black buildings crumbling at the edges, ivy and moss climbing up their sides and windows. Most of these buildings are filled to the brim with people. When Heaven was first built, every family had their own apartment. But as the population inside the city swelled, two families had to live in the same unit. Things have only gotten worse with time; now we're packing as many people as possible into each home. But anything is better than the alternative.

The only reason people like me, Derrick, and Juliette get the privilege of a quiet space for ourselves is the work we do. We're the lucky ones, and even still, sometimes being trapped in this city feels like a nightmare.

Derrick and I weave through the sleeping city toward the gates that tower above us all. Two stone pillars line either side of it, circular domes atop them both. But the gates themselves are made of heavy dark wood, its edges lined with glittering gold. Carvings of flowers and vines adorn them, climbing up, like they're reaching for heaven itself. The gates are a remnant of the dreams people had when they built this place, the dreams of my parents and their friends. They wanted Heaven to be the place where humanity didn't just survive but thrived. And so they built these gates, looming and gilded with gold, to represent those dreams. They were, after all, the gates to Heaven.

But once the Sunken came, only survival was possible. The last of humanity charged through these gates, locking them shut behind them. Instead of marking the entrance to Heaven, where humanity thrived, the gates became what divided us from the rest of the world. The locked gates that shut out the hell beyond.

Derrick presses the intercom button by the gate. First, there is only the sound of static, but then the operator appears on the line.

"Yes?" The person asks.

"Derrick Wood, and Eshaal Rana," Derrick says.

The intercom devolves into silence for another moment before the operator speaks again. "Okay, go through."

A mechanical whirr sounds as the doors open. Derrick and I have changed into black hazard suits and goggles. They cover every inch of skin, leaving no room for the lethal atmosphere to seep in and harm us. The toxic water that now covers most of the Earth has also polluted the air, with the areas nearest to the water being the most dangerous. Extended exposure means certain death. Still, I can already smell the world outside our gates. It's damp and heavy, like a mixture of earth and water carried in the wind. There's something unsettling about it.

We step outside the gates, and the usual dread surges through me as I peer down the steps of the mountain where the last of humanity resides. Towering walls surround the city, and with the gates marking the main entrance, the separation between Heaven and the outside feels tenfold.

We descend the mountain, farther and farther away from the safety of Heaven. The Sunken never come this close to the city, but with little protection between the gates and the pier, this is the part of the journey that fills me with the most tension. My muscles clench up as we make the trek, and I only feel my breathing relax once we finally reach the end of the stairs and find the boat with our equipment.

"Do you ever feel like one day those gates will leave us out here?" Derrick asks in a quiet voice, as he climbs aboard and picks up the oars to start our journey.

"Gates aren't sentient," I reply, even though that fear has crossed my mind more times than I can count. If one day the doors to Heaven were closed to us, we would be left out here to fend for ourselves. And there's a difference between being out here for a few hours for a shift and being out here permanently.

More reasons why I can't understand why Juliette would risk it.

On the boat, I dig through the pack of supplies and weapons to grab my flame gun, wrapping its strap around me. A wave of relief washes over me.

Derrick begins to row, propelling the boat forward slowly. I turn on my flashlight. The light slices into the darkness, but there's nothing to see except the surface of the ocean, smooth and black, until tiny ripples form to announce our presence. The water makes my heart beat faster. The dead from my nightmares always feel too close when I'm out here, like they're waiting at the seams of my mind, trying to crawl out into reality.

I try to shake their images out of my head. Juliette needs me.

"Should we do a check around the perimeter first, like usual?" Derrick asks cautiously. The perimeter of Heaven stretches five miles from its landmass in all directions.

"No." I know it breaks protocol, but Derrick doesn't seem surprised to hear my answer. It's almost like he expected it.

"I found something in Juliette's bedroom." I dig into the pocket of my suit and remove the photo, then flip it around to show him Juliette's note on the back and the map she hastily drew. "This is a map from Heaven to . . . somewhere. Out north. We have to follow it. We have to find this place."

Derrick's frown deepens. I half expect him to say no. Each of our shifts has a designated area we're supposed to search, and north of the perimeter is not part of ours. I don't tell Derrick that the map stretches farther north than we've ventured in years, where we have no idea what the Sunken population is, or how much land—if any—remains.

"You know the risks here, Eshaal," Derrick says, though it's not disapproval in his voice, but caution.

The farther out we go, the less likely we are to return. It was only a few months ago that an incinerator and navigator team went out for their shift, broke protocol by going farther than they had been instructed, and never walked through the gates of Heaven again.

"I have to do this," I say, though it doesn't seem fair to saddle Derrick with the risks either. "I can go myself. You can tell Orla that you tried to stop me, but—"

"No." Derrick's tone is firm now. We both know my suggestion was ludicrous; there's a reason why our shifts send people out in pairs of two: one incinerator and one navigator. The incinerator burns the dead bodies, protects Heaven at all costs. And the navigator guides and keeps watch. Each on their own doesn't work—not when danger lurks around every corner out here. "If you're going north, then so am I."

He steers the boat, turning it around. In the moonlight, I can almost make out the gates of Heaven, high up on a mountain. Protected.

With each stroke of Derrick's oars, we move farther away from it. And the dread grows in the pit of my stomach.

It's daylight and several hours before we spot land: a small island, big enough that we can't see the other end of it.

Derrick sways the boat to the side of the island before using a rope to tether it to the trunk of a nearby tree. The shore is close enough that I can balance on the sides and jump off onto the soft, marshy ground.

"I'll stay close," I say, turning back to Derrick.

"I should come with you," he says. "We don't know what's out here or why Juliette would even come here. We're miles out from Heaven. We've never come this far before."

In our three years of working together, Derrick has never left the boat behind. But we've never broken protocol before. We've never come this far out.

"We haven't come across any Sunken yet, but if we do, I can protect myself," I say, though I'm not sure I believe the words I'm speaking.

There's little we know about the Sunken, truly. It's difficult to study a creature so dangerous and so out of reach. One we can't kill, only briefly scare away or injure with the threat of fire. But we do know they need water to survive. They've never ventured far inland, never attempted to trek up the mountain to Heaven.

"It's not just the Sunken I'm worried about," Derrick says, though his face turns ashen at the mention of them—I can make it out even under his goggles. "Even if Juliette really drew a map to here, you don't know what you could find. She was working on research for Orla before she left. Maybe she found something dangerous."

I sigh. "I don't even know if this is the place. Whatever's here, I can protect myself. But you have to stay with the boat, you know that."

Derrick nods, though his pallor doesn't return to normal.

He always gets that look of fear when it's time for us to separate, no matter how many times we've done this together. Instead of letting me go, he asks, "Why do you think she came out here? She must have told you something."

"If I could answer that, I wouldn't be here breaking protocol, would I?"

Derrick doesn't look amused by my answer, but he doesn't say anything else. Instead, he grabs the emergency telecoms device and hands it to me. "Radio me if you see anything weird."

I slide it into the pocket of my suit, nestled beside the photo of Juliette, before making my way toward the trees. Derrick's question burrows into my mind—*why* would Juliette come here?

The land on this island is similar to what I've seen before. It's all swampland, a place where water and earth meet.

I keep my weapon hoisted and ready as I jump over puddles of water, through damp grass, and under the boughs of trees. There's nothing here, but that thought sets my teeth on edge more than anything else. The Sunken can creep up on you when you least expect it, especially in marshlands like this. And if they manage to take you by surprise, there's little chance that you can defend yourself. They can kill in an instant, drowning you in the same water their bodies are made of as you writhe in pain while the toxic, burning water fills your lungs.

I smell the dead body before I see it. It's not a scent you forget once you've encountered it—the rancid odor of decaying flesh. I hesitate in front of a thicket of trees. The body must be somewhere on the other side. My stomach twists, thinking about the possibility of the body belonging to Juliette.

I take a deep breath, steeling myself for what lies behind the shelter of trees. Then I push aside the tall grass and low-hanging branches and march forward.

The corpse lies facedown in the middle of a creek. I edge closer, trying not to think about Juliette and the body as one. Trying to think of the body as a body, not Juliette at all.

Still, it's hard to ignore Juliette's dark brown hair cascading down her shoulders and drenched in the water of the stream. The heart-shaped dark brown birthmark on her arm confirms that I'm not mistaken, as much as I wish I were.

I reach out, my fingers hovering over her body. The odor is overwhelming here. I almost wish Derrick were with me. I turn the body over, trying to ignore the waves of nausea crawling up my stomach. Her golden-brown skin has turned blue black; her hazel eyes, once so bright and full of life, are dull and lifeless. At least the toxic particles in the humid air here haven't yet turned her completely unrecognizable.

I pull my hands back, tears blurring my vision. They say that when you're about to die, your life flashes before your eyes. But they don't tell you that when the person you love dies, their life replays in your head, and you're left asking yourself why and how—endless questions you can never answer.

I swallow my tears, pushing the grief as far back as possible while I hold up the flame gun with shaky fingers. I try to steady myself as I rest my finger on the trigger, looking at Juliette one last time, even though she barely looks like herself anymore. At least she won't become one of them. That's the only reassurance I have.

A twig snapping in the distance stops me in my tracks. My breath hitches, and I turn the flame gun in the direction of the sound. The thicket of trees nearby moves slowly, and my heartbeat hastens. My fingers hover over the trigger, ready to spew fire at a moment's notice. I step gingerly across Juliette's body, shielding it from whatever's approaching. Derrick's words from the boat ring loudly in my head: *She was working on research for Orla before she left. Maybe she found something dangerous out here.*

Finally, a brown hand emerges carefully from the thicket of trees, followed by a girl who can't be much older than me. Her arms are raised in surrender, and she's unarmed. No protection at all—no suit or goggles. Her short brown hair is messy and tangled with twigs and leaves, and her dark brown eyes are sharp with fear as she takes me in. Somehow, she's unharmed from the toxic atmosphere.

"Who are you?" I ask, still aiming my flame gun at her.

She's unfamiliar to me—and I thought I knew *everyone* at Heaven. With our dwindling numbers, it's not exactly difficult. It's been years since Heaven has accepted any new refugees.

"I'm Sona," the girl says. "I'm a scientist. I've been researching landmasses. I recently tracked down this island, and I've been camping out here for a while, and then *she* showed up." Sona nods at Juliette's body. My stomach clenches with anger that Sona was the last person to see Juliette alive, not me.

"How did she . . . ?" I can't bring myself to say the word *die* because admitting that aloud would make it too real.

"She washed up on shore. I think she might have drowned. I was just as surprised as you to find her. I didn't think I'd come across anyone else this far out."

"And so you just left her body here in the creek?" I ask, anger seeping into my words. I half want to pull the trigger on Sona. "Left her to be taken by *monsters*?"

Sona hesitates, looking to Juliette's body instead of at me.

It dawns on me before she can say any more. "Did you say you're a scientist?" I ask. "Were you using her body as bait to draw the Sunken out? So you could study them?"

Sona's face loses some of its color, telling me that I'm right. She doesn't even try to deny it, to defend herself.

I step forward, the flame gun heavy in my hands. Now her dark eyes flicker toward me, a renewed glint of fear in them.

"How stupid could you be?" I ask.

"I just wanted to see exactly what the Sunken do where a human body is concerned. It's never been observed before, and I wanted to make sure we really had it right. When they take the body, what do they do with it? How can a human being be changed like that? The whole thing is a scientific marvel."

"You're going to get yourself *killed*," I say. "Do you understand how dangerous the Sunken are? And you have nothing to protect yourself—no suit, no goggles, not even a weapon."

In the early days of Heaven, there were people who fancied

themselves brave, venturing out into the unknown lands to try and take on the Sunken. Not a single one returned. I didn't know there were still people foolish enough to risk their lives in similar ways.

Sona frowns. "That's a rather primitive way of thinking. Their methods are a bit unorthodox, but . . . look, this is why I'm here. It's for research, to understand them and their methods better. Maybe if we do, we can find better ways to adapt to this new world."

I wonder for a moment if this is the effect of the toxic atmosphere. If the death settles on you like delusion at first, until you lose sense of everything, lose your grasp of reality entirely. I heard it was one of the symptoms, though the more brutal ones were what gave me nightmares as a child—the toxic particles slowly crushing your lungs until your body struggles for air, clouding your eyes until your sight turns to nothing but blackness.

"You should come back with me to Heaven," I offer. "We can give you shelter, protect you." Even as I offer this, I wonder if she's beyond help already.

"Heaven," Sona says, as if there's something distasteful about the name. "The great city closed off from everyone and everything since the floods started. A *refuge* isolated from everything and everyone."

"Isolation was the only way for us to survive," I say, my voice hardening with defensiveness. Heaven may not be perfect—isn't perfect—but we do what we have to in order to survive. "How did *you* survive? We thought the last of humanity outside our gates died a long time ago. The refugees stopped coming soon after the Sunken appeared. We thought everyone outside Heaven was dead . . . or taken."

Sona studies me closely in a way that feels jarring. "The refugees didn't stop coming. Heaven wouldn't let anyone else in. They said they were 'at capacity.'"

I blink at her slowly. "What are you talking about? We kept our gates open until the Sunken emerged, and then . . . it was too risky to transport anyone inside without risking our own lives, risking our survival. Once we figured out we could use the fire to keep them away, we sent out search parties to find anybody else left alive. There was no one left . . ." I still remember when teams of people returned to the city empty-handed, their faces grim. They had many stories of terrifying encounters with the Sunken, but none of human survivors.

"There was no one left," Sona repeats with a chuckle, but there's a darkness underneath it. "Your government told us we would find protection in Heaven if we could pay for it. People like my family didn't get in. Your people watched as thousands of us died, to the floods, the hunger, the cold. They watched as the Sunken took us, not caring what happened. I guess our lives weren't as precious as the ones who bought their way into Heaven. And those search parties? Death parties were more like it. The Sunken were growing in number, and so they sent you people out to incinerate anyone they could find, dead or alive. If they weren't citizens of Heaven, they didn't matter."

"That doesn't make any sense," I insist. Her words feel like a fog in my brain. I was born in the new world, but if there's one thing I know, it's the story of Heaven. The last city on Earth, housing the last survivors of our planet. And Sona's story isn't true. It can't be. "Nobody bought their way into Heaven. We were *all* refugees. There were supposed to be more cities after ours so we could save as many people as possible, but then the Great Flood happened and the Sunken arrived and it was too late. Otherwise—"

"That's a nice story," Sona says, though pity colors her sarcastic tone. "But that's not the truth. Whoever your parents were, you were lucky they had the money to get in." She pauses and adds, "Or maybe *un*lucky."

I shake my head again, as if that'll make Sona's words disappear. Make it like I had never met her or heard any of this. "You shouldn't even be here. You shouldn't—humanity outside Heaven doesn't exist. There's no one left."

Sona raises an eyebrow. She almost looks bored by this conversation. "*Or* we found another way to survive."

"Nobody else survived," I insist. But the more I say it, the less convinced I become. Sona is real. I'm not hallucinating. The toxic air hasn't killed her. She's alive and standing in front of me, speaking to me. Telling me lies . . . or truths . . . Either way, I can't make any sense of her claims. And what about Juliette? If she came out here, maybe it was for the same reason as Sona. To find the truth the rest of us didn't know.

I think back to Juliette when she returned from her research trips. She was always more subdued then, quieter. Like she'd returned but left a part of her outside the city. I thought it was just the fear. That in the same way I was haunted by nightmares of the dead, she was haunted somehow by the outside world. But maybe there was more to it than she'd ever let on.

"Well, I'm here, and I have never set foot in your precious city. And after everything they've done, I wouldn't want to go there either," Sona says.

I want to say more, demand the truth, but it's just then that the air around us shifts. It's not a visible change. It's a certain stillness that infuses itself into the environment: The wind stops, the soil under my feet becomes less solid, the sound of water becomes louder than the blood pumping in my ears.

"No." It's all I can whisper as I turn back around, toward Juliette. But I find the monster instead: the Sunken.

It's the first time I've seen one of them this close. Its blue-green skin glows in the sunlight, and hard scales line its body, glinting sharply when one catches the light.

Murky brown mucous drips from its webbed hands and feet.

But the faces of the Sunken are what haunt the dreams of every resident in Heaven: shaped like a human's but resembling no human *I've* ever met. Soulless black eyes, no nose to speak of, and rows of vicious teeth.

I scramble back, almost tripping over the edge of a tree, pulling the trigger of my flame gun as I double back. The flames rip out of my weapon in a flurry, engulfing the Sunken in front of me.

It lets out a roar and stumbles back. Then its eyes sway from me, to Sona, to Juliette on the ground.

I can't let them turn her into a monster.

I pull the trigger once more, launching toward the monster instead of away from it. For a moment, all I see is the wall of fire in front of me, feel the heat of it prickle my skin.

"What are you doing? Stop!" Sona screams from somewhere in the distance, but I barely register her words.

In the wake of the fire, the Sunken is still there, hunched down to protect itself. The scales on its skin have charred and blackened. I feel triumphant for a moment, but the monster rises again in a flash. It lumbers forward, toward me. My heartbeat quickens as I reach for the trigger again, but the gun lets out only a cough of a flame. It's jammed.

"Shit, shit," I mumble, pulling the trigger again, harder. But that single moment is all it takes. The Sunken sways away from me and toward the body on the ground.

"No, don't!" I cry, but it doesn't listen. I don't even know if it's capable of listening.

Its webbed hands find Juliette's body, the murky brown mucous already beginning to envelop her. I rush forward, pulling the trigger of the gun with all my force. The fire finally rips out again, but it's too late.

The Sunken flees with Juliette's corpse, and I watch through the orange flames as it disappears downstream in the blink of an eye.

"She's gone." The words are a whisper on my lips. I had the chance protect her—what remained of her—and I couldn't. I was too late. She was right here in front of me, and I was *too late*.

"This is *your* fault," I cry to Sona, needing someone to blame for my failure. "*You* lured that creature here, and *now* look what happened."

Sona just frowns at me for a moment before shaking her head. "You people never change," she mumbles, pushing me aside and beginning to follow the stream down, on the trail of the monsters.

I reach out to stop her but hesitate. I wait instead, half expecting her to come back. Because if she doesn't, if she's not a refugee who needs our help to survive in this new world, what does that mean about the world I've known my entire life?

What does it mean about Heaven?

I have more questions than answers when I get back to Heaven. The city that once seemed like the only place for survival now feels like a trap. When the gates slam shut behind us, my heart jumps to my throat. The alleyways we walk through seem too narrow, like they're closing in on us. The people in the streets have the look of the haunted. I wonder what they know, if they know anything. If the things Sona told me are true, I wonder who in this city is a liar and who is being lied to.

I head to Orla's office as soon as I'm back in the city. It's a place that's intensely familiar to me. While she's risen in the ranks in headquarters, I first knew her as my trainer. She taught me everything I know about my job, my duty. Everything about how to protect Heaven. Usually, Derrick and I meet with her quarterly, though occasionally special circumstances require an impromptu meeting. Juliette being missing for a week definitely qualifies as a special case.

"Eshaal." Orla welcomes me in with a smile. Her office has only become grander over the years. Once, it was little more than a cubicle in a corner of headquarters, but last year she was moved to this central office. There are leather chairs stationed at her desk and a plush velvet carpet on the hardwood floor. Portraits of the founders of Heaven line the wall behind her, alongside a picture of Heaven's gates, when they were first constructed.

"How did everything go?" Orla asks, once we're both seated. Her piercing blue eyes look right through me, and there's something unnerving about her smile. I've always found comfort in Orla, but now I can't help the way my skin prickles at being in her presence.

"We broke protocol," I confess. "It was my idea."

Orla doesn't seem as perturbed by that as I would have imagined. "I take it you were successful if you are admitting to breaking protocol." She holds my gaze, a glimmer of something in her eyes that I can't read.

"We went farther north than Derrick and I have ever been before. It was a long way away from Heaven. She was there; she was dead," I say.

Orla's face falls as she reaches out to touch my hand. "I'm sorry, Eshaal. Juliette was . . . She was one of our best scientists. And I know she was on the brink of some kind of breakthrough about the Sunken. Some way to finally eliminate them."

"I still don't understand why she would leave," I say. "You must know something. She was seeing you more often than anyone else for her research."

Orla smiles sympathetically. "I know you want to make sense of this, but sometimes these things happen. Juliette was . . . unwell, in those last few days. Her research was all she thought about. I overlooked it because she was about to discover something big. I didn't think she would do something so drastic. But maybe she went too far. Maybe she tried to . . . find a way to eliminate them on her own."

Orla's words make no sense. If Juliette had really been obsessive during her last few days in Heaven, I would have noticed it. I realize Orla is only trying to appease me, trying to find a way to make me see the false reality she's creating for Juliette: an obsessed scientist who took her research on the Sunken too far. That would be her story now.

"But we found her body intact. If it were the Sunken that killed her, then we wouldn't have found her at all," I say, in an attempt to refute Orla's lies. "In fact, there hadn't even been any damage to the body. It was like . . . I don't know, the olden times. Normal decay. There was no reaction to the toxic water particles."

Orla shifts in her seat, the discomfort in her expression obvious, though she doesn't drop the smile. "This is why we need scientists like Juliette. This new world is so unknown to us, we're still making discoveries about the atmosphere, how it's changing, how the Sunken affect everything."

But her words don't assuage my doubt. Not after everything that's happened today.

"Why would her body not be affected by the atmosphere?" I ask this time, my voice firm. Demanding an answer.

Orla clears her throat. "It's possible that where you found her, the water particles could be significantly less concentrated. Without studying the body, there's no way for us to know for sure."

"Can I see the research?" I ask, changing my tactic. Orla may not give me a straight answer, but the research can't lie. Juliette had to have found *something* that led her to leave this place.

"I'm afraid that's not possible," Orla says with a sigh. "Eshaal, I understand you have questions, that you want to understand *why* this happened. But sometimes there is no answer. Sometimes it's better to stop digging, for your own peace of mind." She says it kindly, but there's an underlying threat in her voice. "I know this is a troubling time for you. You should get some rest, and I'll speak to Dr. Valasquez about getting you some grief counselling."

Somehow, I very much doubt that Dr. Valasquez will provide me with anything but platitudes. But I know someone else who might answer my questions.

Rowing a boat is no easy feat, though Derrick always makes it look effortless. At least tonight, the new moon hangs above the sky, casting a dim glow over everything as I row out of sight of Heaven. I worried that Orla would shut down my clearance at the gates but the operator had opened the doors without any questions.

I know it's ridiculous to believe the word of a stranger over the world that I've always known, seen with my own eyes, and heard with my own ears, but I need answers. And I fear the only one who can give them to me now is a monster.

I stop the boat outside the perimeter of Heaven, but the city and mountain have disappeared into the dark night already. Around me, there's nothing but the vast ocean of toxic water. No matter how many doubts plague my mind, fear burrows deep in my bones as I stare out at the dark liquid every which way.

I sit there for what feels like hours, every sound sending shivers down my spine.

Finally, I feel it. The hair rising on the nape of my neck, a chill in the air, and the churning sound of the water.

My breath hitches as the monster rises from beneath the surface.

In the dark of the night, its blue scales shimmer, water glinting off it where moonlight hits.

The green mucous on its webbed hands is congealed around the fingers, though splashes of it drip into the midnight-black water below us.

Its canine mouth leers at me as it approaches my boat. Its beady eyes regard me coldly.

My heartbeat quickens, and I raise my flame gun, my only protection against the thing in front of me.

The creature's cold eyes stare down at my weapon, then up at me. Unlike the one on the island, this one doesn't stagger back in fear, but it doesn't grab me and drag me underwater either. Instead, it hovers in front of my boat as if waiting, though it doesn't speak.

I try to ignore my fear, study the monster in front of me. That's when I notice the darkened spot on its arm. A heart-shaped birthmark.

"Juliette?" I ask in barely a whisper.

It nods, as if it understands me. But the thing in front of me *can't* be Juliette. Aside from her birthmark, it bears no resemblance to her.

The creature lifts one of its webbed hands, and I flinch. But it doesn't reach for me. Instead, it points to its beady eyes, black irises never leaving my own.

I touch the glass of my goggles, and the creature makes that motion with its head again—a motion of agreement, I realize . . .

I hesitate.

On my first day of training, Orla told us that the most important thing about leaving Heaven is our protective gear: the suit and goggles. They protect us from the hazards beyond the gates of Heaven, the outside world that's been ravaged by climate change. The new, horrible, monstrous world we inherited. But I'm wondering now if that was part of Heaven's collection of lies.

I reach toward the tightened straps on the back of my head, taking a deep breath before I undo it. I pull the goggles off slowly, even as Orla's warnings ring in my ears.

For a moment, dark spots dance in front of my vision, and I see a monster in the shape of Juliette—the monster's teeth with Juliette's bright eyes, the monster's claws but Juliette's brown skin. But I blink and the image disappears. The dark spots clear to reveal Juliette's familiar face. The one I've known for my whole life. No sign of any monsters. She smiles, and everything seems to still. Her hands, the same delicate ones I've held a million times, reach forward. Her fingers link with mine. Despite her being submerged in water, her hands are warm, like human blood still flows through them.

The new world too seems brighter in front of my eyes, more alive. The darkness in the air and water doesn't seem so pressing anymore. And the scent of the water, which was so foreboding before, now smells sweet and the air feels warm. Unlike anything I've sensed before.

"Juliette." I sigh. "I don't understand. I *saw* you. You were *dead*."

"A first death," Juliette says. "A death you have to die if you want to come underwater and start a new life."

"You mean with the Sunken—as one of *them*?"

"Not Sunken . . . *people*. We're human. When the rest of the world sank underwater and Heaven shut them out, they adapted," Juliette explains. "And when I found out that we've been lied to about everything, I decided to join them. You must have figured it out if you're here. There is no toxic atmosphere, Eshaal. Humanity has carried on outside the gates of Heaven."

I shake my head because even though I can see it all with my own eyes, I can hardly believe it. "But I've *seen* them, the Sunken. They are monsters. That's why we burn the bodies, so the Sunken don't get their claws into more of us. So they don't keep growing their ranks while our population dwindles; so they can't take over what's left of the world, including Heaven."

But even as I say these words, they don't ring true anymore. I've never seen the Sunken with my naked eyes, only through goggles. Everyone in Heaven knows that to go outside without protective gear would mean death; we heard the horror stories from headquarters, saw the pictures. And the people at headquarters are in charge after all; they're the ones venturing out into the world with scientists, trying to protect us from the danger outside our gates. We've never had reason to question them. The only ones who leave are the ones headquarters employs, like me and Derrick and Juliette.

"We don't care about Heaven," Juliette says with a sad smile, almost like she pities my disbelief. Like she and I are not the same anymore. And I guess we aren't. "We just want to live. That's what we're doing. *This* is the new world, Eshaal. Not Heaven. This is how we survive now: underwater, not on top of a mountain, fearing everything outside the gates of a man-made city."

"But we built it so the human race wouldn't go extinct. So we could survive."

"First, Heaven shut out the rest of humanity to protect themselves. Now they want to kill the Sunken because they're afraid of us. It's never going to stop. I met other humans when I was doing my research trips. I didn't believe anything they told me at first, but the proof was always right there in front of my eyes. Once I started asking questions, I couldn't stop. I told Orla that I was zeroing in on a way to eradicate the Sunken, but really I was trying to find a way to communicate with them. To understand. When I finally managed to get in contact, I knew there was nothing else for me to do but join them. What I discovered was that there were never any monsters out here, only up there, in Heaven," Juliette said.

"That's why you left?" I press. "Why didn't you tell me anything?"

Juliette sighs. "I didn't think you'd believe me. You were entrenched so deep. We all were. I knew that if it were the other way around, if you'd told me all this without the proof I'd seen, I wouldn't have believed you. So I tried to find proof, something to show you, but I knew I was running out of time. It wouldn't be long before Orla became suspicious of what exactly I was up to, and I was afraid of what she would do if she knew."

"So you didn't even try? You just left me alone there, *knowing* that everything I believed was a lie?" The words are out before I can think about them, and once the anger simmering in my veins has weight, I can't suppress it. "Do you know what it was like for me? You just disappeared without so much as a note! I searched for you . . . I broke protocol for you. But all I found was your dead body, and I watched that—that *monster* drag you away. I thought I'd failed you."

Juliette at least has the grace to look ashamed. She glances down instead of at me. "I'm sorry, Eshaal. I didn't think I had another choice. But . . . I can make it up to you. You can join me here. We can still be together, live the life we're meant to, out here instead of locked inside the gates of Heaven."

She looks up, meeting my eyes once more. Some of my anger washes away at her plea. I look at the water glinting silver in the moonlight, and I imagine what it would be like if I shed my old life. I could share this entire new world with Juliette. What do I have left in Heaven, other than lies and the blood on my hands? I think about the nightmares that haunt my sleep, and an unfamiliar feeling of freedom begins to itch in my skin.

"Yes, I want to join you," I find myself saying. "But . . . I need to say goodbye to my old life first. I was born there; I grew up there. It's all I've ever known."

"Okay," Juliette says, nodding. "You just have to die your first death, and then I'll come find you."

My mind is whirring as Heaven comes into view. There are so many people in this city who are just as ignorant as I was, whose bodies will be burned to a crisp when they die. Who'll never know the truth because people like Orla will keep it from them until their dying breath. It doesn't seem fair that Juliette and I get a second chance at life when none of them do.

I pull on my goggles as I get closer to Heaven, more out of habit than anything else. Immediately, I feel the shift around me. The goggles feel heavy, like a burden more than protection, now that I know the truth. There has to be a way I can show everyone else the truth too.

A familiar figure is shadowed in the dark when I pull up to the docks. Derrick, wearing a grim expression I haven't seen before.

"Eshaal," he greets me, while I climb out of the boat. "I thought you had decided to follow after Juliette."

"What?" I ask.

"She left in the dead of night, and so did you."

"You told Orla." I can already see it in his eyes.

"What was I meant to do? She asked me to watch you ever since Juliette disappeared. She told me you were saying weird things in her office earlier today. She feared the worst, and maybe she was right to. The rules for our job aren't to be taken lightly, Eshaal. You're lucky to be alive, you know."

"No, I'm not," I say. "Derrick, Juliette is alive."

He blinks at me slowly. "You know Juliette is gone. She's probably already one of those monsters."

"No, she isn't. I just saw her; I talked to her. She's not a monster, Derrick. She's still her."

Derrick frowns. "What are you talking about?"

"We've been lied to our entire lives. This job, being an incinerator, is a farce. We've been burning bodies, but not to save them from the Sunken. We've just been *killing* them."

Derrick shakes his head. I can see in his eyes that I've lost him.

But I know something that could still convince him. I pull off my goggles in a rush, throwing them into the water where they land with a splash. Derrick follows them with wide eyes.

"Look, Derrick, I've taken off my goggles, and I'm going to be okay. I took them off earlier on the boat, and I was fine. The goggles . . . they change things, what we see. If you take yours off—"

"This is what you call okay?" he asks. "We need to get you back inside before you die. You're already talking nonsense. You're delusional."

"I'm not," I insist. "If what Orla said is true, the toxic particles of the water should have already set into me, but I'm the same. Nothing has changed."

"You're talking nonsense. I should have told Orla to get you help a long time ago. You're obviously overwhelmed by everything. I know the job isn't easy, and losing Juliette . . . talking to a psychiatrist can help you deal with all this. It's my fault, really. I should have seen what this was doing to you, but I thought you were strong enough to handle it."

"I'm leaving. Tonight. I only came to say goodbye, and Juliette said she'd come find me after—"

Derrick dashes for me, snatches the flame gun out of my hands, and aims it at me.

"I'm not letting you leave, Eshaal. As your friend, I'm going to take you back to Orla, and she will decide what kind of treatment you need," Derrick says carefully.

I know trying to explain anything to him is fruitless now. Instead, I turn away from him, bounding down the steps of the mountain. A moment later, I hear Derrick's heavy steps following behind.

"Burn me alive if you want. You're not going to stop me," I say through gasping breaths, even though I know if he pulls the trigger, my first death will be my final. There will be no body left behind for a second chance.

"I don't want to do this, Eshaal, but I'm just trying to protect you," Derrick says, his voice punctuated by sadness. I understand it more than he could know. If Derrick had come to me just yesterday, claiming everything I've known about the Sunken was wrong, I would have held a flame gun to his head too.

If only I could take him to Juliette, will him to take off his goggles and *see* her for who she is now.

But maybe there's more than one way to show Derrick the truth.

I come to a sudden stop, and Derrick almost loses his balance as he stops on the step just above mine. I turn to face him now. He's gasping for breath too, but some of his anger seems to have subsided as he looks me over.

"Good, you've come to your senses," Derrick says.

I step forward, toward him. He backs away slowly, like he's unsure of what's happening.

"I'm sorry," I say, unable to keep the tremble out of my voice.

A crease forms between Derrick's eyebrows, but he doesn't get longer than a moment to consider my apology. I brace myself against the cliffside and sidle past him, pretending to surrender. But once I'm on the other side of him, I gather all my strength and push him as hard as I possibly can. I look away, but that doesn't stop me from hearing the awful thuds and cracks of his body hitting the concrete steps, one after the other, as he tumbles to his death. The sounds echo into the night. Once they stop, I hurry down the steps toward Derrick, in a rush and far too slow all at once.

There is no life left in his eyes. They're glazed over. There's no breath in his lungs, no pulse in his throat.

My heart throbs painfully at the sight. For three years, Derrick and I have worked side by side. Not quite friends, but not just colleagues either. Now Derrick is dead. But what had Juliette called it? A first death. He could still live, just as Juliette had. And then he would understand the truth—he would be living it.

I drag Derrick's body along the dock. Juliette promised me this was true, and I had to believe it. I roll Derrick's body into the water. At first the waves pull him in slowly, washing away the blood still on his clothes. Finally, they pull him in completely, and I watch his body disappear.

I take a deep breath, ready to join him in his first death. But then I look up for one last glance at Heaven, at the gates still visible from down here. The last bastion of the old world. A cruel dream that we all helped construct. It's worse than any nightmare.

I climb back onto the boat and thumb through the emergency supplies—weapons meant to obliterate gangs of Sunken if we were ever attacked on a shift. Among the supplies, I find grenades. After grabbing them, I climb up the steps once more. This time, I don't stop until I reach the gates. Once upon a time, it brought me comfort to see these gates, knowing that they protected the last city on Earth. Now the sight fills me with a burning rage.

I pull the safety pin and throw one at the gates, then hurl more incendiary grenades at the walls surrounding the city. At first, there is only silence. Then the explosions begin. Flames start to consume everything.

Heaven is tinged orange. Fire alarms blare from every corner. I can picture the inside of the city: Panicked residents pushing past one another to get to safety. Rushing out of their homes and trying to find a way outside the city's walls. Their survival instincts making them forget they believe the outside to be the most dangerous of all.

The gates of Heaven are now gone forever. Maybe the people inside can finally learn the truth. Maybe they can finally be free.

I glance down at the bottom of the mountain, where Derrick's blood stains the earth. Now it's my turn to die my first death.

I wake to a new world. I look around for the crowded buildings of Heaven, the streets weaving through them, the gates closing off everything. But instead, I find a place vast and unfamiliar. The water stretches every which way, the surface nowhere to be found. In the distance, I can make out a small cluster of houses, paths weaving between them, and people—not monsters, both outside and inside—peering at me, curiosity alive in their eyes.

It feels unsettling to see them, even though they bear no resemblance to the monsters I thought they were. It's because they feel so familiar, so human. Like there's no difference between the Sunken and the citizens of Heaven.

It takes me a moment to realize that I'm one of them now, that I'm no longer a citizen of Heaven. The thought sends a shiver down my spine.

Juliette sits in front of me, her brown hair floating in the water. I glance down at myself, and I realize I'm the same as always. Human, brown skin, black hair. But I'm somehow different too, breathing in the water instead of air. I sit up, feeling the rocks of the ocean floor below my feet.

"I didn't think you'd really do it," Juliette says, taking my hand in hers, pulling us both up to stand. "But I'm so glad you did."

"I had to. I didn't have anybody else up there. My parents, you, Derrick . . . you were all gone. Is he here?" I ask. I look around at the endless stretch of water around us. I half expect Derrick to swim up to us, ready to finally accept that I was telling him the truth.

"Is who here?" Juliette asks.

"Derrick?" I ask. "He died a first death. I rolled him into the water. I thought . . . someone would come take him, and I'd join him here. Maybe it wasn't you, but there must be a way to know who and—"

"He's not here, Eshaal," Juliette says. Her voice is unusually cold.

"Why not?"

"People from Heaven only die one death. I made a deal to come here. I told them that I would destroy all my research, make sure Orla and the rest of the people at headquarters never got hold of any of it. But the deal was only for me and for you. The rest of them? When they die, they die. They can rot just like they left the rest of humanity to rot."

I think about Heaven and its people, the faces I saw every day of my life. All of them doomed to that hellish city, until the water claimed them too. Except the water wouldn't make them its own; it would wash them up and spit them out, leave them to die. If not for Juliette, that would have been my demise too, in the end.

"Come on, we have so much of this world to see," Juliette says, pulling me along.

And I follow, having nowhere and nobody else to turn to.

BREAK THROUGH OUR SKIN

NASEEM JAMNIA

NINE HOURS UNTIL THE BEGINNING

When I was twelve, my mind developed the ability to hear my real name and pronouns whenever someone deadnames or misgenders me. It's come in handy over the past three years since I don't want to go to prison for patricide.

Tomorrow—Sunday—is Norooz, marking the end of spring break but beginning of spring, and I'm supposed to be helping with the haft-seen. Norooz is my favorite holiday on principle: Marking the new year on the spring equinox is some next-level new age shit, and our people have been doing it for literal millennia.

But instead of setting the table with the seven-plus items beginning with the letter *seen*, Maman is lecturing me because of the phone call she just got from one James P. Hudson, PhD in being a pain in the ass, who happens to be my supervisor at the OI (undergoing a name change but technically called the Oriental Institute, which, I mean, yikes on bikes).

"He must not have confirmed it, **Farz**-joon," she says, after I remind her that I already told him I couldn't come in today.

I've been volunteering at the OI, located in the middle of UChicago's campus, since last summer. Dr. Hudson, asshole though he is, is sort of a big deal. Smithsonian internships—my dream—are rarely given to high school students, but he's all but said an official recommendation from him would remove that hurdle.

"It's spring break!" I argue. "Besides, we still have to cook." Plus, I sort of stayed up until two in the morning reading a 150 thousand-word fanfic. (Under the covers, of course; I don't have a death wish. Maman makes me read a study on the importance of sleep for teens every time she catches me staying up late.)

"I can make everything myself." Maman purses her lips and switches to accented English. "If I was still doing experiments and one of my techs left me stranded, I would fire them. You made a commitment, **bacheh-ye-man**." While my dad teaches music theory at the University of Chicago, Maman is the lab director in the very fancy Pritzker School of Molecular Engineering, focusing on teaching after years of research with too many acronyms and prefixes.

Having impressive immigrant parents is a lot. Having impressive immigrant parents who push you to pursue this archeology thing you've been into lately without knowing why you're into it is a whole other matter.

And then Maman adds the absolute kicker: "He said you promised to help set up the new exhibit."

That lying sack of shit. I've been asking to help with the new exhibit on the Shahr-e Sukhteh for *weeks*, and he kept saying he'd "get back to me." *Now* he wants my help? The weekend before it opens? The day before it's shown to investors?

I was wrong: The real kicker is when she adds, "And you need his letter of recommendation."

Seven months of weekends after those three-ish months in the summer. I've talked to every graduate student, sat in on as many lectures as I could, and even done some of the college readings. What other high schooler is this dedicated?

"Chee shodeh?" asks Baba. I hadn't even heard his heavy footsteps on the stairs. He picks up the red-gold tea I made for him before this argument started and pops a sugar cube between his front teeth. "Don't talk back to your mother. That's not becoming of a **person**."

Why would he ask what's up and then immediately take her side? And then bring gender into this, of all things? My ability could have short-circuited if it weren't such a common refrain. *That's not becoming of a* ***[ERROR]****. Carry yourself like a* ***[ERROR]****. Sit like a* ***[ERROR]****. Dress like a* ***[ERROR]****.*

There's no way I can ever come out to my folks.

EIGHT AND A HALF HOURS UNTIL THE BEGINNING

I'm panting and sweaty by the time I get to 58th and University, shirt plastered to my back underneath my coat. When I burst into the museum, Dr. Aiber, who looks like a Nordic Viking, is saying something over his shoulder as he steps out. Despite not being part of the original *Iranian* team, he's somehow our visiting contact. "Oh, hello, **Farz**," he says. "Glad you could finally join us." He quirks an eyebrow over his shoulder and heads out.

In the lobby stands Dr. James Hudson, professor emeritus in the Department of Near Eastern Languages and Civilizations. The flap of skin under his chin, the one old people sometimes get, wobbles. "Well. You've made it," he says with a sniff. I hate that sniff. "While I appreciate the importance of preparing for Norooz, I cannot help but wonder why, with Chaharshanbeh Soori already behind us, you have waited this long to set up your haft-seen?" He gestures to the one in front of the Suq gift shop, decorated with the vinegar and apple and wheaty samanoo and garlic and sumac and oleaster fruits and the ever-tricky sprouted sabzeh—all symbolic items for spring.

I want to tell this Bastion of Academic Knowledge that he's missing items on his haft-seen—the hyacinth and coins and special book and mirror and eggs. And goldfish, I guess, though it feels cruel to get a fishie and then abandon it to its fate. But I know he'll lecture me about weird diasporic inaccuracies and that as an *institution*, which he'll say in that way I hate, the Oriental Institute—he objects to the impending and more specific name change to the Institute of the Study of Ancient Cultures because the "Oriental Institute" has *history* and *meaning*—vows to uphold truth and accuracy. Never mind that those things are subjective.

"**Farz-jan**, I know you've yet to visit the country of your ancestors and survey the sites," he blathers, "but surely you understand how important this tradition is to the Persians."

I hate how he fully enunciates *chaharshanbeh*, and I hate that he rubs in my face that he's been to Iran and I haven't, and I hate that he looks at me like I'm some sort of fake Persian, and I hate that he says *jaan* with the long aleph sound instead of my Tehrani *joon*, and I hate that he adds that totally inappropriate affection only when something Persian is brought up, to show that he, too, Knows Farsi; that he, too, is Knowledgeable About [My] Culture™ because he studied it.

God, I am so freaking tired.

Dr. Aiber pushes the door of the lobby open with his back and wheels in a wooden box on a dolly. "Got her right here, James, as promised," he says.

"Excellent." Hudson rounds on me, his eyes gleaming. "**Farz**, you can make up missing your earlier shift by staying late tonight to finalize the exhibit, and you can begin by looking through the exhibit listing." He shoves a binder at me.

"Late?" I don't hide my dismay. I'm going to miss out on the Norooz prep with my mom. "But I had plans—"

"Could they be more important than preparing for this astounding discovery? I suppose"—he gestures grandly, scoffing—"all *this* is run-of-the-mill to you now, eh? Frankly, I expected more from you, **child**. I am giving you remarkable and unprecedented access to resources on your people's rich history, and yet . . ." He sighs dramatically. "When I took you under my wing, I had hoped to share with you the wonders of what the Persians have created. I am disappointed you have not jumped at this opportunity."

He should be grateful I don't sink my teeth into that excess skin at his throat and tear it off. I've sent him emails. I've caught him before *and* after staff meetings. I have all but begged to be involved in the Burnt City exhibit. But I'm sure if I said that, he'd tell me he can't remember anything of the sort and then smirk off into the sunset. "Took you under my wing" my ass.

Letter of rec. Letter . . . of . . . rec.

Taking a deep, shuddering breath, I clutch the binder. "Fine."

EIGHT HOURS UNTIL THE BEGINNING

The sign for the special exhibit room proclaims, WORLD'S OLDEST PROSTHETIC EYE. Underneath, in smaller letters, reads, *Burnt City, Iran: One of the world's oldest cities.* And under that, an image from an archeological dig showing a curled skeleton: *Who Is She?*

Dr. Aiber rolls the box while Hudson micromanages. I follow them into the special exhibit room off the lobby. I flip through the binder, dismayed at everything still unfinished. I could have done this necessary bitch work *weeks* ago.

In this pile of disorganization, I finally find the text for the introduction label.

Shahr-e Sukhteh, or the "Burnt City," is a Bronze Age urban settlement first excavated in 1915 by British archeologists. It is estimated to have been founded around 3200 BCE and abandoned between 2350 and 2100 BCE. Spanning four eras of civilization, Shahr-e Sukhteh was sacked three times, hence its name, and was in trade contact with regions as far as modern-day Turkmenistan and Pakistan.

"Gentle, gentle!" moans Dr. Hudson, as Dr. Aiber moves the box to a table. "She's so delicate!"

"Mansour wouldn't have lent her if he thought she couldn't survive the trip from Iran," says Aiber.

"Ah, forgive my overeagerness. I've heard so much about her. I assume Mansour has told you his current theory of her being a woman of high socioeconomic class."

I hate the way Hudson says the name *Mansour.*

"The gold filigree on the eye did alert me to that possibility," says Aiber. "Quite luxurious for 2800 BCE!"

Both men chortle.

How are old cishet white male professors so annoying? I flip through the binder of doom to find the description for the main attraction.

"Indeed, indeed," says Hudson, "which causes me to wonder whether there is more to her story. What if, instead, we're witnessing evidence of an ancient form of taarof, where she received the eye in exchange for services rendered?"

Uh—what? How the hell would you even find evidence for taarof, the Iranian back-and-forth show of hospitality via humble servitude? I glance over to see the remains, but they're wrapped.

"Or could she be an Elamite priestess, perhaps?" asks Hudson, not doing anything to help with the unpacking. "Such a stature! Six feet is no small feat." He guffaws at his terrible not-pun.

"Is there enough information to know whether the Elamite pantheon was worshipped in the Burnt City?" I interrupt. I've never argued directly with Dr. Hudson before, but he must have asked me here for a reason—maybe my perspective? At least on Persian and proto-Persian things? I mean, this time period is *way* before the Persians, but many Elamite cultural practices were absorbed by the Achaemenids. "Wouldn't that imply the Elamites influenced Jiroft culture and not the other way around?" And then I take a deep breath, even as my stomach drops, to add, "Also, is there any reason to suppose these remains are from a woman? Pelvis size doesn't necessarily correlate to gender."

Recent work by bioarcheologists has said concepts like sex and gender are relative depending on culture, and when looking at skeletons, archeologists use a five-point scale to determine "most likely male" or "most likely female." I've brought this up in multiple staff meetings, but Hudson mysteriously never hears me, even when some of the archeology students have taken my side. But he can't ignore me when I'm talking to him point-blank.

Dr. Hudson's back stiffens as he turns to me. Dr. Aiber, who hasn't heard me make this argument yet, strokes his chin. Hudson's jaw quivers. "The tablet found in the proto-Elamite language makes clear that the connection between the Elamites and the Shahr-e Sukhteh is not incidental. And as there is overlap with the Mesopotamian pantheon—"

"But it's not even clear whether there was a Mesopotamian influence that far east!"

"—we can postulate that the contradictions are due to regional variations, which does not mean those gods were not worshipped in that era or area, nor does it contradict the thought that the so-called 'Jiroft'"—he actually uses air quotes—"culture, unsubstantiated though the claim is, was established first." He gives me such a scathing look that I wish I'd kept my big mouth shut. "And this idea of *gender* . . ." He shakes his head. "My **child**, do not import these modern ideas onto ancient peoples. Political correctness has no place in ancient history."

Because nonbinary genders are only a thing from the modern era; got it. As if this isn't the entire reason why I've been into archeology in the first place—because I know there have been people like me since the beginning of time.

I just *know* it.

Last year, when I was waiting to hear about volunteering at the OI, I tried to tell my parents about this idea: that there are genders outside the binary across time and space. Usually, when I argue queer issues, my parents humor me, but this time, Baba laughed and said these ideas are "issues of a full stomach." That in countries like Iran, where people are desperate for access to water as climate change worsens or struggle to feed their family as sanctions are enforced or are fighting for their lives and liberty against an unjust regime, they aren't so concerned with issues of identity.

But he's wrong. Plus, there are plenty of nonwhite nonbinary genders. "Political correctness," bah.

Speaking of, I hate the way Hudson says *political correctness*. Actually, I probably just hate when he opens his mouth.

"The youth nowadays have these ideas," he says to Aiber, shaking his head. "It is important to mentor young diasporic folk"—uh, since when has he thought that?—"but it is difficult to instill in them academic integrity."

"I think you've done well mentoring **them**," disagrees Aiber. "**They're** challenging old ideas like any scholar should—you've taught **them** well." Aiber smiles at me. I can't tell if it's condescending or encouraging. "Perhaps that's methodology your generation could further, young **person**. I admit, when James told me he'd specifically sought an Iranian intern for this project"—he pronounces it *eye-rain-ee-an*, which should be illegal if you're a Persian scholar—"I was expecting someone a bit more experienced. But he has a lot he can teach you, so perhaps it's for the best."

My jaw trembles. My body flushes hot, then cold, and if I could Hulk-smash Hudson, I would. What other lies has he fed Aiber about me?

Aiber snaps on gloves and begins the painstaking process of unwrapping the remains. He goes through layers of paper and Bubble Wrap before revealing a brown hemisphere. It's small, almost black, roughly the diameter of a quarter, with sunburst markings running along it.

It's a bit anticlimactic.

"The eye," breathes Hudson. "Behold."

I stand there and shake, wishing desperately to be someone—some*thing* I'm not. To escape my body by making it no longer mine. Wings to lift my fat body effortlessly. Extra limbs to flex and bend in every direction, to express what I cannot with my pathetic mouth. Crafty fingers that don't fumble and extra eyes to see everything coming.

The room becomes very still. I have the peculiar sensation of time stopping, dust particles floating midstream, all breath suspended for this moment.

Then the eye's markings flare to life, golden radial bursts that, as I stare, collect into a single beam, and that eye, that convex hemisphere once gilded, focuses that beam onto me. Neither of the others reacts like they notice as Aiber places it on a purple velvet cushion.

Blood of my blood. I name you kin.

SEVEN AND A HALF HOURS UNTIL THE BEGINNING

I'm alone in the bathroom, and the lights flicker as I splash cold water on my face. How did neither Hudson nor Aiber see the eye *light up*? Did neither hear that weird echoing voice? Am I just sleep-deprived? I mean, damn, it was only one night of staying up late; I shouldn't be freaking hallucinating.

The bathrooms are in the basement, which is nice since no one can see me do the "which bathroom do I go into" dance. The emptiness means I can scrutinize my reflection in peace. Coarse facial hair, which I can't decide whether I should get rid of. That big Iranian nose with its hook at the end. Thick eyebrows coming together in the middle—I've been teased for that as long as I can remember, but I'm torn between honoring my heritage, where a single eyebrow is traditionally beautiful, and freaking hating it.

A cold wind stirs the hairs on the back of my neck. I stiffen. There aren't any windows down here. So how—?

A stall door slams shut, then another. I whirl around, but no one's there. I bend down to look under the three stalls, but there aren't any feet. I tiptoe and throw open one of the stall doors, but still—nothing.

When I turn back to the mirror, a skull with gleaming teeth hovers over my reflection's shoulder, its forehead broken so the eye sockets merge into one space. A glowing golden ball hangs suspended in the middle of that gaping cavity like a cyclops's eye. I shout, throwing my hands up to bat around my head, but I only connect with air. When I get ahold of myself, I'm alone.

What the actual *fuck*?

FIVE HOURS UNTIL THE BEGINNING

My head is going to split open like I'm about to birth a god. I need caffeine, but the staff room's coffee pot is broken. At least I'm away from Hudson's narcissistic babbling. My hands shake as I slide the box cutter down the foam to finish making the labels. Since my phone has like 15 percent battery, I've been working in silence for the past few hours; the work computer is too slow to stream music.

My kin?

I'm so startled by the warped sound slicing through the silence that the box cutter slips. It bites into the webbing between my thumb and forefinger, and I yelp and shove my hand into my mouth. The tang of warm pennies floods my tongue.

Shit—I'm bleeding fast. Blood drips on the foam board, on the papers I've printed, and I clutch several tissues and hurry downstairs to the bathrooms. I stick my hand under the open faucet, hissing. It stings, but there should be a first aid kit somewhere.

Pink water fills the sink. There's a trail of red dots on the floor behind me, and on the white porcelain, and smeared on the metal faucet.

Static fills the air before resolving into a high-pitched wail. Chills race down my spine as the temperature in the tiny room plummets.

It's like I'm outside during a Chicago winter without a coat, my hand a block of ice under the running water as my breath fogs the mirror.

I've been waiting for you, my kin.

I shriek and flail, blood flying in an arc, splattering the floor and bathroom stalls. When I spin around, the broken skull from earlier floats in front of me—except it's different from when it last appeared. Flesh now hangs on sunken cheeks, the forehead, gaping red and brown. A centipede crawls from the nose through the open, bruised mouth with yellowed teeth. Maggots squirm in one cheek. Only the golden eye in the center of the forehead remains untouched, glowing.

I scream.

I fall to my knees.

The room blurs and spins, centering on that shining light.

When my world comes back into focus, I'm frozen in a field, a clay city in the background. A bonfire dances in the center of a crowd, but no heat reaches me. A tall figure steps onto a pedestal, wearing a dark dress patterned like fish scales, the white collar flaring with triangular rays like a sun. They lift their arms in a noiseless chant, and the dagger in one of their hands glints before plunging down—into their left eye. Blood spurts down their face as they scream soundlessly, lifting the dagger back up with an eyeball skewered through the end of the blade, the optic nerve resisting its pull. With a fierce yank, the nerve snaps, flopping onto the bleeding cheek like a fish out of water. Blood darkens the sun collar as the eye is raised for all to see, then thrown in the fire.

I stagger back and bump into the rigid porcelain of the bathroom sinks, and my vision clears. I'm half panting, half squeaking, my hand clutched to my own eye as blood winds its way down my wrist. For a moment, my fingers meet an empty cavern—but no, I'm imagining it. There's my eye, whole and intact. The smell of smoke is thick in my nostrils, and the taste of ash is heavy on my tongue, laced with the copper tang of blood.

My legs take me to a stall, and I vomit the little I've eaten today. The bathroom is no longer freezing, but cold sweat breaks out on the small of my back. What is happening to me? Am I experiencing psychosis? Has Hudson drugged me? Is it worth staying and risking another episode of whatever this is?

Or else do what, go home and have my mom freak out at me? Yeah, right.

When I crawl back out, the skull is nowhere to be seen.

THREE AND A HALF HOURS UNTIL THE BEGINNING

I'm in the exhibit room, and my body is breaking. I watch it happen in the ridiculous mirrors Hudson suggested I hang up for "stature comparison" between visitors and the remains.

Another hallucination for me, I guess. Oh boy.

First one wrist snaps, then the other, splinters jutting out like fish bones. Then each shoulder unhinges, arms rotating up and around. I've become a doll with too many joints. One knee bends to the side, then the other, femurs twisting in their sockets until each leg faces backward. The pain should be astronomical, but I feel like I'm floating in water. A lightness I've never experienced that has nothing to do with my weight.

Finally, the spine—my spine—flexes up until it tears along the fault lines and shoves the—no, my—ribs through my skin, the snapped curves protruding through my chest. Blood fountains over my body, splashing the mirrors. My guts are tight under my skin but eager for escape, intestines pulsing and writhing, longing to spill out and smear viscera on the beige tile floor. It tickles, the only sensation besides floating.

What's happening to me? Am I going to be stuck like this forever? How am I alive? Disgust wars with fear.

In the mirror, I look like something from that "humans getting fused together" movie I refuse to watch. My hands support my body like I'm doing the most fucked-up gymnast bridge pose: brokenly quadrupedal with my knees facing backward, my head upside down as the gaping maw of my torso drools and my ribs jut out like fangs.

The grotesque, naked shape I've become should rip a guttural scream from me. But it doesn't.

A part of me is curious. My lips curve into a smile.

Crablike, my body shuttles one way, then the next, lost in its transformation. It is nothing like walking or crawling; it's an awkward flailing of limbs smearing red in my wake. Slipping, I collide into an exhibit stand, sending it crashing to the floor. Glass shatters, and as I scuttle away, I smack into another stand, which careens. This time, it's easier to steady myself.

I should care about the destruction, but instead, I'm hyperfocused on settling into a rhythm.

It feels *good* to move like this.

For so much of my life, my body has been a meat cage. A thing that defines me but that I have little control over shaping. But now,

now, my jiggling thighs bounce free instead of being constricted in jeans. My joints have no trouble hoisting me aloft, even though I've never been flexible enough to try a position like a bridge. My spilling belly barely holds in my guts even as my ribs reveal the cavern of my heart.

This feels freeing. This feels *right*.

Blood of my blood. I awaken, booms a voice, a resonant gong.

An eye, reddish-brown turning black from being buried for five thousand years, floats above me and multiplies, doubling, tripling, quadrupling in the mirrors. It pales into a golden color as bleached bone bubbles out of thin air around it, centering the eye in the middle of a forehead as a skull assembles. Like a bad PowerPoint transition, vertebrae fade into view and stack together, clicking into place, followed by the other bones. Then come bundles of nerves, a thin webbing of vessels; then ropy red muscles layer over the arms, the legs, the hollows of the cheeks. The skinless body suspends itself against the ceiling, looking down at me as I gape at the unmoving heart suspended inside the ribs, where no flesh hides it.

The skull rotates 360 degrees before spinning back in record speed like a windup top. The golden eye fixes on me.

Like recognizes like, says the voice. **I see you, child of my blood. I see you as you are meant to be seen.**

The distorted words flex the bulging veins in my disjointed hands. My hair, hanging limp, rustles.

Neither man nor woman, child nor full grown: you are the in-between and the both-and and the beyond. You are the past and present and future. You are the liminal space.

The ribs poking out from my skin move with my breath, twitching with each heartbeat. I allow the garbled words to run through my mind, until slowly, the speech resolves into modern Farsi—not exactly what was spoken in Eastern Iran five thousand years ago. Even the words I don't know in Farsi are clear in their meanings.

And when I comprehend the message, I want to laugh until I scream. Shocker, of course I've invented someone—the only someone—who knows my truth! A thing I rarely allow myself to confront. Wherever it came from, I'm grateful for my ability; it keeps me safe. I don't have to hear my parents tell me it's an issue of a full stomach or that I'm confused. I want to give them the benefit of the doubt, but I also don't know how to even begin the conversation when it's centered around *me*.

The cyclops eye roams over me. From the skeleton's back, black legs unspool, spider limbs as thick as my arm and covered in fine, twitching hairs. The legs descend toward me, and I scream for real, my wayward organs vibrating with its force.

If I could run away—if I believed in prayer—if I were a good Muslim (whatever that means)—

And then my body lifts, chest up. I droop, arms and legs dangling, and my vision goes white.

Your body does not know yet how to take its shape, explains the skeletal remains from the Burnt City. *This may cause you pain.*

Fire lances through my torso. I struggle, but my body flops uselessly. Whereas turning crablike had been painless, the stabbing agony of crunching bones now makes me howl, like the time I dislocated my shoulder, except now, my shoulders—rotating back; my knees, twisting forward—aren't the only things that hurt. I am such a nightmarish ball of sensation that I don't know where it begins and

I end, or vice versa, and is this how I die, with the giant person found with a prosthetic eye who maybe was a priest or maybe was a rich person or—

All at once, the fire burning through me extinguishes. My body steams and pants. Bones are no longer broken; skin has been reknit. I'm back to "normal."

But the mirrors remember. They're splattered with blood, smeared with viscera, a thick mucus pooling where I stood—lay?—moments before. The glass from the broken cases glitters like fallen confetti.

My body begins to shake. Someone is calling. **Farz. Farz. Farz. Farz.**

"**Farz**!" snaps the angry voice of Dr. James Hudson. "For heaven's sake, wake up!"

I startle. "Huh?"

I'm in the special exhibit room, draped over the case where Aiber had set up the skeletal remains—including the eye. My breath fogged the glass where my head lay, some drool classily left behind. And *blood*—blood smeared from my hand through the gauze.

Shit.

"This is *most* unprofessional," Hudson continues, flustered. "What on *earth* are you doing here? You're supposed to be finishing the labels, not taking a nap! And on the display case, of all places! Why is there blood everywhere? Good grief, **child**."

Was I . . . sleepwalking? A trail of blood stains the floor, leading from beyond the room's entrance and ending in a pool by my feet. My chest aches.

"—first aid kit in the bathrooms." Hudson's voice reels me back to reality. "Do not get blood on any of the labels, I implore you. Redo them if you must."

My hand is bleeding again. I stumble to the door and look over my shoulder.

The eye stares back at me.

TWO HOURS UNTIL THE BEGINNING

"I'm sorry, Baba, I had my phone off since the battery is almost dead." I barely contain my sigh as I cradle my phone between my shoulder and ear and pace. I finally turned on my phone when I saw how late it's gotten and was greeted with fifteen missed calls, seven voicemails, and thirty-two texts from both my parents.

They probably thought I'd been murdered. I should have known my *gonna be late* text hours ago wasn't going to cut it. Nice going, asshole.

"Dr. Hudson gave me a lot of work," I cut in when my father takes a breath mid-lecture. "And—"

And then I started hearing voices and seeing a disembodied skeleton and watching my body break itself from the inside out to free the *real* me.

I called Baba instead of Maman because his lectures are way less intense than Maman's rants. But now I sort of wish I'd sent another text and turned my phone back off.

"I'm sorry, Baba," I manage again, and something in my voice takes him off guard, because he doesn't respond for a long moment.

Then he sighs. "*How long will you take?*" he asks in Farsi, which is a good sign because my parents always lecture me in English to "make sure you understand."

"A couple hours at most," I say. A hopeful estimate. "I just need to finish setting up the room."

Another pause, then: "*All right. Two hours, and we'll come get you even if you're not done. Bacheh-ye-man, please don't scare us like that again.*"

I hang up knowing I'm the worst kid in the world.

Unsurprisingly, my feet have led me to the exhibit room during my call. Blood still stains the exhibit case and floor; I run downstairs and bring up the janitorial cart via the elevator to clean up.

It's not until I start wiping the glass of the remains case that my vision blurs, a sudden headache roaring to life. I drop the spray bottle and clutch my forehead, the pulses sharp—until they abruptly stop.

When I look up, I'm back in the field from earlier, another bonfire blazing. This time, the person in the scaly dress, whose left eye is now wrapped in bandages, no longer holds a dagger. Instead, they watch as someone else throws a bound and gagged person atop the fire; the figure wriggles like a worm as they burn.

There are others wrapped and piled, forced to be next.

A sacrifice, willingly given, was once my price, says the luminous voice from before—tied to the remains of the same person I see before me. *When the Seer sacrificed their eye, they gained my voice for a time, on condition of their willing death after. But their leaders, greedy for eternal prophecies and futures, used the lives of their captured enemies to desecrate the ritual and shackle my spirit to the Seer's body.*

Though no sound reaches me, I see the crowd cheer with each new victim. The one-eyed Seer looks afraid.

I know I'm not really here. My lack of smell or taste or anything other than vision, like I'm watching a silent movie in a sensory-deprivation tank, tells me I'm not. But I still shake. "Who are you?" I croak.

Some called me the voice of our creator, a manifestation of the power of our deities. I was the mouthpiece of the divine.

My temples pulse; my body fever-aches. "What should I call you, then?"

To be named is to submit. My name is the vastness of the waters of chaos. My name is the height of the Tree of All Seeds. My name is the cosmic mountain that reaches out of this sphere and into the next. A pause, then: *That is to say, should you wish to bestow upon me a name of your choice, I will accept it as a proxy.*

A stand-in name. How does one encapsulate an idea? I catalog the little I know of the person found in the Burnt City, and my chest flares hot—not with pain, but with righteous fury.

"Dr. Hudson thinks your Seer was an Elamite priestess"—I sneer the words—"despite there being no indication that they identified as a woman. So I guess a good name would flip that off. I mean, Farsi doesn't even have gendered pronouns."

Oh. Of course. *Ou* makes sense as a pronoun for the skeleton. A commonality in ancestry. A commonality in tongue.

Womanhood or manhood is beyond the likes of me. Another person is thrown on the pyre. The crowd silently sings its bloodlust. *As it is beyond the likes of you, my kin.*

I flinch.

There is no shame in who and what you are. Do your people not celebrate your unbridled potential?

"No one knows," I whisper, my throat dry. The fire is larger now. How could a disembodied voice see my truth before anyone else in my life? It's almost unfair. It's almost painful that an ancient spirit understands when my own family doesn't. "I . . . don't know how they'd react. I mean, I don't think my parents would disown me or anything. My guess is they'll dismiss it. It's just . . . easier not to tell anyone."

Yet there is more to this, I think. Do you feel at home in your body?

At home in my body?

I consider the way my stomach muffins over my jeans, the flaps under my arms. The hair coating my belly and chest. My stubby fingers and how the bones of my big toes poke out like bunions, like Baba's. My body doesn't bother me, not exactly. What bothers me is how caged I feel. But human bodies aren't made to be expansive. Human bodies are made to be simple and symmetrical, not monstrous.

I'm bound in flesh, and I wish I could break through my skin—grow tall to survey a space for safety or extra arms to swoop all the groceries and Maman's gigantor purse at the same time. Be able to pluck my musician dad's daf and setar and tombak and ney with delicate spindle fingers. Empty out the abandoned lab next to the one my mom has to share with three colleagues so she can move into it, finally ridding it of unused centrifuges and disconnected fume hoods and broken freezers and incubators.

"I don't know." The last victim is tossed on the flames, and bile surges in the back of my throat. "I have to think about it." I hug myself. "So they killed their enemies instead of allowing your host to sacrifice themself, and that kept you caged. You're . . . not human, are you?"

I am beyond such designations. Ou gives a haughty sniff. *But I have been bound to these bones for millennia, and such time has eroded the distinction between human and non. My spirit was meant to be freed in that final sacrifice willingly given. Those were the terms of our bond that were not honored—and so the Seer passed into the hereafter, and I remained.*

"The modern Farsi word for freedom is *aazaadi,*" I say. "I could call you Aazaad—free." Not much of a name, and I'm sure Dr. Hudson would have some thoughts on diasporic linguistic liberties, but it's something.

Preparing myself—for ou's disappointment, perhaps, or lest there be more gore awaiting me—I turn. But behind me isn't a stretch of field, the towering city, but instead, the empty exhibit room. I look back to the case, and that eye—the eye made of tar and animal fat that only I seem to see whenever its focus moves—swivels its golden light and stares straight at me.

That is a profound wish upon me. I thank you for it, blood of my blood.

Oh. That's relief I feel, isn't it? That, for once, I've done something right?

"You can call me *Farz.*" I haven't spoken my real name aloud to anyone. Its weight feels right on my tongue. "That's *fe, re, ze.* Although I guess you didn't use those letters in—" I blank what to use here and switch to English. "Elamite, if that's what you spoke. How are you understanding me right now, anyway?"

Blood ties transcend language. Hello, Farz.

I've never heard someone else speak my name.

In another context, I would object to equating blood and family. But in this case, because *blood* could refer to our shared culture or our shared language or other similarities—in this case, I'm okay with being claimed in this way.

When I daydreamed about coming out, I never thought it would be to someone outside my parents or friends. And I never thought it would be to someone who is beyond being a someone or something. Tears prick my eyes, and I bat them away, even though what I really want is a hug.

Someone *sees me.*

I place my bandaged hand on the case, near where the skull sits. This time, it does not bleed through. "It's nice to meet you, Aazaad."

TWENTY-SEVEN MINUTES UNTIL THE BEGINNING

After sunset, a spring storm pounds on the high-up courtyard-facing windows as I finally, *finally,* finish setting up the exhibit. Aazaad kept me company with quiet observations, but mostly allowed me my silence. Now I survey my handiwork: pottery, including what we're calling an early form of animation; scraps of clothing; an early backgammon set. I can't help but feel a surge of pride that my ancestors created this.

Dr. Hudson sweeps in, Dr. Aiber on his heels. Aiber whistles, looking around the room. "Well done, **Farz**," he says. "James has taught you well."

Dr. Hudson hasn't taught me jack shit.

"**Farz's** work does add a layer of authenticity to the whole thing, doesn't it?" says Hudson, his chest puffed. "Our goal, after all, was to honor our Persian brethren."

Oh, so bringing me in last minute to do the bitch work adds *authenticity* and *honors* my people, huh?

"We'll be sure to mention your contribution to the investors," adds Aiber, clapping me on the shoulder. "Well, I'd better head home before the missus gets angry." He chortles. "Good night, James, **Farz**."

Aiber's footsteps fade. Hudson says, "A word, **Farz**, before you leave for the evening."

To remain calm, I press my fingers to my wrist and count my heartbeats. Just a few more minutes.

"I've been mulling over our earlier conversation, when you insisted that a widened pelvis may not correspond to womanhood." Oh, great. "In my extensive work on Persia"—oh, great times two, we're back to being *Persia* again—"there is no indication of such an idea. Nor have my colleagues encountered evidence to suggest our modern understanding of"—his lip curls—"*gender* applies to such ancient peoples."

Lightning cracks across the sky in the window behind him.

"Projecting such *agendas* onto the past is not only a fallacy but also intense hubris on your part," he continues, as if he hasn't made me three inches tall. "And, furthermore, it's unbecoming of an archeologist. You have brought these objections up before, and your spirited defense has long felt personal. Being unable to separate your emotional state from academic work leads to messy scholarship."

Thunder clamors belatedly. My breath shallows, trapped in my chest. "But how can you separate scholarship from lived—"

"And that," he interrupts, "is precisely why I cannot in good faith write you a letter of recommendation for the Smithsonian. I am sorry, but this situation feels for you, **Farz**, an expression of your own . . . questions and insecurities. What is it called nowadays, transvestites?"

It starts slowly, so slowly, and then all at once: rage envelops me. The way he looks at me as he spits a slur, as if his colonizing impulse, his academic knowledge, is superior to centuries of my people's history in inherited memory. As if it's unusual to think that transness has taken different forms across cultures with different degrees of acceptance over time. As if he's justified in using my identity to excuse barring me from my future.

I tremble from head to toe, clutching the keys to the exhibit cases. Wait, when did I pick the keys back up?

Foolish, arrogant human, sneers Aazaad in my head. *How fortunate for him that my true powers lay dormant as long as I do not have a human host.*

What does . . . ? I want to clear my throat, but I'm not speaking aloud. *What does having a host mean for the human? Do they always have to die?*

The eye, sitting on its purple cushion, spins its golden gaze my way. *It unlocks your potential. I will not lie: There will be unfathomable pain as your body adjusts. You must expand yourself to become vast enough to hold me. But that is enough—from you. You do not ask for my voice, so I am happy to take another to fuel our joining. Five thousand years is a long time without . . . sustenance.*

Sacrifices willingly, and unwillingly, given.

I raise my chin to meet Hudson's smirk.

In the dream, my body had tried to uncage itself but couldn't go all the way, forced back into the form I know. Aazaad, I named ou, but really, I wished that for myself.

Rain pelts the windows as more lightning snakes across the sky. My resolve hardens. Ou feels it. *First, what binds us; then, my eye.*

What binds us?

Oh.

Before I can doubt myself, before I can talk myself out of this, I unwrap my hand and tug. Gauze glued by clotted blood rips open my broken flesh. Dr. Hudson splutters, but I unlock the glass case and shove my bloodied hand inside. Ignoring Hudson's shrieks, I grab the eye.

Hudson leaps back and shouts as the glass enclosure explodes.

Ah, at last . . . thank you.

Golden light washes over me.

Free yourself, my blood. Become who you were meant to be.

My body shifts.

My back itches and itches and itches as something wiry runs over my shoulder blades before it releases, the way pus erupts from a wound. First one bony branch unfurls, then another, then a third, and a fourth, and finally, my shoulders open wide as if my back has been cracked for the first time.

A pimple blooms in the center of my forehead, the skin growing taut until it bursts open with a wet *sploosh*. Liquid oozes down my face as extrasensory information floods through me—an awareness of heat, of motion, of the air shifting. The edges of my skin are peeled back and raw to the touch when I finger the writhing wound's perimeter before easing the eye, convex side out, into its place of honor. It settles onto its fleshy throne with a *squelch*.

Sharp pain lances through my legs and arms, then my pelvis, then my chest. The ground falls away as my growing legs shoot my torso to the ceiling. I can feel every bone in my body break as I encompass the space in the room.

I look into the mirrors Hudson insisted I set up. They cannot capture my full monstrousness, and I twist to see every angle they obscure. Extra spider legs and bat wings and giant arms throbbing with muscles. I do not need to see the eye shining in the center of my forehead to know this hybrid creature I've become is the embodiment of power. Of freedom.

Now there's a transformation worthy of gods.

I can feel Hudson's miasma. Gingerly stretching two of my new legs, I reach over and pluck him up from where he cowers on the floor. He squeals and demands to be put down. Entitled, even now.

I dangle him, holding his calf with the careful consideration of a scholar. His face, pale and horrified, stares back at me.

"Norooz pirooz, Dr. Hudson," I say, my voice transformed into a deep rumble, a spidery whisper, the growl of a monster in the dark.

First, I tear off his small human arm. His screams pierce the air as thunder booms in the distance. Blood squirts from his shoulder as excess flesh dangles from the ends, and I slurp the arm like I would marrow. The blood is warm and fresh in my mouth, and Aazaad sighs in relief as I crunch phalanges and chew on muscle fibers.

Hudson wails, flailing his remaining limbs in my grasp. His face is sheet white. "Please, let me go, let me *live*—"

Try the thigh next, Aazaad suggests, so I grip the knee and jerk it outward as I might a chicken leg. Hudson weeps, begging for mercy, howling with each tug as I wiggle and eventually rip open his skin like a banana peel. The consistency is like beef, but it doesn't taste like beef—kind of like veal? A little stringy, a little tough, but a meaty kind of tough to sink my many teeth into.

Hudson's whimpering now, his body slack, beyond shock. He'll pass out from blood loss soon. I'm more preoccupied with the bitter aftertaste in the back of my throat and the tender flesh of the buttocks, the sweet melt of the ribs. Is this what pork tastes like?

The blood flowing from his limb stumps has slowed; he is no longer responsive. I raise his body and allow the blood to drip down my mouth, onto my face, into the stringy remains of my hair, tart like warm tomato juice.

The vibrations from oncoming steps hit me as Aazaad says, *Someone approaches.*

Hudson's half-eaten remains drop to the floor. Despite my bulk, my wings beat once to lift me, and my beautiful spindle legs twirl my body around before rearing up, poised to strike. If it's Aiber, he should have come back tomorrow.

The figures at the glass door are familiar. Before Aazaad can attack with our shared body, my parents step into the room.

My parents look from the monster I've become, to the blood splattered everywhere, to the remains of James P. Hudson, PhD. Their brown faces pale into an unhealthy sheen.

I completely forgot Baba said they'd pick me up.

Are their expressions of shock and fear because of *me*?

My mother swallows and steps forward. "**Farz**?" Her whisper is unsteady.

My body contracts. My back rends itself as the spider legs retract. My arms shrink back to their normal sizes, and my extra ones retreat with my wings. My legs shrivel until I'm just me again, normal Farz, covered in blood—on my mouth, on my hands, down my chest, in my hair. I can smell it like someone smells dog shit or vomit or the carcass of the supervisor they just ate. I want to regurgitate everything, but Aazaad has already absorbed the meal as the sacrifice for our binding.

I tremble. The transformation shredded my clothes; I stand naked before my parents, and that, more than anything, fills me with shame.

"**Farz**-joon," whispers my mother, her steps hesitant and careful as she moves toward me. She takes off her coat as she does, swallowing as she puts it over my shoulders without touching me. "Azizam, what happened?"

Baba's lips move in what is probably quiet prayer as he looks up to the ceiling. I put on Maman's coat, and at the sound of the zipper closing, Baba drops his gaze to me. I can't tell if he looks afraid or disgusted, but he surprises me when he says, "You didn't pick up your phone again. We got worried."

"We were supposed to make reshteh polo and koofteh ghel-gheli." Maman sounds on the brink of tears, unsure and untethered. I did that to her—me, her only kid, whom she and my dad have sacrificed so much for as immigrants. But carefully, so carefully, she brushes back a strand of my blood-matted hair. "Are you okay?"

Am I okay? Inside me, Aazaad purrs and curls up like a cat, satiated. But is the danger gone?

My mom keeps her attention on my face. My dad steps toward us, a paper towel in hand from the janitorial cart outside the door. She takes it without looking and begins to dab at my cheeks.

I want to explain, but my voice catches in my throat. How do I explain to my parents that I entered a pact with a millennia-old spirit to transform into a monster and eat my racist colonizing professor-boss?

Baba brings the cart inside and lifts the mop from the grimy water from my earlier cleaning. He drops it onto the ground with a heavy thud. The blood, not yet settled, stains pink. He makes a wide berth around the corpse in the middle of the floor.

I try again to speak but fail. My mom licks her finger and smears it against my nose. She tsks. "Where's the bathroom?"

I numbly half follow, half lead her downstairs, where she washes my face. She gets paper towel after paper towel and rinses my hands, my arms, the inside of her coat I've bloodied but which she puts back on me once I'm wiped. She doesn't bother with my legs, but once we're done, she does take more paper towels up to my father, whose bucket of dirty water is now a filthy gray-brown.

The room looks as spotless as it did an hour ago. The glass from the broken exhibit case has been swept up, and that missing cover is the only sign that anything happened here. Wiped clean, the eye lies nestled on its pillow, placed beside the remains. The body of James P. Hudson is nowhere to be seen—I don't want to know how Baba got rid of it.

The results of what I've done bowl me over. I whimper, cover my mouth. My mother wraps her arms around me as Baba chokes out, "God forgive me, but you're my **child**."

TWENTY SECONDS UNTIL THE BEGINNING

"I'm not," I blurt. It tumbles out of me, and I let it free. "I'm—I'm not a—I'm just your child. I'm transgender. I'm nonbinary. I'm not a boy or a girl. I'm just . . . *me*."

Maman cradles me—without fear or repulsion. "We know." I stiffen, but she doesn't let go. "We saw you researching it on the computer but weren't sure how to talk to you about it. It's okay, azizam. It's okay."

My kin, Aazaad's voice purrs, *they accept you.*

Despite the tears streaming down my face, I smile.

THE BEGINNING

WASPS

MARK OSHIRO

It's freezing in the basement, and Nina's heart churns with hatred.

She sweeps the glass off the concrete floor. Picks up the pieces of the broken table from beneath the window. Tucks the sledgehammer into a corner. Stands in front of the boiler and frowns. She knows it is busted, even though she doesn't know how these things work. But the pipes shouldn't be bent like that, and the temperature in the house . . . that's the other sign. It's the middle of winter in Brooklyn, precisely the worst time for their heat to go out.

But she does the best she can, all while her head throbs and the pain radiates. She glances down at her hand, at the makeshift bandage she's wrapped around it, at the red that's slowly leaking through.

She did the best she could.

But it's still so cold down here.

She is so damned tired of this.

When the front door creaks open, Nina shivers and curls up further into the large cobija, wishing her headache would go away—along with the dread that's as thick and heavy as her cobija. She has to tell Mami about the basement, but she doesn't want to. Doesn't want Mami to bear any more of this burden. The anger beneath Nina's skin flares again.

Mami curses loudly. "Ay, mija, ¿que pasó?" she asks, hugging herself, her breath spilling out like smoke. "Why is it so cold?"

The throbbing in Nina's hand gets worse. "The boiler is busted," she says, emerging from her cocoon of denial.

Her head spins as her mami curses again. She can't just leave it at that, even though she wants to.

"And . . . someone got into the basement. Broke the window and everything."

Mami stills. Then closes her eyes, tilts her head back, and utters a prayer in Spanish. She drops the black duffel she takes to the hospital for every shift and leans against the wall. "Did Hopkins already see it?"

Nina knew this was what Mami would ask first. Not what was damaged. Not if anything was stolen. Not even the barest acknowledgment of the misery they have to experience over the coming days as they live without heat until the boiler can be repaired.

Him. Again. Hopkins.

The very name sends another bout of rage boiling through Nina.

Hopkins, the man who wants to steal their home from them.

"He hasn't," says Nina, brushing aside the cobija and standing. "I took care of it already."

Mami glances at the door to the basement.

"Well . . . not *all* of it," Nina adds, her heart fluttering. "The boiler is still busted. But there's nothing *else* you need to worry about right now."

She stuffs her hands in the big pocket of her hoodie and crosses to Mami.

Her mami pulls her in tight. "I'm sorry you had to deal with that," she says. "Ugh, why is there always *something* happening here?"

Nina can't help but groan. "You *know* why."

Mami rears back slightly. "Don't talk about tu abuela como así."

"Not *her*," Nina says, scowling. "Hopkins!"

Mami deflates. "Oh. You think it was him?"

The pain spikes. "No, I don't. I think it was Tim."

Mami is silent for a moment, and Nina watches the ire grow on her face.

"If it's not one," Mami says, "it's the other."

"I know," says Nina.

She isn't sure if she hates Hopkins or his son, Tim, more. Despite being over twice her age, Tim doesn't seem to have much of a life aside from harassing women in the neighborhood or being his father's attack dog. His most recent favorite pastime was getting drunk outside the Ortiz home and singing loudly at their front stoop. Didn't matter how many times the police were called; he was always only issued a warning. Or his father bought or swindled him out of whatever mess he'd gotten in.

"Do you have any proof it was Tim?"

"No," she says. "But I *know* it was him."

"Nina, this will be over soon," Mami says, her face falling. "In the meantime, we just have to keep our heads down. Follow the rules. We can't give that man any more ammunition."

"But this isn't *fair*," Nina groans. "None of it is."

"I know, mi amor." Mami brushes a strand of hair out of Nina's face. "You doing okay? You look exhausted."

There is a burst of nervous energy in her chest, but she just smiles after tucking her hand deeper into the front pocket of her hoodie. "Yes, Mami. Just a headache. Please go rest. I'll patch up the window."

Mami tries to argue, but Nina guides her toward the stairs. Insists she has it all handled. Assures Mami they'll eat dinner together and discuss what to do next once she's awake. Nina watches Mami ascend the stairs and disappear into her bedroom, the one above Nina's. It still has the complicated moldings along the edges. The original bay windows. The wooden tile floors.

Nina runs her hand up and down on the banister made of iron and curled in delicate patterns along the support beams. She can hear her mami settling into bed upstairs, but as silence falls, she strains to listen.

The home around her creaks a few times. Probably just from the growing cold or Mami's footsteps upstairs. But Nina wonders if this is an acknowledgment, a thankful home desperate to let its occupants know that it is safe. Safe because of *her.*

Nina smiles. "You're welcome," she says softly.

She feels the throbbing pain again.

And she heads down into the basement to clean up the last of the mess.

The basement is always kept pristine. It is, like the rest of their home, a place of reverence. Comfort. And—normally—one of warmth, especially in the brutal Brooklyn winters. Nina cleaned the basement as best she could, but the boiler pipes are still warped like broken limbs. She grabs a broom to sweep up the debris from the broken table, and the light catches more bits of glass she missed earlier.

The dam in her mind nearly breaks.

All this is so unfair. She just wants Hopkins and Tim to leave her family and their home *alone.* What could Nina and Mami have possibly done to deserve this?

Nina's anger is still there, just beneath her skin, simmering.

She's piled the broken table in one corner, knowing she'll have to take it out tomorrow night after the snowfall so that it can be picked up Monday morning. The window . . . that one is harder. She thinks to break down the ruined table to barricade the busted window and prevent all the cold air from rushing into the basement, but then she realizes they don't have the tools for that, nor is it going to be easy for her to hoist something so heavy up there. She tucks her injured hand against her body. She hadn't thought this part through.

It's getting colder. Snowfall is imminent. *Damn it,* she thinks. *It's going to get in the basement, isn't it?*

Nina hears him before she sees him.

His boots scuff on the cement outside in the alleyway. It's absurd to her that she can recognize a specific person's footfall, but this is what Hopkins does. He drags his feet as he shuffles around outside their home. He's inspecting. Looking for things to report. Loopholes to exploit.

He's done this every day since he tricked abuela. Abuela Carmen, who is laid up in a hospital in downtown Brooklyn while the doctors try to save her body from itself. The same hospital that can't explain how Hopkins was allowed access to her room, where he shoved papers in front of her and swore her mortgage problems would be over if she just signed them, and now? Now he's claiming the property deed is in his name. It's why Mami is always gone; she's torn between visiting Abuela and overtime at her nursing gig to fund the legal nightmare Hopkins has thrust upon them.

He says their home is his.

It's not. It won't *ever* be.

It *can't* be.

She backs away from the window as his shadow extends toward it. She doesn't want to talk to him today; she isn't sure she can be who her mami needs her to be. Polite. Law-abiding. Small. But the stairs are too far, so she hides behind the shelf and the altar, then peeks around them.

His shadow grows. His feet shuffle against the ground.

She sees one of his boots through the opening. Then, to her horror, he kneels, pressing his face against the cement, and peers into the basement. She catches a glimpse of his reddened face, beady eyes, and rounded nose before she ducks out of view.

"Tim?" he calls out. "Tim, are you down there?"

Nina clamps a hand over her mouth.

"Tim . . . just answer me," he hisses through the shattered window. "*Please*."

She inches backward, and her shoe scrapes against the cement flooring.

Shit, shit, shit.

"I can see you, little girl."

Her heart drops to her feet. She doesn't move an inch.

"You took him, didn't you?" He grunts loudly. "You have my boy."

Nina rises, and his body is blocking nearly all the sunlight from the opening. He reaches in through it and points a gnarled finger her way.

"I know what you did!" he screams. "Where's my boy?"

"Nowhere!" she shouts back. "What are you even *talking* about?"

"He came over here this morning and never came back!" Hopkins growls. "You did something to him!"

"Please, just *go away,*" Nina cries.

The man reaches in through the window, then waves his arm about as if he's trying to snatch her up.

The anger pushes her forward, and she grabs one of the legs from the smashed table with her working hand and bats Hopkins's hand away with it. "Get out of our house!"

He yanks his arm back. Twists his face in rage. "How *dare* you!" he screams. "That's assault! You assaulted me!"

"Do you really wanna call the cops when *you* stuck *your* arm into *my* basement?"

He pauses. Then he pushes himself up. He kicks at the ground, and something flies through the window and lands on the basement floor. A crumpled-up fast-food bag. Trash.

"This is *my* home," he growls. "You people will see soon enough."

She listens to him shuffle away.

Her head pounds. The pain throbs.

She did the best she could.

Nina leaves the basement door open while she does homework.

It's a beautiful door. It's a deep-colored oak with vines etched into the surface, growing up toward the top of the frame. The Ortiz family has never considered changing it. All the homes around them, they're always being updated and renovated and modernized. Not theirs, though. They repair what is broken, but they leave what remains. It is an act of respect for this place and what it means to them.

Nina starts her history report from the couch, covered in her cobija and within sight of the basement. She stops to listen every so often, certain Hopkins will start shuffling around their property, but he doesn't make another appearance. She then moves to her bedroom to do assigned reading for biology, dragging the blanket behind her.

Her room is the smallest in the house, but it's warmer than the living room. She considers working from Abuela's upstairs bedroom—after all, heat travels upward, and it's surely better than this. But it doesn't feel right. Abuela's room is meant for her return, and Nina believes she'll mess up Abuela's healing if she violates that sanctity. Sometimes, when she lingers at the doorway, she can smell the sweet and earthy scents of Abuela, can imagine her tending to the plants spread around the room that Mami now waters until Abuela returns home from the hospital.

Nina keeps imagining her abuela home, healthy again, and fussing over her plants—and Nina—just like before, because an imagination has power in this family.

In her bedroom, Nina studies invasive species, like cane toads and water hyacinths and vesper mandarina, those terrifying murder hornets in Japan. She knows that these creatures are just trying to survive and that she shouldn't moralize them, but she can't help it. Why can't they just stay where they belong? Why must they always crave more and more?

Her mind drifts, and she gazes up, tracing the patterns in the room's molding with her eyes. She loves the high ceilings and the light-yellow paint on the walls, the markings in the closet that show how Nina has grown over the years. She remembers the faded smoke stains on the ceiling in the kitchen, from when Mami burned the pork roast on Christmas, that are now behind layers of paint.

Nina grew up here. Mami grew up here. Abuela grew up here, as did her mami before her. This home has belonged to the Ortiz family for a long, long time. It is theirs for a reason.

Hopkins is an invasive species. Yes. But what truly infuriates Nina is the greed.

He lives next door at 250 Tompkins in an ugly modernized brownstone that looks like it was modeled after something in *Gentrification Monthly*. But he also owns 246 Tompkins on the other side of the Ortiz family home. The Johnsons used to live there. Nina wasn't ever close to them, but one of the moms—Regina—was Mami's close friend. They're out in Canarsie now, which means it takes two trains and a long, unreliable bus ride to see them. Mami has only managed to visit them once since they were forced out.

Two doors down, at 252 Tompkins, was a Haitian family who occupied the top floor. Nina had a crush on the youngest one, Phara, but they also had to move. Nina never even built up the courage to say anything, and now they're gone. Hopkins pushed them out, too.

Nina's childhood friend, Victor Cardenas, was in a basement apartment at 276 Tompkins with his papi, at least until that big storm last year flooded lots of New York. They begged their landlord to fix the windows and the ceiling and the sagging walls, but no one listened. And then Hopkins swooped in. Bought the place right out from under the previous landlord and promptly evicted everyone. Claimed the building was a "hazard," which legally meant no one could fight it. Now Victor and his family live halfway across Brooklyn.

Hopkins has fourteen buildings.

The Ortiz family has one.

Why does he need another? Why isn't one home good enough for him?

When will he stop?

Why can't he leave them *alone*?

Nina hears Mami making noise upstairs and stirs; she nearly dozed off. She puts aside her biology book and rises from her bed. Stretches.

Makes a quick stop to the bathroom to change the bandage, then spends too long staring at the bloody mess underneath. She cleans the wound, bandages it again, then heads into the kitchen to make something for Mami to eat. The ache is back behind her eyes, and she wishes it would go away. There's still a broken window in the basement, and Nina has no solution.

Her heart leaps. She has to tell Mami about everything eventually, but for the moment, she can shove it all away. Hopkins isn't bothering them, and she'll figure something out before the snow falls. She did her best.

But then Mami comes rushing down the stairs as Nina is taking out a pot to reheat leftovers, and Nina's confidence withers. What if she *didn't* do her best? What if this is all a mistake? She turns and sets the pot down, then quickly hides her left hand behind her back.

It doesn't make sense: Mami is grabbing her puffy black coat.

"I'm sorry, mi amor," Mami says. "I have to head out again."

"¿Otra vez?" says Nina. "¿Por qué?"

"It's Abuela."

Now Nina's heart sinks to her feet. "What happened?"

Mami's mouth curls down, and Nina braces for the worst.

"I don't know," she says. "She says . . . she says she needs to come *home*."

"What?"

"I don't get it either," Mami says, shaking her head. "I just got a frantic call from her, and she says she needs to be here *now*."

"So she's fine?"

Mami gives her a disappointed gaze. "I spoke to her attending," she says, "and her treatment this week was harder on her than usual."

Ah. She's still dying.

Cancer. That rotten poison.

Nina nods. "Well, let me go get dressed."

"No."

Nina stills, and her mouth falls open a bit. "Why not?"

"You need to stay here, Nina."

"No!" she cries. "It's *Abuela*. I have to go, too."

"We can't both go," explains Mami. "Is the window fixed in the basement?"

She wants to crumple to the floor. "No. I was going to tape something over it. Maybe a garbage bag so the snow won't get in."

"I'm not worried about snow, mija. Someone has to make sure no one gets in there."

Nina groans. "It's only a few hours, Mami!"

"And that's all he needs," Mami snaps. "You know how Abuela is, Nina. Every time she goes in for treatment, she tries to find some way to leave. I am gonna do my best to convince her to stay, but I could be there all night if she's as stubborn as she usually is. We can't risk leaving this place unoccupied. You *know* what's at stake, mija." She zips up her coat. "Besides, National Grid will be here in the morning. At eight. And someone has to be here to let them in so we don't freeze our asses off."

"Mami, *please*," Nina says.

Mami pulls Nina into a hug. "Protege nuestro hogar," she whispers.

"You know I will," Nina mutters. "I'm just tired of doing this."

"And what's with this no-arm hug? Are you too embarrassed to hug your mami now?"

She flinches. Then she removes her hands from her pockets and embraces Mami for a few seconds.

Mami pulls away. "I need you to do your best to make sure *nothing* happens to this place. No matter what that man does, he cannot have what is ours."

"I know, Mami."

"This is ours."

"I *know*. So why can't we—?"

Mami raises a hand. "Don't even suggest it. I already know what you're going to say."

"What good is it protecting this place if we can't—?"

"By the rules!" Mami shouts.

Nina's skin prickles. "Okay," she says, her voice low.

Mami grimaces. "I'm sorry for yelling," she says. "It's just . . . there's too much to lose here. Not just this home, but *you*."

Nina tries to ignore the thrums of pain.

She tries to see things through Mami's eyes.

But all she feels is an unending, vicious river of rage.

The house that night—quiet and full of shadows—has never felt so empty before. Nina watches dark clouds rolling in over Bed-Stuy from the window in the living room. A ferocious storm's coming. The wind picks up, and the bones of the house whine from the forceful gusts.

God, she hates the winter.

It will get colder soon. More snow will fall upon what's left over from the week before, and she dreads all the shoveling they'll have to do. She already had to suffer in the cold to salt the sidewalks and walkway outside their building for the last half hour, most of it done with one hand. If she hadn't, Hopkins would have reported them.

That was his new thing: calling up any city agency that would listen to him and reporting the Ortiz home. Mami says the city isn't going to do anything—they're not breaking the law. But they still have to keep up with his nonsense because Mami is worried that any slipup can derail the court case for the deed to the home.

So, for these past few weeks, no mistakes have been allowed. Yet it feels like Hopkins finds a new thing to complain about or threaten them with every day: The way they store their recycling bins. How late they put their trash out. Who comes in and out of the building. How much noise they make.

Nina watches from the front window as Hopkins inspects the sidewalk. He gazes up at the house and yells at it. "You missed a spot!"

She does not answer. She only lets her anger grow.

He eventually shakes his head. Putters off back to his house next door.

In the kitchen, she takes out the leftovers she was going to give to Mami before she left. There's curtido and masa, so she assembles some pupusas with quesillo and frijoles, cleaning up as she goes, doing her best to ignore the mounting thrum in her hand. She eats in silence, thankful that Abuela taught her how to cook like this before she got too sick to stand for long periods of time. Nina pushes the burst of despondency away; her abuela is still alive. There is no sense panicking over what has not happened.

After washing her dishes and silverware, she heads down to the basement. Stretches a cut-up garbage over the broken window and tapes it down with duct tape, hoping the seal will stick overnight. Then she checks to make sure the basement door is locked. Once. Twice. Three times.

She brushes her teeth, tries to curl up in bed with her reading for English, but minutes later, she's standing in front of the entrance to the basement. Her cobija is draped over her shoulders and she's still as ice. She listens. Doesn't hear anything.

She raises her left hand and places it against the door. Even in the shadows, the red is obvious, glaring.

She changes the bandage again.

Nina ends up on the couch, the wind howling outside and the naked oak branches scratching on the side of the house. It still groans every so often.

"I know," she says to it. "We'll get through this."

Her eyes don't leave the basement door until the storm whips against her home, and then she's staring out the window, watching as snow flurries are flung about in the wind.

It's here.

Nina settles in.

She waits.

She doesn't recall drifting off to sleep.

She opens her eyes to light from the streetlamp pouring in the window across from the couch. She silently curses herself for not drawing the curtains. A lot of the white folks who have moved to this neighborhood—many of them tenants of Hopkins—have no curtains or blinds in their windows. She doesn't understand this.

Why would you want someone on the street to be able to see everything you own?

Abuela once told her that was the whole point.

Nina stares at the streetlamp's light. Her mind registers the window. The shadows. The dust in the air.

And then . . .

There's someone here.

She isn't sure at first. It looks like the outline of a tree, or maybe it's the streetlamp itself, but . . . no. There's a shape there. In the corner of the window, and it looks like—

She doesn't move. Doesn't breathe. Can't think.

She is still for an eternity.

And then it *moves*.

A person's head. They look in through the window, and Nina stares into the whites of their eyes. They place their hands against the glass.

The frame rattles.

Nina remains unmoving, her body frozen in terror. Do they see her? No. The couch is mostly tucked away in the shadows. But she still feels exposed. It's only a matter of time.

The person outside moves away from the window suddenly, leaving a painful, chilling silence behind. She realizes the storm died down sometime while she was asleep. Did she imagine all this? Is she dreaming? Her heart thumps in her chest, threatening to break out.

She hears scuffling outside. Then the crunch of boots on a sidewalk lined with salt.

Nina bolts upright and crawls over to the window. She lifts her head slowly until she's able to see out, hoping desperately she won't be spotted.

There's one man at the bottom of the stoop, bundled up in a puffy coat and a large beanie. His mere outline is unmistakable.

Hopkins huffs. Rubs his hands together. Turns back.

She ducks out of sight. *What is he doing?*

His footsteps on the sidewalk grow quieter. She hopes desperately that he is going home. But then she hears the echo of his steps in the alley between their properties, and it all comes back to her:

The window to the basement is on that side.

Nina curses and tries to find her phone. It's wrapped up in the cobija, and when she taps the screen, she sees a text from Mami. She's still at the hospital. Abuela is stable but argumentative. Nina glances at the time. It's just around midnight.

She tiptoes toward her room at the foot of the stairs. At the doorway, she freezes again.

There's a shadow over her window.

She moves to the side at first, then gazes up the stairs. Her mami's room. She can go there. Can film Hopkins if he tries anything. She makes quick work of the stairs, which thankfully do not creak, and then she's inside Mami's bedroom. Her scrubs are piled on the floor next to the bed, rather than thrown inside a hamper. Mami must have been too exhausted. Nina makes her way over to the window and peels the curtain aside.

Hopkins's beanie bobs up and down below her. She raises her phone, opens the camera, and is dismayed when there's a terrible glare caused by the glass. It makes it impossible to film him.

He gets on his hands and knees at the broken window.

She tries not to panic, tries not to let the unbearable fury push her to do something foolish. She gently places her phone on the windowsill, then grips the small indentations at the bottom of the frame. The window doesn't budge, and her hand screams at her to stop. Shit. It's locked. She flips the locks open with aching slowness, terrified she might be making too much noise, but as she inches the window up, she can hear Hopkins grunting below.

The frigid air hits her and washes into the room. Her shiver is instantaneous. But she doesn't stop. Nina grabs her phone and holds the lens over the edge of the sill while she looks at the screen.

Hopkins lies prone on the cement below, his head out of sight and . . . damn it. *He's in the basement.* She watches as he squirms back slowly, and then she hits RECORD. This is it: evidence that Hopkins is the one breaking the law, not them.

He grunts again. Then he whispers harshly, "Tim? Tim, you in there?"

Nina knows he is not going to find his son down there.

He scoots farther into the Ortiz basement. She sticks her phone out more, grateful for the bright security light at the end of the alley. What she's capturing on camera . . . it's damning. She knows it. Her nerves flutter at the thought of getting to show this to Mami. They aren't the kind of family who calls the police, but even Nina can't deny how satisfying it would be to see Hopkins arrested. Maybe they can use this to get the deed challenge dismissed.

There are so many possibilities, and she is drunk on them.

He swears. Lurches back out of the basement and tries to go in feetfirst. Yanks his legs out of the basement, swears again.

Then he looks up.

He sees her.

Hopkins narrows his eyes and sits up, and she frantically pulls the phone back, but her bandaged hand is clumsy, misshapen, and the phone tumbles out the window.

And lands on Hopkins's chest.

It bounces. Clatters on the cement next to his body.

She scrambles back. Maybe she imagined that he saw her, but—

"Where is Tim?" he screams. "I saw you, you little rat. Where is he?"

No. No, no, no! She had him! How could she have messed this up so badly?

Mr. Hopkins is still shouting, but she pushes herself up with her right hand, then darts down the stairs, just in time to see the shadow cross over the window in her own room. She slows, then waits. Listens.

She thinks she hears the man's boots on the salt, but she isn't sure. Where is that sound coming from?

Another shadow falls over the living room window. "Nina," croons Hopkins. "I have something of yours."

Fuck!

He seems to float into view, and all she can see is a dark figure standing there, his outline illuminated by the streetlamp. He's holding something up.

Her phone.

He remains there, her phone held aloft, and her muscles tense, freezing her in place. She can't call Mami. Can't call for help.

He disappears again. Nina takes a few cautious steps forward, but she can't hear him anymore.

Are the doors locked?

Of course they are, but the thought burrows deeper beneath her skin, and she rushes to the front door to make sure. Then she's thinking of other windows. What if he finds another one to creep into? He's clearly not above breaking and entering.

You know what he wants.

She does. The only thing Hopkins wants more than their house. But she can't *give that* to him. Not anymore.

She stills. Hopes to hear that familiar scraping sound.

Nothing.

Maybe he went home. Maybe he'll come back in the morning, and Mami will be home by then, and she—

There's a rattling.

She spins. Listens again. Creeps back toward the stairs.

It's coming from the kitchen.

She realizes she forgot about the door that leads to the alley behind the building, out where the trash bins are, and her heart heaves in her chest as she dashes across the cool wooden tiles. She peers around the cabinets and—

He's there. At the back door. She can see his outline through the pale curtain on the door's window.

He knocks, softly at first, and then the raps are loud, repetitive, like gunshots.

"Open up!" He presses her phone against the glass. "I know you want this back."

She does, but she *can't* let him in.

Hopkins tries to open the door again. "Just tell me where you're keeping him," he says. "I know Tim was here. I sent him over. He never came back."

Her blood boils.

"Fine," he says.

He steps back. Holds up her phone. "Then I guess you don't need this."

He drops it. Nina hears it hit the ground.

He lurches back, and she rushes to the door, ripping the curtain aside, but it's too late.

He stomps on it, the phone crunching beneath his chunky snow boot.

"No," she whispers.

It is a crack in the dam. All that pent-up rage presses against her, begging to be let out.

Then he's gone.

Nina wonders if she should grab a weapon but then feels silly. That's what happens in all those slasher flicks; does it ever turn out well for the victim?

She presses her face to the glass. Can't see him anywhere. Where did he go?

She hears his boots on the cement.

And when Hopkins's body slams into the door the first time, it shakes the whole house.

Something falls and shatters in the kitchen.

Nina can't help but scream. "Go away!" she cries. "Leave me alone!"

"I know your mother is gone," he calls out, and then his shadow grows smaller for a moment.

BANG! He throws himself against the door again, and this time, there's a loud crack that follows. The frame splinters and splits.

He's going to get in.

"Give me my son!"

BANG.

"Give me my *house*!"

BANG.

The frame snaps. It's going to give way any moment.

Her left hand throbs then, and that's when she knows what she has to do.

What her mother *can't*.

Because she will not let this man have their home. It's been in the family since her ancestors discovered what lay beneath the foundation. What prompted the home to be built. What necessitated her family's protection.

She cannot imagine a worse person to lay claim to what is *theirs*.

Hopkins pants on her rear doorstep. He's running out of energy, but there's a long crack running down the wood.

She thinks of everyone else forced out of the neighborhood. Who moved away. Who disappeared from their lives. There must be others. How many have Hopkins and Tim tormented to get what they want?

Nina understands why her mami wants to play it safe, to let this unfold in court so they can get their deed back. Up until now, playing it safe has kept this family alive. Has kept this home under their control.

BANG.

But Hopkins knows he can do whatever he wants. Ultimately, he has the world on his side, doesn't he? He will smash every phone he needs to. Break down every door. Crush every family's dream to get what he craves.

He is an invasive species.

Her rage is singular. Focused. Sharp.

So Nina decides to imagine a different ending.

She strides over to the back door. Unlocks it with a single click of the dead bolt. Then steps back.

Hopkins's shadow is still for a moment, as if he can't believe what Nina just did. Then he pushes the door inward slowly. In the dim light, she can see the confusion on his face as he steps into the Ortiz family kitchen, his brows furrowed, his eyes darting from side to side.

"Don't pull anything funny," he says.

She doesn't respond. Only glares at him with contempt.

Hopkins pauses. "You better not have hurt him," he says, his body heaving as he breathes rapidly. "Just take me to him. I won't report you to the police, and we'll forget about your phone, okay?"

She nods, then points toward the door in the living room. "The basement," she says.

"I *knew* it," he says, then removes his beanie. "You savages are all the same."

Nina doesn't give Hopkins the reaction he wants. It's not like she hasn't heard this before. People like him think they're being original when they say shit like that.

She knows *they're* all the same.

Nina's keys are on a hook by the front door, so she grabs them, then unlocks the door to the basement. When she swings it open toward her, the house exhales, hits her face with a rush of warm air.

It knows.

It is ready.

"Tim!" Hopkins calls out. "Tim, are you down there?"

They are both met with silence.

He shivers. "Where is he?"

"Come," she says, her voice radiating calm. She is certain about this, even as her nerves flare up. She flicks on the lights, then holds the door open behind her. "Down."

He grunts and then follows her, descending the steps cautiously. At the bottom, she looks up at the remains of the garbage bag flapping gently in the breeze.

"Your son did that," says Nina, pointing to it, and she decides to tell him part of the truth. "I caught him down here this morning. Using a sledgehammer on our boiler."

Hopkins's mouth hangs open, and then he tries to sputter some excuse about repairs and ownership and deeds, but Nina no longer cares what this man has to say.

Her blood pumps faster, coursing through her veins like a rushing river. The throbbing rears its head.

The house groans in the wind.

Yes. Her home is speaking to her.

She glances at the mangled boiler and notices something she didn't clean up that morning.

A lone gym shoe, on its side, spattered with blood.

"Tim?" Hopkins shuffles around the basement. "Tim?"

Wide-eyed, he turns to Nina. "What did you do to him?"

She ignores him. Steps to the far corner, where the sledgehammer sits leaning against the wall. That isn't what she needs, though.

There's a door. Black. Mahogany, actually. No etchings or carvings. It is plain, even though what it protects is anything but.

She finds the keys that unlock the dead bolt and the safety locks, and as soon as she is done with the last, she places her right hand on the handle.

Hopkins shoves her out of the way. "Tim!" he cries out, and he wrenches the door open to—

Darkness.

There is nothing but darkness inside.

He's digging in his pocket. "Tim, can you hear me?"

He produces his own phone, flicking on the flashlight, and it's the perfect distraction for Nina. She picks at the edge of the bandage, then begins to unravel it, exposing the stump where her pinky finger used to be.

Hopkins waves the phone around, but he isn't stepping forward. She didn't either, the first time Mami showed her this. How could anyone?

The darkness devours the light. To Hopkins, it looks like utter nothingness.

But she can see the truth.

She can see possibility.

The bandage falls to the floor. The wound still oozes.

And Nina grabs the cleaver hanging from a hook on the back of the door.

"He's not in there anymore," she says, and Hopkins whirls about, his eyes wide as they fall on the cleaver.

"What did you *do?*" he whispers. He glances over his shoulder. "What is this?"

El ancla. That is what her ancestors named it nearly three hundred years ago when they found the darkness, when they discovered what the sacrifice would do for them. It is a means to an end, a way for her to anchor her thoughts and bring them into reality.

She moves toward Hopkins, and he rears back, right up to the edge of the darkness.

"I'll show you what happened to your son," she says.

Then she shoves him inside.

His scream is cut off as the darkness swallows him up, and then she is quick to drop to her knees, to fall forward, and she isn't sure which hand to use. One finger from each hand? Two from the left? She accepts that she wants at least one hand with all five intact, so she sticks out her ring finger, tucking the others as best she can under her palm, and she breathes in. Out. In. Out.

There is always a price. You cannot conjure something from nothing. You must give it a part of yourself. That's what her family discovered. They are the only ones who know of this, and they've been protecting it ever since.

It is hungry.

Do it.

The house groans.

And she gives it what it wants.

The cleaver comes down fast, and the pain is a flash. Redness spurts forth, and the darkness drinks it. She holds her hand forward so that her blood sprays into el ancla, then uses the other to pick up her finger as she chokes back a cry.

She tosses it beyond the doorway.

Then:

A light. A heat. A breath of relief and satiation.

The darkness recedes, and Hopkins is curled in the fetal position in that space, sobbing, begging for God to save him. He glances up, his eyes red and puffy.

"*Witch!*" he spits out. "Is that what you are?"

She stands. "No," she says.

Hopkins is suspended there. There are no walls, no floor, no *anything*. And just beyond him . . . darkness.

El ancla waits for Nina's imagination.

"What did you do to my son?" Hopkins chokes out.

She is pleased at how easy it was to lure him down here. He has no imagination for people like her. It is their perpetual underestimation.

She opens her mind as she gazes in, and moments later, she feels this house latch on to her, hook into her mind, and a comfort radiates throughout her body. It knows she is part of the family that has protected it for hundreds of years.

It begs her, *Tell me what you want.*

She stares at Hopkins, who is shakily pushing himself upright, sobbing like a lost child.

He is a thief.

He is an invader.

She knows. She knows exactly what to bring into this world, and she pictures it in her head, borrowing the image from the biology textbook she was reading earlier.

"Vespa mandarinia," she intones.

There is a low rumble, and it builds into a terrifying pitch. Her ring finger, sitting still at Hopkins's feet, splits apart, the skin tearing off muscle, the muscle tearing from bone, and the darkness rushes in as Hopkins screams again, falls back, but this time, the darkness catches him, holds him in place as her blood and flesh and bone reform, as they become yellowed wings and legs, become the striped thorax, become the hideous black mandible and the stinger.

It grows and grows and grows and grows until Hopkins is cowering beneath it, blubbering, his hands over his face.

It is *angry*, buzzing and hissing.

But she is not the object of its ire. It is worshipping her back, thanking her for the summoning.

She nods. "Now," she utters.

He shrieks as it rears up, and when the stinger pierces his hand, the hornet slams Hopkins's body down, and pinning his palm to his right shoulder. Something snaps.

It tears itself free.

The next sting is in his thigh. When it removes the stinger, blood sprays from an enormous gaping wound, and then it stings again, and again, and soon there is nothing there but red and yellow and black.

Such beautiful colors together.

He finally stops moving. His face has swollen so much, he no longer looks human, just an inflated mass of flesh, and blood seeps from the many, many entrance points until it slows to an ooze, and the hornet observes. Waits.

She stumbles over to the boiler and picks up Tim's shoe. She returns and tosses it into the darkness.

She gives el ancla her gratitude.

"Te protegeré," Nina promises.

The conjuring vanishes. The darkness begins to claim it all, to swim over Hopkins's body, and—

"Nina, are you down here?"

She spins around as Mami comes down the stairs, and Nina crouches, tries to pick up the cleaver, but the pain rushes back as her elation evaporates.

Mami is there, still in her puffy winter coat, staring. She gasps. "Nina, what have you *done*?"

Exhaustion weighs Nina's body down, and she wobbles. The summoning is costly in more ways than one.

"I solved our problem," she mutters.

When she glances back at el ancla, she sees nothing but darkness.

She thinks Mami is angry at first. Can't quite read the expression on her face. But then Mami crosses over to Nina and closes the door. When she pushes it shut, Nina looks at the space where there were once two fingers on her mami's hand.

Now they match.

Mami reaches out for Nina's bleeding hand, examining it closely.

"I need to know everything that happened," Mami says softly. "Please."

Nina nods. Tells her mami about what she found when she heard a banging sound in the basement and discovered Tim. How she ran for the door to el ancla, and she was sloppy, cutting her pinky finger off at an angle, but at least Tim had been so shocked by what she was doing that she was able to threaten him to get inside.

She tells Mami about the reticulated python.

There is a long silence. Mami rubs the pad of her thumb over the back of Nina's hand.

"What now?" says Nina.

She expects rage. Fury. Nina has done what Mami asked her *never* to do.

"Abuela is fine," she finally says. "She's still with us."

There is some relief in that, but Nina is still tense.

"We should go see her together. You need to tell her, too."

"Why?" Nina asks.

The corner of Mami's lip curls up. "So she knows that you did our family proud tonight."

Nina sags. Leans into her mami's body. "I had to," she says, pressing her face into Mami's coat.

"You did good, mija. They're gone now."

"What about the police?" Nina says. "What about our *case*?"

"We can deal with complications later. Right now, I think you need to be with your family."

Mami guides her up the stairs. Around her, Nina feels the house contracting. Maybe it's in her mind, but she doesn't think it is.

Her home embraces her.

And Nina smiles because she knows she did the best she could.

HELL IS OTHER DEMONS

KAREN STRONG

When Ivy first told me her boyfriend was planning to summon a demon, I thought she was joking, but it didn't surprise me.

Every time Brett embraces a new fixation, he goes in for the deep dive, and then, when the novelty wears off, everything he's collected ends up in a forgotten box at the back of his closet. He's been this way since we were kids. Demonology is just his latest obsession. And if this goes like the others, he'll burn through it fast.

In Brett's attic, I sit next to Ivy. Her bare knee touches my thigh, and I feel the heat through my jeans. In the center of the room, Brett draws archaic symbols in white chalk.

"Using a pentagram to summon a demon is kind of basic, don't you think?" I ask.

Brett gives me one of his wide bright smiles. His blond hair, blue eyes, and athletic frame are highly desired by other girls in our senior class, but I'm immune to his pretty privilege. Always have been.

"The pentagram is part of the ceremony, Evelyn. It's been performed this way for *thousands* of years."

"So now *you* want to try it?" I turn to Ivy. "This is a dumb idea."

Ivy says nothing, watching her boyfriend's pale hands move in the low candlelight. I let out an inpatient huff because I know this entire thing is going to be a waste of time. Ivy should be at Bible study at her father's church, and I should be at home doing my AP Calculus homework. And anyway, demons don't exist. Satan isn't some fallen angel who helms a winged army. He's a myth. Not. Real.

Humans are the *real* demons.

When Brett finishes the pentagram, he motions for us to join him. He sits next to Ivy and gives her a quick kiss. My face burns with the memory of another kiss. A secret one.

"Does this demon have a name?" Ivy asks.

"[redacted]," Brett tells her. "He's very powerful."

"Of course, he is," I mumble under my breath.

Brett Lewiston knows all about power—or at least the entitlement of it. In Cedar Falls—our small town known for its Blue Ridge Mountains, fall foliage, and harvest festivals—the Lewiston farm is nestled in a fertile valley. The property has been in Brett's family for six generations. Hardworking hands tilling stolen land claimed with blood and terror.

"You know this probably won't work," I say. "Even if this [redacted] is real—which he's not—I'm sure he's too busy to be summoned by you."

Brett gives me a full smirk. "What's wrong, Evelyn? You scared? I thought you were an atheist."

I ignore him and turn to Ivy. "Your father won't like it if he finds out you're playing with demons. Does he know you're here?"

Ivy pulls her long box braids over her shoulder as she looks at me, and I feel a quick flurry in my stomach. Last summer, things changed between us, and it was magical. I'd always had a crush on her, but I'd never thought she could like me too. Everyone in Cedar Falls already knew about me and my past girlfriends; but Ivy didn't want anyone to know about us—and I didn't want to be a secret. Not after enduring so much in this backwoods town. So, when summer ended, we broke up.

And then she started dating Brett.

I've tried to stay away from her, but I don't have the strength. So, earlier tonight, when she called and asked if I wanted to come to her boyfriend's demon summoning, I couldn't refuse. I wanted to see her—even under these ridiculous circumstances. And after Brett's summoning inevitably fails, I'm planning to see if there's still a chance for me and Ivy to get back together.

Her bare knee touches my thigh again. This time she leaves it there, gently resting against me. "My daddy doesn't know the *real* reason I'm here," she finally tells me. "He thinks we're studying."

Ivy's father has a lot of silly rules and harsh judgments burrowed into his righteous heart. He's made it perfectly clear he hates me—especially after the night he caught me kissing his daughter in her room. Ivy has followed his rules and feared his judgments all her life. It's why she can be with a white boy but not with me. Bishop Joseph Owens of Cedar Falls Church thinks I'm an abomination, but what he doesn't know is that his daughter is just like me. And one day, I'm going to convince Ivy that her father is the real monster.

Brett pulls out a folded piece of paper from his pocket. "The ceremony is fairly simple. This chant will summon [redacted], and when he appears, he will grant me fame and fortune."

"You're really going to ask this demon to make you rich and famous?" I scrunch up my face. "This isn't about the demon at all—it's about *you*."

Ivy shifts next to me. In the attic's murkiness, candlelight flickers over her brown face, but she doesn't say anything. Now I understand why she called me. Ivy knows I don't believe in this bullshit. She's scared and wants me to stop Brett from summoning the demon. But I'm not going to stop him. Ivy needs to see the true character of her boyfriend and break up with him.

I return my focus to Brett. "Do you think that's what everybody wants? Money and attention?"

"Yeah," Brett scoffs. "It's the gateway to everything worth having in the world."

"That's not what *I* want," Ivy says softly.

My hearts speeds up at her words. What *does* Ivy want? Does she miss kissing me as much as I miss kissing her? The lightness in my chest quickly disappears, and the usual heavy burden returns. Ivy could have me if she didn't care what other people thought about her. If she weren't so afraid of her father. If Ivy were brave—a fighter like me—we could both have what we want.

Brett starts the ceremony, speaking in an old dead language. It sounds like Latin but not quite. He fumbles over the pronunciations, and I bite my lip to keep from laughing. He repeats the summoning phrases. I'm quickly getting bored and stifle a yawn. The full ceremony lasts about twenty minutes. When Brett finally finishes, he glances excitedly around the attic for [redacted], then turns back to us, his shoulders slouched, a look of disappointment on his face.

I slowly smile in triumph. "I told you this was a waste—"

A whoosh of wind blows the candles out, and I grab Ivy's hand. Cold dread runs down my arms as the faint scent of sulfur fills my nose. From the lone window, the moon casts the room with silver light. Wisps of candle smoke rise in the air.

Brett slowly stands, still searching for his demon. I pull Ivy up off the floor and away from the chalk pentagram. A floorboard creaks behind us. Moving carefully, Brett walks in the direction of the noise.

"What the *fuck* are you doing?" I whisper.

Brett puts his finger to his lips to silence me. I frown as he moves toward one of the dark corners of the attic.

I squint and barely make out a shadow. I gasp as it scatters apart and then comes back together to form the shape of an ominous hulking form.

"*Shit.*" I stumble backward.

What is unmistakably a demon emerges from the shadows and stretches upward to its full height. Far taller than the average human. Monstrous. Wrinkled hairless skin the color of cold ashes. Long legs that end in razored claws. Bony spindles rise from its spine, and two muscular wings are closed tight across its back. Its head is shaped like that of a long-beaked bird, and red orbs burn like glowing embers inside the eyeholes of its skull.

"[redacted]." Brett falls to his knees in awe. "I summoned you to give me—"

In one fell swoop, the demon tears off Brett's head. Ivy screams as it rolls across the attic's floor and stops in front of us. Brett's face is frozen in eternal surprise, his blue eyes glazed and lifeless.

Brett's headless body wobbles to the floor, and dark blood spurts from his severed neck like an erupting volcano. The demon quickly gulps from the red shower before tearing open Brett's stomach. Rolls of intestines spill to the floor with a sickening *plop*, and an awful stench erupts into the air. I cough and swallow down bile as the demon bows its head and eats greedily from the bloody carcass.

It takes a few seconds for the initial shock to wear off, but then I grab Ivy's hand and pull her toward the attic door.

Ivy lets out a small whimper when she slips on the bloody floor, and the demon lifts its head. Jagged pieces of Brett's flesh cover [redacted]'s sharp beak.

I wrap my arms around Ivy's waist and try to drag her out of the room, but the demon moves with supernatural speed. Its muscular wings fully expand and block out the moonlight. Red eyes glow in the darkness, and a deep fear cracks open in my chest.

[redacted] snatches Ivy by her neck, and I strain to keep her in my grasp. But the demon rips her away.

"Hey!" I shout. "You don't want her. Take me!"

[redacted] drops Ivy, and she falls hard to the floor. My body fills with panic as the demon rushes toward me, its massive beak open wide, revealing a forked black tongue.

I don't have time to scream.

When my awareness returns, I'm no longer in the attic but in a blank void.

I have no body, but there's still an unexplainable sense of a phantom one, as if my physical self is invisible. I turn in a circle but find no beginning or end to the bright whiteness surrounding me.

Then I slowly start to remember.

The summoning of the demon. Brett's headless body. Ivy in danger. My death.

A swirl of darkness appears and forms into the shape of a man with pallid gray skin and yellow serpent eyes. A pair of spiraled horns jut from the top of his head, and curly dark hair frames his face. He's groomed his long beard to a severe point, and even his crooked fingers end in manicured claws. Dressed in an elegant all-black suit, he adjusts a silver infinity pin attached to his silk tie. This man isn't human, but he has immaculate style.

"Is this the afterlife?" I ask.

"Now that's a question for the ages," the not-human man answers in a pleasant cultured voice. "You seem a bit disappointed."

"I thought—I always believed death would be a cold dark vacuum where you cease to exist."

"You're going to be a fun one." The strange man inhales deeply before speaking again. "You may call me *the Valet*. It's what I do here. Do you remember what happened to you?"

"I remember everything," I tell him.

"Good, Evelyn. Knowing about your human life will make this process go much faster."

He turns and walks away from me; his footsteps are loud in the blank void. I quickly move to follow him.

"How—how did you know my name?" I ask once I catch up.

He chuckles softly. "It's my job to know everything about you, Evelyn Lear."

I pause as the revelation quickly comes. I stare at the Valet's nonhuman appearance: serpent eyes, spiraled horns, long claws. "Is this—am I in *Hell*?"

The Valet smiles wide and reveals sharp, pointy teeth. "Of course not, Evelyn. The amenities are *so* much better in Hell."

He touches the infinity pin on his tie, and I slowly transition into my familiar physical form. I'm wearing the same clothes I put on this morning: T-shirt, hoodie, jeans. My skin is the same dark brown as it's always been. I tentatively touch my head and feel the tight coils of my cropped hair. My hand shakes as it moves down toward my neck—but there's no open wound from [redacted]'s lethal attack.

The Valet lets out a long weary sigh. "Feel better? I'm assuming you have more questions."

"If this place isn't Hell, then what is it?"

He purses his lips. "A crossroads. There are many places you can go from here. Hell is only one of them."

"Where's Ivy?" I ask. "Is she here?"

"Ivy Owens is still alive."

The demon didn't kill Ivy. At least my death wasn't in vain. I close my eyes in relief but quickly open them again as more questions flood my brain. "What about Brett? Where's that asshole? Is he here?"

"Finding a missing human soul isn't in my job description," the Valet answers coolly. "My workload is already full enough."

Although it's Brett's fault I'm dead, he's not my major concern at the moment. I need to figure out my own situation. "What other places can I go besides Hell?"

"Humans are so predictable." His voice fills with exhaustion. "Are you referring to Heaven? Are you requesting to speak to an angel?"

"Are—are you a demon?"

"Isn't that obvious?"

I'd always thought the "pearly gates of heaven" and the "eternal damnation of hell" were fairy tales to keep people under control. I believed you only had one life, and you should make the most of it. Now, in death, I realize how wrong I was—not just about demons, but *everything*.

"Am I a demon now, too?"

The Valet's face darkens. "Absolutely not. You're a human soul, and it's all you'll *ever* be."

A tremble of fear rattles through me as I stare at his sharp claws. He could probably kill me easily if I weren't already dead. I take two steps backward.

"I didn't mean to offend you," I tell him. "Since you're the Valet, do you decide where I go next?"

"Judgment isn't a part of my job description either. I don't have that kind of authority. But what I can tell you is that my superiors feel [redacted] has become a nuisance. Since his demotion from his previous position, he's been killing summoners and pushing them into Hell before their time. This type of chaos has caused a major bottleneck for the crossroads, so they've decided to give you an opportunity to take care of him. From time to time, we do indulge a few of you in a little revenge, if you desire, and if it serves our purposes."

Memories flash of [redacted] gripping Ivy's neck. The look of raw fear on her face. I feel anger start to rumble inside me. "You're giving me an opportunity to kill him?"

"No, Evelyn. [redacted] can only be banished back to Hell."

The demon killed Brett—good riddance—but [redacted] also took *my* life. I was relishing my plan to escape from Cedar Falls after graduation. I would've made it out too, had I been able to resist Ivy's call.

"How am I supposed to banish [redacted]?" I ask.

"He's still in the human world, so first, you'll return there." The Valet closely examines me. "You'll retain your soul and your memories. But first, more protocol. Follow me."

We travel through the featureless void until we come upon a door and walk into an office. The Valet sits behind a desk scattered with papers. The room is full of metal file cabinets, cheap wooden bookcases, and worn textbooks. It's an exact replica of my guidance counselor's office.

The Valet looks up at me. "You don't like it? Would you prefer the beach from when you were five? Or perhaps that wretched cabin at summer camp when you were twelve? I only chose this because it was the last place you were happy."

"No, it's fine." I sit in an orange plastic chair.

Ms. Bonner's office is where I told her about my college acceptance letters and scholarships. She cried with me because we both knew it was my ticket out of Cedar Falls. She was a mother figure to me because my own mother didn't care about my grades or my future. But those other places hold good memories for me too. The beach was the last family vacation before my father left. The cabin at summer camp was where I finally French kissed Lola Hampton. But there are also happy moments from that magical summer I created with Ivy, and I wonder why the Valet didn't choose one of *those* memories.

"[redacted] is an ancient demon. Stuck in the antiquated, barbaric ways of consuming human flesh. He doesn't understand possession now requires a more subtle touch—and less *blood*," the Valet says as he organizes papers on the desk. "But it also makes his banishment very straightforward. We should be able to use his pride against him."

"Brett is the one who summoned [redacted]. Why don't you make *him* fix it?"

"At the moment Brett Lewiston's soul is missing. And since we can't find that idiot, you're the next best thing. Think of it as outsourcing." The Valet pushes a stack of papers across the desk to me.

I stare down at consent forms. "Is this a joke?"

"No, Evelyn. It's protocol." He lets out a tired chuckle and mutters something under his breath. "You're not the only case I'm handling right now. Working at the crossroads is not the most desirable job, and as a result, I don't get much help. Also, if you don't sign these papers, I won't be able to send you back to save your girlfriend."

"What?" I look at him. "Are you talking about *Ivy*?"

The Valet touches his infinity pin, and Ms. Bonner's office disappears.

Brett's attic is bright with the moonlight, and the floor is streaked with blood. My spirit hovers over my dead body, which is strewn at a ghastly angle on the floor. I stare at my mangled neck and the blood pooling around my head. In the corner, there's only a grisly outline where Brett's body once lay. I search for his severed head, but it's also missing.

[redacted] is nowhere to be seen either.

The white boy and the demon are gone.

But Ivy is still here.

She kneels in my blood. Her eyes flash red as she tears out a damaged ligament from my neck. She shoves it into her mouth, chews and swallows the tough muscle, then slowly licks her fingers. I watch in cold horror before crying out to her.

"Ivy, what's wrong with you?" I shout. "What are you doing?"

She doesn't respond to my terrified voice. Instead, she burrows her face deep into my bloody neck and tears off another string of flesh with her teeth. I try to get close enough to grab her—I want to push her away from my body—but I can't move. I scream her name again, but she doesn't hear me.

The attic disappears, and I'm back in my guidance counselor's office. The Valet sits behind the desk, waiting for me to respond.

"*Shit.*" I take a shaky breath. "That—that wasn't Ivy, was it?"

"[redacted] has possessed her body," the Valet confirms. "But there's still a chance you can save her—if you exorcise him and then banish him back to Hell."

The consent forms tremble in my hands. "Give me a pen."

In Ivy's bedroom, I watch her sleep. She looks peaceful—almost like an angel, but I know what lurks inside her.

I hover over her bed. The Valet says I'm only the essence of my soul in the human world. A wisp of a ghost humans can sense—an uneasiness trickling down a neck, the rising of goose bumps on skin, the building dread of something wrong. But for me, my existence feels like it did in the blank void of the crossroads. I still have all the sensations and movement of a phantom body.

Ivy has pushed the sheets down into a messy nest at her feet. I move closer and listen to her heartbeat and the blood pulsing through her veins. Her chest rises slowly with every intake of breath, and her eyelids flutter with dreams. I want to touch her warm skin and rub my fingers over the texture of her box braids.

I sneaked into this bedroom so many nights. Every morning leaving a little more heartbroken after listening to Ivy's promises that always evaporated in the daylight. Before my death, I wanted to save Ivy from her father and prove he was an abomination—the real monster. But tonight, I'm here because I need to save her from an even more dangerous monster. Despite every broken promise and every disappointment, I still love Ivy—and I'm going to banish [redacted] back to Hell.

A low moan escapes her lips, and she shudders awake. I wait for the recognition to appear in her brown eyes, but then I remember Ivy can't see me.

But demons can.

The color of Ivy's eyes shifts to bloodred, and her mouth contorts into a sneer of malice. I veer away from the bed into the dark corner of the room.

Ivy sits up and cracks her neck sharply. She stretches her body, long and lean, before looking in my direction. "Go away. Find someone else."

[redacted] is using Ivy's soft, sweet voice.

The demon cackles when I remain in the shadows. I realize [redacted] isn't aware I'm one of the humans he's killed. Maybe he believes I'm a lower-caste demon summoned into the human world. Too weak to be a threat. The Valet explained this might happen. [redacted] won't give up his newest prize so easily—especially if he thinks another demon wants it.

A forceful moan rises from Ivy's throat, and her terrified cries fill the room. Her body writhes in agony as she struggles for control. She rises into the air, her arms and legs flailing. Ivy can be a fighter when she wants to be.

Heavy footsteps pound down the hallway, and I surge upward to the ceiling. Ivy's body falls in a heap on the bed. The door opens, and the room fills with light as Ivy's father races toward her.

"Baby girl, what's wrong?" he cries.

Ivy's tearful eyes are now human and brown. No trace of [redacted]'s bloodred shade. She searches the room frantically, and I wish she could feel my presence.

"It's okay," he tells her. "You're awake now."

"No, there's something—there's something *inside* me!"

Her father's face fills with alarm, but he struggles to wipe his worry away. With effort, he projects composure as he strokes her braids. "It's just another nightmare." He consoles Ivy with a hug until she calms down.

When he leaves and turns off the light, the darkness of night returns. I descend from the ceiling to hover over the bed again.

I want to reach out and touch Ivy. Tell her I'm here to save her. But I can't do either of those things. My current ethereal form can only observe in the human world. It's only through a possession that I'll be able to deal with [redacted].

Ivy's eyes stay vacant for a moment. Then they glow amber and slowly simmer to red before she smirks at me.

I move through Ivy's house, down the familiar hallway to the den, where a TV blares the late-evening news. Joseph Owens is sitting on the sofa bathed in blue light.

A thick Bible lies on the table in front of him, along with several wood crosses and smaller pendants—even a huge gold cross encrusted with rubies—although I'm sure the gems aren't real. It's probably a gaudy gift from one of the faithful members of his congregation. The good bishop of Cedar Falls Church has a very loyal flock. But I don't focus on the holy trinkets.

Instead, I closely inspect the twelve-gauge shotgun on the table beside them.

On the TV, a news anchor relays the latest about my homicide investigation. The Valet has told me everything that's happened in the three days since I died, but it's a different reality when I can witness it myself. My death has become a spectacle.

"The satanic-cult murder of Evelyn Lear still stuns the small town of Cedar Falls." The anchorwoman's voice is comforting mixed with just the right amount of shocked. "Brett Lewiston remains at large and is the main suspect of the grisly crime."

The screen cuts away to a video of police swarming Brett's farmhouse. Then it switches to his senior class photo showcasing his "perfect golden boy" image followed by snippets of interviews from classmates and neighbors—all of them agreeing how out of character it would've been for Brett to brutally kill someone. When my face finally appears on the screen, it's my driver's license photo, where my expression is blank and unsmiling. No one speaks on my behalf—not even my mother. The anchorwoman doesn't mention I was salutatorian of my senior class or accepted to three Ivy League universities with full scholarships. In death, I'm a voiceless victim. Another murdered Black girl. A blink of consideration on the news.

Ms. Bonner put together a very small memorial service for me, but Ivy wasn't there—only a few of my classmates and my mother, who didn't shed one tear. Before coming to Ivy's house, I went home because I think I wanted to see if my mother would show some proof of grief in private, but she wasn't there. I went to Leo's Grill and found her drunk at the bar. I watched as my mother claimed in slurred words how everything had been my fault before I left the restaurant in disgust.

Ivy's father continues to sip whiskey from a stout glass and watch the news. His eyes are empty, but when ice unloads in the freezer, he jumps at the sound and grabs his shotgun.

After a few moments, he finally relaxes and rests the gun in his lap. Does he think Brett is still in Cedar Falls? Maybe Joseph Owens thinks Brett is the true threat instead of a demon summoned from Hell. I want to tell him this type of thinking is the reason I'm dead.

When the Valet told me I needed to possess a body to deal with [redacted], the first logical choice was Ivy's father. He would be the perfect vessel because if I mess up and [redacted] kills him, I wouldn't feel any remorse. Joseph Owens is the reason Ivy wanted to keep me a secret. He's the reason she chose Brett. If Ivy's father dies while I'm trying to banish a demon back to Hell, then I would be fine with it. Maybe even delighted.

All I have to do is slip into his body, take it over, *possess.*

Joseph Owens turns off the TV and then goes around the house, checking the locks on doors and windows, his shotgun gripped in his right hand.

I hover over him as he fixes a sandwich in the kitchen. As I move closer, he senses my presence. He slowly puts down the butter knife and reaches for the shotgun. But when he jerks around, he finds no one. Several heartbeats later, he shudders and then laughs. Nervous energy. He thinks he's being paranoid—but he's not. Joseph Owens is being haunted.

I move closer until I feel the warmth of his skin. He tenses again, but I don't stop. Closer. And closer still, until I permeate his body.

He cries out in surprise.

Possessing a body is like diving into ice-cold water. Shocking and unsettling, then invigorating. Blood pounds around me with each of Joseph's strong heartbeats. There's a *swoosh* of breath as he hitches it in terror. Muscles twitch and bones grind in resistance. When his tension releases, I can feel limbs—arms and legs. Fingers tingle. I realize now how much I took my own physical body for granted. I've missed being a full living human.

When Ivy's father screams in protest, I can only hear the booming echo inside his brain. It grates, waves of harsh sound bouncing off the walls of a small enclosed room.

"Stop it!" I say sharply. "Your body is *mine* now."

The screams turn into whimpers as I walk around the kitchen to get familiar with this new form. I roll his shoulders and inhale deeply through his nose. I stick out his tongue, and it's slippery and warm between his fingers. But when I pull too hard, the pain sparks tears.

I go back to the kitchen island and finish making the sandwich—pastrami on rye. I take a bite. So delicious. But then I think of Ivy eating the torn flesh from my neck, and I put the unfinished sandwich back on the plate. I quickly move to the sink and vomit until there's nothing left but a yellow string of bile. I can still hear Ivy's father sniveling like a child.

"Remember me?" I whisper sweetly. "Evelyn Lear, the abomination?"

He cries harder, and I have to admit I'm disappointed. At least his daughter is a fighter. I bet she didn't let [redacted] usurp her body this easily.

"*What's happening to me?*" Joseph Owens bawls.

"I've possessed you." I take a breath, suddenly very tired. Now I know how the Valet feels. "Listen to me carefully. There's a demon inside your daughter, and we need to get him out."

Steering clear of the shotgun, I leave the kitchen and walk into the den. I scan the table of holy trinkets and choose the large ruby-encrusted cross. I'm surprised at the weight of it in my hand.

"Let's go banish a demon."

I head upstairs to Ivy's bedroom.

I don't turn on the light when I open the door, so the room is layered in muted darkness. As I approach the bed, Ivy's rumpled sheets are still pushed down, but she's nowhere to be found. Inspecting closer, I find a splatter of blood on the quilt. I quickly search the room and then rush to the window but find it's still locked from inside.

I glance at the dark corners of the room before heading to Ivy's closet. I push around hangers of clothes, but she's not hiding behind them. When I hear a shuffling noise, I turn back and slowly approach the bed. Kneeling on the floor, I jerk the quilt up and look underneath.

Two glowing red eyes stare back at me.

Ivy rushes out from under the bed, and I quickly scuttle away until I hit the wall. She cackles as she lands on top of me, knocking the cross out of my hand. Ivy's arms are riddled with bite marks, and she bares bloodstained teeth.

I push her off me and scramble to retrieve the cross. I thrust it out in front of me like a holy shield, but the demon only laughs at me.

"Do you not know who I am? That has no effect on me. Your ignorance is insulting."

In his slide presentation, "Demons and Human Souls: An Introduction," the Valet shared that religious symbols don't have any adverse effect on ancients like [redacted]. Since I didn't have time to read the centuries' worth of pages in the demon's files, the Valet provided a TL;DR recap: [redacted] thinks humans are dumb. So I formed my banishment strategy around his belief that I'm a clueless human—until he realizes I'm not.

Ivy stands up and takes a deep bite of her arm. The teeth marks leave gaping holes in her skin, and blood drips in large blots on the floor. "I decided to slowly eat this one alive."

"I know who you are, or rather, who you *used* to be. Now you're a bottom-feeder." I rise from the floor, and we circle each other as if we're in some kind of morbid dance of predator and prey. "You hate it every time you're summoned into this world—but no one cares about you in Hell."

Ivy's body stills, and her red eyes flare in anger. "*You . . .*" She raises a bloody arm toward me. "You were in this room before, trying to steal the girl from me. Now you are inside the father. *Who sent you?*"

"No one sent me. I volunteered to come here." No longer needing to keep up the charade, I lower the cross to my side. "You don't belong here, Lamech. You're a trespasser. Leave this world."

The demon screeches in irritation at the name, and I know I've hit my mark.

When I asked the Valet about [redacted]'s old job, he told me it was one of the highest summoning positions in Hell. Naturally, his superiors gave the coveted job to his rival Lamech, a demon [redacted] had been feuding with for centuries. Now, in the human world, the rich and powerful summon Lamech to worship him in satanic temples, while the opportunistic assholes summon [redacted] to ask for handouts. Demoted and disgraced, he's been eating his feelings in human flesh ever since.

"You dare disrespect me." The demon growls, low and deadly. "*That is* not *my name.*"

Ivy's eyes fade from bloodred to brown, and she lurches back and forth in jerky movements before a horrible scream escapes her throat.

"Get it out of me, Daddy!" Her desperate plea fills the room with torment. "*Get it out!*"

Ivy continues to fight as she thrashes to the floor. Viscous black liquid spills from her mouth, and a putrid smell fills the air.

The demon quickly regains control, and Ivy's eyes burn fire red again. She quickly scrambles toward me and spits. I wipe the sticky black goop off my face, but I repeat another variation of the mantra.

"You're a trespasser, Lamech. Leave this world. You don't belong here."

"That is not my name!" the demon roars in fury. *"I am Gazidun!"*

When I smile, the demon looks at me in sudden realization. He knows he's made a mistake. The Valet was right. Gazidun's pride would not allow him to be called by the name of his most hated nemesis. There's power in a name.

"You tricked me!" He glowers at me.

"Thanks for claiming your name," I tell him. "You don't belong here, *Gazidun*. You're a trespasser. Now leave this world."

The demon bellows in agony until his shadow rises from Ivy's body. It scatters apart and then comes back together into Gazidun's true form. The demon is just as terrifying as I remember.

Gazidun roars and bursts into flames. But before he's completely gone, he lashes out with a razored claw and punches it straight through Ivy's father's chest. I feel the horrific pain before I'm ejected from his body. Hovering in my ethereal form, I watch Joseph Owens fall to the floor. Dark blood pools quickly around him. Gazidun cackles as the last of him burns, then dissolves into clumps of smoldering embers.

"Daddy!" Ivy screams, and runs to her dying father. "Daddy! Don't leave me! I'm so sorry. I should have listened to you. I should have prayed more. All this time, you tried to tell me."

Joseph Owens opens his eyes, and blood spurts from his mouth. "You're gonna be all right now, baby girl."

Ivy frantically presses both hands onto her father's chest, crying and reciting the Lord's Prayer. After he suffers a few convulsions, a cloudy froth erupts from his mouth, and his eyes roll back into his head. When he dies in her arms, Ivy weeps in anguish. She thinks her father exorcised the demon. She doesn't know it was *me* who banished Gazidun back to Hell.

Joseph Owens used his last dying breath to disrespect me.

I quickly swoop down and try to enter Ivy's body. I need to possess her so I can tell her the truth. She has to know that I saved her from two kinds of monsters at once—human *and* demon. Ivy needs to hear that the girl who loves her more than anything just saved her life.

When I try to enter her body again, I'm snatched violently away by an unseen force. Before I can react, I'm shoved back into the blank void of the crossroads.

The Valet waits for me, his face is full of what I can only comprehend as pride.

"Gazidun has been banished back to Hell," he tells me. "Good work, Evelyn."

"You have to send me back now!" I shout at him.

The Valet cocks his head in confusion. "There's no further need for you to return to the human world at the moment."

"Ivy thinks her father saved her!" My voice is high and loud in the blank void. "She doesn't know it was *me*!"

The towering demon moves closer and touches his infinity pin to bring forth my physical form. "I thought you would be pleased Gazidun killed Joseph Owens. He was such a messy human. Ivy will mourn her father, but she'll be fine without him."

"You don't understand. I—I love her." I turn away from him.

The Valet gently touches my shoulder. "You must know, I've had a long tenure here, and most human souls don't succeed when given this type of opportunity. The way you handled Gazidun's banishment makes me believe you have a natural gift. In fact, you're part of the reason I've been promoted. This is my last day at the crossroads."

When I turn back to the demon, his sharp teeth are gleaming in a wide smile.

"That's good . . . right?" I pause. "Congratulations?"

"Thank you, Evelyn. My superiors were also very impressed with your efforts." The Valet examines me closely. "They want to know if you would be interested in a job."

"What kind of job?"

He straightens his tie. "When you first arrived here, I told you that we sometimes let humans banish demons if it serves our purposes. After your swift disposal of Gazidun, my superiors would like to offer you employment."

"So they want to give me a job banishing troublemaking demons back to Hell?"

"Make no mistake, there's still much for you to learn, but you'll be provided with further training. However, I'm ready to send you on your way if you're not interested."

I let the proposition linger between us. I did get to banish Gazidun, which avenged my death and saved Ivy, even if she doesn't know it was really me. I will always love her, but the Valet is right. Now that her father's gone, Ivy can have the kind of life she deserves—one without secrets, rejection, or shame.

"I'll take the job," I tell him. "Do you think you could set it up before you leave?"

"Of course, I can serve as your escort to meet my superiors."

The Valet offers his arm, and I walk with him through the blank void until we approach a black gate. In the distant horizon, a red sun rises.

"I must warn you, there'll be a *lot* of paperwork with this kind of job," he says.

"It's fine. I have plenty of time now. An eternity."

"Very well then, Evelyn." The Valet bows his head. "Are you ready to enter Hell?"

THE ROAD TO HELL

TERRY J. BENTON-WALKER

I loved you once, but now I fucking hate you.

I've had time to think about what happened between us, and I might finally understand why you did what you did. Even though I *really* wish you hadn't.

Even now, I wonder whether you would have made a different choice that night, if you truly understood me. Or perhaps it was foolish of me to ever think I could have you and your family, damned as I was.

It was sometime in the 1600s, right here in the swamps of the Florida Everglades that I came to be. The exact date eludes me because, unlike your kind, I have no need to measure such things. A Spaniard by the name of Sánchez built me. I was to be a grand dwelling—for a grand motherfucker. He gave me a new and exciting life, then plagued my belly with endless violence. Sánchez had a reputation for being vile but saved his exceptionally depraved antics for the privacy my walls granted him.

And then, one night, having reached their limit with my master's sadism, a local mob descended upon our property and sprayed my handcrafted oak front doors with liquor-laced spittle as they shouted a myriad of profanities and vowed to do all manner of gruesome things to Sánchez—and even worse to his corpse. That mob teased me with the promise of freedom from my master's never-ending and ever-escalating abuse.

I let them in.

Sánchez's blood and viscera dried in the crevices of my floorboards, so malevolent that even fungus avoided it. And Death bound that dirty bastard to me for eternity, a cruel repercussion of my attempt to divorce myself from Sánchez—who became my first haunt.

But he was not the last—nor the *worst*.

As you very well know.

In our final moments together, you judged me rather harshly for my paranormal proclivities—but you didn't understand how lonely it could get when even the alligators and vultures gave my estate a wide berth. My only crime was trying my best to survive the only way I knew how.

For centuries after Sánchez's demise, darkness found its way to this swamp again and again. The murky waters surrounding my estate now run deep with the blood of many who met a grotesque end here. I lured the most intriguing spirits of the deceased to remain with me as friends, their companionship meant to keep depression at bay. I became a lighthouse, perpetually beckoning to those beyond, until I would meet my forever family, a someone or "someones" who would fill with unconditional love the many holes Sánchez had stabbed through my hopes and dreams.

For hundreds of years, I yearned desperately for it—*love*. Many masters came and went over that time, but they all eventually abandoned me, deeming me unlovable, unworthy . . . *haunted*.

And once I'd finally resigned myself to the gruesome fate of knowing only loneliness . . .

. . . *you* appeared.

And you were a dream.

If only I'd known back then you'd turn into a nightmare more malignant than Sánchez, I would've had one of my friends snap your neck in your sleep.

But for some reason, I couldn't help myself. You and your family were unlike any to ever walk my halls. Your energies felt different. It was hard to describe.

Your family's white SUV pulled up outside, and your dads got out, both smiling, brimming with unadulterated hope. That was familiar. An emotion long since rotted with mold, after being pissed on by my birth master.

However, you, far more reserved than your parents, hung back near the rear of the vehicle, biting your full lips beneath the centuries-old willows that dappled sunlight across your bright walnut skin. I lost myself among the mottled earth tones in your eyes because they didn't bear the promise of violence like those of so many others. Instead, I found a gentleness there, which propelled me back to a very brief time in my past—before I was desecrated and bound to an endless cycle of violence.

Your innocence captivated me at first sight. I wanted to love you.

And I wanted you to love me too.

I longed for your entire family to make me your home and never leave.

And during those initial moments where y'all stood in my front yard and looked me over, assessing my worth, I ran through decades of potential memories—joyful celebrations, tearful moments of regret or grief, tender displays of the many, many types of love humans can express with one another. And I imagined each of you taking your final breaths at the end of your very short lives within my walls, after which your spirits would rise from your corpses and become one with me for the rest of my life—as eternal friends. That sounded absolutely *divine*.

I was willing to do *anything* for it.

"Sooo, what do you think, Danger?" asked the copper-skinned one you called *Papa*, the shorter, lighter-complected of your parents. He removed his mirrored sunglasses and hung them on the button of his shirt.

Danger—I thought it such an intriguing name. Still do, frankly, despite my present desire to slowly peel away every bloody thread of sinew making up your scrawny teenage body.

You grimaced and looked over my facade with cold indifference that made my ancient joints creak with shame.

I'd never felt that before.

And suddenly, I became hyperaware of the shutters that'd fallen off or been ripped away for firewood before my friends chased those squatters away. And I wished I'd stopped that gang of kids before they threw stones through my windows, leaving jagged holes and beds of shattered glass like flakes of dead skin.

My friends did catch one of those little shits, though.

And we took him up to my attic.

As you stood on my front lawn, one of the many species of moth that've made my estate their home ever since He arrived, fluttered in front of you, and your eyes followed it with an air of curious disdain.

"Yo," your papa said. "Earth to Danger. I *said*, 'What do you think about the house?'"

You shrugged, your expression unenthusiastic.

"It's a big change for all of us," said your dad, the older bald one, whose skin was dark mahogany. "But only temporary." *Temporary.* That word made my insides groan with dread. "Once the conservation site's up and running, we can get back to the city—and our next project."

"How long is that gonna be?" you asked.

"Uh, that depends on what shape the house is in, kiddo," Dad answered. "We bought this place 'as-is' and have a bunch of sealed rooms to open."

You glanced at your phone. "Please, tell me there's Wi-Fi."

Papa shook his head. "No one's lived here full-time since the eighties. We're going to have to get the house wired for internet. No worries—we'll drive to town and use the Wi-Fi at the public library. Maybe they'll have a summer reading club too!"

You sighed. "Great. I'm cut off from D and D at the climax of a *year*long campaign to save an *entire* realm *and* my AO3 before I could release the last of my short story collection, which I promised my readers I'd do as soon as I got here, except I had no idea *here* would be the dark ages." You chewed your lips again and glowered at me.

Your words didn't anger me. Because I already wanted you to love me.

"I know it sucks right now," Dad said, "but there's a silver lining—you just haven't found it yet."

"Unless it connects to the internet, I'm good," you said.

While the three of you explored my interior, pointing out every one of my many blemishes and flaws, a moving truck trundled down the dirt path and backed up to my front porch. Two white men got out and began off-loading your belongings, which hardly filled my grandiose rooms.

Pete—the tall lanky blond freelance contractor, an acquaintance of your dad's—reminded me of the stick bugs that lived in my attic.

I wanted him.

I knew I shouldn't have. Not when I was trying so very hard to be good and presentable . . . to do better . . . to impress you.

But I couldn't help myself.

And there was Sean, your papa's people-pleasing, husky sandy-haired assistant, who'd been studying botany at university just like your papa, Dr. Sebastian Anthony-Carmichael.

Pete and Sean both toted in their own small suitcases and each took one of the many empty bedrooms sparsely furnished with random pieces left behind by my previous masters, who always seemed to leave in a hurry, never to return.

Those who actually got to leave.

As your family settled, I realized that after so many decades of only my spirits to keep me company, I might have a real chance at being your forever home. I couldn't mess that up by scaring y'all off, so I locked my friends away. They didn't like that.

Especially Him.

But I would deal with the consequences later. You all were far more important.

You would probably say it was selfish of me, but I was glad your parents had both lost their big, important city jobs—because it brought y'all to me. Looking back now, I think what I felt those first few weeks of your stay was what people call *joy*.

I liked it.

Your dad and Pete began clearing decades of cobwebs from my corners, sweeping away layers of dust from my floors, and washing the grime from my windows that hadn't been broken.

Within days, sunlight and life flooded my interior, and I felt rejuvenated!

I wanted more.

Your papa and Sean found time to lend their hands to my restoration when they could break from their studies of the ghost orchids indigenous to my estate. Those enchanting white flowers that glow dimly in direct moonlight and give off the impression of tiny dancing sprites have captivated people for centuries. And like many other scientists before him, your papa wanted nature to reveal her secret—how the orchids thrived in the muck of the swamp.

You *all* would find out soon enough.

During your time with me, you floated about the property, occasionally offering to help your parents' separate endeavors, but only when extreme boredom drove you from your bedroom and your books and your journal and your sad sleeps. You tried to hide your depression from your parents because you didn't want to make them feel bad about the move. After all, they'd only been doing what they thought was best for your family.

But you couldn't keep secrets from me.

You wrote about your special friend a lot—when you weren't crying about him.

> Micah. MICAH. Micah Castillo. MICAH HUGO CASTILLO. mr. micah h. castillo. danger & micah. Danger AXLE Carmichael-Castillo ♥ Micah HUGO Carmichael-Castillo.

Dozens of pages. I watched this boy torment you day after day and wondered how that must've felt. I expect it was akin to the cold emptiness that pervades every square foot of me the moment right after a master abandons me.

You wrote in your journal that you would turn seventeen this fall and had never had a boyfriend. Micah was the first boy who'd made your dick hard with only a thought and the first whose dick you could make hard with only the gentle brush of your fingertips against his neck.

I'd locked all my friends up—even Him—for your ungrateful ass to let that insipid boy haunt your every waking moment and even your dreams.

I hope it hurt like a motherfucker.

And by the way, you did a real shit job of hiding your unhappiness from your parents, because on the eve of your third week here, they got in bed together with the weight of more than fatigue heavy on both their faces. They looked in each other's eyes, and it was as if they could read the other's mind. I'd never seen two people so in tune with each other before.

"Did we make a mistake?" your papa asked in a hushed voice.

Your dad sighed and took a long time before speaking, also in a whisper. "Sometimes I'm not so sure, Bass. It's definitely a shit ton more work than I anticipated. Pete thinks there's a solid plate of metal blocking the attic door. That creepy garden shed in the side yard is likewise impenetrable. And every single locked room we *did* manage to bust into is a funky mess. The wood's all rotted with mold in three rooms so far. Those areas have turned into a complete gut job, which means a bigger crew, more tools and equipment, and a lot more money. Pete and I have already gotten a head start on it, but there's only so much we can do."

"Sean and I haven't had much luck either," Papa admitted. "We've analyzed soil samples around the clock and spent *hours* reviewing field-cam footage and found nothing. We haven't spotted a single moth interacting with a ghost orchid. It just doesn't make sense." He threw up his hands. "How else are the orchids being pollinated? Am I just wasting our time and money with all this?"

Dad turned on his side and raised an eyebrow. "You know, it's not too late to start that drug cartel."

Papa let out a heavy breath and fell back onto his pillow, staring up at my ceiling. "Danger's depressed."

"I know," Dad replied. "He denies it though. Doesn't wanna talk about it either."

"What should we do?"

"About Danger or the house?"

"Both."

No . . . *NO!*

Y'all couldn't leave me. I wasn't going to let them take you away.

In my moment of panic, my massive frame shuddered, and the moans of ancient wood echoed in the stark quiet of nightfall. Both men fell silent and craned their ears to listen. A terse moment passed before they relaxed again and continued their conversation.

"It's only been three weeks," Dad said, his brow furrowed. "Danger just needs time and space—as do you and the ghost orchids. In the meantime, let me assess the damage before we make any big decisions. Pete's reached out to his cousin, who's already agreed to come out and help for a decent price. We might still be able to salvage this."

Your papa sealed their agreement with a kiss. I'm sure you're not interested in the intimate details of what your parents did next, so instead, I'll tell you how I occupied the rest of my night.

You'd probably say it was serendipity, though I believe it was forethought with decades-long precision, but a few of my friends possessed precisely the trade experience your dad required. Freeing them even for a night was a risk, but I took it. For you.

But letting them out enraged Him. He knew your papa was fucking with his flowers. So, to assuage his fury, I gave Him one night only with His beloved orchids.

While you and your parents slept soundly, my friends toiled throughout the night, ripping out the decayed bits of my flesh and tossing them into the swamp. By first light, the sickness that'd spread through my previously sealed rooms was completely gone, exposing my skeletal frame and foundation to the soft morning sunlight that bounded in through the refurbished windows.

And I wondered then, *Is this how it feels to breathe?*

Your parents were first to stir the next morning, but by then, I'd corralled my spirits back into their respective hiding places—all but one. He had an extra-special assignment.

Your dad assumed Pete and his cousin had pulled an all-nighter on the mold job. While happy to have had it taken care of so quickly, he was also peeved Pete hadn't told him they were working through the night. Your papa convinced your dad not to make a big fuss about it, but your dad still brought it up to Pete, who didn't hesitate to take the credit or the check your dad handed him to pay his cousin an overtime rate for the work *my* friends did.

But my annoyance with Pete was a small price to pay for effectively putting the brakes on your parents' thoughts about leaving and taking you away from me.

You often slept later than the others, so I instructed Alfred to wait patiently and not wake you. The morning dragged on, and the light bursting through the gap in your partially drawn curtains intensified until you could no longer ignore the golden strip of sunlight across your sleeping face.

Your eyes opened to the sight of a teen boy with a friendly narrow face, kneeling by the side of your bed, watching and waiting for you to wake. At your sharp intake of breath, he clapped a frigid, ghostly white hand over your mouth. "Don't scream," he whispered. "*Please.*"

You nodded, and he lowered his hand. You sat up abruptly and asked, "Who are you?" Your voice shuddered. "And why are you in my room?"

"I'm Alfred," he said. "The house wants me to be your friend."

Your eyebrows pinched as if it were preposterous that I might exist. "The *house*?"

Alfred nodded.

"Where'd you come from? And how'd you get in my room?"

A soft knock at your closed bedroom door interrupted your inquiry. At your consent, your papa opened the door and poked his head in.

Alfred turned briefly toward him, revealing the jagged piece of rebar that'd pierced the back of his skull like a metal skewer through a cube of raw pork. You gasped under your breath at the ringlets of auburn hair matted with blood and bits of torn pink flesh bedding the sharp metal rod plunged into the boy's brain.

"Morning," your papa said, smiling. "Did I hear you talking? You manage to get cell signal in here?"

Your eyes shifted from Alfred to Papa, until Alfred said, "He can't see me. House rules."

"I, uh, was talking to myself," you told your papa.

You fucking liar . . . Good boy.

"You sure you're okay?" Papa asked. You nodded, and he said, "Someone knocked down all my field cameras yesterday. Did you happen to see anything?"

You shook your head. "I was in my room all night."

"All right," he said with a sigh. "Well, your dad and I would like to see you for lunch if you and yourself could break away from your stimulating conversation for a bit."

"I'll be down in a few minutes."

Papa left, and you turned back to Alfred. "So, you're dead?"

He nodded.

"How'd it happen?"

"Plane crash."

"Shit," you mumbled. "When?"

"In '72," Alfred replied. "We went down in this swamp. Everyone aboard died—all hundred and one passengers."

"I'm sorry. How old were—are you?"

"Seventeen."

"Are the rest of the people from the crash here too?"

He shook his head. "But there are others."

You swallowed hard. "Others?" Alfred nodded tentatively, and you asked, "Where?"

He pointed to your bedroom window.

I could feel the heightened thump of your heart echoing off my walls. *Oh!* How I wish I could've ripped it, still beating, from your scrawny chest.

If only I had hands.

You got up and crept across the room.

Alfred appeared next to you at the window and pointed down to the side yard—and the weathered garden shed, the building your dad had been trying to open.

"It's kept us all shut up in there since y'all moved in," Alfred said. "But the house promises to let me out more if I hang with you."

"Was it you then? Did you knock down my papa's cameras?"

Alfred tensed. "That wasn't me."

"Do you know who it was?"

He stared up at the decorative tin ceiling of your bedroom and mumbled, "I gotta go now."

And he was gone.

Over the next few days, you and Alfred spent more time together—and Alfred kept my secret about our friend in the attic, per the terms of our agreement regarding his temporary freedom.

Installing Alfred as your new haunt effectively expelled the ghost of Micah from your mind; and with him gone, your spirits were lifted enough that your parents no longer worried about your mental health. And thus, I'd resolved another major problem.

Though the largest remained concealed in my attic.

I couldn't let Him out. Not after what He'd done to your papa's cameras. But I also didn't know how much longer I could contain Him. Despite their own feelings about being confined, my friends had all begun to worry that I would lose control of Him soon.

At that particular time, I needed another problem like I needed a massive termite infestation; so, naturally, Alfred—that little pale, mortality-deficient fucker—betrayed my trust.

You and he often took lengthy, meandering walks together around my wooded estate, marveling at the various species of moths flitting through the forest, lost and dazed, lamenting the absence of their beloved caretaker. Alfred thought himself clever, taking you outside my walls to talk without pretense.

He knew I was listening.

That day, y'all walked farther than you'd ever gone before. And Alfred showed you a spot where you could get a blip of cell phone signal. I hadn't realized before then that spirits could sense electromagnetic fields. But what Alfred *didn't* know was nowhere on *my* estate was sacred. The trees have always whispered things to me. They were more loyal than even my oldest friend. They were my blood, you see.

So imagine my fury when I learned that you nailed one of your funky-ass socks to the trunk of one of my kin to mark the spot that traitor had shown you—all to impress you. That was when I discovered Alfred had taken an extracurricular liking to you, and that annoyed me.

He needed to understand—you were *mine.*

But his trespasses didn't end there. In exchange for the friendship you should've been giving *me,* Alfred spilled the *one* secret I'd expressly forbidden him from speaking about.

"Your family's in danger," Alfred warned, leaning against the tree you'd just mutilated.

"Huh?" you asked, rightfully confused—because what the *fuck* was Alfred doing?

"All the ghosts aren't in the garden shed," he said. "There's another—a *really* bad one—that the house keeps isolated in the attic. And ever since y'all got here, He's been *pissed.*"

"But why though?"

"Mainly because the house won't let Him out. And the rest of us are afraid of Him. Before the house locked us all up, no one dared set foot on the staircase up to the attic. Not even Sánchez."

"Who is this spirit?" you asked, curious. "Or who *was* He, rather?"

"He lived here in the early 1920s. His name's Booker Baldwin, and He was best friends with the master of the house at the time, some white industrial investor who lived here with his white wife. She was six months pregnant when all three of them died on this estate."

"Do you know what happened to them?"

"The master was a dick to everyone, even his wife, who was widely known to be as hateful as him. Booker was the only person the master consistently treated with kindness. He'd lured Booker away from a shitty sharecropping situation up north in Georgia that had turned violent and hired Him to look after the estate grounds—and his homoerotic desires. After some time, he grew to love Booker, but Booker only coveted the ghost orchids. Booker spent more time with the moths and flowers than the man who claimed to love Him.

"When the master's wife found out about her husband and Booker's affair, she lost her shit. She would've burned the house down if the master hadn't stopped her. So she set him on fire instead. It happened in the attic. And then she went outside to where Booker was tending the orchids, clubbed Him across the back of the head, and drowned Him in the swamp. Then she took her husband's shotgun to the garden shed and shot herself in the face—close range."

You gasped. Such a delicate breath trapped in the back of your throat. If only it'd choked you so you fell back onto the ground, clawing at your neck until your fingertips turned red and your lips blue.

"What does He want?" you asked. "The ghost of Booker Baldwin?"

"All He's ever cared about," said Alfred. "His flowers."

"Why are you telling me this?" you asked.

Alfred's sallow cheeks blushed. "Because I don't want anything bad to happen to you. Please watch out for the Caretaker—that's what we call Booker's ghost. He's really, *really* bad news, Danger. I'm not sure how long the house can keep Him shut away in that attic."

And that is why you didn't see Alfred again after that transgression. I had to punish him *real good* for talking too damned much—and overstepping my boundaries.

To my abject horror, his little warning sent you straight to your parents. My trees were updating me on the situation right around the same time you were snitching.

"A bad spirit is trapped in the attic," you proclaimed dramatically to your dads. "*He's* the one who knocked down the field cameras!"

They shared a concerned expression.

"*Please,*" you begged. "Do *not* open that attic. This house is haunted. We need to *leave*. Now."

Ah, but it wasn't going to be quite that easy, Danger. I'd already made sure of that.

"Unfortunately, we've passed the point where we can easily cut our losses," your dad said, and looked to your papa. "We need to stay at least through the rest of summer."

Papa shivered slightly. "As grand as it'll be when we're done, this house does give me the creeps. Sometimes it feels like the walls have ears *and* eyes."

"How about we go on a little family excursion to town tomorrow?" Dad suggested. "We can take a break from this place for a bit. Being cooped up here so long might be starting to get to all of us. And maybe while we're out, we'll even find some sage to take care of any pesky poltergeists."

"So, we're *not* leaving?" Disbelief sharpened the edges of your voice like the blade of a guillotine.

Your parents shared another look, and your dad said, "Yes, we're leaving, but not until the end of summer. I'm sorry, Danger. We hear you, kiddo. I don't expect you to fully understand what your papa and I have been through, but I can assure you, the living have done far more harm to our family than the dead ever could. One future was already stolen from us. We're not giving up the next without a fight."

After all I'd done for you ungrateful dicks, you were scheming to sage away all my friends and abandon me before the leaves on the trees started changing colors. My frame rumbled with barely checked rage. I'd done so much to make you fuckers love me, but none of it was enough: I ripped out my diseased innards and discarded them in the swamp. I confined and infuriated the only friends I'd ever known. And I even gave you a friend of your own.

My worst fears had come true. I began to believe I was too damned for anyone to love. But even then, I still didn't want to completely believe it.

It was clear, if y'all weren't going to make me your forever home, I would make you my friends. And then you'd never leave again.

I should've let Him have you all from the onset.

You woke uncharacteristically early the next morning and joined your parents on a trip into town, leaving Pete and Sean behind.

Pete, feeling guilty for duping your dad, wished to surprise him on his return by opening the attic and getting a head start on the renovation up there.

And what a wonderful surprise it would be!

He sat his thermos of black coffee and bourbon on one of the stairs, hung his lit work lamp on a hook on the wall, and plugged in his blaring headphones. As he hacked away at my wooden attic door with an axe, something stirred just on the other side.

Once the wood was out of the way, Pete sat the axe aside and huffed an exasperated breath at the solid plate of metal blocking the attic's entrance. He disappeared and returned with welding equipment. I'd never seen someone so determined to perish.

After a while, a large portion of the metal barrier fell away, revealing the dank darkness of the attic beyond. Pete dropped his torch, removed his face shield and headphones, and stared into the black hole that may as well have been a portal to Hell.

He climbed up carefully and poked his head through to assess the space.

A spectral hand grabbed a fistful of Pete's blond hair and snatched the man through the hole. Poor Pete didn't even get the chance to scream.

A single brown moth fluttered down from the attic and wavered in front of the still-burning lamp hung on the wall.

You and your parents returned on the cusp of dusk, everyone's spirits somewhat renewed from your little jaunt—the last you'd smile that night.

Sean met you three on my porch, a pair of muddy boots in one hand, his tackle box of beakers, vials, and various instruments in the other. Humidity and sweat had already slicked his sandy hair to his head. "Hey, hey!" He smiled and lifted the box. "Headed to get soil samples."

"Need a hand?" your papa asked.

Sean shook his head and glanced up at the couple of moths

thumping into the porch light, which had been switched on in advance of the encroaching sunset.

"You seen Pete?" asked your dad.

"Not since morning," Sean said. "He was lugging a bunch of equipment upstairs earlier though." His phone alarm went off, and he set his boots down to silence it. "Sorry, but I gotta hit this collection window."

"Of course, go ahead." Papa stood aside to let Sean pass.

The young scientist went about his usual winding course, stopping at each little orange flag that'd been meticulously planted where the ghost orchids grew along my property.

The three of you shared a moment of anxious silence before going inside. But you, Danger, reemerged after several minutes, having realized you'd forgotten your phone in the car.

But you didn't make it off my porch.

The setting sun lit the horizon in fiery oranges and reds that burned beyond the towering trees, beneath which the ghost orchids resembled fairies dancing in the air around a bonfire.

A few yards away, a man staggered toward you on unsteady legs, his eyes wide and laden with horror.

"Sean?" Your voice was small, frightened.

Your papa's assistant gagged and opened his mouth wide. Then he gripped the bottom of his jaw with both hands and pulled it down, farther and farther, until tears burst from his bloodshot eyes and rolled down his reddened cheeks. He stumbled closer until you could see the dark creature wriggling up from the rear of his throat. It walked across Sean's pink tongue and over his white knuckles, then took flight at the same time the sun disappeared from the sky and darkness took over.

"A moth?" you whispered, then gasped.

Sean vomited an eclipse of moths.

They spewed from his mouth like water from a burst pipe. You shielded your face, but they weren't after you. The moths doubled back and swarmed Sean.

I felt your weight swaying from foot to foot against my floorboards. Shock rooted you to the spot; it was as close to holding you as I'd ever come.

Sean's airways finally unobstructed, he released a scream that was more like the high-pitched squeal of a pig being flayed alive. The moths covered him, forming a writhing second skin. They filled his mouth, silencing his shrieks. He dropped to his knees, and you let go of a pitiful whimper. You opened your mouth to call for help, but fear gutted the words before they left your tongue.

The moths drained the blood and fluids from Sean's body until he was nothing more than a pruned heap of skin and flesh around a limp skeleton. A few gorged themselves to the point of being blood drunk and flew straight into the air, only to plummet back to the ground, where they splattered, bulging stomachs exploding like blood-filled water balloons.

And then you threw up on my goddamned front steps.

"Danger—" your dad said, appearing in the doorway behind you and noticing Sean's pruned corpse. "What—the—fuck?! BASS! SEBASTIAN!"

He pulled you back over my threshold as your papa bolted into the foyer and screamed.

A few hundred yards away, the ghost of Booker Baldwin stood at the edge of the marsh near a patch of ghost orchids, His arms spread wide, His head thrown back. What must've been hundreds of moths fluttered to Him contentedly, each kissing His body before zooming off to feed the army of ghost orchids around my estate.

Papa gasped. "I was right. It *was* the moths."

"And Him—the Caretaker." You rounded on your parents. "I *told* you!"

Dad shut the door on Booker's ghost and announced, "We need to leave."

"I literally said that yesterday!" you shouted.

How dare you.

Every inch of me shook with vehemence, and your family clung to one another in my foyer. Windowpanes rattled in their frames. Paintings fell from hooks and crashed to the floor. Heavy furniture bobbed and slid from their stations. Vicious cracks ripped across my foundation like lightning streaking the dark sky.

After I calmed, you broke away and scrambled to the parlor window overlooking the front yard and screamed, "NO!"

Alfred yanked out the starter relay of your parents' SUV and, leaving the hood propped up, ran into the woods.

I told you I wasn't letting you leave.

"What the fuck is going on?" asked your papa, who stood next to your dad, both watching the scene from a nearby window.

"We might be able to call for help," you said. "There's a spot down the road where I sometimes get a single bar. I nailed an old sock to a tree to mark it."

"About how far?" Dad asked. Panic clamped your mouth shut until he snapped his fingers in front of your face. "Danger! How far?"

"I—I dunno," you stammered. "Maybe a mile?"

"Okay," he said. "I'm going to try and get the neighborhood first responders on the phone. It's been a while since I've run track, but I can still jet."

"You're not about to leave us here with that creepy-ass Caretaker running around!" Papa shouted. "What if He comes in here?"

"He won't," you said. "All He wants are His flowers."

"We're wasting time," said Dad. "I'll be back."

He snatched open the door and sprinted down the dirt road. A muggy, tepid breeze blew in from outside, the dark of night bringing with it a shy chill that still managed to charge the terror hovering thick in the air.

I slammed my doors, which made you and your papa jump.

Y'all were really starting to piss—me—off.

"Let's be ready to get the hell out of here when Dad comes back," Papa said. "Go pack your overnight bag. Just the essentials."

You nodded, and you both ran upstairs, your papa splitting off to the master bedroom.

In your room, you ripped a duffel from the closet and began frantically shoving your belongings inside. Determination to betray me set your face to a frown the whole time.

You couldn't wait to abandon me.

You hefted the bag onto your shoulder, then something outside your window snagged your attention. You crept closer to see what it was.

A gust of wind picked up outside. The open doors of the garden shed *thwacked* into the frame and swung back open. A pitiful overhead light flickered to life, immediately drawing a moth toward it.

Look what you made me do.

Shadows gathered within the building. Molded pine straw carpeted the floor. A haphazard pyramid of red gas canisters was stacked against the inside wall, veiled in very thin shadow. The translucent figure of a woman crawled forward from the dark, dragging her mutilated body across the straw. The top half of her head was missing. Blood and bits of brain fragment soiled the front of her white nightgown.

"Fuck me," you muttered, and dashed to your parents' bedroom.

Papa zipped two bags shut and went rigid when he saw the look on your face. "What's wrong?"

"The shed," you said breathlessly. "It's open. The ghosts are out. *All of them.*"

Papa snatched up both bags. "Let's go find Dad. Now."

You led the way down the hall and to the stairs, but you tripped over your own feet halfway down. Had your papa not grabbed you, you would've fallen the rest of the way.

How nice it would've been to see your bones snap and their sharp edges punch through your taut skin, leaving behind tiny shards of bone and marrow marinating in thick bubbly pools of your blood. *Mmm.*

Instead, the ghost of my birth master stood at the foot of the staircase. The sight of Sánchez stole both your voices. He towered at seven feet. Most of his body was burned, his clothing charred tatters that clung to the craggy blackened canvas of what was once skin. Under an arm that ended in jagged bone and frayed flesh at the elbow, Sánchez had tucked his bloated, severed head, also burned, so the face was melted and unrecognizable. Above a hair-raising, lipless grin of mismatched brown teeth, Sánchez's eyes shot open, revealing two rotted orbs.

"THIS IS *MY* HOUSE!" the head bellowed up at you and your papa. Sánchez stomped one heavy boot onto the first step, and the entire staircase trembled.

"MINE!" the head screamed again.

Papa grabbed your arm and hauled you back upstairs. He headed for the master bedroom, but you yanked away.

"No!" Your heartbeat thudded as Sánchez's heavy footfalls drew nearer. "We should hide in the attic. It's the only place the other ghosts won't go."

"And what if the Caretaker comes back?"

"We'll just have to be gone before then."

As Sánchez arrived on my second floor, you and your papa slipped through the hole into the attic.

You screamed, but your papa put a hand over your mouth and held you close until you calmed.

I was disappointed you two couldn't appreciate the beauty of what lay before you. And that was all the evidence I needed to realize neither you nor your dads would ever love me.

More ghost orchids than either of you had seen in one place made glowing curtains along the walls and ceiling in the attic, all of them drinking in the moonbeams pouring through the window facing the full moon, bright in the nighttime sky. Dozens of fat moths floated from one flower to the next, exchanging blood for pollen in a never-ending cycle of carnage.

Pete sat slumped in one corner of the room. You nearly missed him because he almost blended into the wall. Orchids sprouted from every visible orifice of his body, and the little stick bugs that I enjoy so much were lounging in the tangled blond nest of hair on his head.

"Dear God," muttered your papa.

You went to the window and cursed aloud when you looked down at the front yard below. "Sean's gone."

"What?" Papa rushed forward to peer down at the mangled,

blood-soaked patch of grass where Sean's dead body lay not long ago. "What happened to him?"

I'll never tell.

You stuck your head through the hole in the attic door and listened for a moment. When you came back up, you said, "I think it's clear. We should go now."

Papa climbed through the hole first, helped you down, then grabbed the axe left behind by the late Pete. Sánchez was stomping around in the master bedroom, flinging curses and your parents' belongings, the crashes muffled through the walls. As you and Papa crept along the upstairs hallway, another ghost wearing a hard hat dipped their head in passing before disappearing into a room where two others were installing new crown molding.

When you and Papa made it downstairs to the front door, you yanked it open, and you and your dad shrieked together.

You threw your arms around him.

"Lawrence!" Papa pulled your dad inside. "Thank goodness you're okay."

"I couldn't get anyone," he said. "Y'all good?"

Papa tossed Dad one of the bags he carried. "It's time to go."

The three of you turned to the door and paused.

The Caretaker stood in the center of the road a few dozen yards away. A cloak of moths floated around His bare body. His eyes smoldered like two full golden moons, brighter than the one above. He pointed at the three of you, and His voice was a layered hissing composed of thousands of tiny wings beating; it roared with the intensity of hurricane-force winds. "My moths are hungry. And my orchids need sustenance."

At the top of the stairs, Sánchez's head roared, "WHO FUCKED WITH MY HOUSE?!"

"*Whatthehellarewesupposedtodonow?!*" came your papa's frantic whisper-shout.

"It's the house," you said. "The only way to end this is to burn it down. I saw gas cans in the shed. We just need matches."

Your parents looked at each other, and the unspoken communication they'd once had devolved into static.

"No time to argue," you said as you darted outside. "Get the matches!"

I sealed my front doors shut in your parents' faces. My foundation trembled and emanated raw heat. I wanted to bake them like hens until their skin seared and peeled back from their flesh.

You kept your eyes on the garden shed, not the Caretaker, who'd begun trudging after you, nor your parents, whose screams came from inside me as Sánchez hunted them.

You charged into the shed and sneezed at once from the dusty air. You grabbed two gas canisters, one in each hand, and shrieked when the ghost woman clamped her icy thin fingers onto your wrist. You stared wide-eyed into her open cranium, a bony bowl filled with shredded brain matter and fetid blood.

And then you kicked her in the throat.

She let go, and you rounded—and came face-to-face with the Caretaker. The woman withdrew into the shadows, leaving a trail of gore behind.

The ghost of Booker Baldwin blocked the entrance to the shed, His haggard face stoic, His golden eyes shining two spotlights aimed directly at you. The noise of the moths' wings generated a constant rustle, which built to a gentle din that echoed in the space behind you.

You gripped the containers and took a step back.

You were trapped. We *had* you.

"Hey! Booker!"

The Caretaker turned, and you peered around Him at Alfred, who stood back, cradling an armful of ghost orchids.

"What have you done?" hissed the Caretaker. He clenched His fists, and His moths flew all around Him in a frenzy.

Alfred dropped the flowers in a pile at his feet and looked at you. "Forgive me, Danger. I didn't want you to leave either."

The lump of anxious terror in your throat kept you from speaking.

The Caretaker growled.

And then Alfred unzipped his pants and pissed on the flowers.

The Caretaker charged at Alfred, who took off running, his ghost dick still out.

"Thanks, Alfred," you mumbled, "but fuck you *and* this house."

You ran back and emptied one of the gas cans along my porch. You tossed the spent container aside, grabbed the other, and pulled on the front doors. They were sealed tight.

That's right, you little fucker. Burn me down, and you'll kill your parents too.

I said you're NOT LEAV—

The axe blade crashed through my door, lurched free, and slammed into me again and again until you saw your papa's face through the splintered hole. He hacked at my handcrafted oak with his axe, and you pulled away pieces until there was an opening large enough for you to fit through.

"Where's Dad?" you cried, peering at your papa through the hole.

Before he could answer, your dad bolted from the direction of the kitchen, a box of matches in each hand and Sánchez pounding close behind, his head spitting curses.

"Go, Danger," shouted Papa from inside. "Run and get help!"

"No!" you cried. "I'm not leaving y'all behind!"

Your dad sprinted by and yanked your papa along with him as Sánchez chased them both into the next room.

You grabbed the gas can and squeezed through the hole in my front door. Dad and Papa, having circled the first floor with Sánchez screaming after them, burst from the kitchen again.

You brushed past your parents, unscrewed the top of the can, and doused Sánchez *and* my goddamned foyer.

Dad lit a fistful of matches and tossed them over his shoulder. The accelerant ignited in wild flames that engulfed everything inside me. He grabbed you and your papa by the hands and pulled you both back through the hole in my ruined door.

My last image of y'all is of your backs disappearing into the night as the three of you ran from me, your dads on either side of you.

I'll see you again someday, Danger—in Hell.

My road there was paved by my own delusion. How foolish of me to think that I could love. That I was worthy of such a thing. That I could love you.

That I could be your forever home.

And as penance for my encroachment, you reduced me to a mound of ashes, the remnants of my centuries-long existence left to the whim of the goddamned wind.

If I could've said one thing

to

you

before

you

left,

it

would've

been

.

.

.

"Fuck

you too,

Danger Carmichael."

EPILOGUE

ANONYMOUS EMAIL

To: William Harrington
From: [Undisclosed Sender]
Subject: Ghoulfriends

Hello William.

I've been a follower of your blog for quite some time and must say that I am quite impressed with you and your devotion to the world of horror. Regarding your most recent post about the disappearance of Jakobi Warren, I would like to suggest a potential scenario for your consideration.

The White Guy Dies First was inspired by true events, yes? Well, that would mean Nona, the witch from *The Protegé*, could be real. And so could her power. So what if she and Jakobi had a secret arrangement? What if Nona could grant any wish—for the right price? And let's say that price was thirteen souls, thirteen bodies that would bear the cost of fame for the unsung filmmaker.

Perhaps Jakobi went into hiding after fulfilling his deal with Nona, waiting to bear the fruits of his bloody wish. And maybe after some time, he redefined his definition of fame, realizing that it is not shiny awards or bright accolades or even piles of money; but instead, fame—in its most authentic form—is the impact his work had (and continues to have) on the lives of people across the world that he would've otherwise never gotten the opportunity to meet. And even if the ripple he makes touches only one person, that is still one life forever changed. That is fame. *That* is power.

Just a thought.

Be easy, kid. And stay weird.

ACKNOWLEDGMENTS

Faridah, Kalynn, Kendare, H. E., Lamar, Chloe, Alexis, Tiffany, Adiba, Naseem, Mark, and Karen—it has been a privilege and an honor to work with each of you. Thank you for lending your light and your talent. And to Mark, especially—thanks for gifting me the title! <3

Ali Fisher, I couldn't have imagined a better partner to edit this anthology with than you. Thank you for your impeccable trust and guidance as we waded through the terrifying realm of anthology editing together. It was a grand time, as always.

Dianna Vega, it continues to be an honor and privilege to work with you each and every day. I appreciate you very much for all you do.

Patrice Caldwell and Trinica Sampson-Vera, thank you for championing me and this collection from the very beginning. We couldn't have done it without you.

Many, many thanks to the brilliant teams at New Leaf Literary, Tor Teen, and Macmillan Audio for bringing another project of mine to life in such an amazing way.

Much appreciation goes out to all the booksellers, librarians, and educators who've worked and continue to work tirelessly to put this and other stories into the hands of the kids we write for. I couldn't do this without you.

And to the readers and everyone who blurbed, reviewed, or shared this collection—thanks for rocking with me this long. Be easy now.

Terry J. Benton-Walker